KU-335-394

A Midsummer Night's Gene

ALSO IN LEGEND BY ANDREW HARMAN

The Sorcerer's Appendix
The Frogs of War
The Tome Tunnel
One Hundred and One Damnations
Fahrenheit 666
The Scrying Game
The Deity Dozen

A MIDSUMMER NIGHT'S GENE

Andrew Harman

LEGEND

Published by Legend Books in 1997

1 3 5 7 9 10 8 6 4 2

Copyright © Andrew Harman, 1997

The right of Andrew Harman to be identified as the author of this
work has been asserted by him in accordance with the Copyright,
Designs and Patents Act, 1988

This book is sold subject to the condition that it shall not, by way of
trade or otherwise, be lent, resold, hired out, or otherwise circulated
without the publisher's prior consent in any form of binding or cover
other than that in which it is published and without a similar condition
including this condition being imposed on the subsequent purchaser

Paperback edition first published by Legend Books in 1997
Legend Books

Random House UK Ltd
20 Vauxhall Bridge Road, London, SWIV 2SA

Random House Australia (Pty) Limited
20 Alfred Street, Milsons Point, Sydney, New South Wales 2061, Australia

Random House New Zealand Limited
18 Poland Road, Glenfield
Auckland 10, New Zealand

Random House South Africa (Pty) Limited
Endulini, 5a Jubilee Road, Parktown 2193, South Africa

Random House UK Limited Reg. No. 954009

A CIP catalogue record for this book is available from the British Library

Papers used by Random House UK Limited are natural, recyclable products
made from wood grown in sustainable forests. The manufacturing processes
conform to the environmental regulations of the country of origin

ISBN 0 09 978881 0

Typeset by Deltatype Ltd, Birkenhead, Merseyside
Printed and bound in the United Kingdom by
Mackays of Chatham plc, Chatham, Kent

For all those who wrestle with adversity …
… and win.
Hold that dream.

Contents

Per Adua Ad Astra

18th June, Next Year

Forty-eight thousand tons of cutting edge alien technology slowed to sub-light and, with all the grace of your average calving glacier, fell out of the sky.

At that very instant the driver of the red Chevrolet grasped at her temples and slammed her foot on the brake. The car slewed across the interstate on a haze of burning rubber and ricocheted off an innocent conifer. 'Oh god,' whimpered Lorelia Auric rubbing her temples and grimacing in the way beloved of level eight telepaths the universe over, 'they're here!'

Her passenger pulled a meaningful face and looked up through the sunroof. 'You mean . . .?'

'Yes,' interrupted Lorelia, 'they've finally tracked me across the wastes of space and are even now preparing their devilish war engines to complete their mission and conquer my home world.'

'Just as I feared,' cursed the professor slamming his fist into an open palm.

Tara Ness cringed at the dialogue, winced at the acting and edged forward on the sofa. She knew the good bit was coming soon. She'd seen the trailer only last week.

A streak of crimson spacecraft arced across the tiny square of sky which glistened on the tv. The scene shifted and showed the deadly iridium-alloyed invader surfing in on a bow wave of ionising atmosphere. Tara winced again and, suspending disbelief from the highest gallows she could muster, told herself repeatedly that she couldn't possibly see the strings casting shadows on the backcloth. No, not at all. That *was* forty-eight thousand tons of cutting edge alien technology she could see hurtling in over Yosemite Park to

1

kidnap the cloned sister of Princess Aurelia and take her back to the rebel planet. Honest.

The action cut unceremoniously back to the interior of the now steaming Chevrolet.

'For the good of your people, we must save you, Lorelia,' expounded the professor earnestly.

'But, how? It's too late now!' wailed the platinum blonde Ms Auric.

'Nonsense. I have a plan! Pull yourself together and follow me,' declared the professor with great charisma and fiddled with the door handle. With one bound he was standing by the side of the interstate, gesturing for Lorelia to follow.

'But we can't outrun those cunning alien fiends,' wailed Lorelia. 'There's no hope for us.'

'You're right, of course. On our own, alone here in Yosemite Park, our chances don't look good. But help is on its way!'

There was a full screen shot of Lorelia looking at once shocked and not a little hopeful. 'But how . . .?' she pouted, in a way she had when playing a heroine in times of acute danger.

'By now that evil ship will have triggered every early warning tracking system the world over. Even as I speak the brave boys of the US Marines will be scrambling to our defence,' announced the professor with earnest encouragement.

Sure enough the scene flicked to a vast airbase somewhere in the Nevada Desert. Claxons screamed, small figures sprinted in all directions and whole squadrons of F-18 Eagles roared down the centre of the runway on full afterburner. All it needed was for the main air traffic control tower to begin descending into the ground and Tara would have been in sciffy heaven. Sighing regretfully that Gerry Anderson hadn't produced this she turned her attention back to the action.

The professor reached out, grasped Lorelia's hand and stared meaningfully into her eyes. 'If we can only stay out of the evil enemy's sight for long enough, then maybe, just maybe . . .'

His words were cut off by a wobbly red saucer racing across the studio sky.

'Run!' shouted the professor and tugged hard on Lorelia's hand.

In strangely exaggerated moves the fleeing pair headed for the forest.

Unnecessarily, the car exploded behind them.

'That was close,' offered Lorelia panting once again to the camera before a background of curiously grainy looking flames.

Tara cringed. It was blindingly obvious to her that the makers of this slice of cinematic mediocrity had certainly run out of money for special effects long ago. She knew a cheap colour separation overlay when she saw one, but . . . ah, what the hell, it was science fiction. Not very good science fiction admittedly but what else would you expect from BBC 2 on a Tuesday afternoon.

'Target in visual range, commander,' announced an F-18 Eagle pilot staring at a horizon filling spacecraft.

'Fire when ready, troopers,' came the crackled reply.

A screenful of thumb flicked a safety catch off the joystick and, pausing just milliseconds too long for dramatic effect, pressed the red button.

Curiously a Polaris missile erupted on a plume of seawater. Instantly a Letraset laser flashed from a cardboard invader, the screen burned crimson and an explosion, burning with all the ferocity of a damp sparkler, was all that remained of the F-18 Eagle.

'Run!' reminded the professor helpfully and skipped over a large tree root. Lorelia attempted to follow but, pencil pleat skirts and high heels being what they were, caught her ankle and sprawled onto the forest floor. 'Professor!' she cried, milking her *femme fatale* role for all it was worth.

Forty-eight thousand tons of cutting edge alien technology wobbled shakily into view overhead and once again Tara went into denial over those strings.

This was it, she knew it. The moment she had been waiting for and nothing, not even a few bits of string were going to spoil this. She clutched her knees in feverish anticipation and edged even further forward on the sofa.

Sure enough a blue beam flashed down from the centre of the craft and focused on the prone Lorelia Auric.

'Professor!' she cried as the beam grasped her under the armpits and began raising her skywards. 'Professor, what's happening?'

'You're in some sort of beam,' offered the professor helpfully. 'I . . . I can't reach you, Lorelia.' Tara's heart was pounding. At last, Lorelia had been captured. Any minute now she'd be snatched into the invader's saucer and, for the first time, Tara would see inside the alien craft. Her heart pounded a couple of beats faster. This was the bit she always loved. Flashes of *This Island Earth* and *The Day the Earth Stood Still* zipped across her mind whetting her appetite to glinting sharpness.

Lorelia dangled desperately above the treetops, wailing. Above her loomed a cardboard orifice glinting with silver foil.

Suddenly a Meccano grab extended from nowhere, clutched her around the midriff and, looking like an out-take from *King Kong*, dragged her inside.

If Tara could have sat any closer to the edge of the sofa, she would have. She stared intently at the screen, mouth open, desperate to know what the inside of the alien craft was like. The scene changed and suddenly, there before her was a setting that looked uncannily like a typical house in suburban Australia.

'Forgot these, did you? How many times do I have to remind you?' announced Tara's mother dropping a pair of size nine police dress boots in her lap and collapsing onto the sofa with the panache of an average avalanche. 'Clean 'em now and don't make any noise while *Neighbours* is on, d'you hear?'

Tara stared dumbfounded at the tv remote in her mother's hand. 'I . . . I was watching that,' she spluttered, her mind spinning down to earth with a crash. Thoughts of alien ship's insides shattered, crashed and burned . . .

'Exactly,' her mother waved her arm dismissively. '*Was* watching. It's my turn now.'

'It's always your turn,' grumbled Tara in the way teenagers have.

'Who pays the licence fee?' snapped her mother, her eyes already glued to the goings on in Ramsay Street.

'Dad,' glowered Tara.

'Er . . . yeah. Exactly. So clean his boots. He's going out tonight. It's an important Community Police Meeting.' She jabbed the volume control with an expert thumb and hiked the grating antipodean accents up a few decibels.

'Surprise, surprise,' tutted Tara miserably. It was always an important Community Police Meeting. Ever since her father had been promoted to Chief Inspector he had embraced the beliefs of raising the police profile. Especially amongst the local business fraternity. Well, they always provided the best buffets. Vol au vents, Courvoisier, the lot.

To all but the most blinkered of folks, the last three years had served to raise little other than the dimension of Chief Inspector Everett Ness's waistline. But tonight would be different. He had assured everybody of the fact.

'My boots ready yet?' snapped fifteen and a half stone of half dressed Chief Inspector as he burst in through the door, fiddling desperately with his cufflinks.

'Sssshhh,' hissed Rosemary with a dismissive wave of her hand. 'Everett, do be quiet, he's going to propose, I can tell!' An antipodean handyman fiddled with his electric drill and stared longingly at the leotarded keep-fit mistress.

'Have you done my boots?' whispered Everett advancing on Tara. 'You know I need them gleaming tonight. I can't launch the "Big Friendly Uncle Copper Crime Hotline" if my boots aren't up to scratch. The media will be there.'

Miserably, with thoughts more on the plight of Lorelia Auric and her Battle Beyond Infinity, Tara rubbed her sleeve across the size nine's steel reinforced toe caps. She had given them a good seeing to for last night's community policing

5

bash so all they needed was a quick wipe. In seconds they reflected back her daydreaming face.

Behind her Everett buckled on a small cellphone pouch in the exact place a holster should be. For a moment he stood still, arms poised at his sides, three inches away from his belt. Then, suddenly, as if in response to an insistent warbling his right hand flashed to his cellphone pouch, snatched the tiny Motorola out, flipped open the mouthpiece and clamped the phone to the side of his head. 'Hi there, you're through to the Big Friendly Uncle Copper Crime Hotline. Nobody's keener to solve that misdemeanour. How can I be of service?'

'By shutting up!' snapped Rosemary jabbing the volume button for a few more essential decibels.

'A genius is never appreciated by those around him.' Everett was wounded. 'You simply don't appreciate the work that went into that opening speech, the inspiration and devotion needed to come up with something seemingly so simple and yet catchy. Nobody's keener to solve that misdemeanour ... ah, perfection. I can almost hear Nick Ross saying that at the end of *Crimewatch*.'

'Shut up,' hissed Rosemary captivated by the Australian's toolbelt and fittings.

'You won't be saying that when I'm made Commissioner, will you? I tell you, the "Big Friendly Uncle Copper Crime Hotline" is my ticket to that promotion. When Divisional Headquarters hear of my success I'll ...'

'Haven't you gone yet?' frowned Rosemary, irritation writ large across her forehead. 'Don't be late, will you? You don't want to miss the buffet.'

'I have plenty of time in hand,' expounded Everett, a model of efficiency. Nonchalantly he flicked back the sleeves of his dress shirt and glanced at his Timex. 'Oh, god. Ten to already!' he panicked and wriggled his toes. 'Ten to!'

Trying her best to ignore her parents' usual sparkling conversation Tara dropped the boots onto the carpet and snatched at the *Radio Times*. Desperately she flicked to today's scheduling in the vague hope that there just might be a picture of the interior of the alien invader's ship. Maybe, just maybe, if she tried hard enough she could imagine every single fitting on the bridge. The magazine lay in her lap. She scoured the double spread of evening's viewing eagerly and ... Unsurprisingly, she was disappointed. The pages were covered with full colour shots of this year's Wimbledon hopefuls chatting to Desmond Lynam. She cursed and flung it away as her father finished tying his bootlaces and headed for the door.

'And don't forget the doggie bags!' snapped Rosemary. 'Make sure you bring back a *decent* selection of vol au vents this time. You know I hate those caviar and cream cheese ones you brought in last night.'

'Yes, dear,' answered Everett through the door.

'And, Everett!' she called, her eyes still glued to the goings on down under.

'Yes, dear?'

'Do bring some nice wine tonight. You know how I hate Claret.'

'Anything you wish, dear.' There was the sound of the front door being snatched open and a jangling of car keys.

'I fancy a nice Australian white,' she called as a certain Aussie handyman stripped and dived into a backyard pool.

Tara tutted to herself and frowned as her mother spread herself on the sofa and obviously began daydreaming about things he could come to fix around their house anytime he had the urge. She shook her head in disgust, why couldn't her mother dream of normal things? Proper things. Things like the utter thrill of first contact with an extraterrestrial species. Or standing on the bridge of an interplanetary craft. Or being abducted by creatures from beyond the fringes of the Solar System.

'Tara? Are you still here?' scythed her mother's voice through her dreams as the *Neighbours* theme tune blasted into earshot. 'What are you waiting for? You should be out fetching my regular portion of chips. The place has been open for a good half hour. Go, now and be back before *Brookside*!'

Miserably, Tara took a fiver from the mantelpiece and trudged out of the door leaving her mother spread on the sofa, devouring popcorn like some distant suburban cousin of Jabba the Hutt.

'I'm sorry but registration is closing now!' insisted the clerk at window four of the Patent Centre.

'Take the damn papers will you,' snarled the figure in the white lab coat attempting to thrust a vast wad of crumpled papers beneath the glass screen. He had about as much success as the average paperboy wrestling with the supplements on a Sunday morning.

'Now, now, Mr Striebley . . .' began the clerk peering up over her hornrims and tapping an officious pen on the mahogany of the desk.

'*Doctor* Striebley!' insisted the one in the lab coat. 'I'm a Doctor. As well you know!'

'Well, behave like one,' hissed the clerk scowling at the shredded mess of Patent Registration papers which now lay before her. 'You scientists are all the same. Bursting in here at five to six with half filled out registration forms, expecting us to jump to attention and stake your latest claim for a new discovery.'

'But that's your job!' squeaked Striebley looking at his watch. 'C'mon, take the papers, please!'

'Come, come, what *is* the hurry, hmmmm?'

'Competition,' hissed Doctor Striebley clawing at the worn front of the newly converted Benefits Office.

'A bit of healthy competition is good for you,' smiled the clerk.

'Not if they register first. Do you know how much we stand to lose if somebody else claims this as their own?'

'Ooooh, no. Do tell.'

'Millions. Millions!'

The two clerks inhabiting windows three and five stifled a giggle. It was like this at least once a week at the Patent Centre. Ever since the new Science and Technology Park had opened up on the outskirts of the ancient University Town of

Camford there seemed to be a constant stream of desperate scientists dashing in to put their name to brand new discoveries. And all of them had that same worried look. The paranoid stress of the certainty that decades of research and purification and analysis and application could be turned into a costly waste of time by somebody else pipping you to the post. Oh, it happened alright. Industrial espionage. A quick hack into a database here, a sneaky brick through a lab window there, and a monthly million pound cheque for life was destined to have someone else's name on it. Folks were even patenting genetic codes nowadays. Raking in the cash from dozens of labs every time an innocent mouse did what came naturally and popped another litter.

'Look are you going to register this as another victory for Splice of Life Patentable Biosciences Ltd. Or not?' insisted Striebley wincing as he thought of the trouble he'd be in if he went back to Professor Crickson and admitted defeat.

'It's not just as easy as that, you know,' replied the clerk. 'There's the searches for previous claimants . . .'

'. . . checks on the validity by peers and the three days for the cheques to clear. Yes, yes, I know! Do you want our money or not?' Striebley waved a cheque for several hundred pounds as if fly fishing.

He hated having to pay quite so much for the privilege to register a new discovery of vital scientific and cultural worth but ever since the Mayor had introduced his bid to establish Camford as a seething hotbed of research and development, things had certainly changed thereabouts.

It had to be said that Mayor Tony Keswick had surprised almost everyone with the rate and scale of the changes he had somehow managed to tug out of a host of political top hats. As well as the stunning taxbreaks and grants for anything even remotely scientific he'd wrenched from a bewildered European Parliament, he had single handedly pioneered a shake-up of the patenting system.

Now that Keswick's 'fast-track to patentable security' scheme was well in place there was only one way to go. Let's face it, if you were offered the chance to cut the normal three years of bureacratic faffing down to seven working days what would you do?

Already Camford was looking like it was poking its nose ahead of other, more established, centres of excellence and the knock-on effects were delighting Mayor Keswick. With all the layabout graduates being snapped up by new and shiny laboratories he was able to close a Benefit Office and convert it into a Patent Centre. Suddenly, not only was money not being shelled out to a host of scarf-wearing types but . . . it was actually being handed back by them.

Quite who it was that was pocketing all the proceeds wasn't entirely clear. Although, it did seem more than just a mite coincidental that the Mayor was currently zipping about town in a spanking new Jaguar XK8.

'Of course we want your money,' smiled the clerk dishing out the Patent Centre's new corporate slogan with casual aplomb. 'But we have to check on previous registrations.'

'I've already done that. Believe me, there are none,' begged Striebley, his fingers tangling themselves in his scarf. 'This is a very specialised field of research.'

The clerk lined up her hornrims and peered at the top line of the partially shredded paperwork.

'So I see,' was all she said, and flashed it at her colleagues. The strain of barely contained eruptions of mirth was almost tangible. Yet again Splice of Life Patentable Biosciences Ltd had come up trumps.

'And you are absolutely certain that there has been no prior claim for this particular . . . er, discovery?' asked the clerk.

'Checked every blasted database I could think of. Even sent out gophers on the Web. Nothing. This is a breakthrough!'

'The Japanese? Checked them? They're pretty inventive you know?'

'Yes. Yes!'

'Very well then pass the rest of the paperwork through and we'll accept it for preliminary registration.'

Striebley's shoulders relaxed visibly as he set to jamming several shrubs' worth of forms through the gap under the bulletproof glass. This task completed he whirled on his heel and began to dash for the door. Before he had gone three steps an alarm erupted into life, warning lights flashed on, and a vast uniformed gentleman stepped out of a convenient shadow. Nonchalantly he tapped a truncheon on his palm.

'Forgotten something, sir?' he asked with enforced politeness.

Sheepishly Striebley looked at the small sheet of paper in his hand and forced a smile. 'Whoops. Forgot,' he offered and handed the cheque over.

In that very instant two highly significant things happened. One, the preliminary registration of Oven-Bake Sushi became official and, two, the bank account belonging to Splice of Life Patentable Biosciences Ltd slipped into nothingness.

Striebley knew damned well that if things didn't start improving soon he'd be out of a job. And with the sudden shortage of Benefit Offices thereabouts, it didn't make the future look too rosy.

He shuddered as he thought of poor Edward back in his tank at the lab.

Whistling a tonally dubious version of *The X Files* theme, and dreamily debating whether David Duchovny was *ever* going to get his kit off on screen, Tara Ness trudged towards Luigi's Fish Emporium, a scrunched fiver rustling in her pocket. She was half way past the tiny row of turn of the century shops when it happened.

For about the first time in a week and a half, reality got a look in.

Like a bolt from the blue a fourteen and a half inch wide scale model of USS *Voyager* winked at her from the shop window.

Stunned, Tara stopped in mid stride, left foot hovering six inches above the pavement, and shook her head.

It couldn't be, could it? Had she really been watching *that* much tv science fiction. Was this the first signs of madness?

Bracing herself for acute disappointment she took a deep breath and risked a look.

There, squatting casually on acres of galactic curtaining material, was a perfect scale model of the Intrepid Class Starship *Voyager*. Almost instinctively her brain flashed up technical details as she checked off its registration number. NCC74656. Yup, that was it.

But what the hell was it doing in a shop window which up until very recently had been concerned with the sale of footwear?

And why was there a Romulan Warbird and a Dalek next to it?

'Do come inside if you wish to browse,' offered the black-clad and remarkably young looking shopkeeper who had mysteriously appeared at her side. 'No obligation,' he added and smiled with all the trustworthiness of the average life assurance salesman.

'Well, I really ought to . . .' Limply Tara pointed at the chippy.

'Nonsense, nonsense,' smiled the shopkeeper and held open the door for her. Inside she saw enticing glimpses of things with lasers and obvious faster than light capabilities.

'Er . . . Just a quick squint won't hurt, I don't suppose,' she whispered and stepped over the threshold, her teenage eyes wide.

'Welcome to "Fitments of the Imagination". My name's Regan,' grinned the shopkeeper walking backwards, steepling his fingers beneath his chin and bowing gracefully. In a flash Tara found herself thinking of a dozen different alien inhabitants of countless spacestations brought to her through the magic of television.

'We can cater for *all* your internal decorating needs,' smiled Regan sweeping his arm proudly around the interior of the packed shop.

'Decorating?' spluttered Tara.

'Of course. Bored with your bathroom? Why not make each trip a real adventure? Come . . .' Regan vanished behind a pyramid of carefully arranged Daleks, beckoning with an index finger.

Her mouth an 'o' of wonder, Tara followed. She found Regan proudly holding another fourteen and a half inch wide plastic *Voyager*.

'Look at it,' he expounded cradling the disc shaped craft like an overjoyed father with his three week old daughter. 'Perfect in every detail. Fashioned from heavy duty plastic to withstand the heaviest punishment and bleaches. Warp nacelles doubling as hinges for easy attachment to any domestic water . . .'

'Hold on. Did you just say bleaches?'

Regan nodded. 'Of course. Although I wouldn't guarantee the paintwork against some of the more abrasive cleaners. Steer clear of those and your *Star Trek Voyager* Toilet Seat will last a lifetime.' As if to demonstrate he raised the saucer section and smiled through the remaining ring. In a second he had snapped it shut again seamlessly.

Tara was stunned.

'Or if *Star Trek* isn't your particular cup of tea we have the *Independence Day* special.' With a flourish he whisked a fourteen inch disc of deadly alien technology out of flat carboard box. 'It comes complete with your very own White House Bog Brush Holder for that authentic cinematic feel. Who can fail to be moved by the very vision of interstellar conflict looming in the smallest room of your house? Yours for only £39.99.'

Bewildered Tara shook her head.

'Or what about the Romulan Warbird Shower Head Fitting and Tholian Web Shower Curtain with . . .?' And Regan would have launched into a full tour of the shop had he not been interrupted by the door being thrust open.

'Everything fixed for tonight?' blurted the intruder sporting a red pony tail extending half way down his back. He advanced impatiently across the shop floor.

'Not now, Farson, can't you see I'm with a customer?' hissed Regan, pointing at Tara under cover of the alien craft.

'Is everything set for tonight?' repeated Farson his foot tapping.

'I'm terribly sorry about this, I must apologise for my friend's behaviour . . .' began Regan, shrugging.

Farson tutted and paced away.

'Don't mind me,' grinned Tara embarrassedly. 'I'll just have a bit of a look round.'

'If you have any questions I'll be over there . . .' offered Regan, shrugging again and rolling his eyes to the red pony-tailed one loitering by the till.

'Yeah, sure,' answered Tara and turned her attentions to the shoulder high pyramid of Dalek Pedal Bins.

'Well?' snapped Farson as the shopkeeper approached him. 'Have you done everything I asked?'

'Er . . . Sort of,' Regan looked at his feet.

'What's that mean?'

'We've had to change site. Sainway's carpark is right out.'

'What? But it's perfect! Level. Out of town. Away from the police station.'

Despite her current interest in the finer details of the Thunderbird Two Closable Soap Dish, Tara's ears pricked up.

'We won't have to move far,' reassured Regan. 'It won't affect the launch window.'

Thunderbird Two slipped out of Tara's hand and clattered noisily on the floor.

'What about the reporter?' pressed Farson ignoring the desperate teenager as she picked up the soap dish and checked it for damage. At £17.99 it did seem a mite on the pricey side. Especially as it didn't come with so much as a free tablet of Imperial Leather.

'The reporter,' swallowed Regan. 'I was going to tell you about that . . . er . . . .'

Farson folded his arms. 'I don't think I'm going to enjoy this next sentence am I?'

Regan shook his head slowly. 'Well, the guy from the

Fortean Times would've come only the Fifty Ninth International Tarot Reading Championships are on in Earl's Court and . . .'

'And the girl from *New Spaceman*?'

'Spent too long looking at the solar eclipse last week and keeps getting migraines.'

'So you're telling me that our most important mission so far is destined to go completely unregarded by the world at large because *you* couldn't arrange to get a journalist here?' Farson's face rapidly turned a similar shade to his fiery hair.

Tara shook her head and wiggled her little finger in her ear. Important mission? Did he *really* just say important mission? Images of self destructing tapes and car chases through European capitals flashed through her mind.

Across the shop Regan took a defensive step away from Farson, raising his palms. 'Look. I've had a lot on my mind lately. You should try moving shop without interrupting cashflow. It's not as easy as . . .'

'That's just typical of you. Concentrate on the profits. You don't really care about *The Adversity Project*, do you? Not deep down.'

'Don't care? Who's financing it all, eh?' bridled Regan. 'I work my fingers to the bone here, you know? If it wasn't for the generous funding from "Fitments of the Imagination" all this searching for extraterrestrials would have packed up years ago.'

Suddenly Tara forgot completely about the eighteen quid's worth of Thunderbird in her hand as her curiosity leapt kittenwards towards imminent destruction. Excitedly she peered around the edge of the pyramid of Dalek Pedal Bins.

She couldn't have heard that right? Searching for extraterrestrials? These two were searching for aliens? Surely not?

'Without much more funding it will pack up,' groaned Farson.

'What?' gasped Regan. 'What are you talking about?'

Behind the Daleks Tara mouthed a similar question. What *were* they talking about?

Farson was looking worried. 'We can't possibly afford to

go geostationary without big money. We don't get a decent sponsorship deal soon and *Adversity VI* will be the last shot. Your profits just aren't enough. We just can't afford a big payload uplift.'

To Tara's ears all this sounded remarkably like the type of conversation two chaps at NASA would be having. If NASA was a cottage industry, of course. But that was just her imagination again. Wasn't it? Nobody in Camford discussed satellite uplifts and interplanetary coffee mornings, did they?

'Can't afford it? How long have you known this?' squeaked Regan sounding genuinely alarmed.

'Three months,' admitted Farson fidgeting with his crimson pony tail. 'Why the hell d'you think we needed that publicity. An article in *New Spaceman* would've been perfect to let the world know of our cause. People would've been flocking to join SOFA. Proudly showing their friends and family that they too believe, that they have joined the Search for Offworld Friendly Aliens.'

Tara squeaked in awe. It *was* true. They *were* talking about first contact scenarios. The floor seemed to sway beneath her feet as the reality hit. She shook her head violently, staggered forward and, with a sickening clatter, several squadrons of aluminium Daleks spread themselves across the shop.

Instantly the conversation stopped.

Farson and Regan glared accusingly at the prone figure of Tara adrift amid a sea of pedal bins. 'These are quite tough aren't they?' she spluttered pathetically. 'It's good that. A bin needs to be tough, don't you think?' She attempted a feeble grin. She failed.

Farson and Regan simply stared.

Tara's stomach squirmed and the vast majority of her body had the desperate urge to be in a distant galaxy, far, far away, right now. She was almost on her feet dashing through the door, never to darken that particular part of Camford ever again. Almost.

There was only one thing that stopped her in her tracks. The sure and certain knowledge that if she didn't find out what these two guys were really rabbiting on about then she'd regret it. Maybe not now, but soon. And for the rest of her life.

This required some quick thinking. Immediately. Now what would Joe 90 do . . .?

With a struggle she hauled herself to her feet, casually picked up a black and gold Dalek and, through trembling teeth and a whirling mind, said in as casual manner as she could muster. 'Look, look, the paint hasn't even chipped. I . . . I must mention that in my review. Yes. That's right. My review. Of course,' she said, winging it for all she was worth. 'My readers *will* be impressed. Sorry about the mess boys, do you want me to clear . . .'

'Readers?' gagged Farson suddenly taking a step forward and staring at the brunette teenager through new eyes. 'D . . . did you say readers?'

'Oh, yes, yes. Hundreds of them. Thousands . . .' she suddenly found herself embroidering. 'They voted my column the best in the whole magazine last year.'

Farson's eyes lit up. '*You're* a journalist?'

'Yes,' she lied in as haughty a manner as possible and handed him the Dalek. 'Don't tell me, I know. I don't *look* like a journalist!'

'Well, actually . . .' began Farson before he was cut off by her eyebrows arcing into a 'v' of vexation.

'We don't *all* wear scruffy raincoats, have five o'clock shadows and carry little pads about, you know?'

'I . . . I didn't mean any offence . . .'

'It's alright. Happens all the time. Don't worry about it.' Tara shrugged dissmissively and headed towards the door carefully stepping over a dozen or so Daleks. 'Anyhow, I've got a deadline with some presses and front pages and things, so if you'll just excuse me, I really must be . . .'

'No!' squawked Farson leaping deftly in front of the door. 'I mean, er, not just yet. What magazine d'you work for? I might have a great story for you.' He winked meaningfully at Regan.

The black haired shop owner shook his head and looked at the floor. There were times when he wondered about

17

Farson's leadership abilities. Okay, so they needed the publicity, but there were ways of getting journalists. Press agencies, that sort of thing. You don't just chat up the first brunette teenager who happens to confess to being a reviewer of pedal bins.

Suppressing a shriek of terror, Tara halted in her tracks. 'What magazine? Er . . . er . . .' And suddenly she realised that perhaps she hadn't thought this through to quite the degree the situation demanded. 'Er . . . ha . . . you might not have heard of it.'

'Try us,' pleaded Farson not wanting to let the call of the printed word slip away. 'We read a lot of magazines, don't we, Regan.'

'Yup,' snorted the shopkeeper. 'Tons of them.'

Tara swallowed and the palms of her hands began to sweat. 'I work for . . . um . . . um . . . *Amazingly Unfeasible* Magazine,' she blurted.

The silence in the shop was underwhelming.

'It . . . It deals with all the weird and wonderful goings on just left of life's mainstream,' she added. 'A bit like *The X Files* . . . only much, *much* weirder.'

Farson stared at her, rubbing his chin thoughtfully. He cast an inquiring glance across at Regan. Tara's brain was fizzing with desperate fabrications. 'B . . . Buzz Aldrin reads it all the time,' she hazarded with only the slightest quiver in her voice. 'And . . . er, it's William Shatner's favourite magazine! He recommended it to Leonard Nimoy and . . .'

'*You're* the expert on magazines, Regan. Buzz Aldrin's heard of it. Have you?' challenged Farson.

'Well, er . . . *Amazingly Incredible*, did you say?' hedged Regan desperately not wanting to appear ignorant when faced with such a quality readership.

'*Amazingly Unfeasible*.'

'Yeah, yeah, of course, that's it,' grinned Regan uncomfortably. 'Course I've heard of it. There was one of those almond-eyed aliens on the cover last month, wasn't there?'

Tara swallowed again. 'Er . . . was that *last* month? D'you know, it's *so* hard to keep track of covers sometimes. Aliens this month, spaceships the next, crop circles the month after that . . . life as a journalist is *such* a whirl.'

Suddenly Farson could stand it no longer. He leapt forward, flipped the shop sign to 'Closed' and pulled down the shutter. She was a journalist, he was certain. 'How would you like the biggest story of your life?' he asked, half insistent, half desperate, wholly overdramatically.

Mutely Tara nodded, her stomach churning.

'Meet me here at three in the morning and I'll take you for a night you'll never forget,' whispered Farson hoarsely.

'Three?' she gasped.

Farson nodded. 'And bring your pad and pencil. You won't want to miss a thing!' Beaming he tugged open the door and showed her out. 'Three. Don't be late!' he reminded her and slammed the door with a forceful flourish.

'You sure you know what you're doing?' cautioned Regan a moment later.

'Course I do. That's why I'm the president. It's time to prepare. T minus eleven hours forty-five, and counting.' And he was heading for the store room in a clatter of Daleks.

Outside the front of 'Fitments of the Imagination' it took Tara Ness a good ten minutes to remember why it was she was standing in the street next door but one to the aromatic premises of Luigi's Fish Emporium. Her mind spinning with speculation she set off for a bag of chips.

Doctor Striebley pedalled up the hundred yard long stretch of 'Edison Boulevard' with somewhat less than his normal degree of enthusiasm. At almost any other time he would have been racing up towards the gleaming lab brimming with eager keenness, desperate to roll up the sleeves of his lab coat and dive headlong into the heady world of research, straining his intellectual shoulders against the forefront of science. But, not today. There was a dark cloud hovering over his intellectual horizon – the looming spectre of finance. Or rather, the lack of it.

Ever since he had handed the last few hundred quid of Splice of Life Patentable Biosciences Ltd's liquid assets over to the clerk at the Patents Centre his thoughts had been on the darker side of miserable. Okay, so Oven-Bake Sushi *had* been Professor Crickson's invention but Striebley had agreed to shell out that final bit of cash on getting it patented. He was only too well aware of the fact that it had been his signature on their very last cheque.

Nervously he halted before the tinted security doors of the lab, leant his ageing bicycle against the wall and tugged out his pass card. With a swish he passed it through a slot in a box screwed to the right hand of the frame and watched apprehensively as the uPVC door slithered open. He knew that very, very shortly he would have to break the news of their financial situation to Professor Crickson. It was a prospect he relished with a minimum of glee – the Prof was certain to take it badly.

Striebley stepped into the central atrium of Splice of Life, stared at the tropical foliage strewn decorously everywhere and idly wondered just how much he could get for the cheese plants at the weekly car boot sale. Miserably he concluded that it probably wouldn't even be enough for a pair of magnetic fleas. He shrugged and headed towards his lab.

He didn't get there.

The white coated figure waiting on the top of the stairs saw to that.

'Striebley! Aha, Striebley! There you are at last. Where the hell have you been?' yelled Professor Crickson and clattered down the flight of metal steps. 'I've been trying to find you for hours. Been hiding from me, have you? Scared I won't like some of your results, eh?'

Striebley edged away from the foot of the stairs and tried desperately to hide behind a suitable aspidistra.

Crickson leapt off the bottom rung and, like a bush-hatted explorer in a Saturday matinee, hacked the foliage away with a rolled up magazine and appeared panting before Striebley. 'Well, where've you been? What've you been doing that was so important, hmmmm?'

Striebley swallowed and tried to avoid the piercing eyes

peering over the bifocals. 'I ... er, just popped out,' he offered in as non-inflammatory manner as he could.

'Just popped out?' snapped Professor Crickson prodding Striebley in the chest with the rolled up magazine. 'You're a scientist. You don't just pop out whenever you feel like!'

'I didn't *feel* like,' complained Striebley. 'You told me to. Oven-Bake Sushi doesn't patent *itself* you know.'

Crickson's face suddenly brightened. 'All the paperwork was in order I take it. Everything alright?'

'Paperwork was fine,' cringed Striebley sensing the moment of revelation taking a giant step nearer. 'The Clerk accepted it after a bit of persuasion, but ...'

'But what?' asked Crickson pouncing on the Doc's hesitation suspiciously. 'Wasn't registered by the Japanese, was it? They're always there with something new ...'

'No, no ... they haven't a clue about it.'

'The Americans then,' squawked the Prof suspiciously, chewing the earpiece of his bifocals thoughtfully. 'It's them damn yanks, isn't it. Prior claim from Harvard or UCLA or ...'

'No, no. You're the first. You've invented something new!'

'So what's the problem, eh?' scowled Crickson peering up at Striebley as if he was some specimen under a microscope. 'Sounds fine to me. Another patent registered to Splice of Life Patentable Biosciences Ltd ... What? Why are you looking so damned miserable?'

'Because ... because there won't be any more, that's why,' blurted Striebley with more of a whine in his voice than he really would've liked. 'We're out of money. No more cash in the bank. Penniless!'

'Oh, is *that* all,' shrugged Crickson putting his specs back on. 'Thought there was something serious amiss.'

'Didn't you hear me? We have no money. That means no more reagents. No more research. No more job!' shrieked Striebley.

'Yeah, yeah,' tutted Crickson dismissively and thrust the

21

rolled up copy of today's *New American Scientist* at him. 'Page thirty-six. Read it.'

'Didn't you hear what I just said . . .' began Striebley in complete confusion. This was not the reaction he had expected.

'I heard. I heard. Now read.'

Striebley swallowed and, humouring Crickson, turned to page thirty-six. The headline 'Cracking the Highway Code: Born For Life In The Fast Lane' leapt from the glossy paper.

'Read, read!' chivvied Crickson barely hiding a strangely excited grin. Despite his bifocals and balding pate he looked all the world like a overwound nine year old waiting for the girl next door to discover the glistening mass of frog-spawn lurking in her sandwich box.

Dreading what he would find, Striebley fixed his gaze on the first words.

On the highways of the future, speed cameras will be a thing of the past. Within two years you'll be more likely to be pulled over on the basis of your family history rather than the actual speed you're doing. At least that is the radical claim of a group of scientists who have been investigating the so called genetic predisposition of a heavy right foot.

For decades, geneticists have shown that certain individuals holding certain genes will always have an unshakable tendency to behave in certain ways. There are genes for gymnastic ability, chromosomes for creativity and allegedly sequences for public speaking. But now, to these ranks comes another. The recently discovered 'speed gene'.

Following extensive testing of persistent moving traffic violators, scientists have discovered a direct causal link between the presence of one specific gene and an overwhelming tendency to break every speed limit in sight. Carriers of the so called BMW 535i gene are six hundred times more likely to travel in excess of ninety-eight miles an hour than those without . . .

Striebley pulled a face and snorted. 'What *is* this? Speed genes?' he snapped derisively. 'Who the hell does research into things like that? Waste of bloody time. And I bet they got a massive grant off somebody at Scotland Yard.'

'Not at all. There's been not a penny of external investment,' offered Crickson. 'So far,' he added significantly.

'Well, it won't be long before the coppers are offering them loads of dosh for that little nugget of information.'

'Hmmm, my thoughts exactly,' nodded Crickson, stroking his chin.

'I bet they had ideas on government money right from the start,' snarled Striebley gnashing his teeth enviously. 'That's just typical of the way science is going these days. Forget research for research's sake. It's all down to money nowadays. How much cash can we get for the fewest questions?'

'The best part of a million quid, I reckon,' smirked Professor Crickson.

'What? That much? Where does it say that?' spluttered Striebley scouring the pages of *New American Scientist* for pound signs.

'It doesn't. At least not officially anyway. But I'm sure they'll want to negotiate me down from my opening bid of a million and a half.'

Suddenly Striebley's jaw fell open. '*Your* opening bid?' he gagged staring bewilderedly at the Professor. 'What d'you mean *your* opening bid?'

'As Director of Research it seems fitting that I should open the bidding. Oh, come, come, stop looking so blank. Don't you recognise your own results? Look at the top of the page.'

Striebley's eyes slithered up the glossy page to the tiny list of contributing scientists. If anything, his jaw dropped even further open. 'You? Me? . . . but, but, I haven't been doing any research into this!'

'Neither have I,' grinned Crickson rubbing his hands together joyously. 'But the coppers don't know that, do they?'

'Are you mad? You can't ...'

'Already have. Any minute now and the phones will be ...'

The shrill warbling of an incoming call echoed around the inside of the atrium.

Crickson picked up the receiver. 'Yes? ... Yes. This is Professor Walter Crickson speaking ... Oh, hello minister ... A fascinating piece of research? ... I couldn't agree more ... Tomorrow morning at nine thirty it is, then. Certainly. Goodbye.'

And as the receiver rattled in its cradle Crickson punched the air and Striebley sank onto the bottom rung of the stairs.

'Million and a quarter, no problem,' chirped Crickson. 'No civil servant schedules a meeting at nine thirty in the morning unless he's *really* keen about something.'

20th June, Next Year

2.55 a.m.

Holding her breath, Tara Ness eased her wardrobe door shut and pulled on her warmest anorak. Risking only the shortest bursts of torchlight she snatched up three pencils and one of W.H. Smith's finest flip-top writing pads. And there she stood for a moment, her mind spinning with questions, wondering what else she would be likely to need as a journalist reporting for *Amazingly Unfeasible* Magazine. She snatched up an elephant shaped rubber and a protractor and desperately stuffed them into a suitable pocket. And then she was off, heading for the bedroom door with the stealth of the average SAS trooper on an embassy raid. She reached out, grasped the handle and suddenly froze.

A massive question floated before her, taunting, fixing her to the shag pile of her bedroom in a ferment of worry. Had her father remembered to set the burglar alarm when he had rolled in at well gone midnight?

She knew only too well that one foot on the landing and she'd trigger the motion sensors and polaroid security cameras. There was no way past it. The number of times she'd been snapped in her nightie and woken the entire street when heading off to the loo in the middle of the night was testament to the system's sensitivity.

Desperately she wanted to be off down the stairs, skipping over the creaky fifth step from the bottom and dashing out the front door. But only one thing stopped her. The wall mounted polaroid. How would she explain being photographed on her way to the loo wearing her warmest anorak and Doc Martins?

Cursing the fact that Joe 90 never encountered such problems she decided there was only one solution.

She spun on her heel, scuttled across the carpet, swept back the curtain and shoved open the sash window. All as silently as possible, of course. In seconds she was out across the moonlit roof and scrambling down the clematis covered trellis on the side wall of the garage.

Half a mile away, the red haired figure of Lance Farson tapped a Sonic Screwdriver Propelling Pencil and Biro Set irritably against a cash register. 'She's late,' he grumbled.

'You didn't really expect her to turn up, did you?' tutted Regan.

'Of course I did, she's a journalist. She's bound to be hungry for a decent story. She won't be able to stay away.'

'Correction. She *said* she was a journalist,' pointed out Regan petulantly. 'I didn't see any identification. Did you?' During the nine hours since turning over the 'Closed' sign of 'Fitments of the Imagination' and busying himself with the final preparations for tonight's historic launch, Regan had begun to harbour a veritable fishing fleet of doubts relating to the journalistic qualifications of the mysterious girl. After all, did it not seem to be trusting the fickle powers of coincidence a mite too much in believing that she just *happened* to turn up by chance, just *happened* to overhear their conversation and just *happened* to be exactly what they wanted, right then ... a journalist? And then there was the question of

25

Amazingly Unfeasible Magazine. He prided himself on the sure and certain knowledge that he had annual subscriptions to every magazine, journal or fanzine that had anything even remotely to do with science fiction, fantasy, the mysterious and the paranormal . . . so why, pray tell, had he never heard of *Amazingly Unfeasible*? Add the nagging feeling that he'd seen her face somewhere before and Regan was beginning to smell creatures of an unmistakably rodentish nature.

'I didn't see any identification because I didn't ask,' countered Farson scribbling irritably on a till roll with the Sonic Screwdriver Biro. Secretly he hated himself for this omission. Why was it that whenever he was faced with brunette members of the female persuasion he always forgot to find out vital information like name, telephone number and favourite flavours of ice cream? 'If she's a journalist, she'll be here,' he added hopefully, mentally putting her in the chocolate chip cookie and fudge category.

'She's already late, you said so yourself . . .' began Regan and he would have started ranting on about the critical timing of launch windows and how they had really better get moving, sharpish, right now for the benefit of *The Adversity Project* and ultimately, mankind. Fortunately, at that very instant, the shop door was shoved open by a certain panting teenage girl sweating in her warmest anorak.

'Ha. What did I tell you?' grinned Farson lancing victorious daggers at Regan and leaping to his feet. In a few steps he was across the shop and hovering excitedly next to her. 'So glad you could come, Miss . . .?'

'Ness,' she panted. 'Tara Ness.'

Over by the recently rebuilt pyramid of Dalek Pedal Bins Regan sniggered derisively and pulled the type of prescient face for which Mystic Meg was justly famed. 'Let me guess. I sense that your parents are fans of the last series of *The Avengers*?'

'H . . . How did you know that?' asked Tara shocked and not a little impressed. 'They've got all the videos.'

'Amazing what you can learn about a parent's viewing habits from an offspring's first name. You just have to know

26

what to look for,' he grinned smugly. 'In your case, it's the delicious Tara King. Good job they weren't mad about Emma Peel otherwise you'd've ended up sounding like a chain of high street undie stores,' chuckled Regan.

Tara scratched her head and looked confused.

'Well, now that we're all here let's get moving,' declared Farson, trying to ignore Regan's idiocy. 'Time is of the essence.' He cracked the door, peered covertly into the street and dashed out to a waiting 2CV. Beckoning madly like some failed extra from a cancelled cop show he leapt into the driver's seat and fired up the engine.

Regan bustled Tara across the street and dumped her unceremoniously in the back seat next to a sticky forty gallon oil drum. Worriedly she stared at the glistening goo coating its filthy sides and began to wonder if she hadn't just possibly let her imagination run away with her. She was alone in a car with two strangers, in the middle of the night, heading who knew where, to do who knew what. She swallowed nervously and pondered the possibility that maybe her definition of first contact scenario was somewhat less carnal than theirs.

With only the slightest crunching of gears Farson dropped the clutch and raced the mustard yellow motor away as fast as he could. What with the three ten gallon oil drums of rocket fuel on the roof rack and the one in the back seat it took a good few minutes to wind it up past thirty. Idly he wondered if perhaps he should have used a few gallons of that in the car instead of Tesco's Unleaded. He'd been working on that sugar-based fuel for the last year and a half, honing its bond-energy release coefficients to perfection, heightening its power output to the maximum, putting in countless hours of overtime. And now, tonight, it would finally be used.

Nervously steering the top heavy vehicle through the narrow streets of ancient Camford and earnestly hoping that he wouldn't be called on to perform an emergency stop, Farson headed out toward the fens and a glorious date with destiny.

The 2CV's suspension complained in no uncertain terms as they trundled over the humpback bridge which marked the outskirts of Camford. The street lights stopped, plunging the road into almost complete darkness.

Suddenly, a frantically waving figure sprang from a privet hedge and began leaping about in the car's headlights like a stage struck lunatic desperate for a nightly fix of limelight. Farson swore and slammed his foot on the brake. Tara screamed.

Two hundred yards later, the car finally shuddered to a halt and the panting camouflaged figure caught up with them.

'What is it?' hissed Regan winding down the passenger window.

'Intruders,' came the terse reply.

'Damn. There can't be anyone still at it,' grumbled Regan.

'Fraid so, sir. Couple of late arrivals turned up about an hour ago.'

'An *hour*!' gasped Regan with not a little jealousy. 'What *are* they doing? No, no ... don't answer that.'

Up a tiny lane the shrieks of ecstasy reached a muffled climax and, with a shudder, a white Sierra rocked into satisfied motionlessness. There was a scuffling inside, the unmistakable sound of Wrangler zippers ascending and the palm of a hand wiped at the lust-steamed windscreen. Moments later the engine coughed into life and the last of the night's newly deflowered students was driven away into the still night air, grin plastered to bewildered face.

It was the same every night on 'Rumpy Row'. A column of fifteen or so cars turned up, gyrated in sticky franticality and drove off again, sated. It was a popular little spot. Especially with the students. And especially just around Finals time.

Regan had hoped they'd have all cleared off by half three. They normally had.

Farson drummed his fingers irritably on the steering wheel and snorted. This was just *too* much. How could such a vital mission to the stars be delayed by the sticky nocturnal activities of a Sierra driver?

'Lights off,' hissed Regan suddenly as the Sierra growled into earshot. The road plunged into darkness and a ghostly vehicle floated into view. It turned left, shifted a gear and sped off towards Camford, all windows opaque with moisture.

In the back seat of the 2CV Tara's mind whirled with a snowstorm of questions. Had she really heard what she thought she had earlier in that shop?

Cursing under his breath about NASA not having to put up with such trivial events causing mission delays, Farson reached into the glove compartment and snatched out his trusty Kennedy Space Center Baseball Cap. 'Right, synchronise watches at T minus twenty-five,' he announced importantly and flicked his cap on. He always wore it on special occasions like tonight. After all, it was a genuine piece of NASA merchandise. He revved the 2CV and spitting at least three pieces of gravel, he turned into 'Rumpy Row'. The camouflage-clad one scurried behind.

In minutes, to the casual observer, the scene had returned to the normal nocturnal stillness of the early moments of a typical morning. Slight flicks of supernatural mist licked over the edges of the fens, stroking the ankles of the distant Ancient University City of Camford. In the distance a cluster of feral tabbies mewled hoarsely. All was as it should be. But that was about to change.

The balding radials of the 2CV crunched up the incline of 'Rumpy Row' powered by a struggling engine. Farson peered out into the cool gloom, his eyes peeled for a covert signal which would guide him to the camouflaged entrance prepared by the advanced troops of SOFA.

Suddenly a section of privet hedge moved, lurched excitedly forward and waggled a high-powered torch light up towards the car.

'Bugger,' cursed Farson blinking uselessly beneath the brim of his Kennedy Space Center cap. 'How many times have I told him not to point it so high! I'll kill him, I'll . . .'

'Later,' hissed Regan. 'There are far more important things to do first. The universe awaits!'

'Good point,' agreed Farson and jammed his foot on the brake. With a sharp squeak of struggling discs the 2CV shuddered to a halt and in an instant a dozen sections of privet hedging lurched forward in a flurry of torch beams and attacked the trio of oil drums on the roof rack.

'What the hell . . .? What's going on?' shrieked Tara as ropes and bungees clattered on the roof. 'No time to explain,' declared Farson, flicking his pony tail over his shoulder and leaping out of the driver's seat. 'C'mon. No time to lose.'

In seconds, under Farson's waved instructions, an impromptu opening appeared in the reinforced concrete walling ahead and the drums vanished through it. Tara's jaw dropped in awe as, magically, a diesel generator, a bank of Marshall stacks and a Portakabin all followed, hauled stealthily by the swarm of privet sprouting forms. She barely contained a squeak of delight. This was even better than *Thunderbirds*.

Farson grinned to himself and slapped the side of the Portakabin. Everything was running as smoothly as a greased ferret on roller blades.

'You getting all this?' hissed Regan suddenly from the passenger seat, his voice cutting through Tara's growing sense of wonder like a soldering iron through Flora. 'I'm sure your readers will want every detail.'

'Er . . . I . . . er, of course,' she spluttered, tugged out her flip-top pad and began rummaging for a blank page. 'Er . . . do tell me about the generator . . .' she began, licking the tip of her pencil in what she hoped looked like a professionally journalistic manner. 'How many ccs, does it have, hmmm?' She looked up at a now empty vehicle.

'Ask your questions on the move. We're already running late,' hissed Regan tugging her out of the door and staring importantly at his watch. Only forty minutes remained of the launch window. Things would have to work like clockwork from now on. One hitch and the entire mission would have to be aborted. Cancelled until at least the middle of next week. 'C'mon,' he snapped and pointed into the gloom of the night.

Ahead, through the gap in the wall, Tara could just make

out Farson barking whispered orders at a group of oddly humanoid looking privets fidgeting around him. In seconds they had saluted and squirmed back into the cover of the night.

Trembling with pent excitement he shook his head and pushed on after his team straining with the Portakabin. Then suddenly he caught himself, slapped his forehead in the universal gesture of the terminally forgetful, whirled on his heels and dashed back towards a certain anoraked brunette. In a rare moment of chivalry he took Tara by the arm, smiled and, with growing thoughts of getting her telephone number as soon as possible, he whispered, 'Welcome to the start of the Experience of your Lifetime! You'll like this. Believe me! You'll like it.'

Fizzing with excitement, Farson led her away from the 2CV blissfully unaware that the heel of her left Doc Martin had contacted a carefully positioned strand of high security, translucent fishing line.

In a small hut at the edge of a distant expanse of grass, a makeshift string of discarded coke cans rattled noisily in the still night air. In a millisecond the sound of snoring had stopped and the figure on the camp bed was up and hopping across the floor in his mustard yellow sleeping bag. He stared accusingly at the alarm and cursed under his breath.

'Intruder in sector thirteen,' he mumbled to himself. 'More bloody students I'll bet. Why do they always go so wild after Finals?'

Pupating rapidly from his sleeping bag he sprang across the hut, leapt into his trusty wellingtons, hurled his wax jacket over his fleecy pyjamas, donned his flat cap and lurched towards the door. Pausing only to snatch a torch and his baseball bat from the shelf, he was off in search of vandals in sector thirteen, anger rising within, seething like a blocked drain in a rainstorm.

How dare they wake him up at this time of night? It wasn't right. Not half an hour had passed since his last inspection. Couldn't they have broken in just a bit earlier?

Every night he did his rounds. Strolling around, sweeping his industrial Eveready torch through the gloom, rays blasting every three-quarter inch blade of the immaculately tended grounds. Every night he searched tirelessly for any sign of abuse, any misplaced divot or suspect sod. Night-time was the only chance he had. Folks *would* insist on playing golf on his pet turf all the rest of the time. Bloody golfers.

His anger boiled as he stalked across the fifth green and thought of someone breaking in. It was bound to mean there'd be damage. His professional pride was on the line here. Of all the acres of lawnage which covered Royal Berkshire, no turf was as well cosseted as these expanses of enviable green. Every hole of the Regal Greens Golf Course had its very own verdant Axminster huddling around it in clover free perfection. Reg Treadly, Head Groundsman and Certified Lawnophile, saw to that on his rounds. Here he could be found, stalking tirelessly across his acreage, communing silently with his tiny green charges and occasionally whispering phrases of tender encouragement before the onslaught of the coming day. And today his darling greenery was being attacked by saboteurs. Well, he'd see to them. It was his job.

He hurried on towards sector thirteen, and the hordes of vandals who were *surely* hurling empy Moet and Chandon magnums over their shoulders in the traditional post-finals frenzy.

Reg suddenly stopped in his tracks, bent and, with a practised oath, snatched a stray leaf off the otherwise debris free expanse of the fifth green.

'Trees,' he tutted as he hurled the leaf into his litter sack. 'So untidy,' he grumbled and gently patted the uncovered blades. But this morning he had no more time for extra encouragement. Sector thirteen had been invaded, violated. If they were hurting his turf . . .

Thrusting his trusty Eveready deep inside his waxen pocket and drawing Betty, his faithful baseball bat, with a ninja-style flourish he crept silently towards the source of the covert rustling. Not for the first time did he wish that the Regal Greens Golf Course was sited somewhat further from the Ancient University City of Camford. One of the incessant problems he encountered on his morning perambulations was couples of bonking students. Precisely what it was that lured them in droves to the edge of the thirteenth rough, he hadn't a clue. But he knew what got rid of them. His teeth glinted in the night as he patted the end of his baseball bat. The number of naked buttocks that particular rod of willow had contacted was well into triple figures. And rising.

With practised stealth he crept onward, his footfalls shrouded in complete silence and, curiously, an oddly rising mist.

Ahead, the rustling sounded again through the dense undergrowth and was followed by a series of hisses for silence.

Reg Treadly grit his teeth together at the sound. So, there were a whole gang of them tonight, eh? Well, he and Betty had dispersed orgies of pot-smoking psychology students before. A grin of something more than mere job satisfaction flashed across his face as he paced vast stick-insect strides across the green.

Unseen, the mist around his ankles was deepening rapidly, almost like theatrical dry ice pouring over a stage edge. Suddenly Reg's expert ears latched onto the unmistakable sound of metal against metal, the jangling of chains and the fastening of bolts. A shiver of revulsion ran icy fingers up the nape of his neck as his imagination kicked into overdrive. What acts of kinky perversion were they engaging in? Was it legal? Should he just hang about in the bushes and watch for a few minutes? After all, it wouldn't hurt to just take in the sight of firm female flesh being shackled to . . . NO! NO! This sort of thing just shouldn't be allowed. Not on his thirteenth hole anyway.

Working himself up to his most ferocious snarl and wielding his baseball bat above his head in practised circles he leapt through the opaque curtain of rhododendrons. 'Okay, you filthy pack of bloody st . . .'

It was as far as he got before his words were drowned by the suddenly powered up pa system announcing. 'Two ... two ... Testing. Aha! See I told you it was the yellow wire and the red button. Right then, er ...' Unnecessarily, the voice cleared its throat. 'Ahem ... T minus three minutes and counting. Auxiliary power units commencing charge-up.'

Cheers went up from clumps of privet all across the thirteenth fairway. Somewhere a generator coughed into life. Arrays of halogen lights sprang into blazing glory, each focusing on the clump of hastily cobbled together scaffolding and plywood perched on the green baize of the thirteenth green. And Reg Treadly's jaw dropped almost faster than his faithful baseball bat slipped out of his hand.

'Flight pressure charging. O-two flow at 22 kPa,' declared the voice with only the slightest hint of impending feedback.

'Welcome to Ground Control,' grinned Farson, his red fringe wagging untidily beneath the peak of his Kennedy Space Center cap and, like some groom leading his recently enspoused across the legendary threshold, he pulled her inside. Tara's boots clattered into the open-sided Portakabin and she stood momentarily bewildered by the twinkling of red LEDs on banks of baffling equipment, radar screens and a myriad of angle-poise lamps. 'Impressed?' whispered Farson enthusiastically into her quivering shell-like. Mutely she nodded. She hadn't expected this. She'd never dreamed that such things happened in Camford.

Suddenly an intense figure in bottle glasses and fuel-stained lab-coat cleared his throat, leaned closer to a microphone and blasted across the pa system again. 'You! Don't just stand there. Help them!' he screamed through the dozen cones of the Marshall stacks, gesturing wildly at a dumbfounded figure in a flat cap and wax jacket.

Treadly turned an index finger towards his chest. 'Me?' he mouthed.

'Yes. You! Give them a hand with the fuel. We haven't long until the launch window closes. And get that flat cap off, you know it isn't standard issue uniform. Telemetry uplink activated.'

'You'll have to forgive him,' offered Farson into Tara's ear. 'He always gets a bit over excited on launch nights. Not surprising really. He's designed and built the entire *Adversity* series.' Tara watched the lab coated figure peering at arrays of dials and valve settings and found herself thinking of the resident bespectacled genius of Tracy Island. 'The *Adversity* series?' she asked as two silver dungareed figures rolled a forty gallon drum out from a hijacked golf trolley and headed off into the gloom.

'Ahh, of course, you haven't met our latest baby, have you? Do forgive me.' Farson reached out to a large switch on a panel and flicked it with an unnecessary flourish. Instantly banks of halogen lights flooded the thirteenth hole of the Regal Greens Golf Course. 'Miss Ness, meet *Adversity VI*!' he declared.

'Oh my god, is it real?' she squeaked as she stared into the night. She rubbed her eyes and squinted again at the gleaming white column of three-stage liquid-fuel rocketry perched atop a hastily cobbled together array of scaffolding and plywood. Silently it vented plumes of vapours into a pair of genuine Sahara sand-filled bunkers. The two silver dungareed figures shoved the oil drum onwards towards the metallic growth of the spotlit launch pad.

'T minus two minutes thirty,' came another hundred decibel announcement over the pa.

'Impressive, huh?' smirked Farson, spreading his hands across the humming scene of activity like Caesar surveying his empire.

Tara fought with her rapidly weakening knees and nodded mutely. To her, and the binocular toting crowds of advance troops gathered on the boundaries of the thirteenth rough, *Adversity VI* seemed to stare expectantly heavenwards, as if every atom of its being was already straining desperately to leap into the wild blue canopy above and lurch into whatever lay beyond.

'T minus two minutes fifteen and . . .oi! Are you going to

get helping, or not?' accused the voice of the lab-coated one once more.

Reg Treadly took three shaky paces towards the silver dungareed figures straining behind the barrel and suddenly caught himself. Help them? Help them destroy his grassy babies? No way! He snatched Betty, his faithful baseball bat off his tender lawn, snarled and strode imperiously towards the Ground Control Portakabin.

'Uh-oh. Intruders,' mumbled Farson and stepped bravely before Tara. This was his show, he wasn't going to let it be ruined by ignorant members of the public.

"What is the meaning of this!' growled Treadly, moments later, tapping his rod of willow meaningfully across his palm and peering into the Ground Control Portakabin.

'Never seen an interplanetary device before?' asked Farson attempting withering sarcasm.

'Interplanetary device, is it? Looks like an overgrown firework to me. And it's still months till Guy Fawkes Night.'

'This is no Fawkesian prank,' hissed Farson. Behind him, Regan ground his teeth.

Quicker than everyone expected Treadly leapt sideways and lay Betty significantly across a glinting control panel.

'Mind my knobs!' shrieked Regan angrily lurching forward. 'That's delicate equipment, that is. And bloody expensive, too!' He swept Treadly's weapon away. 'One false adjustment and mankind's future will . . .'

'What about the future of my bloody grass!' yelled the Head Groundsman. He knew from years of experience that the only way to deal with students was to shout. It was the same with foreigners, too. Shout. They always got the message soon enough.

'Grass?' squeaked Farson. 'How can you think of grass at a time like this?' He stared from the vapour venting tip of *Adversity VI* to the stars above, his eyes misting with the glory of the moment. 'Here we stand on the brink of the Universe, poised at mission status go for a main engine start and you're concerned about a few bits of turf!'

'It's my job to worry about bloody bits of turf,' growled

Reg Treadly with a riptide undercurrent of menace and a nonchalant flick of Betty.

Farson, in a show of what he hoped Tara would consider macho defiance, flicked open the mic channel on the control desk, cleared his throat and declared, 'T minus one minute fifty and . . . your job!' The words echoed around the thirteenth fairway before the lab-coated one, in a rare moment of understanding, closed the channel.

'My job,' confirmed Treadly tapping Betty threateningly against his weathered palm. 'Reg Treadly, Head Groundsman of the Regal Greens Golf Course, the thirteenth hole of which you are now trespassing upon. And *you* are?'

'Er, look, I can explain . . .' spluttered Farson.

'I'm listening,' scoffed Treadly.

'Well, it's er . . . Vital SOFA business. You wouldn't understand,' said Farson, peering out from beneath his Kennedy Space Center Baseball cap with a sneer of what he sincerely hoped passed for intellectual challenge.

'Try me,' growled Treadly returning a firm gaze of horticultural superiority. 'I want to know precisely why my prize thirteenth fairway is being destroyed!'

'Er . . . It's not our fault we're here,' began Regan. 'We would've used our favourite launch site except, er it's been tarmacked over to form the new Sainway's car park and there's a height restriction on the way in and . . .'

'*Launch site*,' choked Treadly. 'You mean you're actually going to launch that thing?'

'In a minute and a half actually,' insisted Farson. 'It's a bit hard to continue our search without it. Mankind needs . . .'

'Search? What are you on about?' Treadly shook his head and wished for a simple orgy to clear.

'Our Search for Offworld Friendly Aliens, SOFA, see?' smiled Farson feeling the reassuring nudge of firmer territory. Tara thrilled. It *was* all true.

Farson pushed onwards. If he could waste enough time it wouldn't matter what arguments the groundsman came up with. Eighty-odd seconds and *Adversity VI* would be on its way. 'Once we've established a geostationary satellite we'll contact any residents of neighbouring galaxies . . .'

'And ask if you can borrow a cup of sugar, I suppose,' snarled Treadly oozing sarcasm.

Farson held up his finger and declared. 'An interesting idea although there is at present no evidence to suppose that any alien civilisation will find sucrose as pleasurably sweet as we humans . . .'

'I believe we have found a kindred spirit here,' growled Regan trying a different tack, advancing towards Treadly palms wide. 'Let us embrace him into the ways of our belief. The Founding of a Universal Village!'

The Head Groundsman took a step backwards and waggled Betty, threatening.

'Oh, come, come,' soothed Farson staring at Treadly. 'Don't you believe that the Truth is Out There?' He pointed towards the moonlit heavens above Camford.

'Well, I . . .'

The baseball capped one grinned and pressed on as the figure in the lab-coat monitored gauges and flicked switches importantly.

'And if the Truth is Out There, let's not leave it shivering on the Cosmic Doorstep of Infinity. Invite it in for tea and muffins, I say.'

'Tea and muffins?' spluttered Treadly.

'Tea and muffins?' mouthed Tara.

'Or chocolate hob-nobs if you prefer,' smiled Regan with the charm of a bouncer.

'T-minus one minute ten!' came another announcement with only the slightest squeal of feedback. 'Hurry up with that fuel!'

The silver dungareed ones put on a burst of speed.

'Fuel!' screamed Treadly and in an instant his mind was filled with images of searing flames torching his thirteenth green as *Adversity VI* lurched its way heavenwards. 'My grass!' That would really muck up the arrangements for the Prince Fahad El-Fannagil Open today.

'Ah, I shouldn't worry yourself about that,' reassured

Farson. 'It's a specially formulated sugar based fuel – a formula of my own devising actually – specially calculated to burn at a temperature safe to all organic matter. After all, we don't want to barbecue our alien cousins as soon as we meet them now do we?'

'It's safe? No acres of charred lawnage?' spluttered Treadly.

'Not at all. Perfectly, perfectly safe,' smiled Farson and casually hid his crossed fingers in his jacket pocket. Perhaps he should have actually tested the stuff first but there hadn't been enough time. The work load at Splice of Life had been terribly heavy recently and besides, testing wasn't necessary. All his calculations showed the bond energy would be way below the inflammability constant of organic . . .

'T-minus forty-five seconds. All systems in go-mode. Radar tracking operational. Powering up ignition generator.' A quivering digit reached out and flicked a yellow and black striped toggle switch. Almost instantly a battery of red lights began flashing along the entire height of the launch gantry. The silver dungareed fuel operatives gasped and sloshed the last few gallons of Farson's sugar based goo into the primary ignition tanks. Moments later they tugged the funnel out, screwed on the filler cap and legged it towards the relative safety of the nearby rough. It had to be said that they had taken a massive dose of salt with all of Farson's reassurances regarding the safety of the fuel.

'T-minus twenty,' announced the one in the lab-coat and stabbed the play button on the cassette recorder.

'Hey, that's my job!' snapped Farson, shoving him out of the way.

Much to Treadly's disgust the overplayed strains of Richard Strauss's *Also Sprach Zarathustra* reverberated through the gathered Marshalls. He tutted to himself. *2001* definitely had a lot to answer for.

'T-minus ten and counting. Primary ignition coils warmed and ready. Auto-sequence start.'

Despite himself not understanding a word of what was blasting from the Marshalls, Treadly found himself getting caught up in the mounting excitement. His mind flashed cliched images of Apollo stages tumbling away from thrusters in sheets of flame, grey expanses of lunar surface spun by as viewed from the LEM's window, golfers swiped birdies on the moon.

Tara also found herself getting aroused by the whole nocturnal scenario, but that could have had something to do with the fact that she was now sitting on top of the sub-bass woofer and those tympanis were giving it loads.

'Nine.'

'Are you absolutely sure my grass'll be alright?' begged Treadly with mounting doubt, the ugly head of impending unemployment leering at him.

'Eight.'

'Trust me. I'm a scientist,' grinned Farson.

'Seven.'

'Isn't that supposed to be. "Trust me, I'm a doctor"?' quivered Treadly.

'Six.'

'Doctors know nothing. Scientist make all the discoveries,' insisted Farson.

'Five,' bellowed the pa and the venting of vapours increased from the first stage.

'Four. Auxiliary power units at optimum.'

A host of cables were released from *Adversity VI*'s nose cone and swung towards the gantry with a clatter.

'Three.'

Tara hugged her knees and rocked back and forth on the speaker stack.

Deep inside the bowels of *Adversity VI* a grumbling of turbines sounded.

'Two.'

Farson was trembling like a first-time father to be. His eyes wide in the final moments before launch.

'One.'

'Through Adversity To The Stars!' he yelled punching the air as the lab-coated one fisted a fire button pirated from his Nintendo console.

The gleaming column of interstellar rocketry rumbled for the last time on the thirteenth hole, coughed dramatically and an NGK spark plug crackled into life. Tara held her breath, feeling the abdominal wrench of tangible excitement.

A sheet of vapourised fuel blasted from each of the four boosters, hit the pilot light and caught with the ferocity of a rabid dog. Crimson aerosols of flame erupted earthwards, fighting gravity, wrestling inertia and igniting the plywood launch pad faster than a petrol soaked barbecue on Midsummer's Night.

And slowly, the roar of exploding gases drowning the desperate screams of Reg Treadly, *Adversity VI* shook itself loose of the shackles of gravity and lurched towards the infinity of the heavens.

The Marshalls joyously blasted out the SOFA anthem, twelve hundred watts of Karen Carpenter hailing any listening 'Occupants of Interplanetary Craft'.

Adversity VI was a scant four foot six inches towards geostationary orbit before the tidal wave of noxious black exhaust fumes engulfed the whole of the thirteenth fairway. In seconds visibility was a distant race memory as billows of syrup smelling gases wrapped the scene in blankets of vapourised molasses.

Unconcerned, *Adversity VI* powered onwards, its gaze fixed nobly on the vast starry yonder. And beyond.

It took a good half hour for the smoke to clear from the Ground Control Portakabin. And when it did it was heralded by the combined wails of Reg Treadly and the whoop of extreme delight from a soot covered Farson dragging enthusiastically on a tightly wound joint.

'Look!' he shrieked, pointing at the bank of less than pristine circular radar screens before him. None of them showed any trace of an identifiable signature. Not a green dot even so much as glistened behind the iridescent bow wave of rotating light. 'It's gone!' he announced with a little dance of impending interstellar success and took another drag.

Behind him the lab-coated one wiped a small tear of

separation from behind his bottle glasses. 'G ... gone,' he whimpered.

Chivalrously Farson offered the lazily smouldering joint to Treadly.

'*It's* gone? So's my thirteenth hole,' wailed the groundsman, his faithful baseball bat dangling from his hand forlornly, his shoulders sagging in defeat. The charred remains of the plywood launch pad pulled insulting tongues of flame at him. Quivering, he snatched the offered joint and, mistaking it for an Embassy Number 6 set about getting as much calming nicotine into his system as was physically possible.

Farson's ears were deaf to the cries of a mere Head Groundsman. He was gripped in the intense rapture of victory. 'It's gone. Up there. Out of radar range! Way past the ionosphere! To Infinity and Beyond!'

'What about my grass!' wailed Treadly on his third drag.

Farson lay a consoling hand upon Treadly's wax jacketed shoulder as the auto-reverse mechanism clicked and Karen Carpenter struck up again. 'Those blades are martyrs to the cause, a tragic but vital sacrifice upon mankind's rocky path to the Universe. Forget not that the needs of the many far outweigh the needs of the few. Our planet earth will benefit manyfold from their demise when contact is made.' And he would have eschewed a million more sciffy cliches if he'd had the chance. Things about last, best hopes and the forging of interstellar brotherhoods. Fortunately he was interrupted by a strangely grinning Treadly.

'And what about my job, eh? How'm I supposed to get the Prince Fahad El-Fannagil Eighteen Hole Open running smoothly with only seventeen holes, eh? Didn't think about that, did you, man?'

'Got any green paint?' offered Regan. Warily Treadly nodded. 'Quick couple of coats on the slightly scorched bit and it'll be right as rain. Nobody'll notice.'

Everyone who heard Treadly's reply blushed.

'I feel our mission here is complete,' declared Farson, inhabiting other worlds of his own. 'Let us away to Mission

Control and await first contact over a few pints of lager. Come, Tara and I'll show you many lithographs of previous launches.' And in a matter of seconds the generator had coughed into silence and droves of troops sprouting privet began hauling away the Portakabin and the charred remains of the launch pad.

'We'll, er, close the fence on the way out,' offered Regan helpfully before having it away on his toes pursued by the suddenly aerial Betty.

As Tara scrambled away towards the 2CV in the lane beyond, goose flesh gathering about her ankles, she thrilled. What a night!

Farson fired the ignition of the 2CV and roared off in a shower of gravel. He was happy. As predicted, *Adversity VI* had blasted off out of radar contact and was seeking out as many strange new civilisations it could tip its boosters at. At least, that's what he believed. Unfortunately, due to a nought point three degree misalignment of the lower left hand stabilising fin it would be a very long time indeed before *Adversity VI* made contact with any passing extraterrestrials. Unbeknownst to anyone, except a particularly confused family of woodpeckers, the eighteen inch rocket was currently lodged half a mile away deep inside the blackened interior of an ancient and hollow oak.

On the thirteenth hole of the Regal Greens Golf Course Reg Treadly waggled his trusty Eveready torch and stared through tear stained eyes at his tape measure. Fifty square yards ruined! Swiftly, hysterically, his mind whirled as he tried to calculate precisely how long it would take him to throw fifty square yards of B&Q's special offer sods over his wounded babies. Panicking he realised he hadn't a clue what time they opened. He collapsed onto his backside, propped his back against a nearby tree and puffed his way desperately towards dawn.

The Thirteenth Hole

Another glug of crimson was hurled into the pot of paint and stirred in with a flourish of a multicoloured brush. The artist held up his candle and squinted at the resulting colour, sucking his teeth thoughtfully and grumbling critically. The pressure was on, he could feel it. This had to be just the right shade. It had to say 'scorching flame, searing heat'. It had to scream 'conflagration' from every molecule of hue. The whole final panel depended on it.

He held up his brush and squinted at the ceiling way above him, comparing. Suddenly he cursed, tutted and snatched at the pot of vermilion.

'*More* red?' spluttered Lupin peering over his shoulder and shaking his head. 'It looked just fine and dandy to me.'

'Oh, did it, now?' grumbled the artist whisking the paint pot as if making a meringue. 'And what would you know, eh?'

'I know red when I see it,' defended Lupin, feeling hurt.

'Ah, well there you are, then. It *wasn't* red,' hissed Calabrese squinting at the pot. 'It was vermilion. There's a *world* of difference. Philistine.' He tipped in a tiny glob of cerise and homogenised it with frantic vigour.

'You're just being picky now,' complained Lupin, cradling his lute sulkily.

'I am *never* picky,' snorted Calabrese. 'I am an artist and, as such, I am precise. Correct chromatic balance is essential at all times. Even *you*, a mere musician, should appreciate that.'

'Yeah, yeah, but there's precise and then there's spending the best part of a day getting just the right shade of red for a tiny little patch ...'

'Are you suggesting I'm wasting time? Fiddling about

44

unnecessarily, hmmm? Prevaricating?' Calabrese ground his teeth as he stared accusingly at Lupin.

'I'm sure it doesn't always take other artists this long to mix . . .'

'Ohhhh, speak not to me of other artists,' wailed Calabrese slapping the back of his hand against his paint splattered forehead and adopting the tortured expression of the creative. 'What care I if they choose to hurl together shades in sloppy balances of colour? It is no concern of mine if their work exhibits the tonal depth of the average finger painter or the realism of the nursery artist or . . .'

'Hit a nerve there, methinks,' grinned Lupin strumming a victorious chord.

'Nonsense, nonsense,' grumbled Calabrese scooping up a brushful of russet and plunging it irritably into the pot before him.

'Oh, no?' pressed Lupin. 'You mean you're *not* decorating the Royal Nursery free of charge and at great personal discomfort to wheedle your way into Her Highness's Good Books, hmmm?'

Calabrese made a noise in his throat and continued whisking.

Lupin forged on, sensing a chink in the artist's defensive armour. 'You saying you couldn't care less who becomes Official Court Artist, are you?'

'Alright, alright! So I want it!' snapped Calabrese gnashing his teeth. 'Which artist wouldn't ache for that highest of accolades?'

'I knew it. I *knew* it,' chuckled Lupin plucking an arpeggio of delight from his favourite instrument. 'I had you figured right from the start . . .'

'And you consider yourself to be less than transparent, do you?' countered Calabrese his eyebrows arching.

Lupin's arpeggiating clattered to a discordant halt. 'What's *that* supposed to mean, eh?'

A wry grin of victory slithered across Calabrese's face. 'You think an artist has no ears? You think I'm deaf, do you? Well, I've got news . . . I've heard you.'

'Heard what?' scorned Lupin with far less confidence than he wanted.

Calabrese screwed his voice up an octave and in a remarkably accurate impersonation of his lute-toting companion began to sing. *'Mine angelic Hellebore, none other dost I hunger for . . .'*

'No!' whimpered Lupin holding his head. 'Stop it!'

'Pierce my heart for wanting more,' continued Calabrese his finger in his ear.

'Ssssh, somebody might hear,' pleaded Lupin. 'Shutup!'

'Mine pulchritudinous, Hellebore.' And with a remarkably wobbly fifth at the end the artist stopped. 'Done the second verse yet? Can't wait to hear it.'

'It's not meant for you.'

'I think I could have surmised that one. But pray, do tell when the fair princess will hear that refrain?'

'Soon enough,' sulked Lupin, clueless as to how he would ever manage to get the Princess Hellebore alone with just him and his lute. 'But . . . but, when I do, it'll melt her heart and . . . and she'll be mine. You'll see.'

'You've been playing with too many ballads, you have. They've gone to your head,' tutted Calabrese scowling critically at his pot of paint.

'Isn't that the right colour yet?' growled Lupin attempting to steer the conversation off the tender subject of his dearly belusted. 'C'mon, slap it up there.'

'Slap it up there?' gagged Calabrese turning his artistic gaze angrily on the musician. 'I am protecting our heritage here, I do not *slap* paint *anywhere*! Clear?'

Lupin nodded and tried to hide a grin of satisfaction. It was always so easy to steer the conversation with Calabrese.

'Recording the finest moments of our history for all to see requires the greatest of care,' ranted the artist, waggling his brush.

'And I suppose it's deliberate that all the illustrations featuring any of Their Highnesses' ancestors just *happen* to be five times the size of any of the others?' baited Lupin.

Calabrese took it. 'Of course it's deliberate. They deserve

the recognition. Their Highnesses' ancestors made our nation what it is today,' insisted Calabrese earnestly. 'They performed deeds of infamy *way* beyond the call of duty. They ensured our name was feared across all the shires . . .'

'Oh, come on, you cannot be serious. What's so infamous about tying someone's bootlaces together?' He pointed accusingly at the ceiling and waggled a finger at a vast panel depicting a regal looking figure writhing on an ornate throne, inches from the rapidly advancing sea. Sprinting away towards the dunes was a tiny grey-skinned figure.

'They're not just *any* old bootlaces! You think King Canute *wanted* to nearly drown himself?' snapped Calabrese feeling hurt that his choice of subject matter was being questioned by a mere musician. 'If it hadn't been for the bravery and heroism of Her Majesty's Great-Great-Great-Granduncle Samphire showing us the way, it would have been generations before we discovered the value and delight in royalty baiting.'

Lupin shrugged and pointed to a large panel depicting a smoke-filled medieval kitchen and a very embarrassed looking chap searching for a pair of oven gloves. 'What's that got to do with royalty baiting?' he frowned.

'Everything,' hissed Calabrese, despair hovering at the edges of his voice. Was it really true what they said about artists not being appreciated in their own lifetime? Had all this work decorating the ceiling of the Royal Nursery been a complete waste of time? Should he add little explanatory captions under all the panels? 'Am I the only one who knows of the past achievements of our ancestors?' wailed Calabrese.

'Looks like it,' shrugged Lupin playing stupid. It was wicked, he knew, but he did derive an enormous amount of pleasure in watching Calabrese squirm. 'Now, about that guy in the kitchen . . .?'

'Alfred! King Alfred.' Calabrese's face was flushing redder than it had been for years. 'A King destroyed for want of a thermostat. Thousands of his finest troopers deserted him that day and all because of the actions of Titania's Great-Great-Grandfather Charlock. Who would have thought

a couple dozen logs could have ruined a reputation!'
Calabrese almost went misty eyed as he stared at his
painting.

Lupin feigned being lost. 'Er, could you expand on that a
bit, eh?'

Calabrese rolled his eyes and slapped his high forehead.
Suddenly he whirled around and stared at the musician
across the top of his pot of paint. 'Would you follow him
into battle?' he waggled an angry finger at the smoke-filled
kitchen. 'Would you trust your life on the strategies of a man
who is incapable of keeping an eye on a bunch of cakes?'

'Well, er . . . I . . .' hedged Lupin readying himself for a
real ranting session from the artist.

'Exactly!' declared Calabrese and flung another brushful
of cerise into his pot and set about whisking it to a froth,
silently.

Lupin stared open mouthed. 'Is that it?' he asked.

'There's nothing more to say,' mumbled Calabrese. 'If
you can't see it . . .'

Confused, Lupin looked at the arching expanse of coloured panels and for the first time the message of it all hit
home. For the first time the joyous C major of realisation
struck home in his heart. There, all across the ceiling of that
nursery was laid out vital moments of history. Battles,
uprisings, plagues . . . and one common theme ran through
the lot. Sabotage, betrayal – the grey-skinned hand of
deliberate direct interference. Here its deadly digits flicked
extra logs on stoves, there it deftly tied bootlaces together.
Above him its interfering palm patted a grinning rat and a
tiny circus of fleas whilst behind were thousands, struggling
in the grips of the black death.

And in that moment Awe snuck under the tent-flap of
Lupin's heart and settled in on the front row, open-mouthed
in wonder.

'Aha! That's it, that's it!' cried Calabrese staring into his
pot of paint. And suddenly he was leaping across the room,
jumping into the rickety basket and tugging hard on the

ropes. Blocks and tackles tightened, creaked and miraculously carried him high into the gaudily decorated arch of the ceiling. In moments he was securing the rope around cleats on the basket and lying back, waiting to stop swinging. With his nose inches from the gently oscillating expanses of recently applied paint, he readied himself for the final finishing touches. It was all there before him, countless hours of painstaking work. Vast figures were spread across the ceiling, at once animated and yet utterly motionless, terror filling their eyes as they scattered in all directions, fleeing the deadly nightmare of tongues of plaster-grey flame.

Calabrese took a proud breath and knew that, armed with his inestimable skill and that pot of flame-hued paint, the entire panel would somehow come magically to life. Soon no one would be able to look at that expanse of colour without having their emotions wrenched with unquenchable pride. His brush snaked out towards the ceiling and, in a mute repeat of those glorious deeds of some distant ancestor, he ignited the kindling in the corner of the baker's in Pudding Lane.

Lupin stared up from the grey skin on his hands and watched, amazed as the final strokes of red underlined the part similar anatomy had played in history. In a matter of minutes Calabrese's vision would be complete and, there for all to wonder at, the Great Fire of London would be added to the Royal Nursery catalogue of the Glory Days of Feyrie.

He watched in awe as Calabrese's hand lashed across the ceiling, daubing, flicking, leaving trails of uncannily realistic flames on this, his tribute to the setting of the Great Fire. Unconsciously he stroked a chord of delight from his lute.

Lupin had wondered if Calabrese had flipped completely when he'd revealed his plans to him. There were some things one definitely expected to have decorating the walls and ceilings of a Royal Nursery – perhaps legions of small furry animals, wide-eyed and smiling, or maybe squadrons of laughing butterflies swooping over fields of dancing sunflowers – but seventeenth-century Londoners in the throes of being toasted? He never would've expected it to work. But somehow, here, amongst the dozens of other celebratory depictions of the Glory Days of Feyrie, it was utterly perfect.

Deep inside the lower depths of Camford Constabulary Headquarters, far more than six feet under street level, lurked an infrequently visited office. None but the most firm of stomach or the sick of nature set foot inside this organ lined room. Well, except, that is, for those who were on the receiving end of the attentions of the office's occupier. And their opinion didn't count any more. It was too late for that.

All around the shelves of Doctor Boscombe's Forensic Lab there were cloudy flasks of interesting organs, charts of poisons and their side effects, reference manuals, and, Blu-tacked to any available surface, there were the photographs. Hundreds of them. Glossy colour images of variously decomposed torsos, mutilated limbs and a host of unrecognisable glistening things grinned out from the walls. Perversely Boscombe positioned the messier ones carefully on the wall behind his desk. It always gave him a feeling of immense satisfaction as he watched any visitor's attempts to studiously ignore the Kodacolour carnage leering at them over his shoulder. For him, it was therapy. Especially on a Monday morning.

Since the Art of Forensic Science had been the latest profession to receive the unwanted attentions of the dreaded early evening Sunday Drama Squad and had suffered a rash of pre-watershed bloodless murder stories Boscombe had elected himself Envoy of the Cause. It was his task to raise the black-bagged art once again to utter incomprehension by the unwashed masses. Forensic science was most definitely not the sort of subject matter that should be enjoyed, let alone understood, by those more attuned to the pleasures of Jane Austen. There was, in short, no way on God's Earth that Boscombe was going to allow Forensic Science to slither down to the soapy levels of the post-Herriot vet.

First thing this morning, his mind still seething with the banality of last night's episode of *Grave Conclusion*, he had breezed into his office and caught a satisfying eyeful of those

Kodacolour shots behind his desk and snatched the comforting whiff of formaldehyde. In that moment he had been happy.

Sadly, it hadn't lasted long.

This morning Doctor Boscombe was not alone. He peered at a large photograph in his hand, and, keeping it close to his chest said, 'Extreme signs of trauma. Evidence of last meal in lower intestinal tract. Blood staining consistent with extreme violence.' He squinted quizzically over the top of the ten by eight and looked uncannily like a very young Boris Karloff. 'Well?'

The hopeful applicant sat opposite in an interview suit five years out of fashion. Bewildered, he shrugged and looked away from half a dozen exposures of an unidentified body arranged like a halo around Boscombe's head.

'Come, come,' tutted Camford's Senior Scene of Crime Officer. 'Every scrap of evidential data is present. I should not have to supply more.'

'Er . . . no . . . no,' spluttered the graduate nervously. 'Er . . . are any of his colleagues holding anything that could be construed as murder weapons?'

Boscombe pulled a face and made a show of examining the photograph once more. Of course it was unnecessary. He knew every detail of that frame. It was one of his favourites. So unexpected the way one minute he's complaining of stomach ache and then . . .

'No, no. Think!' snapped Boscombe irritably, secretly bemoaning the standards of tuition at forensic schools. 'The subject is flat on his back, disarranged upon the table and the killer has fled the scene. Screaming!' The interviewee shook his head. Boscombe sighed. 'Rib cage shattered. Signs of lungs. Kidneys upon the serviette. In short, extreme trauma. Come on.'

'Er . . . er . . .'

'You shall kick yourself. It is undoubtedly one of the finest examples of its kind.'

The graduate screwed his eyes shut, mouth working hard, brain whirring. 'It's . . . it's . . .'

'Yes?' urged Boscombe desperately. Twelve times in the last two days he'd asked this very same question and this looked like being the twelfth failure. What were they teaching them at University these days? Did nobody appreciate the subtleties and forensic accuracies of cinematic murder anymore?

'Er . . . Juan Sanchez Villa-Lobos Ramirez played by Sean Connery who's just been murdered by Clancy Brown as the Kurgan . . .'

'No, no!' bleated Boscombe all semblance of dispassionate discourse evaporating. 'That's bloody *Highlander*. And Ramirez had his head hacked clean off. Nothing to do with chests exploding.'

'What is it then?' growled the graduate angrily. He knew there and then he had blown it. Mind you, he thought, did he really want to work for someone whose interviewing technique for a Forensic Technician involved twenty questions about movie murders? Boscombe grinned and showed him the photograph with the irritating relish of a liar on *Call My Bluff*. The graduate slapped his forehead as he stared at an exploded John Hurt scant moments after twelve inches of screaming Alien had just burst through his chest and fled into the rest of the Nostromo.

'You didn't say anything about it being in the future,' complained the graduate.

'You didn't ask. I'll let you know about . . .'

'Wait a minute. Gimme another chance,' begged the interviewee, sitting forward desperately on his chair. 'See that fingerprint on the wall up there, the big strangely elongated one, I know that one.'

Boscombe raised a quizzical eyebrow and steepled his hands on the desk before him. He didn't need to look around at the fingerprint. His mind's eye supplied all the necessary detail. Four inches long, oddly similar to a humanoid standard but strangely different. At first glance it looked almost smudged but clearly illustrated all the classic whorls, ulnar loops and tented arches. 'Well? Go on then.'

'Eugene Victor Tooms from *The X Files*. He can stretch

himself and must eat five human livers every thirty years in order to ... What? Why are you shaking your head?'

'Woefully incorrect,' tutted Boscombe. 'Do you not recognise the index digit impression of everybody's favourite alien, ET?'

Snarling angrily the graduate leapt up and whirled on his feet.

'Slam the door on the way out, will you?' called Boscombe and was treated to that very thing. The glass rattled precariously in its frame. In a few moments the sound of stamping feet had subsided and Boscombe was alone in his Forensic kingdom. It looked like he would have to stay that way. No suitable candidates again.

Reluctantly his eyes drifted towards the heap of paperwork lurking on the far end of his desk and a twinge of regret writhed somewhere around his spleen. Perhaps he shouldn't have been so hard on the latest interviewee. Maybe he should have given him the job. At least then he wouldn't have had to do all the paperwork himself. At least then he would have had some time to get down to the important things in life and death, like finding an accurate and reliable method to determine the time of death. This was almost the twenty-first century after all, there should be a better way than having to ram thermometers up the deceased's backside. It really wasn't dignified.

Alternatively he could have spent a relaxing morning up to his elbows in some recently deceased member of the general public. Miserably he sighed. It seemed to have been an inordinately long time since his last post-mortem.

Sighing wearily, his finger tips aching for a decent dissection, he reached across to the pile of papers, paused and changed direction. Idly his fingers clasped around the front cover of a three week old edition of *Forensic Forum* and dragged it towards him. Attached to the front was a sticky yellow strip of paper with a scrawled message:

Read page 8 before Monday's meeting. Or else. Ness.

A brief grin squirmed across his face. Today was Monday. It was just the excuse he needed. An order from the Chief Inspector, the paperwork would have to wait.

Slurping noisily at his coffee he flattened the journal open at the relevant page and wrinkled his brow. A bifocalled face leered out of the magazine at him, grinning with immense smugness. The caption below did little to cheer him up:

Camford's finest crack Speed Gene.

'Camford's finest?' snarled Boscombe. 'What are they on about? I'm Camford's finest. Nobody knows Forensics the way I know Forensics. Finest, pah!'

Reluctantly, and more through the slim possibility of tearing whatever it was they were being hailed as the finest for into the tiniest of shreds, he read on. It didn't raise his spirits much:

In a press conference today, Professor Crickson speaking on behalf of himself, Doctor Striebley and their technician Lance Farson of Camford's Splice of Life Patentable Biosciences Ltd announced that he believes they have taken the science of DNA Profiling into the next century.

'We have pushed the barriers of Genetic Understanding back and heralded in a new era of comprehension,' declared Crickson.

Boscombe tutted disgustedly. Such verbosity shouldn't be allowed from a scientist. ' "Barriers of Genetic Understanding". Pah!'

'Following massive studies into the genetic predisposition towards highway maldemeanour and persistent velocity transgressions . . .'

'Speak english, idiot,' complained Boscombe chewing the rubber off the end of his pencil.

'. . . we can now announce that we have isolated the gene responsible for that scourge of the late nineties. Our data shows that we have found the gene for road rage and that it is readily . . .'

'What? Oh, pull my other metatarsals why don't you? What idiots are going to believe this load of . . .'

And moments before Boscombe got up a full head of derogatory steam, the phone rang. With the lightning reflexes of a praying mantis on speed his hand lashed out and snatched up the receiver. 'What?' he bellowed and then winced. 'Ahh, Chief Inspector, yes. Just reading it now, sir. Absolutely fascinating.' He rolled his eyes and mimed stifling a yawn. 'Utterly amazing what advances they're making these days. The meeting today? Change of venue? Er . . . fine, fine, I . . . Upstairs? Now? Yes . . . but I . . . Immediately? Yes, sir.'

Pausing only to decorate the picture of one Professor Crickson with a Mexican moustache, he stood, thrust his hands into his pocket and trudged off upstairs for the regular monthly forensic progress meeting with Chief Inspector Everett Ness.

Idly he pondered precisely why there was a change of venue. It wouldn't be too long before he found out.

There was a penultimate flourish of flame-red bristles, a final dab of adjustment and abruptly the Royal Nursery was filled with an earsplitting whoop of delight. In seconds Calabrese had unfastened his work basket and was plummeting floorwards. Snakes of rope leapt ceilingwards into the blocks and tackles as he descended. Lupin crunched a chord of alarm from his lute and snatched his head upwards to see Calabrese's basket expanding before his widening eyes. Squealing he rolled sideways, cradling his lute. Inches from the floor Calabrese looped a rope around the cleat, tugged and slowed the basket's fall with a shriek of protesting hessian. He leapt out, hurled his head back and surveyed his masterpiece, casting a self-critical eye over every line, assessing every hue, swelling with pride at every perfect portrayal of the past.

'Finished!' he declared punching the air and spinning around on his heels.

'You could've given me a bit more warning,' complained Lupin. 'You nearly hit me.'

'Stupid place to be, under my cradle,' tutted Calabrese and headed for the door.

'It's the only place safe from your stray drips ... Hey! Where are you going?'

'My work here is complete,' declared Calabrese pompously, his grey-skinned hand perched on the door handle. 'It is time for my audience to be made aware of their viewing pleasure.'

And for the first time in far longer than he had ever imagined it would have been, Calabrese set foot outside the nursery. A wave of peculiar agoraphobia crashed over him as he stepped into the small passage. For a second he wanted to turn on his heels and run screaming back into the comforting haven of his world and throw himself onto the welcoming bosom of his painted friends. But only for a second ...

Steeling himself he leapt into the passage and dashed off, secure in the knowledge that minutes after the gracious and beauteous Queen Titania saw that nursery he'd be offered the job of Court Artist. It was, to use the vernacular, in the bag.

Lupin watched him vanish away down the dark passage, his jaw hanging limply as silence fell like snow around him. Nervously he shook himself, snatched his lute and sprinted off in hot pursuit.

'Hey, hang on. Wait for me ...!'

Far away down the passage, deep below the thirteenth fairway of the Regal Greens Golf Course, accessible only via a secretive hole which was a rumour to even the canniest of badgers, there was a desperate air of pre-natal tension.

A grey-skinned creature peered through almond shaped eyes at an array of potions and tinctures and hoped it had remembered the ancient lore correctly. Nervously it fingered a pale green phial and attempted to smile reassuringly at the bloated writhing female on the bed of ferns.

'Well?' growled another of the creatures imperiously. His voice echoed around the large cavern, bouncing off the arching roots of the soil ceiling and shaking a clump of truffles dangling in a distant corner.

'Er ... yes. She's fine,' answered Cobweb the wrinkled apothecary hesistantly and limply took the pulse of the patient.

'Fine? I don't feel fine!' snapped Queen Titania writhing on the ferns as if to prove the point. 'In fact I feel *far* from fine. Can't you give me something?' she begged in a less than regal manner. 'Is there none of that toadstool gin left?'

'No!' snapped Oberon in a heavy whisper adjusting his crown of thorns. 'You can't have any of that. Remember what happened last time?'

'Of course I remember!' bellowed Titania and grimaced with the agony of another contraction. Cobweb dabbed a strip of lichen across her sweat glistening brow. 'These bloody contractions won't let me forget!' ranted the Queen. 'It was bloody agony then and it's bloody agony now. Give me the gin! Now!'

'But Tanny, darling. It might affect the dear child. You've hung on so long, a few more minutes won't do you any harm.'

'A few more minutes of agony?'

'Yes, dear. I'm sure it smarts but ... We don't want another Hellebore, do we? Now, I'm not saying she's ugly but ...' he whispered hoping earnestly that the dozen or so other creatures in the cavern didn't hear.

Titania writhed and turned unhealthily red. 'Oh, that's just typical of you, that is! Blame Hellebore on me, why don't you?'

'Ssssh, keep your voice down. I'm not blaming you. It's just that ... well it *was* you that gave birth to her and ...'

'You've tried to wash your hands of her for years. You're her father, like it or not. It's your fault as well! Where's that gin?'

'Are you absolutely sure I'm to blame?' asked Oberon fiddling with his crown. 'I mean there was that all night dewdrop hanging party when you and Puck . . .'

'If you're suggesting that Puck had anything to do with Hellebore you've got another think coming. Where do you think she got that taste for truffles, eh? You!' Titania shouted angrily. 'I hate the bloody things! And you can't ignore the fact that she's got your nose!' Her stomach squirmed violently and her face screwed itself up in agony. 'Give me the damned gin!' she screamed and grabbed Cobweb around the throat.

'I . . . I can't,' choked the apothecary under Titania's overwhelming grip. 'You know what'll happen in your condition.'

'I don't care! Give me that gin before I die!'

'Tanny, darling, don't say that. You've always survived before. I know childbirth is painful and smarts a bit, but . . .'

'How the Hell do *you* know what it's like?' snapped Titania turning crimson.

'Your descriptions are very graphic, dear,' winced Oberon. He knew he wouldn't have a moment's rest in the next few months what with the new brat to feed and Titania's endless reminders of these hours of agony. But, it would be worth it if they could only get a girl. Then there might be a future to look forward to.

'Gin!' squealed Titania. Cobweb's eyes were bulging unhealthily as the Queen's grip tightened still further.

'No,' said Oberon firmly. 'You know what'll happen if you use artificial aids.'

'I don't care. In fact I don't believe that ancient lore. I don't care! I don't care! I just want it out! I've had it long enough!'

'Breathe,' choked Cobweb. To all present it wasn't entirely clear if this was an order or a request.

'But Tanny, dear. The ancient lore is true. It will be a boy if you have a gin. You know it!' insisted Oberon desperately.

'That's just coincidence,' writhed Titania, sweating.

'The only girl you've had in the last twenty years was Hellebore; she was the only gin-free delivery. That's proof.'

'Sheer coincidence. Don't blame the gin. I want it now!'

Suddenly, away across the hall, a door burst open and two figures bowled in panting desperately from the mad dash through miles of underground passages. They knew Queen Titania had planned the Nursery to be 'out of the way' so she wasn't disturbed too often by the screams of children, but they hadn't realised it was quite that far. Calabrese exploded into the hall, fizzing with expectations, bursting with the overwhelming desire to throw open the doors to his newly painted nursery.

He was half way across the floor when his eyes focused the fact that perhaps everything was not precisely as it had been when he had left to decorate the nursery for Titania's first born. For one thing there was the clump of four occupied cradles gathered in the corner.

Calabrese's head reeled, could he really have spent that long on his decorative mission? His gaze settled on Oberon's midriff and the large beard tumbling towards it and inklings of confirmation struggled to the forefront of his mind. Still, he thought, better late than never. After all, everybody knows that you can't hurry art.

He took a deep breath, smoothed down the front of his single asterisk of sycamore covering his modesty and strode towards the Royal Mound of Leaves.

'Your Highness, I have excellent news!'

'You've found the gin?' she squealed desperately.

'Er . . . no, no. This is news of a more cultural and heroic nature . . .'

'If it's about last night's *Rootside* don't tell me. I want to find out whether Hyacinth is ready to return Foxglove's advances.'

'*Rootside*?' spluttered Calabrese, confused. 'I . . . er, I don't think this has anything to do with that, er, your Highness, your nursery is complete.'

'Great. Is that your news?'

'Yes, your majesty, I look forward to your viewing pleasure at ...'

'Where's that gin?' she screamed, writhing in the grip of a contraction.

' ... your earliest convenience,' finished Calabrese to his toes and turned away, his future crumbling before his mind's eye.

Behind him, there came a blood curdling scream. It was followed by several ineffectual cries of 'Push, Push. That's it. That's it. Push. Harder!' and, with a shrill squeal a tiny pair of feyrie lungs made everyone aware of their recent delivery.

'Well? Well?' shouted Oberon and Titania simultaneously peering at the wrinkled apothecary. Cobweb, trembling, held out the baby to Titania. He took a deep breath, considered lying for a moment, considered the painful consequences of such a move and forced a smile.

'Congratulations!' he announced. 'It's a perfectly healthy bouncing baby boy!'

'Oh, bugger!' snarled Oberon. 'Not again.'

'Bring me a gallon of gin!' wailed Titania. 'I've got some serious sorrows to drown. Now!'

'Don't you want to hold him?' asked Cobweb offering the writhing infant at arm's length. 'It ... it's good for mother – child bonding and continued well-being ...'

'He's yours. Take him away. Now where's that bloody gin! And bring on *Rootside*! That's a Royal Decree!'

Suddenly, off to the left there was a jingling of bells, a troupe of painted feyries sprang enthusiastically, if shambolically, onto the centre of the vast table and Calabrese's worst fears were realised. *Rootside* was about to begin and all eyes were wide with anticipation. Could the greatness of Feyrie actually have been reduced to this? Looking forward to an endless string of anecdotes and limp storylines cobbled together to appeal to the lowest of mental common denominators. The applause told him precisely what he didn't want to hear.

'Ill met by moonlight, proud Lucy!' declared a particularly

60

effeminate looking feyrie miming hanging dewdrops in the eyes of daisies.

'Hail and well met,' replied a badly made-up chap sporting a pair of acorn cups beneath his tunic in the appropriate places. 'Hast thou seeneth the glances of admiration passing twixt Hyacinth and Foxglove?'

'Nay,' overacted the first feyrie throwing up his palms and grinning as Oberon and Titania laughed with bewildering heartiness. 'That pair surely cannot be trysting?'

'Oh, 'tis true!'

'But at their tender age?'

'Tender age? Nay, thou holdest some misprision, surely. They are well old enough.'

'Marry, time dost take a winged form these days.'

'I dids't not mention wedlock,' announced the second feyrie, hoisting his acorn cups back towards the centre of his chest to the obvious delight of the audience.

And so it would have gone on had not the latest offspring of Titania's not suddenly remembered what its lungs were for.

'Cobweb!' screamed Titania in immediate response to the shrill cacophany. 'Cobweb! Shut that brat up, I'm trying to watch *Rootside*!' The cast stood nervously in their corner and picked at their fingernails.

The panicking voice of the wrinkled apothecary trembled back through a curtain of roots. 'Yes, yes . . . I will, I, er, how?'

'You mean you don't know?' roared Titania irritably.

'Frankly . . . er, no,' confessed Cobweb barely audible above the screaming. 'I normally only oversee the delivery of the little, er . . . darlings and, not having one of my own upon which to practise, I am at a loss to . . .'

'You want practise? You got it,' screamed Titania. 'That one's yours, okay? Royal decree and all that. To have and to hold and to change regularly. Now shut it up!'

'But how?' he yelled over the screaming brat as the actors shuffled uncomfortably upon their makeshift stage.

'The traditional method,' shouted Titania. 'Give it the gin

bottle. And when you're done, give it here, I'm gagging for a swig.'

Sobbing gently to himself in a ferment of melancholy, missing days gone by, Calebrese slunk miserably off into the dark and trudged away up the passage he had all-too-recently sprinted down.

Lupin, though strangely gripped by the events unfolding in *Rootside*, turned and followed. Calabrese looked in need of a cheering galliard, and he knew just the tune to sort him out.

Much to the obvious satisfaction of the two men brewing their first cuppa of the day on a tiny primus, the traffic jam was already close to crippling the Camford ring road. It wasn't quite eight in the morning and already three-quarters of a mile of angrily canned commuters were stacked up nose to tail down the chestnut lined artery of Fenland Road.

'Does your heart good to see just how appreciated we are, doesn't it, mate,' chuckled Derrick the Chief Tarmac Operative over the rising cacophony of blaring car horns. 'Just love the way they all turn out in the morning and greet us with a cheery "parp" or two, don't you reckon?'

'Stop your gabbing and hurry up with that tea,' growled Bob the Operator-in-Charge of Pneumatic Drills. He didn't look up from the tiny hand-held monitor screen linked into the cable laid before the weekend. He had to check all their previous week's work still functioned correctly. Idly his knobbly thumb jabbed a tiny button and scrolled through the dozens of shopping channels and recycled movies which made up CablePix's test signal.

'Perfect,' he confirmed as just the right amount of static flared between channels. With a self-satisfied yawn he tossed the rugged test-monitor over his shoulder and stared ahead down the length of Fenland Road, his hands trembling in anticipation. He knew they had a hard day ahead of them. Half a mile of densely bundled optics needed laying for CablePix before lunch time. And they were the men to do it.

Derrick grinned to himself as the grimily tarred pan came to the boil. With a deft flick of a wrist, more used to shovelling asphalt into burners, he hurled three perforated bags into the water and released the pressure valve on the primus. It hissed its way into relaxation, its job over for at least the next half hour. Bob peered out of the red and white striped tent and weighed up the morning ahead. Fifteen trees stood between him and a hefty bonus. Or rather the roots of fifteen trees.

'Don't know what bugger planted them by the side of the road. Wouldn't've stuck 'em there if they'd ever had to lay cables, I'll tell you.'

Derrick stared at the hundred and twenty year old colonnade of chestnuts and decided against mentioning the fact that cable tv hadn't been around with the Victorians. Digging pavements up for a good night's entertainment hadn't been necessary then. A piano and a glass of sherry was good enough in those days. Philistines.

'How'd the Victorians ever survive without fifteen channels of shopping, d'you think?' asked Derrick, stirring the tea with a trowel.

'Eh?'

'I mean, what did they get up to when they'd run through all the hits in the Victorian Family Piano Songbook?'

'Did they have songs back then?'

'Oh, sure, you know, "How Much Is That Doggy In The Window?" and "When I'm Cleaning Windows" and stuff,' he hazarded a guess.

'You can't play "When I'm Cleaning Windows" on the piano. That's a ukelele thing,' commented Bob, with authority way beyond his actual knowledge.

'Oh yeah,' said Derrick, realisation dawning as he shovelled a few trowels' worth of Marvel into the tea. 'Geez, you reckon the Victorians only had one song for the piano, then?'

Bob nodded with his sagest of expressions. 'Why else d'you think they always look so bloody miserable in the photographs. "How Much Is That Doggy In The Window?" every night would do serious damage to a bloke's sense of fun. Now, where's that tea?'

A chipped enamel mug swung towards him, icebergs of Marvel bobbing gently on the chocolate brown surface. 'Lovely,' grinned Bob and downed it in three gulps. Wiping his mouth with the back of his hand he hurled the dregs of tea out of the tent, cracked his knuckles noisily and creaked to his feet. 'Time to face our public,' he grunted, settled his trousers down to reveal the requisite three inches of posterial cleavage and strode out into the morning chorus of horn blasts.

With a cheery waggling of a pair of calloused fingers to a particularly snarly looking rep in a white Vectra he fired up the compressor, snatched at his trusty pneumatic drill and assaulted the roots of a nearby chestnut.

And as he plunged that blade deep into the Camford substructure he chuckled. He still found it strangely ironic that he should be back doing this so soon after being sacked by the council for damaging the roots of thirty protected sycamores down Finals Avenue. But he didn't care. He was earning twice as much now after being whisked away from the Employment Exchange. It seemed that CablePix considered he had the perfect qualifications and weren't as fussed about gnarly bits of trees' underground plumbing. And quite right too, mused Bob as his fingers went rapidly numb, it wasn't as if trees didn't have enough roots to be going on with. And besides, it was bound to do them good. You pruned roses didn't you?

And as Bob burrowed away towards the centre of the earth he gradually became aware of a curious wailing sound. Years of hands-on pneumatic experience had taught him that the drills of his trade didn't make curious wailing sounds unless something was amiss. With a reluctant shrug he shut off the power and stared at his clay-covered bit. Oddly the noise continued and was definitely getting louder. Could it be the compressor?

He turned towards the grumbling yellow monster on the kerb and screamed as two of Camford's fastest squad Rovers mounted the kerb, sirens blaring, lights blazing and hurtled past him scant inches between wing mirrors and certain premature evisceration.

Cursing volubly as he extracted himself from the bottom of the cable-lined trench the Operator-in-Charge of Pneumatic Drills shook an angry fist after the pair of rapidly vanishing Rovers. It was all much to the obvious delight of the snarly looking rep in the Vectra.

'I saw that,' fussed Derrick rushing to the scene. 'I saw that. Oooh, shocking that. Shocking. Didn't even slow down! You need a hot cuppa after a shock like that! Geez, bloody coppers getting road rage now ... It's not safe being out on the streets.'

And without further ado Derrick dashed back into the shady confines of the red and white tent and busied himself over the aging primus.

Bob hauled himself out of the trench, and, accompanied by a barrage of irate hornblowing, he resettled his trousers to their correct altitude with professional pride, staggered towards a reviving brew and a few more minutes' gazing at the tiny screen of the test-monitor. With forty eight channels to choose from there should be something on to take his mind off that near miss.

Cotterpin creaking and rear mudguard rattling with somewhat more gusto than usual, the white lab-coated figure swerved into the entrance of the Camford Fens Science and Technology Park and ploughed unstoppably onwards. In moments he had flashed past the Scud'U'Like Army and Navy Suppliers, whistled by the heap of radials mounded outside the Tyres'R'Us Puncture Repair Outfit and vanished around the corner of the corrugated frontage of his own place of employ. The bike shed was in his sights.

Across the two hundred yard length of the grandly titled 'Edison Boulevard' a blue-overalled pair of tyre mechanics slouched against each side of a vast Michelin. Expertly they nursed their first coffee of the working day. Behind them a distorted tranny spat Radio One into the morning air. In unison they shook their heads and slurped.

Every morning they stared across 'Edison Boulevard' and pondered precisely what went on behind the corrugated exterior of Splice of Life Patentable Biosciences Ltd. That it was ecologically dodgy they were certain. That it was highly immoral they were positive. Well, the logo gave it away. A double helix of crimson neon above a conical flask. Nothing environmentally friendly could come out of a company lurking under that banner. It smacked of science. That was always a dangerous flavour.

Throughout Camford rumours abounded regarding the goings on within those walls. Double-headed dogs pulled on thousands of Woodbines and fluttered mascara-plastered lashes at heartless scientists. Vast tanks of human organs were liquidised and canned into mysteriously popular brands of soups whilst lab-coated technicians laughed hysterically. A thousand different breeds of crash-landed aliens were tested in a million different ways. It was a wonder that the FBI or Greenpeace or Amnesty Interplanetary, or someone hadn't closed it down years ago.

Of course, nobody had ever brewed up the courage to find out precisely what was going on in there. Not yet anyway.

The pair of blue-overalled pneumaticists shook their heads again as a white lab-coated figure in plus fours and lab-coat appeared from the direction of the Splice of Life bike sheds and hurried towards the front door. He brandished a tiny credit card sized sliver of plastic enthusiastically. In a second he had run it through the security system and the tinted triple-glazed uPVC door sloughed open. With a glance over his shoulder and a covert wave at the staff of Tyres'R'Us the Doctor disappeared within. The pneumaticists tutted. The rumours must be true. Why else would they need such tight security?

With surly glowers of suspicion the overalled ones drained the last of their Mellow Birds and set about ripping the balding cross-plys off an ageing Allegro.

Within the air-conditioned interior of Splice of Life, Doctor Striebley dashed eagerly towards his laboratory, fingertips itching for another day's science. Today he would have a patentable breakthrough, he was certain. The weather was perfect for it. Utterly cloudless.

Swiping his security card down the side of his lab door he burst in and headed straight for the dark mass of his creation lying on the slab. Complex arrays of pipes bubbled coloured infusions through the one hundred and eighty pounds of the thing in the tank, filling the room with amniotic gurglings. Excitedly his nose tingled with the warm biological aroma which pervaded everything, cloying, barely on the right side of nauseating. And above it all, looping in vast technicolour looms, thousands of wires sprouted, writhed and plunged into its flesh. It looked like a telephone exchange after a typhoon.

'Today's the day, Edward!' thrilled Striebley dashing past the form on the slab and patting its tank gently. He scurried across the lab, drew back the blinds and carefully flicked a bank of switches. Twenty feet above him a row of electric motors hummed into life, gears engaged and, unseen by all but a momentarily startled raven on a nearby satellite dish, a vast panel of the roof slid backwards. Cams pushed, bearings slithered and gradually what looked not too dissimilar to fifty feet of Bacofoiled garage door unfurled. With a click it locked to full extension. And there it halted, a mechanical tulip staring unblinkingly sunwards.

In the bubbling lab below, Striebley was peering intently at a dozen dials and rubbing thoughtfully at his unshaven chin. Twelve needles lounged in parallel against the extreme left stops. Completely dead. But not for much longer. Chuckling quietly to himself in the greatest tradition of a scientist on the brink of a breakthrough, his fingers tapped excitedly against the dials. Still panting from his mad dash to work that morning, he took a deep breath, straightened up and, with a fizz of rusting contact breakers, made the final connection. The good Doctor Frankenstein would have been proud of the results.

Almost immediately things began to happen. Bubbles streamed from the surface of the thing in the tank. The pulsing of the infusions quickened. An eerie aura began to smoulder just beneath the surface of the form. And, to Striebley's immense delight, the twelve needles began to twitch.

'Come on, Edward,' he urged with the seething enthusiasm of a desperate punter at the Grand National. 'C'mon. You can do it!' The liquid in the tank turned translucent with foaming bubbles and the temperature in the lab began to rise. Striebley tapped feverishly at the row of dials, grinning manically as they continued to ramp up into the red.

Suddenly there was a swish of security card in the corridor outside, the door slid open and two figures burst impatiently in.

'There, there. Just like I said. There he is!' declared the red pony-tailed technician dashing into the lab and pointing accusingly at Striebley.

'Not now!' shouted Striebley waving a dismissive hand over his shoulder as he glared at the dials.

'What d'you think you're doing? Have you forgotten what day it is?' growled the taller and far greyer figure of Professor Crickson, Head and Founding Brain behind Splice of Life Patentable Biosciences Ltd.

'Shutup, shutup!' bellowed Striebley, concentration making him forget the pecking order thereabouts. 'Can't you see I'm busy!'

'Obviously,' growled Crickson staring in wonder at the fizzing mass in the tank. 'But they'll be here any minute! Shut it down. Now!'

Striebley spun on his heel, slammed his palms on the slab and peered through the array of pipes and wires. 'Eighteen months I've been working on this. D'you expect me to stop now, when the conditions are perfect?' His eyebrows angled angrily in a ferment of scientific inspiration. 'I could've done this yesterday afternoon but oh no . . . I had to patent your damned Oven-Bake Sushi. Just give me ten min. . .'

'Shut it down. You'll be late for the meeting with Chief . . .'

Suddenly Striebley's fists pounded the workbench with frustration. To anyone with even the tiniest knowledge of body language it was somewhat apparent that Striebley had (a) forgotten completely about any meetings that day and, (b) was mightily hacked off about having to stop his experiment for any such meeting.

'You've got to be there,' insisted Crickson peering imperiously over his bifocals. 'They want to talk to everyone who worked on the Speed Gene Project. That means all three of us.'

'You credited him?' gasped Striebley in shock, pointing through the curtain of wires and tubes at the yawning red-haired technician.

'Of course. Two names on a paper of this importance just doesn't have the right sense of intellectual pedigree to it.'

The red-haired technician nodded his overwhelming agreement and headed towards the bench, stifling a yawn. He hadn't manged to get much sleep last night.

'You're not going through with this,' pleaded Striebley, shaking his head, fear igniting in his eyes.

Crickson nodded. 'Absolutely. We stand to make a million and a quarter here.'

'We stand to end up behind bars!' squeaked Striebley.

'Come, come don't be so alarmist,' tutted Crickson.

'You're trying to defraud the police of a million quid and you're asking me not to be alarmist?' Striebley was rapidly beginning to wonder if it might have been a good idea if he hadn't come into work this morning. He might at least have had the chance to end the day a free man.

'Look, Striebley. You know it's fraud, I know it's fraud, even Farson here knows it, but if we don't tell them, they'll never know. We've got science on our side, let's blind them with it! Trust me, by the end of this meeting they'll be pressing their money on us to carry out more research into the Speed Gene.'

'But they'll want results. They'll be expecting more data. They'll have deadlines.'

'No problem,' smiled Crickson disarmingly. 'You know damn well there's no such thing as a workable deadline in science. If they start getting fidgety we'll just blame the equipment, or the reagent, or something. And if they still won't go away, we make it all up. Easy. Meantime we've got all our financial worries taken care of. We might even be able to get that patented,' he added pointing to the fizzing form on the bench.

'If it ever works,' grumbled Striebley.

'Yes, well, there's insufficient time now so . . .'

Farson looked up from a bank of dials and cleared his throat. 'Erm, I think that now is a really good time to try it, actually,' he said. 'Electrolytic composition and voltage values all look perfect.'

Both Crickson and Striebley whirled around and stared at the dials.

In his lab coat pocket the pony-tailed Farson crossed his fingers. For months he had been desperate to see if this actually worked. All the theories pointed to a roaring success. He wasn't going to let this chance of seeing it slip away.

'There's still a good seven minutes before our guests are due to arrive,' added Farson. 'And the coulomb coefficient is moments from climax.' He rubbed his palms and peered eagerly at Crickson.

'Well?' snapped Striebley, the thing in the tank bubbling furiously. 'Are you going to walk away from the scientific breakthrough of the decade?'

Crickson twitched his head sideways.

It was all Striebley needed. Catching his breath he whirled in a flurry of lab-coat, snatched at the rusting contact breaker, and swung on it. There was a crack of a discharge, a taste of ozone and the umbilical supply from the fifty feet of shimmering solar panels was severed.

Behind him the hundred and eighty pound thing in the tank remained eerily motionless. Its only signs of life the constant pulsing of coloured infusions and the seething of gases around it.

Crickson and Farson took a wary step forward and squinted into the tank for signs of success. Striebley's creation stayed rooted to the spot.

Of course, had it even so much as twitched, they would have been out the lab screaming in horror. Everybody knows that potatoes don't twitch. Not even genetically engineered King Edwards.

'Well?' whispered Crickson with a tremble.

'Perfectly. Look!' shrieked Striebley pointing blurring fingers at the row of twelve dials. 'Five hundred and eighty microelectron volts, fifteen hundred amps. The increased electrolytic availability has worked.'

'You mean?'

'Yes! I've done it! It works! I've invented the world's first solar rechargable potato battery!' He skipped excitedly around the form in the tank, punching the air on a wave crest of euphoria. 'This is it. The end of mankind's dependency on fossil fuels. Potato powered cars here we come!'

'You mean one of them can power a car?' gasped Crickson.

Farson considered powering things less down to earth. What leaps could the Search for Offworld Friendly Aliens make armed with a satellite-mounted solar-rechargeable King Edward powering their radios.

'Power a car, oh yes. Oh yes!' Eyes wide with excitement Striebley tugged a calculator out of his pocket and began stabbing figures into it. Farson's gaze was fixed on the tiny liquid crystal display. 'Assuming an average charge capacitance of . . .' Striebley's fingers blurred as they inputted numbers. 'And electrolytic conversion co-efficient of eighteen point three five . . . A picofarad constant of fifty-five point three three six, then . . . Oh. No. That can't be right?' The Doctor's face clouded over as he glared at the calculator's screen. 'Can't be right at all.' Striebley scratched his head and reassaulted Tandy's finest guessing box. After a few moments he snarled, whirled around the slab and snatched a similar number-cruncher from Crickson's top pocket.

'Well?' frowned Crickson as Farson left the lab shaking his head forlornly.

'Er . . . not really,' whimpered Striebley staring miserably at the figure on the calculator screen.

'Explain,' insisted Crickson.

'It would seem that rumours of my success have been somewhat exaggerated,' confessed Striebley handing the calculator back to Crickson wearing an expression which normally went under the heading of 'crestfallen'.

Crickson peered at the figure on the screen. 'Two point three five eight eight? What's that mean? It doesn't sound so bad.'

'That refers to the mass of the potato battery required to power a stripped out Mini over a distance of three-quarters of a mile in midsummer in the Sahara.'

'Two point three five eight eight kilos is excellent. Stick a few together in parallel and we'll be up and . . . why are you shaking your head?'

Striebley choked back a scream and simply uttered a one word answer. 'Tons.'

Fortunately the screams of Farson in the foyer were drowned by the sudden cacophony of sirens as three of Camford Constabulary's police Rovers raced down Edison Boulevard in their direction.

Almost before the first echoes of the triplet of sirens had rebounded off the buildings lining the Boulevard, two blue-overalled employees of Tyres'R'Us had dropped the cross-plys they were wrestling with and sprinted to the door. They weren't disappointed.

Three of Camford Constabulary's two and a half litre Rovers roared along the two hundred yard dead end at nigh on sixty, lights strafing the corrugated buildings. Without warning there was a screeching of brakes and a racing of engines, and they slewed to a perfect trio of handbrake turns, each positioned the regulation three inches from the kerb. A blue cloud of atomised Michelin floated silently into the morning sky as the engines died and the drivers' doors were hurled open. Constables Skitting and Sim exploded into the air and were off, dashing around the front of their vehicles. PC Plain took a short cut across his bonnet, gaining vital millimetres of advantage in a move more normally associated with chaps from C15. He landed at full sprint, hurling himself towards their target. Much rode on this dash across the final few yards of herringbone brickwork. Pride, the chance to impress their superiors and a means to avoid paying for tonight's drinks in *The Monocle and Asparagus*. They knew the rules, last officer to any scene of crime got the lagers in all night.

PC Plain was a nose ahead as he forged on towards Splice of Life, his effort matching that of any Olympic hundred metre finalist. Three yards from touchdown he surged forward, dipped, extended his stubby index finger and jabbed it victoriously onto the backlit doorbell. 'I won!' he declared panting as Skitting struck the corrugated wall a very close second. 'You cheated!' gasped Sim red faced. 'Jumping over your bonnet like that. It's immoral. Who d'you think you are? One of the Professionals?'

'Just 'cause you lost,' grinned Plain, his quarter-inch corona of hair shimmering in the morning sun. 'Anyway, you cheated on the way here, down Fenland Road.'

'Moi?' spluttered Sim attempting a look of innocence. 'I didn't go down Fenland Road.'

'Exactly,' snarled Plain. 'Keeping quiet about roadworks just isn't on.'

'I didn't keep quiet about anything,' smirked Sim as three figures approached from the perfect dotted line of Rovers behind them.

'No? Well, I didn't hear you telling us about bloody CablePix digging up the whole of . . .' Suddenly he stopped abruptly, whisking a snappy salute out of nowhere as Chief Inspector Ness piloted the top brass into earshot.

'You didn't ask,' mouthed Sim with hollow satisfaction as it slowly dawned on him that, despite his devious attempt at sabotage, tonight's first round of Fosters was certainly coming out of his trouser pocket.

'At ease,' growled Chief Inspector Everett Ness officiously from beneath the dual pelmet of his cap's peak and the continuous line of his overly bushy eyebrows. 'I trust you have made our presence known.'

PC Plain nodded – unnecessarily – as at that very instant the tinted door of the scientific establishment slithered open and, like some re-enactment of a third kind close encounter, a triangle of white coated beings emerged, blinking into the morning sunlight. It would have made Steven Spielberg proud.

'Greetings, gentlemen,' declared Professor Crickson in as important and pleasant a manner as he could muster. In truth he found it rather hard. Being a scientist he wasn't really used to it. 'Er ... Welcome to Splice of Life Patentable Biosciences Ltd. Do please enter.'

Behind Chief Inspector Ness a tall figure, who bore a remarkably striking resemblance to a young Boris Karloff, rolled his eyes wearily and wished he'd been allowed to stay in the Rover. He knew deep in his bones that this couldn't possibly be a good idea. Not a chance. No way. It just wasn't the way things were done. Especially not Forensic things. He risked a scathing glance of resentment at the grey-suited civil servant to his left. How dare he tell him how to run the Forensics Department of Camford Constabulary? Damned ignorant pen pushing son of a ...

' ... visitor's safety badge. We do need you to fill one in. Company policy, you understand.' Farson the red-haired technician waggled a blue plastic radioisotope-sensitive rectangle under Boscombe's nose.

'Company policy, you understand,' sneered a discontented voice inside Boscombe's mind. 'Ideas above their bloody station, if you ask me.' Miserably he scrawled a stubbornly incomprehensible signature on the badge. Well, it was his prerogative. He was a Doctor after all. A practitioner of a profession famed for its legendary illegibility.

'This way, gentlemen,' said Crickson swiping a credit card down the side of a door and ushering his guests into the panelled interior of the board room.

A large table squatted in the centre of the plush carpeted room, laid with six glasses of still water and a pot of mint imperials. As trustingly as delegates at a Middle Eastern peace conference the sextet filed in and took up their places at table, suits on one side, lab-coats the other. 'Gentlemen, may I once again welcome you to our company,' began Professor Crickson laying it on thick. He was determined to make this work. His UB40 depended on it. 'Allow me to introduce my staff. On my left Doctor Striebley, Head of Energetic Manipulation and Patentable Vegetables.' Striebley nodded distantly and desperately yearned to get back to his King Edward whilst he was still a free man.

'And on my right, Lance Farson, Chief Technician.' The red pony-tailed technician grinned and nodded.

On the far side of the table Doctor Boscombe drummed an impatient fistful of fingers. Simeon Yeats, the grey-suited civil servant cleared his throat and flicked open a plastic snakeskin briefcase. Boscombe winced and pulled a face as if a dozen kittens were scraping claws down blackboards three inches from his ears.

'Further to my previous communications with both parties gathered here, I call this meeting to order.' Yeats attempted to subtly edge his chair around to the head of the table. Nobody failed to notice. 'As you all know, since I have informed you via letter, fax and e-mail, the government has recently upgraded the criteria upon which the Criminal Justice Charter is assessed.'

Boscombe sighed wearily. Upgrades! As if he didn't know it. Every week it seemed some new yardstick was conjured up and called upon to criticise his undoubted Forensic Expertise. Ever since some idiot technician had dribbled some Semtex on the bottom of a certain centrifuge and subsequently called into question every single arrested bomber's guilt, he had suffered. In a flurry of public face-saving policy moves the Criminal Justice Charter had been forced kicking and screaming into the world. There were now eight different British Standards to check on his blood grouping ability. BSs 57890 through 57923 were specifically designed to scrutinise his skills in fingerprinting and God knew how many more there were waiting in the wings of the civil service to appear and poke at his skills in poisons recognition or drugs identification.

And now the Charter's inquisitorial eye had swung its unblinking attention on that trendiest of buzz-word sciences. DNA Profiling. Boscombe fought his concentration back towards the monologue spouting from Yeats's mouth.

'... and so, in order that the government can fulfil its white paper pledge to establish a comprehensive DNA Database for every known criminal resident within the United Kingdom it is ...'

Boscombe choked and sat suddenly upright. 'What! What the hell did you just say?' he spluttered his face turning pale.

'Er ... er. Which bit?' asked Yeats staring at his carefully prepared speech and holding an index finger under the current line.

'Every known criminal?' choked Boscombe.

'Yes, yes.' Yeats re-read the passage silently to himself, nodded and looked up. 'What about it?'

'*Every* known criminal?' he gasped imagining himself suffocating beneath a swelling avalanche of tumbling paperwork.

Yeats blinked implacably behind his glasses. 'This was made clear in my previous communication, ref CJC 483 #6–7 I believe, in which it states that "provision must be made for the comprehensive DNA Profiling of all criminal ..."'

'Precisely what do you mean by "all?" ' challenged Boscombe, his brow furrowing as he attempted to pull himself together. 'Would that three letter definition include those miscreants caught doing fifty in a thirty zone, perhaps?' he sneered in dripping sarcasm. He was most disappointed when nobody so much as sniggered with appreciation.

'Er, yes, actually,' answered Yeats. 'Such reckless behaviour is evidence of the genetic seeds germinating within the psyche of ...'

'Whoa, whoa,' gagged Boscombe waving his palms in disbelief. What nonsense was this? What pseudo-scientific gobbledegook? He didn't have to let his Forensically sensitive ears suffer with this. Fuming within, he fixed Yeats with a withering stare. 'Do you, a non-scientist, presume to convince me, a qualified and highly eminent exponent of the forensic arts, of the genetic predisposition towards speeding?'

Yeats delved into his plastic snakeskin briefcase and tugged out a recently published paper. It showed a series of parallel lines glowing fluorescently on a rectangle of electrophoretic gel. A tiny pair had been circled in pink magic marker.

'The lower band is called road rage one, RR1 and has been isolated in over ninety per cent of DNA profiled speeding offenders..'

'And . . . and the other?' spluttered Boscombe feeling the table beginning to spin. A certain article in *Forensic Forum* swam sickeningly to the forefront of his mind.

'BMW 535i,' answered Yeats.

'After the car, I presume?'

Yeats nodded. 'Stick a carrier of those genes in any car showroom and they'll be behind the steering wheel of a BMW 535i, through the doors and away over the speed limit before you can mention thirty-six month repayment plans.'

Boscombe made a strange gurgling sound and turned paler.

'Gentlemen, gentlemen,' interrupted Professor Crickson. 'As fascinating as it is to discuss some of Splice of Life's previous academic studies we are currently here for other, more pressing and lucrative, purposes I believe.'

'Hear, hear,' mumbled Striebley under his breath and absently drew King Edwards in the polish on the table-top.

Crickson smiled as benevolently as he could and leaned across the table. 'It is always immensely satisfying when one has been partly responsible for publishing a paper announcing a momentous discovery, as I'm sure Doctor Boscombe knows.'

Boscombe ground his teeth. He hadn't published a paper in years. And certainly not since the introduction of the

Criminal Justice Charter. The bloody paperwork got in the way, there simply wasn't time. No time anymore.

Crickson was rabbiting on. 'But it is even more thrilling when that paper is noticed and acted upon. Especially by such eminent folks as yourselves. On behalf of Splice of Life Patentable Biosciences Ltd I would be honoured to accept the contract to carry out further research into this fascinating field. We will require an immediate cash injection of one and a half million pounds.'

Under his breath Doctor Striebley groaned. That was it. Crickson had done it now. There was no turning back from the biggest scientific fraud ever coined in Camford. He had wanted to be a famous scientist but ... well, not this way.

'One and a half million? Oh, come now ...' spluttered Simeon Yeats cringing. 'We'll give you a million.'

Boscombe coughed and waggled a finger in his ear. Had he just heard right? A civil servant offering to give a scientist a million quid? The conversation suddenly seemed interesting again. 'Million and a quarter,' pressed Crickson across the table, fingering a wad of scientific looking papers in what he hoped was an intellectually seductive manner.

Yeats flashed a worried glance at Chief Inspector Ness and ran a finger around his collar.

'There *are* other interested parties,' added Crickson.

'Correct,' interjected Boscombe suddenly, his eyes lighting up. 'Me,' he added.

'You?' cried five throats as all eyes turned on him, some in shock, some fear.

'A million pounds for the opportunity of some real research *is* somewhat on the attractive side,' grinned Boscombe rubbing his chin dreamily and imagining a complete make-over for his lab. New freezer, new slab, the works.

'No, no! You can't ...' squawked Professor Crickson panicking.

'*Pourquoi pas*?' pondered Boscombe. 'The art of forensic science is my *forte* after all.'

'Ah, but DNA manipulation and assaying is ours,'

countered Crickson hard on the heels of a fleeing million and a quarter quid. 'Our expertise goes back for decades . . .'

'Yes, yes, we know all that,' interrupted Chief Inspector Ness wearily. 'You detailed it most thoroughly in your letter of introduction last month.'

Striebley coughed again. Letter of introduction? his brain squealed. How long had Crickson been planning this scam?

Ness turned on Boscombe, the lines of his cap peak and eyebrows frowning. 'If you had an interest in this field you should have made it clear sooner. All of this was detailed in a memo last week.'

'Memo?' choked Boscombe. 'When do I get a chance to read memos, eh? There's too much paperwork already and . . .'

Desperately Crickson cleared his throat. 'We can alleviate some of that workload,' he smiled oh-so-reasonably.

Boscombe rounded on Crickson, hope welling inside. 'You'll do my paperwork?'

Crickson swallowed as all eyes fixed themselves his way. Nervously he swallowed as the expectant silence thickened, congealing above the gleaming surface of the table. 'P . . . paperwork?' he began. 'Er . . . er, of course,' he winced uncomfortably desperate to hook the million and a quarter pound pike floating before him. 'Once . . . once the contract is in place you need never worry about any of Camford Constabulary's growing workload of DNA profiling . . .'

'And assays?' added Boscombe.

'And assays,' agreed Crickson.

'. . . or the associated paperwork?' pressed Boscombe.

'*Or* the paperwork *or* the ten new assessment criteria included in the Criminal Justice Charter . . .'

'Ahem . . . fourteen,' interrupted Yeats from the head of the table. 'We've thought up a few more.'

'Fourteen new assessment criteria,' continued Crickson sickly. 'Thus allowing you to continue with the more old-fashioned methods of Forensic Detection.'

'Old fashioned? They're the classical methods,' snarled Boscombe with professional pride. 'Original and Best! As dependable as Hovis! Requiring skills and understandings built up over decades of experience . . .'

'Yes, yes. That's just what I meant to say,' grunted Crickson.

'I take it, then, that Doctor Boscombe has no objection to us issuing the contract to Splice of Life?' asked Simeon Yeats.

Crickson's heart was pounding frantically. A million and a quarter pounds hovered tantalisingly.

Boscombe shook his head and was already turning his attentions to palming off as much of the other routine work as he could. They could have the urine samples for drink drive offenders. That always ruined his Christmas.

In a rare display of civil service efficiency Simeon Yeats whisked a handily prepared contract out of his plastic snakeskin briefcase and flourished it at the panting Crickson, eagerly collecting his signature. Yeats wanted this to start as soon as possible. There wasn't much point hanging around doing nothing when he could be earning his ten percent by next week.

With a lucrative grin he locked the contract away, called the meeting to a close and led the delegates from Camford Constabulary out.

They were barely out of the door when a warbling noise began emanating from Chief Inspector Ness's inside pocket. Flushing with embarrassment he pulled the mobile out and jammed it to his ear. 'Hi there, you're through to the Big Friendly Uncle Copper Crime Hotline. Nobody's keener to solve that misdemeanour. How can I be of service?'

Behind him Simeon Yeats beamed.

'Ah yes, Mr Treadly. Lights in the sky, you say? Last night on the thirteenth hole? Can you describe the rocket?'

Nervously, Farson played with his pen. How dare Reg Treadly be reporting last night's launch. They only damaged the thirteenth green a little bit. There was no reason to waste police time on it.

'Well, if it *was* travelling that fast,' continued Ness with a look of wonder on his face, 'I expect it'll be well into

Metropolitan Police jurisdiction by now. I shall alert them. Goodbye.' He stabbed the 'End Call' button and folded the phone back into his pocket. 'Typical,' he grumbled, 'First call and it had to be a nutter. Still, it can only get better.'

Farson breathed a silent sigh of relief and watched the backs of the disappearing entourage. Moments later as the burning rubber of the three Rovers drifted away on the morning breeze, Striebley turned to Crickson with barely contained fury in his eyes.

'What the hell have you done?' he snarled.

'Secured our future,' grinned the Professor.

'What future? How can we do any of this? We haven't got anything to do with DNA analysis.'

But Crickson heard not a word. Already he was preparing himself for his new project. A scheme which could revolutionise the entire future of the fast food industry. This would outshine his previous, less than luminous successes. Oh, yes. Now that Splice of Life was back on solid financial foundations it was time to go way beyond the groundbreaking inventions of the past. So microwaveable gazpacho and boil-in-the-bag steak tartare hadn't quite hit the mark. His new project would. It couldn't fail to.

'Order me five day-old chickens, a dozen maize seedlings and a liquidiser,' grinned Crickson. 'And get me DN-Aids Inc on the phone!'

'You mean . . .?' spluttered Striebley.

'Yes. Project CFC is back on track!' In a whirl of lab-coat, and a swish of security card, Crickson vanished into his laboratory chuckling.

The door to the Royal Nursery was kicked miserably open and a small grey-skinned figure trudged forlornly in. He headed across to his work basket and slumped into it, painfully aware of the cold emptiness of the echoing room. Right now it should be filled with the admiring 'oohs' and the awestruck 'aahs' of a select band of viewing Royals. He should be minutes away from complete success.

A dribble of flame-red trickled down a casually discarded brush.

Suddenly a cheery trill of notes twanged from a poorly tuned lute shattering the gloomy silence.

'Hey nonny, nonny and a fol-diddle-ol . . .'

'Shutup!' yelled Calabrese kicking a pot of paint across the room. Mustard yellow sprayed up his shin.

'Hey! Mind my lute,' whined Lupin, hiding the instrument from the flying colours. 'I was only trying to help. You looked in need of a good song.'

'Well, that rules you out, then,' sulked Calabrese.

'Thankyou *very* much, you ungrateful . . .'

History never will recall precisely the insult which was ready to launch itself from Lupin's tongue. Calabrese was saved a good lashing by the sudden sound of rapid hammering directly above their heads. It pounded angrily from somewhere behind the Great Fire of London, setting the entire nursery vibrating wildly. Cracks spidered their way across the ceiling, ageing the entire area centuries in seconds. Coloured chunks of plaster showered down sending the feyries scattering.

And suddenly, an entire section of medieval London dropped out of the ceiling, crashing to the floor, smashing inumerable pots of paint into a slick of technicolour. The pneumatic pounding stopped.

A shaft of daylight lanced out of the hole, peppered with motes of dust – an open wound bleeding soil.

Calabrese stared in horror, squinting up between his fingers as a cascade of curses filtered into earshot.

'Damn those bloody Victorians. Damn them all!' cried one voice near the hole.

'What is it, Bob?' called another.

'Why can't anybody make a decent map of all the drains around here,' cursed Bob. 'You'd have thought CablePix could've supplied us with one. I nearly fell down that!'

'Not your day really is it, Bob,' observed Derrick, his voice growing louder.

'If I'd been fatally wounded I could sue them. Bet they never thought of that, did they?'

'Well don't you worry about that right now,' mothered Derrick. 'You've had a nasty shock there. What you need is a nice cup of tea and a few minutes with this.'

Vaguely, Calabrese imagined he saw one silhouette pass a small rectangular object across the hole to the other.

'Good thinking, Derrick. After all I do need to check that the system is still functioning. I'll just put it here by my side while I take my gloves off and . . .'

'Careful, Bob. Mind you don't . . .'

Too late, Bob saw the error of his ways. One slight nudge and the tiny toughened test-monitor succumbed to the forces of gravity and slid into the gaping chasm below. It tumbled fifty feet in free-fall, spinning towards certain destruction, its screen flashing images wildly until abruptly it was snatched to a halt, caught by the cable plugged into it.

And there it hung, swinging gently back and forth, chattering away to itself, its liquid crystal screen writhing in the agonies of the shopping channel.

To Calabrese it was irresistible. In seconds he was scampering across the wrecked nursery staring at this moving picture, awestruck. What magic was this? What treasure?

Already his thoughts were racing. How could Titania not pay him any attention if he was armed with this?

'It's alright,' called Bob, high above. 'I think it's still attached. I'll just have to pull and . . .'

Calabrese leapt for the twitching screen, grabbing at it, tugging.

'Bugger. I think it's caught on something.'

'Give it a tug,' offered Derrick helpfully in the distance.

Obligingly Bob did so. The snaking black cable snatched taut, twanged and wrenched the coaxial plug out of the socket. It whiplashed out of sight.

'Gah! Lost it,' cursed Bob. 'We got another one?'

'Yeah, one each, remember,' answered Derrick.

'That's alright, then. If they want it back they can get it themselves. That tea ready yet?'

The Operative-in-Charge of Pneumatic Drills stood and headed off towards the red and white tent by the side of Fenland Road.

Fifty feet below, a stunned Calabrese ran a long index finger across the now static snow storm of the screen, stabbed the channel select button and shook his head.

He had seen it move with living pictures. He *had*. Hadn't he?

There and then he vowed to himself that he would see them again. Suddenly unconcerned about the state of his nursery, his mind began to whirr.

Project CFC

Two twisted rectangles of static reflected in the pair of almond shaped eyes staring intently at the tiny CablePix monitor. The creature's grey-skinned fingers poked and prodded feverishly at the available buttons, fidgeting desperately.

'Well, *I* don't believe you saw pictures coming alive in there,' announced Lupin waggling a finger at the snowstorm-gripped screen.

'They were there,' hissed Calabrese through determined teeth. 'I saw them!'

'You've been working too hard, if you ask me,' grumbled Lupin and strummed an angst-ridden chord from his lute.

'Nobody's asking you,' came the snapped reply. It was accompanied by the tapping of expensive monitoring equipment on paint splattered floor.

'Only trying to be helpful,' mumbled Lupin sulkily. 'I mean, you've been at that for hours and all for what? Eyestrain.'

'I know what I saw!' insisted Calabrese with a note of hysteria.

'Yeah, yeah, that's what you say. I'm still sticking to the working-too-hard theory. I mean, what am I supposed to think, eh? You see your beloved ceiling caving in and you're up snatching at weird little boxes dangling from bits of string and claiming they're showing you pictures. *Moving* ones at that! ... What? ... Why are you staring at me like that? ... Let go of me!'

'What did you just say?' gabbled Calabrese shaking Lupin by the shoulders.

'Er ... which bit?'

'Something about bits of string?' insisted Calabrese furrows of angst highlit silver in the tv's light.

'Well, it *looked* like string,' offered Lupin defensively. 'I ... I can't be certain. It was snatched away rather fast and ...'

'... and the pictures vanished,' finished the artist staring longingly up at the hole. 'Of course, why didn't I see it before ...'

'See what?'

'The pictures. They're up there!' Calabrese leapt to his feet and slapped across the floor to the multicoloured mess of his work basket with the fervour of a prophet whose mission has just been revealed to him.

Behind him, Lupin was scratching his head, running through the last few minutes of conversation, trying desperately to find the nugget of madness which had fired up Calabrese. 'No, no. You *can't* be serious,' he spluttered as he reached the same conclusion for the second time. 'You're saying the pictures come from the piece of string?'

'It all makes perfect sense,' declared Calabrese unfastening the ascending rope from the cleat.

'No. No. You're getting it all mixed up. Pictures come from brushes. *Music* comes from strings.' As if to demonstrate the fact, Lupin tugged a random chord from his lute.

Calabrese ignored him. 'They're up there. Don't you see?' He started pulling eagerly on the rope and his work basket rose into the air, creaking.

Lupin watched him whisk off towards the shattered ceiling and shook his head. This was sure to end in tears before bedtime.

In moments Calabrese was feet from the ruined image of the Great Fire of London fastening the rope around the cleat. He stared across at the hole through eager eyes, fixing his gaze on the coils of cable fizzing with picture information. It hovered tantalisingly out of reach, taunting, beyond his grasp.

Gritting his teeth he began to swing in his basket, straining against the ropes, setting the whole thing penduluming across the ceiling. Fifty feet below, Lupin stared up in alarm.

He'd definitely been under too much pressure. Typical artist, can't take rejection.

Crumbs of plaster rained down from around the hooks holding the basket to the ceiling as Calabrese increased his arc of swing. At every opportunity he reached out, grey fingers scrabbling scant inches from the cable, desperate to grab it, but constantly failing.

'Come down!' wailed Lupin as a chunk of plaster loosened around the rear peg and tumbled to the floor.

His words went unregistered as Calabrese's almond-shaped eyes judged the distance to the lip of the hole. Suddenly, gritting his teeth, he tugged hard on the ropes, hurled his weight backwards and swung the basket wildly. Plaster dust sparkled down from the straining pegs in the ceiling as he pulled at the bottom of the swing, whooshed upwards and leapt. Legs and arms kicked desperately in mid air, flailing uncontrollably as he arced towards the ledge in the bottom of the hole.

Behind him three of the pegs tugged themselves free of the ceiling and clattered floorwards. The basket seemed to quiver for a moment, then it too was snatched by gravity. With the final rope snaking curves of fear in mid air behind it, the entire basket fell.

Lupin screamed and dashed for any available cover as the rope went taut, ripped the final peg out of the ceiling and hit the floor in a cloud of plaster dust and atomised paint.

For all this, Calabrese cared not a jot. He was trembling with excitement as he cradled a three inch diameter python of PVC coated cabling. Millimetres from his fingertips fizzed millions of bits of information, fifteen channels of shopping, twelve data-compressed movies, half a dozen education broadcasts and far, far, too many quiz shows.

Salivating excitedly Calabrese tore at the tough outer coating of the cabling, his claws ripping away a section in a matter of moments. And there, just as he had expected, were hundreds of strands packed tightly together like the fibres of a tree's root. Well, it *was* long and thin and found underground. He peeled a strand from the bunch, tugged it out and dashed back towards the edge of the hole.

It was only now that he realised why Lupin was screaming his name so wildly. He peered over the edge and looked straight down fifty feet to the wreckage of his trusty work basket.

'Now you've done it!' shouted Lupin squinting up at the tiny head silhouetted above him.

'Nonsense,' announced Calabrese in his finest heroic tone. There was no way he was going to be foiled by a simple fifty foot drop. With a flick of his wrist he tossed the single strand into the void, grit his teeth and abseiled into the darkness.

'Are you mad?' said Lupin in strangled tones a few moments later, as Calabrese blew on his palms.

Perhaps fifty feet straight down had been a bit foolish without a safety harness or gloves . . . still, he'd done it now.

Quivering with excitement he grabbed the CablePix monitor and, taking a breath, he plunged the strand of fibre deep into the tiny socket in the device's top corner.

Suddenly the snowstorm of static and the screaming hiss of random electrons vanished. Snatches of soundbites reverberated around the confined space as his deft fingers turned dials here, stabbed buttons there, tweaked this and fiddled with that. And suddenly, with a blast of colours and a fanfare of orchestral synthesiser Calabrese tapped into CablePix's test signal programme.

'I knew it. I knew it!' he shrieked, skipping up and down with delight. 'Look. It's moving!' Lupin peered over his shoulder, stared at the screen and for once hadn't a clue what to say. His lute slipped out of his hand and rattled on the floor unnoticed as a pair of bikini clad babes, sporting crash helmets and bulges in all the right places charged towards each other wielding vast padded clubs. They screamed aggressively, scything the PVC mallets through the air with great gusto. Sweat gleamed on thighs, highlighted for the benefit of the male audience by deft use of starburst filters on all cameras. Ripples of abdominal musculature tensed and suddenly the whistle blew.

It was just as well the first half of *Warrior Women – The WBAM Network Challenge* ground to a steamy halt when it did. Calabrese's blood pressure couldn't have coped with the excitement.

An unnaturally tanned presenter sporting the type of big hair beloved by American purveyors of power ballads leapt onto the screen. All teeth and chin he babbled over-enthusiastically into his microphone.

'And what a crushing victory there from "Thighgress" using those now infamous thigh holds of hers. Ahhhhhmayzzzzhing! Hey! It's a war out there! But, hold on fight fans, you don't need me to tell you that. Ohhhhh, no! And you don't need me to remind you to join me, here, after the break. You do and you'll miss "Vestal Vyxxen" vs "Gina G-String" vying for victory in the Harem of Harlots. The babes are back in town soon on *Warrior Women – The WBAM Network Challenge*!'

Abruptly the presenter pulled a wildly inappropriate macho pose, grinned the cheesiest of blue smirks and a caption board spun out of left field and slammed into the screen.

Fortunately for Calabrese and Lupin, this broadcast being a test-run for CablePix, there were no advertisements to fill the sudden gaping void. Silence enveloped the tiny soily hollow, broken only by the slight panting sounds coming from the two dribbling feyries.

'Wh . . . what *was* that?' gagged Lupin a few moments later, his eyes still welded to the blank screen.

'"W . . . *Warrior Women – The WBAM Network Challenge*". I thought you were paying attention.' Calabrese's voice was oddly flat and not a little distant.

'I was,' and he made a funny noise in his throat. 'Couldn't look away, actually,' he confessed, his eyes motionless on the screen. 'No, what I meant was . . . er, what were they?'

'Women, of course,' whimpered Calabrese, his voice vibrating unnaturally high.

'But they can't be?' dribbled Lupin. 'They look nothing like Princess Hellebore.'

'I . . . I think you'll find it's the other way round,' offered Calabrese. 'They're from up there, see?' Unblinkingly he pointed at the rooty ceiling.

'Up there? But how d'you know?'

Calabrese grinned a memory laden grin as he thought back to the number of women he'd seen running away, naked, screaming after he'd hidden their undies in wildly inappropriate places. Ahhh, the good old days before he had started painting . . . ohhh the freedom of youth.

'You mean there's more of them up there?' spluttered Lupin, his hormones getting the better of him. 'More? Like that?' In the universal gesture of the terminally lecherous, Lupin stroked a pair of imaginary 38 Ds. A grin spread fungally across his face.

'You *have* led a sheltered life. There's hundreds more,' whispered Calabrese in the meaningful way normally exhibited by ancient sages. And in that moment something deep inside him clicked. A ghostly shadow of the good old days hauled up a net of deeply sunken memories and upended them across the forefront of his mind. Flapping and gasping wildly, like a trawl-net of hake, the memories choked in the sudden shock of revelation. Recollections of pale kidnapped teenage girls hammered at him. Reveries of a myriad japes flooded back unchecked.

'How d'you know there's more of them?' asked Lupin suddenly suspicious, snatching his gaze from the still screen.

'I've seen them!' said Calabrese whistfully. 'I've been there. Stole their undies.'

'Oh, come on pull the other . . .'

'. . . I've danced with them.' Calabrese's voice was trembling, his eyes widening, excited. 'I've held them. I've caressed their tender teenage bodies. I've loosed loveshafts of . . .'

'No! You?' Lupin's eyes were pools of almond-shaped awe. 'I thought you just painted that sort of thing.'

'Paint what you know,' grinned Calabrese tapping his nose.

'But . . . you?'

'Yes! Me! I did all that!' Calabrese's index finger stabbed at his grey-skinned chest, anger and pride jabbing it painfully between his ribs. 'But those days are gone now. The good old days. The finest of times, when I couldst deploy a twist of love in idleness to devastating efficacy . . .'

'Ssh, ssh! Not now!' barked Lupin suddenly. His head turned, captured, as the now familiar theme tune of *Warrior Women – The WBAM Network Challenge* sprang into abrupt life. Already it was having effects on parts of male feyriedom which Pavlov could only have dreamt of. 'C'mon, it's "Vestal Vyxxen" vs "Gina G-String" in the Harem of Harlots!'

'And welcome back to part two . . .!' expounded the grinning presenter with fifty kilowatt powerteeth.

Calabrese stared through the screen, half watching, half reliving a million memories. He flexed his elongated fingers forlornly. He'd spent far too much time decorating this damn nursery. And all for what? He had nothing to show for it. It had been far too long since he had wreaked mischief. *Far* too long. Things would have to change.

But, there was plenty of time to see what form 'Vestal Vyxxen' had. Judging by the wails of lust emanating from his viewing partner's corner, she seemed to have particular promise.

'Nice light run tonight,' grinned Miles the managing director of DN-Aids Inc as he handed over a printed sheet of laboratory items to a remarkably short-haired driver. 'I've loaded up most of the boxes, we just need to collect a few items from TechGen Labs and drop 'em off at Splice of Life. It's alright, it's on our way.' He pointed to a clump of recently ordered items ringed in biro. The driver nodded.

'Now you just grab them things. I don't want you helpin' yourself to any other stuff that isn't tied down, clear?'

Alistair, the part-time delivery driver nodded reluctantly.

'You still got the security blue-prints for TechGen Labs?' The driver nodded.

'Anythin' else we need? Torch? Pliers?'

'Glass-cutters,' growled Alistair.

'Geez, what d'you want them for?'

'Front door,' answered the driver with a grin.

'Sod off. Use a brick like we usually do. Now come on.'

They headed out of the rusting Portakabin of DN-Aids Inc, strolled across the carpark and hot-wired the waiting pale blue delivery van. In minutes they were heading off into the night, order form on the passenger seat, jemmy in the glove compartment.

It was six thirty-two and as usual the girl in the floral print Laura Ashley dress and co-ordinating cardigan flung her apron across the kitchen, trudged into the hall and waited for the start of the tapping. She stood outside the dining room her hand on the brass imitation Georgian door handle and, sure enough, it began. Slowly at first but within seconds the impatient rattling of Sheffield Steel against mahogany table top was unignorable. Dreamily thinking of gleaming rockets and telemetry uplinks being active, she took a deep breath and pushed open the door. The usual torrent of words crashed into her, flooding from her frowning father waggling his Sheffield Steel fork.

'Ahh, there you are, at last. I've been calling you, you know. C'mon now, hurry up or it'll be cold . . .' Idly her lips moved in perfect synch with his words as she trudged around the honeysuckle clothed table and took her place in one of the half dozen mahogany carvers. It was the same speech every night.

'. . . insulting to your mother,' ranted her father, his dense eyebrows quivering darkly. 'You don't know how hard she's worked to put this food on the table. Do you?'

She didn't need to even glance at the plate of asparagus quiche, vegetarian ratatouille and bean salad perched atop the placemat of some fictitious Dickensian pub. Yeah, she'd really put herself out tonight. A plateful of Marks and Spencer's finest convenience cuisine.

Tara knew very well how hard it was to wrench open the packets and slam them in the microwave. As per usual she'd done it all whilst her mother squatted in the corner of the kitchen sucking on a bottle of Amontillado. But try telling him that, he'd never listen. That's what came of yelling orders at his minions in blue all day, every day. It was one of the perks of being Chief Inspector, you didn't have to listen to answers.

'. . . receive, make us truly thankful,' he concluded almost piously and, in a single fluid movement snatched his fork and sliced off a triangle of asparagus and cheese pie. In a second it was down his throat.

'You do make a grand quiche, dear,' smiled Everett Ness sycophantically. 'We never have it often enough, you know?'

Tara pulled her co-ordinating cardigan around her shoulders and cringed. Wasn't once a week often enough? Nobody needed a calendar in the Ness household. If it was asparagus quiche it was Tuesday. Low-calorie cottage pie from Iceland tomorrow. Lasagne on Thursday. Findus's finest breaded cod fillets on Friday. Life was such a veritable whirl of wild unpredictability. 'Such a good little cooker, aren't you Rosemary? Always get it just right,' grinned Everett grinding black pepper enthusiastically over his plate. 'Why do you never learn how to do useful things like this at that school of yours, hmmm?' he suddenly asked staring fixedly at his ratatouille. Tara was unsure whether he was interrogating her or the courgettes. She assumed it was the former.

''Cause I left that bloody place last year,' she complained picking boredly at a kidney bean. 'With a GCSE in Geography. Remember?'

Another mouthful of St Michael's asparagus quiche vanished down Everett's throat. 'Rosemary, dear, do remind me I really ought to talk to Tara's tutors about making sure she can cook a decent quiche before she leaves. It's vital in this day and age that the women of today can cook. Vital. I mean, where would we be if all our food came out of packets, eh?' Rosemary picked an imaginary crumb off the honeysuckle print tablecloth. Everett didn't notice. 'Lost, I tell you. That's where we'd be. Lost. And mark my words

93

that's where we're heading with all these women taking up careers left, right and centre. It's not natural.' A glistening mound of beans tumbled after the quiche.

Tara made a mewling noise and mashed maliciously at a slice of courgette.

'And why are we getting lost, hmmm? Pass the salt, Rosemary, dear.'

'Ecstasy Tablets and Teenage Pregnancies?' snarled Tara just to be difficult. Her mother took a sharp breath and shoved the wooden salt cellar towards her husband, scowling at her. They both knew damned well that wasn't the right answer. Ecstasy Tablets and Teenage Pregnancies were only ever discussed on Fridays, if at all. Rosemary stared expectantly at her husband as he ground the sea salt over his plate.

'Precisely!' he declared, masticating absently. 'The Demise of the Family Meal.'

Rosemary let out a sigh of relief. Tara rolled her eyes heavenwards and tapped the side of her head.

Everett was blissfully unaware as he assaulted his plate again. 'It's a well known fact that families just don't get together around a central table anymore and discuss the day's events, carving up any problems into manageable slices and chewing them over with company. I blame tv dinners. A dining room should be for eating, not watching tv.' And with a final fork circuit of his Royal Doulton plate he devoured the last of his repast, stood and headed off for the lounge and his regular weekly appointment with David Attenborough on the Serengeti. It was so nice of the Rotary Club Crime Prevention Society to rearrange their meetings so he could watch all those small furry animals scurrying around chewing each other to bits. So accommodating.

He was barely out of the dining room when there was a warbling of telephone in his pocket. 'Hi there, you're through to the Big Friendly Uncle Copper Crime Hotline. Nobody's keener to solve that misdemeanour. How can I be of service? . . . Ahh, if it isn't the good Mr Treadly. Again. No, I'm afraid the boys from the Met haven't reported any sightings of strange lights in the sky . . . Of *course* I'm taking this seriously,' answered Ness rolling his eyes heavenwards and reaching for the tv remote. 'Well, if you think the press can help you, then feel free. Goodbye . . .' Tutting, Ness severed the link, disconnected the battery temporarily and settled down for an uninterrupted period of viewing pleasure.

In the dining room things weren't quite as peaceful. 'Ecstasy Tablets and Teenage Pregnancies? What were you thinking?' growled Tara's mother, as she watched Tara clear the table with ferocious efficiency.

'Sorry. Thought it was Friday,' tutted Tara insolently. 'Thought I'd opened the breaded cod fillets.'

'Bring me a cup of tea, Rosemary, dear,' shouted Everett settling himself down for a quick bit of wildlife entertainment at the expense of a troupe of hapless meerkats.

'Yes, darling,' shouted Rosemary reflexively and kicked Tara towards the kitchen. The kettle was on, tea in the pot and the requisite two teaspoons of semi-skimmed slopped into the bone china cup before Tara glanced up at the clock. Three minutes past seven, she'd have to get a shift on, otherwise she'd be late. The kettle pabbled feverishly in the corner and, seemingly exhausted, switched itself off. Tara slopped the water in the pot, whirled on her heel and headed off upstairs. 'And where d'you think you're going?' slurred her mother, her words reverberating in the neck of the sherry bottle.

'My room,' snapped Tara clattering away. 'It needs Hoovering.'

In seconds she was in her room and locking the door behind her. She strode across the magazine strewn floor, flicked on the hi-fi and snatched a plain covered box off the bookcase. 'Where is it? Where is it?' she grumbled as she rifled through the box of cassettes, rejecting 'electric drill', 'sander' and 'shelf erection' outright. And then she came across it, jammed in the corner, last as ever. She pulled out the cassette, rattled it into the hi-fi, selected auto-reverse and stabbed play. The speakers crackled into life with the sound of a plug being rammed into a wall socket, a switch being depressed and suddenly her room was filled with twenty watts per channel of industrious vacuum cleaning in full glorious Dolby stereo.

Wasting no time, she dashed across to her wardrobe, tugged out her warmest anorak and swung it around her shoulders. The smell of burnt rocket fuel and scorched grass rattled into her nostrils reawakening memories of last night's launch. Already it seemed unreal, otherwordly.

She rummaged in her anorak pocket and tugged out the flip-top pad. And there were the words of confirmation in stark undeniable black and white. *Monocle and Asparagus 7.30 GAIA*. It was her writing. It was all true.

With a final check behind her Tara slid open her sash window, stepped onto the garage roof and was away into the evening air in the direction of *The Monocle and Asparagus* her mind fizzing with wild expectations.

Precisely what it was that attracted folks of a more environmentally conscious nature to said public house none of its numerous, and strangely hairy, clientele knew. But attract them it did, in droves. Some mused that it was due to the favourable crossing of some, as yet undiscovered, ley lines. Others that it was due to the fact that the pub had been built upon the site of an ice-age mammoth's burial ground. It could simply have been the fact that the beer was the best for miles around. That and the little known fact that the landlord obligingly injected just enough pot into the air conditioning system to maintain a subtly intoxicating air of relaxation.

Whatever the reason, the infamous 'back room' of *The Monocle and Asparagus* was regularly packed out. On the first Thursday of every month it was the turn of the Ecological Retaliation Army – a band of camouflaged angels dedicated to avenging the crimes wrought upon nature's more vulnerable members, dishing out short, sharp and memorably painful shocks to all transgressors; on the fourth Tuesday there was the 'Friends of the Fens' – a group of folk whose amphibian admiration of the Great Crested Newt led to regular meetings down the pub in earnest attempts to get as pissed as their beloved amphibian; and then there was the bunch that were in tonight. The mob that called themselves GAIA.

The Genetic Anti-Interference Alliance believed it would all end in tears if scientists carried on poking about in the delicate workings of evolution. Darwin would be spinning in his cenotaph if he knew of the travesties that certain scientists were wreaking in the name of science. Having discovered that it wasn't too hard to hurl genetic info across any of the barriers of species it wouldn't be long before some folks were trying to create blue strawberries, bald mice, fields full of absolutely identical goats, glowing tomatoes.

'Look, I'm telling you, if God had intended tomatoes to contain the genes of certain jellyfish to make them light up when they wanted a drink, God would've stuck the bloody thing in there, wouldn't she?' growled Elijah Sacramento the self-elected Team Leader of the Camford Branch of GAIA.

'Still, an' all, it's a neat trick isn't it,' offered a red pony-tailed devotee at the same table. 'It'd save me a trip to the bar if I could do it. Sit here, glow a bit and another pint would miraculously . . .'

'I don't think you're taking this seriously,' interrupted Elijah with a slight eastern European twinge to his accent. 'You have been exposed to the influence of the enemy too long, perhaps?'

'No, no. It was just a joke. Bit of light relief . . . er, no pun intended, honest.'

Elijah scowled at him through his John Lennon glasses, his lip quivering.

'Er . . . look, anybody want another . . .' Six faces lit up and half a dozen empty glasses were slapped onto the table. Farson tutted something about tomatoes and reluctantly headed off towards the bar.

At that instant five foot eight of anoraked brunette teenagerdom burst through the door buzzing with hormones and excitement in near equal proportions. Farson spotted her almost instantly. Well, he had been counting the minutes, waiting for her.

'Ah, Tara, you're here,' he observed unneccesarily as he swept towards her, empties in hand.

'Er, sorry I'm a bit late. Couldn't get away, you know?'

'Of course,' he grinned. 'Headlines to write, deadlines to meet. The journalistic life must be such a whirl.'

Tara shrugged in what she hoped was a nonchalant not-too-worldweary manner.

It seemed to work. Farson was staring at her.

'You going to fill them?' she asked flicking one of the glasses in Farson's hand.

'Er ... oh ... I clean forgot ...' Flushing he turned towards the bar. 'Can I get you ...?' Tara nodded and followed.

'How's the review going?' asked Farson leaning on the bar and waggling a tenner for service.

'Fine, fine,' lied Tara. 'Editor loves it.'

'Knew he would. Those Dalek Pedal Bins are a real hit ...' Farson's voice faded as the barman appeared. 'Er, three lagers, two Abbot Ales and a Guinness. And ... what would you like?'

'Lager and tomato juice.'

'You want Worcester Sauce with that?' asked the barman.

'Of course,' frowned Tara. 'It's not a real Bloody Helga without it.'

Farson cringed.

'So, what's the big secret?' asked Tara impatiently fizzing with questions. 'Why d'you invite me here? What's GAIA want with a journalist? I thought you said you were secret?'

'Keep your voice down,' hissed Farson looking worriedly over his shoulder for prying ears.

'Look, there's secret and there's secret, right?'

'What, like the Roswell Incident?'

'...? ...' Farson began.

'Everybody knows the Americans have got a couple of aliens in a box but no one knows what they look like and nobody knows where they are. Is it that sort of secret?' she asked, her eyes glowing with excitement.

'No,' confessed Farson fiddling with the bar towel and trying to find the right words. 'This is more ... er ...'

'Exciting?' pressed Tara. 'Extraterrestrial?'

'... more like PR.'

Tara's face fell.

'But ... but it will be exciting,' promised Farson. 'Honest. There'll be ...'

'Twelve ninety-eight, mate,' blurted the barman plonking a trayful of drinks on the bar and holding out his hand. Farson rummaged about in numerous pockets and somehow scraped the relevant cash together. Dropping it into the twitching palm he picked up the tray and headed back to the group. 'It'll all make sense in a few minutes,' he offered.

'Better do,' muttered Tara under her breath as she followed him through the heaving pub and past numerous tables. He ducked under a low beam, swung left and placed the tray on a tiny table. Tara tuned into the conversation instantly.

'... blind watchmaker theory discounts the positive deterministic angle proposed by Darwinism and other ...' The speaker stopped suddenly, peered intently through his John Lennon glasses and turned an accusing gaze on Tara. 'Who's she?' he snapped at Farson. 'You went to get a round in, not bring back spectators.'

'Elijah, gentlemen, this is Tara Ness reporter for *Amazingly Unfeasible* magazine.'

The entire group recoiled in secretive horror.

'The press?' hissed Elijah Sacramento with all the relish of the average vampire seeing dawn's early light.

'It's alright, she's one of us,' placated Farson desperately. 'Tell him, Regan.'

'She knows her SF,' he grunted from the shade of the distant corner and snatched at a lager. Elijah Sacramento rubbed the wispy strands of his putative goatee and looked Tara up and down. 'Registration number of USS *Voyager*?'

'NCC 74656,' answered Tara with glee.

'Maximum speed?'

'Warp 9.975 in normal space.' Her heart pounded. Was

this what all the secrecy had been about when Farson had invited her here last night? Were they forming a pub quiz team?

'Okay, she's in,' growled Elijah darkly and turned his attention back to the gathered group

'Aren't you going to ask me any more?' asked Tara sounding a mite disappointed. 'I know all about *Babylon 5*, too.'

Elijah frowned at her and hurriedly Farson fetched her a stool, thrusting her into it and pressing her Bloody Helga into her hand. Tara took the hint.

'Where was I?' began Elijah distantly, trying to shake the worrying feeling that he had seen that girl somewhere before.

'Something about the work of short-sighted watchmakers being destroyed by blind lunatics with oxy-acetylene torches ... or something,' offered a particularly hairy being in the corner. 'I got a bit confused with all them metaphors.'

Tara stared at the speaker and wondered if he wasn't in fact the victim of some evil experiment to reactivate the long-dormant genes of eminent neanderthals.

'Ahhh, never mind that now,' pronounced Elijah with casual imperiosity. 'Now that all of us are here, I declare tonight's GAIA Council Meeting open. Minutes.'

The hairy one in the corner cleared his throat and opened a large leather bound book. 'Much discussion as to the genetic purity of Gillian Anderson. A proposal was made by Brother Regan to kidnap her for exploratory testing. Her agent hasn't got back to us on that one yet. Other topics covered include: Lab rats: has incest stunted their mental capacity? Chimpanzees and Man: if there's such a close genetic correlation between us, how do we know who's running the White House? Woodlice ...'

'Enough,' interrupted Elijah impatiently and cringing at the standard of recent meetings. If only there was something really meaty they could get their teeth into. He hadn't formed the Genetic Anti-Interference Alliance to just sit around in the pub and discuss titbits scooped from the bottom of *New American Scientist*'s barrel. He needed action. Now.

'Any other business,' he sighed and looked around the table. He didn't hold out much hope.

It was the moment Farson had been waiting for. He flipped on his favourite combat baseball cap, spun it around and leant forward. Lowering his voice for increased dramatic tension, he said, 'Operation Surgical Splice must come forward.'

'What? What's this, Operative Farson? Explain!' spluttered Sacramento spraying a film of lager across the table. 'You said, in your last report, they were no threat to the genetic integrity of Mother Earth, bless her cotton socks.'

'They weren't, then. What lines of research they had were simply enhancing existing traits, like increasing the power outputs from vegetables, or . . .'

'Yes, yes, we know about the solar-rechargeable King Edward,' interrupted Elijah. 'What's changed?'

Farson swallowed. 'Cash.'

There weren't the gasps of shock and alarm he had hoped for.

'They've got the contract,' he added as enigmatically as he could. Desperately he squinted out of the corner of his eye trying to gauge Tara's reaction. Was she impressed?

'You mean . . .?'

'Yes. Project CFC is back on track!'

All but Tara were spellbound, adopting gestures of horror and impotent outrage around the table. She just sat there and shook her head slowly convinced that this was either a wind-up, or they were all barking mad, or this was some rehearsal for some very bad am-dram company who'd been kicked out of the local church hall for not being up to scratch.

'Crickson's started ordering new equipment already,' insisted Farson.

'I see . . .' mused Elijah enigmatically stroking his goatee.

'No you don't!' snapped Farson. 'You don't know what he's ordered!' Farson's hysteria was beginning to affect the rest of the GAIA members. They all stared at him expectantly, some with drinks poised 'twixt mouth and table.

'What? What?' spluttered Tara sarcastically. 'Do tell.'

Somehow she resisted the temptation to clap her hands together.

Farson swallowed and turned to her, his face a study in dark forebodings. 'Five day-old chickens, maize and . . . and . . .' He ran out of words.

'What?' pressed Tara, suddenly feeling unsure about everybody else gasping in horror. 'That doesn't sound too bad. Chickens eat maize don't they?' she suggested hopefully.

Elijah shook his head and tutted meaningfully.

'What? What?' flustered Tara.

'He's ordered a . . . a liquidizer as well!' spluttered Farson. Everyone around the table took a sharp gasp and grabbed at their drinks.

Baffled, Tara looked around uncomfortably. 'What?' she squeaked. 'What's wrong with that, eh? Poor little day-old chickens can't eat hard bits of maize can they? Teething trouble and all that. He'll need the liquidizer to mash it up. Like baby-food . . . what? Why you shaking your head? What else's he going to liquid . . . No. Oh no . . .'

And as she stared at Farson, his hands tucked in his armpits, flapping forlornly, the truth hit. 'Not the poor little . . .?' It was more than she could take. Downing her Bloody Helga in one gulp she grabbed hold of Farson's lapels, twisted him around to face her and barked. 'Right, tell me about your Operation Surgical Strike, then.'

Farson shook his head. 'Splice. Surgical Splice,' he corrected, dreamily staring into Tara's eyes. She looked so different when she was angry, so dominant, so . . . oooooh.

'Yeah, yeah. Whatever,' she hissed. 'You've got an awful lot of explaining to do, matey boy.'

'Hear, hear!' seconded Regan from across the table.

And not for the first time in the back room of *The Monocle and Asparagus*, under the gentle intoxicating influence of far too much beer and a subtly narcotic atmosphere, campaigns of war began to be drawn.

'Hold that torch straight,' hissed Miles, the managing

director of DN-Aids Inc. 'How d'you expect me to cut the right wire with that thing waggling around like a Mysteron on acid!' Alistair grunted an apology of sorts and concentrated.

Miles scowled at the blue-print lying on the concrete next to him and traced the line of the main alarm system through the jemmied junction box before him. With a deft snip he sliced through the yellow and black wire, counted three and exhaled. So TechGen Labs hadn't updated their security since their last visit. One day they would. Then it would just have to be another trip back to the head office of Property-Tectors Security Systems plc to get the new blue-prints. But, until then . . .

Bolt-cutters chewed their way hungrily through wire-mesh fencing, glass-cutters ground their way through the front door and within minutes an unmarked two-ton Transit was backing into the car park whilst busy hands set about disconnecting several thousand pound's worth of almost pristine scientific equipment from the walls of TechGen Labs.

A pair of almond shaped eyes stared at the fizzing images, completely captivated by the action unfolding before them in the cavern of their ruined nursery. A pulse of excitement pounded at Calabrese's temples as he revelled in extraordinary viewing pleasure.

He watched fascinated as fingers, strangely short and far too pink, tapped away at an odd cluster of square pads each of which was painted with a letter. The viewpoint switched and showed a dark screen flashing with green letters. The feyrie scratched his head and leaned forward as a message was typed in.

FILENAME: PENTAGON.DEFENSE.NUCLEARLAUNCHSEQUENCE.

Tense music backed it up. Searing strings hovering above a pulsing bass. Somehow it seemed to hook into his emotions, gripping him, thrilling. Behind him Lupin was writhing in ecstasies. Never had he heard a lute get anywhere close to that music. In blissfully hypnotised innocence his grey toes were jigging wildly to the pounding theme tune. Deep, deep inside him a tiny clump of neurones sobbed plaintively and attempted to rearrange a series of notes which were hatching into a jaunty little tune. Desperately they wrestled it into a minor key, slowed the tempo and then wailed pathetically as they realised his lute could never sound like a Fender Strat through a clipping Marshall stack.

Then, from nowhere there was a stab of discord, a rumble of tympanis and the screen flashed crimson. Calabrese gasped.

ACCESS DENIED

Amazed, all his attention focused on the dancing images, Calabrese watched the fingers tap wildly again, filling his screen in high-resolution Hollywood imagery. His curiousity burned to know what would happen next.

CODENAME: ALPHA 1. A1:PRIME.PRESIDENT.

There was a brief shot of a sweating face lit by the glowing screen of the vdu. It pulled on a smouldering cylinder in its mouth. The music hammered on, building the tension, drawing Calabrese ever further into the plot. Of course, he hadn't a clue what words like 'NuclearLaunchSequence' and 'Codename:Alpha 1.A1:Prime. President' meant but some-how he knew that someone was trying to sabotage someone else, and that someone didn't want it to happen and that, for him, was enough. On a deep-down level a good hundred dozen bells of memory were ringing, harking back to the good old days.

Suddenly the screen flashed green and the music shifted up a gear of stirring intensity. Calabrese's heart pounded at the back of his throat as slowly the viewpoint swung away from the sweating face, panning around to show the message on the screen.

104

And the fingers were back in action again, faster, more positive.

SecurityOverride: Alpha a 1 {: Beta Prime} Omega. Target Sequence: Crimson Katana. Engage Launch Procedure

A doom laden chord of orchestral intensity rattled through the speaker and behind him Lupin whimpered and almost wet himself. Having listened to the sounds floating from the tiny speaker, his lute would never have quite the same appeal for him ever again, he was utterly certain. His mind raced with thoughts of the music he could make if he learned to play that box. It could change the whole future of entertainment down here. He might even get himself noticed by his belusted Princess Hellebore. Deep down he knew he had to have it. Now. His heart swelled with excitement and before he realised precisely what he was doing he snatched the CablePix monitor and began stabbing wildly at the buttons.

'Oi! Give me that back!' squealed Calabrese rounding angrily on Lupin. Single frames of colour flashed across the screen between bouts of white noise, music changed key, tempo and instrumentation every other second in a total racket of disjointed fragments. 'That music? . . . How d'you do it, eh? Show me?' growled Lupin jabbing at the buttons in frustration.

'The music?' spluttered Calabrese. His mind was on the plot. What was the saboteur up to? Desperately he wanted to find out. And every second spent with Lupin in charge of the buttons was a second he was missing out on the action.

'That surreal music. That stirring soundscape of intrigue. How d'you do it? C'mon, this is professional interest. I'm the bard, you're not supposed to be able to make better music than me. C'mon.' Every sentence was punctuated by feverish jabbings of buttons.

'Give it back. I'll show you how it's done,' gabbled

Calabrese. What was happening in the plot? He had to find out. 'You just name the tune and I'll ...' Before Lupin realised Calabrese had snatched it back, turned his back and was scrolling back to channel one. In moments that same haunting music was filling the nursery with rhythmic discord.

'That's it, that's it!' shrieked Lupin. 'Oh, it's beautiful!' he enthused jamming his ear next to the speaker, covering the screen. 'And so very, very LOUD!' He shook his head enthusiastically. Hellebore couldn't fail to notice him if he was to compose a symphony of this just for her. 'Get out of the way!' barked Calabrese. 'Move or I'll miss it!'

He wrestled the monitor free of Lupin's ear and stared at the screen. Horrified confusion flashed across his face. 'No, no! Where's it gone?' wailed Calabrese. 'Where's the fingers and "Codename:Alpha. A1:Prime. President" and all that? What's happened to it?' He stared forlornly at the strings of credits scrolling up into the top of the screen. 'It's gone,' he sobbed. And as if in reply a voice boomed out of the grille. 'And there'll be more from *Mission Inconsequential* next week. But stay tuned. It's *Warrior Women* next.'

'You made me miss it!' shouted Calabrese thumping floor. 'I'll never know if he succeeded in hacking into Target Sequence: Crimson Katana.' It seemed that already Calabrese had got the hang of the lingo of *Mission Inconsequential*. 'It's gone!'

Struck dumb with shock Lupin stared at the screen as the last few rows of words vanished into the top of the tv monitor.

Suddenly, without any period of tuning up, another orchestra sprang into action and the images changed. 'How do you do that?' gagged Lupin. 'Show me how you play it. Teach me ...'

'You made me miss it,' moaned Calabrese flicking forlornly through the channels looking for images of fingers on keyboards everywhere. 'It's gone and it's all your fault and ...'

Suddenly his ranting stopped as a snippit of matter-of-fact

commentary slithered into earshot. His attention shifted to the screen, his jaw dropping open in incredulity. 'No,' he whispered. 'No, that can't be . . .'

Lupin was straining to see as the commentary continued. '. . . often to be found perched on the classic red and white toadstools, fairies can be seen dressed in acorn cup hats and shimmering pink gowns . . .'

Calabrese's face was twisting with writhing indignation, his pride snarling angrily within as the catalogue of lies rattled out of the speaker. 'Acorn cup hats!' he spat. 'Shimmering gowns! What nonsense *is* this?' The screen showed a tiny picture of a wand-wielding creature taking to the air on a fluttering of wings and a vapour trail of tinsel. The commentary droned on. 'The most famous fairy figure, of course, is that of Tinkerbell. Beloved by children worldwide, her ability to fly is as captivating as any of the fairy's delightful traits . . .'

By now Calabrese was seething. 'Wings!' he spluttered. 'Beloved by children? What lies are these? How dare they spout this slander?'

'. . . and next week on *The Mystical, Magical, Marvellous Show* for all those who like their mystical creature less on the sugary side we'll be showing you the real truth about gremlins. Here's a sneak preview.'

And as the scene changed to flashes of mayhem wrought by large-eared grinning monsters in small-town America, Calabrese screamed at the screen. 'No, no, that's all wrong. Gremlins aren't like that! We're the evil ones! How can they have got this so wrong?' he wailed, shaking his fists imploringly at the ceiling.

'Maybe they forgot,' offered Lupin with a shrug.

Calabrese turned on him in an instant, fuming. 'Forgot?' he seethed, his heart pounding with waves of hurt pride. '*Forgot?* How could they possibly forget about us? They live in constant fear of feyrie interference, they quiver in persistent worry of where we will strike next, tremble in continual terror of the dangers lurking all around them. Plague, famine, fire. It's all there in our heroic ballads.'

'Our heroic ballads,' enthused Lupin feeling a stirring in his lute-strumming fingers. 'I'd love to meet some of those real heroes, y'know. Where do they hang out?'

'At the Court of Queen Titania. Have you learnt nothing? Hundreds of them gather every night in readiness to set out on quests to disrupt and disturb . . .'

Lupin looked surprised. 'Every night? You sure?'

'Of course. I know my legends.'

'Oh . . . Can't have been doing a good job lately then, can they?' mused Lupin plucking a casual chord from his lute.

'What? How can you say that about our heroes?'

'Easy,' shrugged Lupin. 'Every single ballad I've written recently has been about an ancient hero. Nothing new, see?'

'Nonsense, nonsense,' flustered Calabrese. 'You just have to open your eyes and look around you.' He waved his arms expansively towards his ceiling. 'It's positively dripping with deeds of heroism and courage. They go right back to the very dawn of history,' he answered proudly.

'And the most recent?'

Calabrese stared above him and scoured his ceiling desperately. 'Few years old, at most . . . maybe a decade or two . . . or . . .'

'I think you'll find it's that one,' offered Lupin, pointing to a certain fire in the capital city.

After several minutes of fruitless searching for anything more current Calabrese shrugged. 'Well, I might have missed one or two.'

'You didn't miss them, they're not there. Face it, there just aren't the heroes there used to be. For everyone up there, we don't exist anymore. Our days are over.'

Calabrese's face writhed in a very peculiar way as the truth smashed down the door of his mind, kicked off its boots, poured itself a large drink and settled in for a long stay. He leapt to his feet, fists clenching and unclenching, and headed off for the door. 'Oh our days are over, are they?' he fumed, fizzing with kilowatts of hurt pride. 'We'll see about that.'

Lupin, sensing a ballad opportunity, grabbed his lute and dashed off in hot pursuit.

A pale blue delivery van shuddered to a halt and the uniformed driver slithered out of the cab.

Rubbing a bored finger across the underside of his nose he trudged around the back of the Transit, hauled open the doors and began to unload the recently collected equipment from TechGen Labs. He wrestled them onto a suitable trolley, borrowed from B&Q for this very purpose, turned back into the gloomy interior and groaned as he stared at the last few packages.

'Why me?' he shuddered as he stared at the parcels squatting in the almost empty van. His eyes locked onto the red sticky tape sealing two of the boxes shut and swallowed nervously. BIOHAZARD! It declared in no uncertain terms. 'I shouldn't have to do this. Shouldn't be my job. Not my job at all,' he grumbled, and images of Ebola victims flashed across his paranoid mind.

Swiftly he grabbed the unlabelled box, hurled it onto the trolley and fled from the suddenly claustrophobic back of the van. In seconds he was jabbing a sweating finger at the doorbell of Splice of Life Patentable Biosciences Ltd.

Minutes seemed to crawl slowly by as he peered ineffectually through the opaquely tinted glass door and shuffled from one foot to the other. In his mind, outbreaks of organ dissolving pathology oozed restlessly inside the boxes in his van. BIOHAZARD. BIOHAZARD!

Sweating he pounded once again at the doorbell.

Instantly it sloughed open and an imperiously sneering Professor Crickson stared at him. 'Yes!' he barked and then. 'Ah. It's you! Excellent. Everything there?'

'There's a couple more in the van.'

Crickson snatched the trolley from the van driver's hands and hauled it over the threshold. 'Do bring the others, there's a good chap!'

'B ... bring *them*?' he spluttered, 'But ...'

'You *are* a delivery man, yes?' said Crickson staring implacably.

'Y . . . yes, but . . .'

'Then deliver!' Defeated by logic he turned and trudged towards the gaping malevolent maw of his transit. 'Can't you just come and . . .' he began peering around the edge of the door.

'Deliver,' commanded Crickson.

Attempting to tell himself that there couldn't possibly be anything really dangerous in those packages, honest, he cringed and reached out a trembling hand to the cardboard handles on the top. And so it was that he reappeared moments later from the back of the van, one BIOHAZARD box clutched in each hand at arm's length, his mind spinning wildly as it tried desperately not to consider the horrors contained within.

He knew very well the type of things they dealt with, the things in those boxes. He'd seen science on tv. *Quatermass. Invasion of the Bodysnatchers. Aliens. Critters.* It must be true. No smoke without fire, and all that. He just didn't want to know.

It was almost possible that, had the wind been in the right direction, he wouldn't have found out the truth. But, just as he approached the doorway of Splice of Life a tiny gust swirled out of nowhere, plucked the tiny aromatic fragments of the package's contents and casually inserted them up his left nostril. He stopped in mid step as his olfactory system twitched, shuddered and recognised the smell. Musty, vaguely sweet, botanical.

Horror laden images of Donald Sutherland fighting screaming bodysnatchers flooded through him. They were here! In these boxes! The creatures in the other box suddenly began scratching around and making shrill peeping noises.

It was too much for him. Blubbering desperately he dropped his burdens, spun on his heel and leapt into the cab. In seconds the transit was burning clouds of rubber as it accelerated backwards down the length of Edison Boulevard. It spun and screeched around the corner.

'Don't I have to sign anything?' asked Crickson waggling a pen uselessly into the rubber fragranced night air, shrugged and carried the pair of discarded boxes into the privacy of Splice of Life.

'What's all the fuss?' shouted Striebley across the foyer, peering through the security door of his lab. 'I'm trying to work in here.'

'BIOHAZARD,' grinned Crickson. 'Always freaks them.'

Striebley's eyes lit at mention of the 'B' word. 'Exciting?'

'Oooh yes,' grinned the Head and began ripping open the box from which the odd peeping sound was emanating. 'Project CFC!' he chuckled.

Striebley watched as Crickson peered inside, extended a gnarled index finger and appeared to be stroking something. The peeping increased in volume.

'Don't know why they declare these BIOHAZARD,' grinned Crickson stroking a day-old chick in his hand. 'They're so cute!'

'Salmonella,' answered Striebley authoritatively. 'Riddled with it they are. Worse than iguanas, you know.'

'And what about these?' mused Crickson tugging a tray of maize seedlings out of the other box.

'Hmmm. Poisonous aren't they. Well, if you eat them raw.'

'No, that's kidney beans, isn't it?'

'I can't keep up with all these Health and Safety Regulations. They really get in the way. Only the other day I was trying to write a COSHH risk assessment for tuna fish and . . .'

But he was talking to empty air. Professor Crickson had gone. Vanished upstairs with his three vital boxes. The three essential ingredients to get Project CFC up and running.

The Prof was already sweating with the anticipation of it all. Why nobody had thought of it before he hadn't the foggiest. But that was the way with most folks. Couldn't see the obvious even if it bit back.

Of course, he'd been the same himself once. Pouring all of his effort in one direction. Misdirection.

But he'd been young then and he'd needed his failures. If he hadn't invented the groundbreaking boil-in-the-bag steak tartare then there would have been no microwaveable gazpacho. Secretly he held out a glimmer of a hope that one day those glorious culinary creations would have their time. One day Findus or Crosse and Blackwell or Heinz, or *somebody*, would come knocking on his tinted doorway desperate to license the sure-fire winner from him. Oven-Bake Sushi. Ahhh, that way lay fortune!

And it wasn't that unlikely. After all, look at the phenomenal success of pizza. That was simply glorified cheese on toast when all was said and done. There was no accounting for taste. Witness the millions of bags of Monster Munch that were sold every week?

He ran his security card down the side of his door and burst eagerly into his laboratory, striding determinedly forward towards what he knew simply had to be the glorious future of complete success.

With practised skill he stifled a brief twinge of regret stabbing through his heart. His fists clenched angrily, eyes screwing shut tight as he wrestled to keep out those other myriad moments of previous certain success. So many times it had seemed perfect. Like the time he had conjured up the one product that could unite and monopolise the entire crisps and snacks industry in one fell swoop. It was sheer genius. How could Dry Roasted Peanut Flavoured Crinkle Cut Crisps have failed?

He bit his knuckles. 'Face it. You're just ahead of your time!' he attempted to console himself. 'Ahead of your time.'

He could wait. He still had the patents on them. And fifty-three other little gems of culinary wizardry just waiting to be picked up and thrust at the waiting public for a sizeable fee, of course.

But all that waiting was about to change. With Project CFC, they would be coming to him. They would be begging him for the license to use his patentable biosciences. They would worship at his feet. It couldn't fail.

Chuckling, he patted the head of one of the cheeping, day-old chicks. 'You'll be famous soon,' he grinned. 'Famous!'

Gripped in a ferment of excitement he dashed around the end of the lab workbench and began unpacking the liquidizer. Behind him, high on the far wall, illustrated in full colour flow diagrams and annotated to perfection, was the entire scheme for Project CFC.

Extraction of Chicken DNA. Amplification of essential genomes. Insertion into Plasmid DNA. Trans-species location. Propagation of Transgenic Hybrid. Success! Five short steps to manufacture a foodstuff that would unite carnivore and vegan alike. The breakthrough for the twenty-first century – chicken fed corn.

Biologically it made perfect sense. It was so much more efficient. If one looked at it from a bioergonomic viewpoint it was stunning. For every beam of solar energy landing on his corn-leaves it would go directly to making edible products. None of this messing about making beaks and parson's noses and stuff.

And the benefits didn't stop there. Oh, no. Salmonella would be a thing of the past. Battery farms would vanish. There'd be no need for messy guano disposal.

And here he was, right on the brink of it all, teetering vertiginously on the edge of worldwide fame. All he had to do to get that ball of brilliance rolling was find out which of the chicken's genes were directly responsible for that distinctive and complex flavour they had. Which were the strings of double helix that made the little darlings so finger lickin' good?

There was only one way to find out.

'Here, chicky!' chirruped Crickson, reaching towards the box of yellow fluff. 'Come to science.' His gnarly hand flashed into the box, snatched a bewilderedly peeping day-old and casually dropped it into the glass cone of the liquidizer.

'This is going to hurt you more than it'll hurt me,' he whispered and then, barely hiding a sneer of voracious scientific interest in loads of patentable discoveries, he flicked the power switch. Like the most irritating of traffic lights when one is in a hurry, yellow turned red.

Fifty feet directly above Titania's head the last few golfers of the day had long since debated the choice between a five iron and a mashie niblick, and were now slaking their thirsts with a well earned drink or five.

The Queen of the Feyries yawned and stared at the lattice of roots tangling their way darkly across the ceiling of the central hall. Before her lay the remains of another feast of cockroach-au-vin and minnowstrone soup. A half finished acorn cup of beetle-juice squatted on the table, bubbling gently. Overhead, forests of truffles nestled between gnarly oaken fingers and looked for all the world like inedible navel fluff. She burped, took a swig of gin and clapped her hands noisily.

Across the hall a curtain of roots were tugged back and a grinning feyrie sporting far too much make-up and a pair of acorn cups strolled onto the makeshift stage. 'She' was followed moments later by another.

'Hail and well-met, proud Cynthia,' declared the first feyrie. And in that instant tonight's episode of *Rootside* had begun.

'Greetings, fine Flavian. 'Tis a fine day for trysting is't not?'

'Aye, 'tis, 'tis.'

All eyes, captivated by the action, failed to notice a door fling itself itself open on a distant wall. A panting feyrie erupted through it and charged across the floor, elbowing his way through the audience. 'Your Highness, Your Highness!' called Calabrese.

'Silence!' bellowed Titania shifting on her pile of leaves.

'Your . . .'

'Silence! Can't you see I'm busy.'

'But . . .' Calabrese heard grumblings behind him as the entire audience ground their teeth and pressed forward. It seemed nobody wanted to miss *Rootside* tonight. Well, it wasn't surprising, the truth about Foxglove and Hyacinth's love child was about to be revealed. Hands clasped around his shoulders and a dozen feyries breathed down his neck.

He drew himself up to his full three feet one and a half, snarled and attempted once more to gain an impromptu audience with Queen Titania.

'Your . . .'

It was as far as he got before he was forcibly ejected the way he had come, and after a short period where the actors rewound, *Rootside* resumed.

'Well, what did you expect?' asked Lupin shaking his head a few moments later in the corridor as the dust cleared.

'This is important. She should have listened, she should . . .'

Lupin shook his head and eased open the door. 'There's a time for audiences. It's all there in the second verse of the "Ballad of Bittercress" just before the key change where it goes "Hey Nonny fol-diddle-ol . . ."'

'Shutup. Instantly, or your instrument will regret it,' snarled Calabrese, staring threateningly at Lupin's lute. Barely hiding a look of disgust Calabrese peered across the hall at the captivated attentions of dozens of feyries.

There was a time when this cavern positively hummed with laughter and delight, handsome young bucks of feyriedom regaling the masses with tales of evil wickedness wrought that very day on the bewildered overgrounders. There'd be squeals of appreciation when the latest virgin child was unveiled, stolen from above, kidnapped for their own evil sports of lust. And, oh, those nights of wild orgy when the teenage overgrounders were brought out, pale and bewildered . . .

A wry grin of carnality squirmed across his face as he recalled Puck's delight in 'putting a girdle about the earth in forty minutes' and returning, his arms burgeoning with the flower whose juice could make any creature dote on any other.

The purple pansy, Heartsease.

Snarling he stared across the cavern at the now snoozing

Puck. 'Look at him,' he thought to himself, 'couldn't even get a girdle around himself in forty minutes now.'

Calabrese grit his teeth as he thought of all the lost opportunities, all the maidens he could have had his way with, all the golden chances of practical wickedry which had lain untapped by generations. He hated to admit it but Lupin was right. The heroes had vanished.

And then his scathing gaze fell on the grossly overfed bulk of King Oberon.

It was all his fault. Had to be. The rot had set in with him on a certain Midsummer Night a few centuries back. What a jape it had seemed then, such scope, such perfection! A splendid confounding of magic, mirth and merriment. The finest of risible recipes.

First take one Titania, Queen of the Feyries, sleeping, add one portion of the juice of 'love in idleness'. Leave to one side to marinade. Then, take one over-enthusiastic amateur actor, add the head of an ass and set to singing near the sleeping Queen prepared earlier. Allow the Queen to rise at the sound, become stricken and dote endlessly upon the ass-headed mortal. Serve to an audience of wildly entertained feyries.

Everything had been bowling along according to plan. Tanny was in full gush, promising the ass-headed one jewels from the deep, beds of pressed flowers. She was set to feeding him bags of honey, apricocks and dewberries and he, the dolt, desirest nothing more than hay and dried peas. Oh, such merriment was had by all, such an aching of ribs.

And what does bloody Oberon do in the midst of this delight? Only feels sorry for her and, with nary a by-your-leave mutters a quick spell, turns everything back to normal and then . . . and then, he spends the next few dozen decades making it up to her.

Suddenly Calabrese saw it all clearly. In those few decades the wicked joys of being a feyrie had atrophied, shrivelled and died, evaporated. Gone was the thrill of a night's revelrous sabotage when they'd start many a stampede, burn the odd crop or turn a dozen churns of full-fat milk sour in the flick of a index finger. Ahhh, those had been the days. All the good clean practical wickedness of his youth.

All gone.

Now there was nothing to do but watch *Rootside*.

Well, unless you were into guessing whether Oberon and Titania could pile on the pounds faster than Puck.

Calabrese ground his teeth as his thoughts spun back to the Glory Days depicted on his shattered ceiling. How could he possibly be proud to hold his head up and be counted as a feyrie when nightly soaps and truffles was all that station amounted to?

'You want a brand new heroic ballad?' hissed Calabrese. 'One that'll set the hearts of feyries aquiver for centuries to come?'

'A new ballad?' asked Lupin slightly doubtfully.

'The newest. The most amazing. Chronicling the rebirth of the feyrie nation, the return to its rightful place.'

'I should say so,' grinned the one with the lute.

'Then follow me,' declared Calabrese whirling on his heel and heading off down the passageway.

'You? But, I thought you didn't have a chance to talk to Titania. How come you've got a hero to write a song about?'

'You're looking at him,' hissed the artist and dashed away into the gloom.

Lupin scratched his head, curiousity rumbling in the back of his mind. Had Calabrese finally lost his marbles? What was he thinking of?

There was only one way to find out.

Clutching his favourite lute tight against his chest, Lupin broke into a run.

Professor Crickson drummed his fingers impatiently on the lid of the centrifuge and cursed the thing. Why did it always take *so* long for the damned machine to slow down? It wasn't as if it should be difficult to decelerate almost half a ton of honed metal from twenty two and a half thousand revs per minute to zero, was it? Could the damned machine be deliberately retarding the very forefront of scientific advancement?

He cursed again as he thought of all the wasted hours he had spent in front of this jumped up spin-dryer.

'Just you wait,' he threatened it with a gnarled finger. 'Come my food revolution, you'll be first on the tip. I'll have a brand new one. Inertialess damping. Maglev acceleration. You'll be as obsolete as a dodo with flares and I'll . . . aha!'

The centrifuge lid clicked and unlocked. With a raptorial bound he was on it, ripping open the cooled interior and snatching out the spun down chicken pate. 'Perfect, perfect!' he chuckled to himself as he looked at the razor sharp separations in the ex-farmyard remains. The DNA would be in the crimson solution at the bottom of the test-tube, split from the gristle and feathers by the action of phenol chloroform.

In three bounds he was across the lab, skipping past the vast transparent tanks in which his babies would soon be growing, and prodding a pipette in the top of the tube. To anyone watching he was a study in the influence of feverish excitement and the heady vapours of chloroform. His pupils swam disjointedly in the swirling miasma of his eyes.

Chuckling to himself, his right leg tapping with pent energy he loaded the sample into the top of the PCR machine and quietly cursed this acknowledgement of the inefficiency of his system.

'Polymerase Chain Reaction,' he growled under his breath. 'Damn you, necessary evil. As soon as I get my Hydroponic Isotoning and Development Bar sorted I won't need you.'

And he wouldn't, either. He wouldn't have to spend all night amplifying the amount of DNA present before carrying on along his delicate development process. He hated the inelegance of it all. To him PCR amplification smacked of reliance on a principle which owed more to making poo stick to walls if you hurled enough of it than any decent scientific tenet. It was almost as bad as the botch job employed by countless millions of CD players worldwide, the infamous

'Four-Fold Oversampling'. The things were bound to work if you looked at the same thing four separate times, split the difference and ignored any bit that didn't agree. That just wasn't scientific.

With a grunt he loaded the last of his chicken mousse into the machine, flicked a switch and was suddenly at a loose end. There was absolutely nothing he could do now before morning. He might as well nip off home. Busy day tomorrow after all. It was never a breeze pushing back the frontiers of science.

Shrugging idly, he flung a few bits of corn into the peeping quartet of day-old chickens and grinned wryly. 'You'll be cannibals if you do that, soon. Sleep well and hope that this is a success. Otherwise, you're next!'

The bundles of yellow fluff stared up at him with total incomprehension. In minutes, having checked that the PCR was working to expected parameters he skipped through the door of his lab.

In seconds he was on his bicycle and trundling off down Edison Boulevard attempting to get his Sturmey Archer into second gear.

Unbeknownst to him four pairs of eager eyes peered out of the shadow of the bike shed, nodded to each other and, with only the slightest flash of anorak, scurried off towards the tinted security door of Splice of Life Patentable Biosciences Ltd.

Regan snatched a suitable half-brick from the gutter and, before his companions had realised what he was up to, he had fitted it into his ever-trusty sling and was lining up on the opaque expanse of the front door.

'Out of the way. Out of the *way*!' he barked as the two figures of his GAIA mission colleagues scampered across his line of fire.

The one with the artistically correct goatee beard spun on his heel and stared in horror at the rapidly revving half-brick. 'No, no!' cried Elijah Sacramento. 'This isn't the way.'

'It's *my* way,' snarled Regan, feet apart, brandishing. His black leather jacket creaked ominously in the still night air. 'The Way of the Warrior!'

'I'm telling you,' repeated Elijah desperately. 'This is not the way. You won't achieve anything by wanton acts of . . .'

Elijah was flat on the herringbone brickwork, forearms over the back of his head before he finished the sentence.

With a militant grunt of effort Regan launched the half brick dead centre at the tinted rectangle of the sliding door. It whistled through the night air, spinning like a neolithic circular saw, chewing up the distance with deadly ferocity.

Still in the shadow of the bike shed Tara's breath caught in her throat as the half-brick smashed into the door with a resounding report, hovered quivering momentarily and fell impotently to the ground.

'Told you it wasn't the way,' tutted Farson scowling at Regan and swiping his security card down the side of the door. 'It's bulletproof glass,' he added as the panel hissed open and he swept an arm of welcome cheerily inside. He peered into the gloom of the bike sheds and gestured to Tara. 'C'mon. It's alright, believe me.'

Almost reluctantly she scurried through the door, W.H. Smith's jotter in hand, eyes wide.

'Get every detail, okay,' enthused Farson. 'Tonight will be a glorious strike for Genetic Rights. We want the world to know the truth about these barbaric experiments, and with you as our spokeswoman amplifying our words with the power of the press we cannot fail.' He smiled at her encouragingly.

The red-haired technician quivered inside. It was part excitement, part fury, all annoyance. He hated the way genetics was going these days. After struggling through his degree he knew the potential for the study of DNA to open up huge advances in the future. There were cures for deadly illnesses waiting just around the corner, ways of preventing tissue rejection, but what were current scientists doing? Breeding naked mice, manufacturing alcoholic hamsters and, here, under his nose, they were ready to combine genes from two totally different species. And for what? To rival McDonalds for the fast food crown.

If Mendel had foreseen all this interference in the genetic purity of life he would surely have burnt his sweet peas.

Farson knew that it was time for action.

So did Regan. He was stood staring at the door, every fibre of his body seething with disappointment that it wasn't in a million pieces, his mouth working angrily. Something would have to be smashed tonight. He would see to that. It was utterly inhuman to expect him to come on a raid and *not* smash something just a little bit. That was like going to a rave and not jigging about a bit. Definitely not his style.

Besides, nothing else in here was bulletproof.

'Tara. Up here. Come on!' barked Farson urgently as he sprinted up the open wire stairs through the palm-filled atrium towards Crickson's laboratory. Elijah and Regan were hard on their heels, clattering footsteps matching, when suddenly the GAIA Team Leader skittered to a halt and burst into a side room tugging Farson with him by the ponytail.

'These? What are they?' snapped Elijah pointing at the expanse of gleaming equipment arrayed before them, leds flickering, cooling fans whirring. 'What weird science is being concocted here, huh? What are they doing?'

Farson rolled his eyes hurriedly. 'Nothing to do with chickens,' he snapped. 'That's the DN-Aliaser. None of your business, c'mon.' Farson was ten yards down the corridor and staring backwards in gradually lengthening strides when he realised that perhaps a smidgin more explanation was called for.

'Everything here is my business,' growled Sacramento. 'A smidgin more explanation is called for.' Farson ground his teeth and sauntered back down the corridor.

'You know, what I was telling you about at the meeting tonight. Well, that's it. Arrived today. That's the device they, er, we are going to use for the DNA profiling of criminals. And it's got nothing to do with day-old chickens. Happy? Now, come on.'

'Smash it!' snarled Regan, thumping a fist into his palm and wishing he'd retrieved his half-brick.

'No, no,' squeaked Farson. 'Gods, all Hell breaks loose if we mess this stuff about. Camford Constabulary's finest'll be onto us like a shot. Government agents, Riot Police, the lot!'

'What?' coughed Elijah edging away and keeping a very wary eye on Regan's expression.

'Yeah,' continued Farson trying to herd them away. 'It's the Criminal Justice Charter. DNA profiling of all criminals is a real votewinner, you know. Not to mention a moneyspinner.'

Nervously he thought of how precariously his paypacket hung on that humming machine. 'Now, come on, the chicks are this way.'

And somehow he managed to bundle them out of the tiny lab and towards a far larger one across the corridor.

'May I present Professor Crickson's lab,' announced Farson as he slid his security card down the side of the door and pushed it open.

Immediately Regan was past him in a blur of black leather, antennae of outrage searching for signs of genetic interference. 'Chick-Killer Crickson,' he snarled angrily under his breath, his fist pounding rhythmically at his palm.

'We don't know that for certain,' argued Elijah. 'We need evidence.'

Regan made a dismissive noise whilst Sacramento stared at a pair of vast tanks bubbling gently in the far corner. They had about them the exact air of equipment of which the legendary Doctor Frankenstein would have been proud, pipes, rivets, the works. Wild guesses as to future occupants spun through Elijah's mind as he investigated the large amniotic tanks.

Given twenty questions he probably still wouldn't have been close.

There was currently only one person who knew precisely what they were destined to incubate. And he was right then still trying to get the Sturmey Archer of his trusty cycle into second gear.

Across the lab, Regan was kicking cupboards belligerently and gradually working his way towards a particularly smashable looking rack of test-tubes. There was no doubt that, at that particular moment, he had a test-tube rack shaped knot of stress lurking across his shoulders which could be cheerfully cured by a bit of destruction.

His fingers flexed as he nonchalantly advanced on the rack of used test-tubes. And then with a squeal he recoiled in horror, heart pounding, finger pointing. In three bounds he was joined by Elijah, Farson and Tara. 'What? What is it?' they gabbled. 'Evidence?'

Regan pointed accusingly.

There, clinging to the top lip of a blood-stained tube, swung a single tell-tale fluff of yellow feather. Behind it lurked the liquidizer, similarly enfeathered. All the evidence pointed to one conclusion. Chicken pate.

'No!' screamed Regan as he lurched forward and snatched at a power cable. In a flash, the splattered Kenwood looped across the lab, hit the far wall and exploded in a flare of consumer electronics and a shattering of bulbs. The rack of test-tubes followed suit.

'Regan? What the Hell d'you think you're doing?' snapped Elijah grabbing him firmly by the shoulders.

'One of my psychiatrist's better pieces of advice,' he grinned dangerously. 'Destructional therapy. You should try it. Pass me that bottle, will you?'

'Have you forgotten why we're here?' snarled Elijah folding his arms.

'Never did have much truck with that existentialist stuff,' Regan grinned and whirled on his heels, fingers itching for more destruction. Now.

'But, Regan, have you forgotten our mission?'

'Retaliation,' came the chuckled reply as he snatched three conical flasks off a nearby shelf and decided that it was time to find out if he could juggle. Unsurprisingly he failed to keep them airborne for long.

'This is just wanton vandalism . . .'

'And what Crickson's doing isn't?' screamed Regan,

pounding his fists on a nearby table and conjuring up his best impersonation of irony. 'Take one day-old chick, liquidize . . .'

'We don't know for certain that he's . . .'

'I think we do,' announced Farson as he peered inside a small cardboard box.

'You've found them?' gasped Elijah. 'Are they all there?'

'How many victims did Chick-Killer Crickson order?' hissed Regan, a pulse of excitement pounding at his temples.

'Er, five . . .'

'And how many are left?' growled Regan holding up a large conical flask.

'Four,' answered Farson.

'Got 'im!' shrieked Regan tossing away the flask and snatching a large metal retort stand off a shelf. Several catalogues' worth of glassware orders exploded under sudden impact as he whirled the thing around his head.

'Here's the proof!' insisted Farson above the cacophony of shattering silicates. Eagerly he skittered around the end of the table, tugged open the shrilly peeping box and thrust four tiny day-old chicks under Tara's journalistic gaze. 'Four!' he declared unnecessarily and stared dotingly upon the tiny birds, grinning at the octet of his reflections in their tiny eyes. Behind them a cloud of misery passed over Elijah's face. 'For one of these plucky little chicks, we were simply too late.' He stifled back a sniff, melodramatically.

Poignant silence dripped across the lab, congealing in sticky pools of meaningful reflection.

'But we'll make him pay for his crimes against GAIA!' screamed Regan, suddenly reanimating, shattering the mood as abruptly as he despatched a glass reflux jacket, three beakers and a gross of centrifuge tubes.

'We've got what we came for!' shouted Farson thrusting the package of chickens into Tara's hands and dashing across the lab.

Tara dropped her jotter onto the glass splattered worktop and stared bewilderedly at the chickens. Perhaps agreeing to act as reporter for this raid was a little foolhardy, she thought. But Farson had asked her so nicely . . .

Regan was gearing up to dish out several shades of irreparable damage on the centrifuge, when Farson stepped bravely into the one-man fracas and hauled him bodily out of the lab. His shins didn't really thank him much for it.

'Spray cans!' screamed Regan wildly as he struggled against the red-haired technician dragging him off down the stairs. 'Where are they?'

'What spray cans?' spluttered Farson wincing as another of his toes suffered beneath Regan's boot heels.

'The ones we're supposed to be leaving our messages with. You know, all over the walls, "Evolution not Gene Pollution!" or "GAIA says Hiya!" or . . .'

'He'll have got the message. You saw to that,' grunted Farson. 'I've never seen so much destruction. Well, except at Halkidiki's Taverna down Fenland Road on plate smashing night, but . . .'

'But it's not personalised. There's no message.'

'Tara will deal with that, in her magazine.'

'That'll take too long. We need immediate response. Shock tactics. Claim it as a GAIA victory now!' ranted Regan.

'You can't be worried he'll think it's just vandals!'

'Vandals! Exactly! We can't have that!' screamed Regan wrestling his way free and sprinting back up the stairs.

'Phone him up tomorrow! We've got to go!' shouted Farson up the stairwell.

'Phone? Never. That's the coward's way. I never do my dirty work over the phone.'

'It's good enough for the IRA.'

'Exactly!' he yelled and in seconds he was back inside the lab flinging anything smashable in all directions. A three litre beaker tumbled off a shelf, bounced on a gaping drawer and crashed onto the worktop next to Tara's notepad. The beaker shattered into a mess of fragments and one beautifully scything curve of glinting blade. Tara squealed, cradled the box of chicks to her chest and realised she didn't have her jotter. It wouldn't do to leave anything so incriminating lying around. She had to get it back.

At that very instant Regan's berserker gaze focused on the scything blade on the workbench. Instantly he knew it would be only a matter of a few minutes' work to deftly carve a brief but succinct message into the melamine surface of the lab worksurfaces. The mood he was in right now, it was certain that most of the words would consist of four letters.

He leapt across the lab, his hand making eager grabbing movements in the air. At the very instant Tara snatched for her jotter, he reached out a desperate palm towards the glinting scimitar of deadly glass, and was hit in the back by a rugby tackling Farson. The shard spun away, flashing as it chewed at Tara's hand.

'What are you trying to do? Kill me?' shrieked Tara clutching at her hand and cradling it defensively to her chest. 'That could have taken my finger off. It could've left me maimed, scarred for life, destined to wear gloves for eternity!'

'You should've brought the spray cans!' snapped Regan, shrugging petulantly. 'It's bloody stupid to go to all this trouble and risk nobody knowing whodunnit, isn't it!' He stomped out of the lab grumbling things about Picasso always signing all of his paintings. 'We should do the same, see? We are artists in our own way. How can we get the message of Genetic Anti-Interference across if no one knows about us, eh?'

He was ignored. Farson and Elijah were staring at Tara in shock. 'You okay?' asked Farson.

'What about the chickens?' squeaked Elijah grabbing the box and peering inside.

'Thankyou *very* much,' spat Tara. 'Who cares about chickens anyway?' she snapped and, pausing only to grab her jotter, she strode towards the door.

Behind her Farson was staring in wonder. Such devotion to duty, he thought. Even in times of personal suffering she remembered her jotter, her assignment.

'I could get tetanus from this,' observed Tara as she

stomped down the stairs. 'Or worse, rabies, salmonella . . .'
And so her rabbiting continued. A constant barrage of
arguments and counter-claims bombarding Farson's and
Elijah's tender lobes. She had been wounded for the cause,
she was going to get the most out of it.

Only once they had vanished into anonymity down the end
of Edison Boulevard did she halt under a suitable street-light
and risk a peek at her field injury. With a calculating glint in
her eye she assessed the inch-long scratch on her palm and
wondered what the chances of it scarring were.

One thing she did know for certain, though. It was a good
few beers in the bank of martyrdom. Play her cards right and
Farson would be in her debt for . . . oooh, at least the next
three weeks or so.

'Buy me a pint and I'll show you my scars,' she
whispered, practising.

'No, too tarty,' she mused. 'How about, 'Buy a beer for an
old veteran?' Hmmm, with a bit of work it could have
definite shades of Nancy out of *Oliver*, that one. How
about . . .'

'How about you get a shift on or we leave you behind!'
snapped Elijah cradling his take-away chickens and stifling a
guilty hunger pang as he caught a nostril full of Southern
Savoury Wings hurrying past Kenchucky Take-Out.

'Pah! Gratitude!' spat Tara and quickened her pace.

Behind them a glistening drip of blood hanging on a
scimitar of glass turned opaque and quietly clotted.

From Here to Maternity

21st June, Next Year

With a chuckle of mechanical mischief, a blot on an otherwise meteorologically perfect morning, Professor Crickson's Sturmey Archer yet again stubbornly refused to go into second gear. Grumbling, the Professor waggled the lever and powered on down the two hundred yards of Edison Boulevard. One of the things that Crickson had never got the hang of was easing off on the pedals between gear changes.

In a conspiracy of sadistic cycle parts the ratchet of his gear lever slipped, slackened the operating cable and the Sturmey Archer, with definite malice aforethough, rattled into the normally impossible state of neutral. The Professor's legs whirred around three times in quick succession before he slipped out of his toe-clips and bounced painfully on his saddle. The Sturmey Archer braced itself to enjoy a screaming tirade of morning-fresh bawled blasphemies.

Normally it would have got it. A real blistering ear-bender of obscenity.

This morning the Professor merely spat demurely, re-affixed his toes and charged on towards his beloved place of employ. This morning the Professor had better things to think about than the simple gratification of verbal abuse. This morning his mind was firmly focused on the genetic manipulations he would carry out. His brain was buzzing with the myriad delicate steps he would need to take along the rocky road to International Success. They were spread out before him in dizzying complexity, fixed like the sticky coloured footprints of a maniac ballroom tutor. Before his very eyes the Foxtrot of Fame tango'd in and out of the Salsa of Scientific Advancement fluffing its ostentatious sleeves with gay abandon.

But, before the woodwind of his mind could strike up the Nobel Laureate Merenge, a roaring trio of Camford Constabulary's finest Rovers cannoned past his handlebars in a row, barely enough room to swipe a credit card between their massed wing mirrors. In a whirlwind of dust and an explosion of atomised Michelin, the three growling monsters slammed into a host of handbrake turns and slewed to a perfect parallel-parked halt. A triple helix of rubber curves smouldered on the road surface, eerily mirroring the glinting neon of the Splice of Life logo below which they were etched.

A hail of fulminating wrath caught in Crickson's throat as he pushed hard on the pedals and watched impotently as three jumpered police constables sprang from their Rovers and began garlanding the twiggy elders in the pavement as if Christmas had been moved to the middle of next week.

Still out of swearing range Crickson could only push on harder and watch as the festoons of blue and white 'Crime Scene–Do Not Enter' tape swelled around the trees. Beyond them, the security door sloughed open and Striebley appeared.

'At last,' panted Crickson into his handlebars, 'Striebley'll put a halt to this madness.'

He was wrong. His eyebrows clawed their angry way up his forehead as he watched his traitorous lab-coated colleague shake hands with them and, horror of horrors, invite them in. There wasn't a meeting scheduled today. Crickson knew it. He wouldn't have double-booked anything to interfere with today's breakthroughs. Well, this would have to stop. And now.

'I'm sorry sir, you can't come through here,' ordered PC Sim forcefully as Crickson bounced up onto the kerb and careered towards the wild cat's-cradle of blue and white tape stretched between the trees.

'Oh, yes I can,' countered Crickson fuming with remarkable politeness.

'No,' insisted Sim holding up the tape. 'Look, "Crime Scene–Do Not Enter".' He waggled the roll in his hand. The other two were frantically wrapping their tape around everything that was handy.

Crickson made a strange growling noise in his throat, produced a large pair of scissors from his jacket pocket and, with only the slightest of resistance, hacked his way through the screen of blue and white and stomped off towards the entrance to Splice of Life.

In a second he had swiped his security card down by the side of the door and had vanished inside.

At almost the very same instant, the suede headed figure of PC Plain wound the last of his tape off the end of his roll and leapt into the air with a shriek of delight. 'I won!'

Moments later PC Skitting joined him, his eighteen month old elder sapling groaning under the mass of tape.

'That's not fair!' whined PC Sim. 'I had to deal with the public,' he complained looking forlornly at the three inch thickness still left on his roll.

'Luck of the draw,' grinned Plain. 'One of life's little hazards. Face it, you lost. The lagers are on you.'

'Again,' added Skitting with a chuckle.

Sim gnashed his teeth together in frustration. He'd been ahead, he was sure. He would've won, if it hadn't been for that idiot on the bicycle. His eyes fell on that hated steed of Crickson's, hovered on the tape in his hands and a connection was made. A wicked grin slunk across his face as he advanced.

Inside the palm-filled atrium of Splice of Life Patentable Biosciences Ltd things weren't quite as peaceful. Crickson had rediscovered his voice.

'Striebley! Striebley! Where the hell are you, and what in God's name d'you think you're doing inviting guests into my lab, today of all days?' His feet clattered on the open wire stairs as he powered his furious way upwards, hard on the trail of the group he had just witnessed enter his holy ground. 'Answer me or I'll change my security code. I'll be the only one I allow in . . .' He kept up a constant monologue as he reached the top corridor and bowled onward.

'You'd better have a bloody good reason for having them

traipsing all their feet all . . .' He whirled around the corner of his door and was hit in the face by the full destruction of the scene.

'Wh . . . wh . . .' was all he managed for a few seconds as his eyes drifted over the acres of shattered glassware.

'Well, don't just stand there,' he barked as he realised how much time he was wasting. 'Clear it up! I've got work to do! The barriers of scientific knowledge don't push themselves back, you know.'

'And the perpetrators of such heinous deeds don't normally volunteer for arrest,' growled Doctor Boscombe Scenes of Crimes Officer of the Camford Constabulary Forensic Department wheeling on Crickson with a crunching of pipette. 'It is a remarkably little known fact that clues as to the identity of certain criminals do not simply leap from the debris and offer their services in the furtherance of justice. I would have thought that you, being a scientist, would know that.' Boscombe grinned the type of grin that made the young Boris Karloff a screen legend, and set about milking the situation for all it was worth. He hadn't enjoyed the meeting much yesterday. He had portrayed Forensics, the One True Science, in a bad light. Today, he would make amends.

'Do I detect a whiff of sarcasm, my dear Doctor?' bridled Professor Crickson.

'Sarcasm?' sneered Boscombe. 'I haven't a clue what you mean.'

'Gentlemen, please,' interrupted Chief Inspector Ness, stepping between them. 'A crime has been committed here. Let's work together and solve it.'

'That's fine by me,' grinned Crickson with an effort. 'I'm all for solving crimes and apprehending miscreants and suchlike. But, can't you go and do it elsewhere? I've got work to do and, in case you haven't noticed, you're in the way.'

'We were here first,' mumbled Boscombe.

'It's my lab,' snapped back Crickson. 'And I don't want members of the public poking around . . .'

'Members of the public!' shrieked Boscombe his fists

131

beginning to clench. 'I'll have you know I'm a highly qualified member of a very honourable profession ...'

Crickson was staring at the ceiling and fanning his mouth with the flat of his hand.

'And why don't you want us poking around, hmmmm?' attacked Boscombe suddenly. 'What've you got to hide? Perhaps this wasn't a break in after all. Insurance job, was it? Research not going too well?'

'No, no, it's nothing like that,' defended Crickson and winced as his voice came out at least a fifth too high to be convincing. All eyes looked at him with increased suspicion. 'It's not!' he wailed digging deeper.

'I'll be looking for evidence to the contrary,' grinned Boscombe. 'And, what with you being a very clever scientist, and all, I'll expect it to take a very long time indeed before I complete my investigations. You know, fingerprints and fibre analysis and shatter patterns of glass and ...'

'But, my work!'

'Sorry about that,' said Boscombe, who was obviously not.

'Just let me have that piece of equipment,' begged Crickson pointing at the PCR machine. 'It's vital for my research. You can investigate the rest.'

'How vital?' pressed Boscombe, feeling Crickson on his back foot.

'*Vitally* vital,' spluttered the Professor. 'You've got to let me have it.'

'Have it what?' grinned Boscombe.

'Doctor. Have it, Doctor,' squeaked Crickson.

Boscombe folded his arms. 'Have it what?' he repeated.

Crickson shook his head in confusion. 'Have it, sir? No. Have it, Your Worship? ... No, no. Ah! Please?'

And in that instant Boscombe did a little jig. Got him! Victory!

'Take it,' he muttered striking a Noel Coward pose and staring ceilingwards as if the device was utterly unimportant to him. 'But remember, if *I* decide that *I* need it for *my* investigations, I will have it back, clear?'

Crickson was already across the lab, unplugging it feverishly.

Behind him, fidgeting nervously was Dave 'Trigger' Luger from Ballistics. 'Er, excuse me Professor, but I was wondering if you could answer a question for me,' he asked. 'Well, it's not for me. It's for my boss. See I've only been with the Forensics Department a few days and he suggested I ask you . . .'

'What? What? Can't you see I'm busy,' snapped Crickson tugging the PCR machine off the desk and whisking it away across the lab with a crunching of glass.

'It's just a simple question,' pressed Luger. 'I've come all the way out here 'cause I thought you'd know.'

Crickson halted in the door of the lab. 'What is it?'

Trigger brightened visibly suddenly feeling very important.

'What's the question?' groaned Crickson rapidly gaining a vast insight into precisely why there were so many unsolved crimes in Camford.

Trigger straightened himself up. 'Er, what I want to know is. What bore are "Magic Bullets" and can you use them in a standard service revolver?'

Crickson's screams of anguish as he fled down the stairs were almost deafening.

'What?' shouted Trigger plaintively. 'What did I say? Professor . . .?'

Boscombe chuckled evilly to himself. That lad Trigger would go far. Oh yes, indeed. Very soon now he could see him appearing at his office asking for a left-handed test-tube or an inverted conical flask or some such nonsense. He made a mental note to open a book on the very matter with PC Plain immediately his painstaking Forensic Investigation of this trashed lab was over. Flexing his interlocked fingers backwards before him and cracking his knuckles with a hammering report Boscombe whisked an antique brass-ringed magnifying glass out of his inside pocket and began examining the floor before him. In moments he was dictating a running commentary into a tiny tape recorder fixed to his person by way of a natty mock crocodile hip-holster.

'Excessive littering of fragmented silicated laboratoryware consistent with repeated serial percussions of a type normally issued by those of a more vandalistic demeanour,' he began striding through the wreckage like a caribou stork in a china shop the morning after a visit from a particularly rowdy herd of BSE-ridden bulls. 'Random attack patterning indicative of a non-pre-planned schematic. Negative arson indicators.' He crunched on. 'Absence of aerosol graffiti or other forms of non-verbal communicative epigrams . . .'

'Well?' asked Chief Inspector Ness eager for some news to placate Crickson. This timing wasn't at all conducive to fostering solid links between the police and the scientists of Splice of Life, unless he could just show them how marvellously effective Camford's Finest could be when they pulled their fingers out, got their noses to the grindstone and their men to the bilges.

'Well?' he repeated impatiently tapping Boscombe's shoulder. 'Any conclusions?'

The Doctor turned in slow imperiousity, pinned and mounted the Chief Inspector with the arrogance of a butterfly-collector and, covering his microphone for a second, spat the answer, 'Rustlers.' He raised his trusty brass-ringed Victorian magnifying glass again and resumed his investigation.

'Rustlers?' spluttered Ness incredulously. 'What the hell makes you think . . .?'

Boscombe tapped a petulant foot against a large mound of ex-conical flasks and test-tubes and made a noise in his throat. 'If you will observe the fragment of test-tube perched towards the forward half of this mound.'

'The one with that yellow piece of fluff stuck to it?'

'The portion exhibiting adherent biological matter, correct,' he hissed with a worryingly schoolmistressy tone. 'Biological matter of a distinctly avian nature.'

'Eh? You mean from a bird?'

134

'That is the more normal origin of feathers, is it not?' asked Boscombe with weary pedantry.

'Yes, but what's that got to do with rustling?'

'Look around you,' commanded Boscombe sweeping the wreckage of the lab as if it was his very own. 'Can you currently observe any of our avian brethren in the vicinity?'

'Well, er . . . no . . .'

'Exactly!' announced Boscombe placing his hands victoriously in the small of his back and pushing out his chest.

'Eh?'

'My dear Chief Inspector, consider, if you will, the basic contact trace theory of Forensic Science as proposed by Edmond Locard at the University of Lyon in 1910 which underpins the whole of my chosen profession.'

Ness stifled a groan.

'"A criminal will always remove some trace from the scene of his misdemeanour, and leave some trace behind,"' declared Boscombe waggling the shattered test-tube meaningfully before dropping it into a plastic bag and shoving it in his pocket. 'In this case, a chicken, which I estimate to be no more than a day old, left a feather in the laboratory, proving categorically . . .'

'That the chicken did it?' interrupted Ness with obvious delight.

Boscombe scowled a deadly scowl and forged onwards. He was having to get used to levity around him. He blamed the cancerous spread of tv series starring forensic scientists which poured into the nation's homes unchecked. Now everyone thought they knew all there was to know about the noblest of criminal sciences. If the rot continued at this rate then, by Christmas, forensic scientists would be as highly respected as the average wellington booted group of country vets. There'd be 'A Post-Mortem Christmas Special on Ice' or worse.

'Proving categorically that at least one day-old chicken was present here in the laboratory at, or moments prior to, the time of the incident,' rattled on Boscombe. 'A day-old chicken which is now thoroughly absent.'

Despite himself, and seething because of it, Ness found he had to agree. It fitted the facts.

'It is my contention that this crime was committed by a determined band of dedicated rustlers . . .' began Boscombe before tugging his magnifying glass out from behind his back, slamming it in front of his eye and leaping behind a nearby formica topped table. His commentary barely faltered as he surfaced Titanically from behind the table clutching a shard of gleaming glass. '. . . the identity of one of whom is written upon this!'

Ness only just managed to refrain from blurting, 'What? Pyrex?' He didn't think it would have gone down at all well at that particular moment. Boscombe with a sharp implement wasn't something to goad too liberally.

'Progress,' he declared. 'A blood grouping is guaranteed!'

'And what about a DNA profi . . .?'

'What?' snapped Boscombe, cutting Ness off in mid sentence. 'Are you suggesting that I am incapable of identifying the perpetrator without a DNA profile?' he sneered. 'That I hand this vital evidence over to . . . to . . . these people?'

'No, no. It's just that this is a wonderful public relations opportunity for us both to work on the case. The press will love it!'

Boscombe shuddered. 'No. They'll plaster tacky headlines everywhere. I can see it now. "Boffins' New Brainy Test Triumphs in Chicken Rustler's Rapid Arrest!" or worse we might get a visit from the "Home Secretary!"'

'It'll be good publicity for the DNA profiling scheme. It'll put us on the map of crime prevention.'

'No, no, don't say things like that! *Crimewatch UK* will be setting up an outside broadcast before you could . . . No, no.'

'I could be on telly,' mused Ness. 'You wouldn't stand in the way of that, would you?'

Boscombe snarled and glared at the clot of dried blood. All this fuss over a little scab. 'I can't.'

'You must. I insist.'

'Can't,' insisted Boscombe. 'There's not enough of it,' he

lied and, dropping the shard into a hastily produced bag, he stamped out of the lab and off down the open wire stairs.

Ness's pursuit was only stopped by the untimely interruption of the mobile phone in his top pocket. Snarling, the Chief Inspector stiffened. It had been warbling irritatingly all morning. As soon as Simeon Yeats, the grey suited civil servant, had handed it to him in the interest of presenting a 'more accessible face of the police force to the public at large' he knew it would be real trouble. Especially when he'd cheerily trotted out the phrase, 'With this new service it'll be less Big Brother watching you and more Big Cuddly Uncle Copper watching over you.'

Ness took a deep breath, shuddered again and tried to conjure up a smile as he flicked the 'Call Receive' button and answered, 'Hi there, you're through to the Big Friendly Uncle Copper Crime Hotline. Nobody's keener to solve that misdemean . . .' His chirpy friendliness didn't last much longer as the caller cheerfully chatted away about seeing this morning's edition of the *Camford Chronicle* and definitely recalling lights in the sky above the Regal Greens Golf Course in the early hours of yesterday morning. 'Not another one!' cursed Ness to himself.

'Look, I know all about the bloody lights in the sky and the engine noises, yes, yes, thank . . . What? . . . Do about it? Nothing. They're miles away by now! Did Reg Treadly put you up to this?

'Hello? . . . Hello? . . .' He stabbed an irritated thumb on the 'End Call' button and jammed the phone back into his pocket.

Several feet below, Boscombe was being grilled by a pack of feral reporters spitting questions as he ran the gauntlet across the herringbone pattern pavement.

'Can you tell us what happened?'

'Is it true that Splice of Life Patentable Biosciences Ltd are currently experimenting on live captives from the Roswell UFO Incident?'

'Are the rumours of rivalry between you and Professor Crickson true? Did you trash the place?'

'What is the motive for the break-in?'

Boscombe stopped suddenly in his tracks and three reporters ran into his back, one badly bruising his nose with an unfortunately positioned microphone.

'That I will answer,' he declared. 'The motive is rustling!'

In the stunned silence that followed he wheeled on his feet, sprinted past a strangely mummified bicycle wrapped in several thousand feet of blue and white 'Crime Scene–Do Not Enter' tape and leapt into the nearest Rover.

In seconds Plain had autographed the surface of Edison Boulevard in his own inimitable manner.

Two thousand miles' worth of Michelin.

'Are we there yet?' complained Lupin in the traditional way of the whiner.

'What d'you think?' growled Calabrese as he kept out of sight in the shadow of the suburban fences and privet hedges of Camford.

'Let me guess. Just a bit further? Just around the next bend? Another three on the left?' panted the thin grey form of Lupin.

'Something like that,' came the grumbled reply as Calabrese dived into a squirrel's backside made from privet and scrambled up through it. In moments he was squinting out through the nose of the mad topiarist's creation, attempting to get his bearings. It had been a long time since he'd been thereabouts. This had been a hare the last time he'd been by this way, he was sure. Or was that on the parkland over by . . .

'You're lost, aren't you?' sniped Lupin, still blinking far too frequently as his almond-shaped eyes attempted to adjust to the brightness of a June day. A lifetime spent underground made it a bit blinding up here.

'Not lost exactly,' he hedged from the privet squirrel.

'Well, where are we? And *don't* say "on the brink of a revival", again!' Over the last few hours Lupin had begun to feel far less confident that Calabrese even had a clue what he was up to. He had been regaled with grand tales of the past as they had sprinted down dead-end passages, turned around and headed off up another long unused track fifty feet under the Regal Greens Golf Course. At first Lupin had been really fired up at the thought of wreaking some evil in the name of feyriedom. But now . . .

'Don't rush me,' snarled Calabrese. 'It's not my fault they keep changing things around. I'm sure there weren't this many buildings around . . .'

'I don't want excuses . . .'

'Aha. C'mon, this way,' announced Calabrese suddenly. In a flash of grey forearm he had pointed vaguely, sprang out of the privet squirrel's nose and was tightroping his way along a handy clothes line.

Lupin took an executive decision that he hadn't meant it absolutely literally and sprinted across the lawn vanishing through the dense privet hedge directly beneath the spot Calabrese had leapt it.

For minutes they ran on, dodging this way and that, swerving right, dashing left, working their way uneventfully through the outskirts of the Ancient City. Well, *mostly* uneventfully. There was only the once when they slapped their way around a corner, screamed and vanished back the way they had come pursued by a crimson something the size of a hill. Fortunately for them the driver of the number 63a had his eye on the schoolgirl in his mirror.

Their progress had been a little more on the cautious of sides from then on until, upon rounding a corner, Calabrese spun a full one hundred and eighty and stopped in his tracks facing the oncoming Lupin. He pulled a mocking bow and announced, 'Here we are!'

Lupin clutched at his lute excitedly, quivering as he thrilled at the thought of being one of the first feyries in centuries to do what feyries do. Calabrese had painted perfect pictures in his imagination of them stealing a naked cavorting virgin. And they were going to do it here.

He rubbed at his eyes and stared at the scene revealed across Calabrese's back. A small privately shaded nook of ancient forestry? A smoke screen of the palest bluebells? The heady scents of seduction filling the air and scantily clad maidens dancing playfully between the fronds of hanging ivy?

Not a hope.

The nearest Camford District General got was the distorted pictures of the Seven Dwarves plastered on the Children's Ward walls.

'You've got to be kidding,' gagged Lupin a moment later from the relative cover of a clump of overlong grass by the perimeter fence. 'You telling me I'm going to kidnap the woman of my dreams from there?'

Calabrese nodded.

'It wasn't quite what I had in mind.'

'Well, if you want to go back and live out your days with only the company of a few bawdy ballads to help you through the long dark nights ...'

'No, no! Er, appearances can be deceptive, I suppose.' Lupin squinted at the monstrosity of neo-Concretian functionalism and hoped that deception was indeed in the ascendant.

'C'mon then,' whispered Calabrese and in a flash of grey he was off across the lawn, keeping low and using the tubs of randomly strewn geraniums as cover. The pair swept around to the left, knees almost colliding with their chins.

Suddenly, Calabrese ducked behind a large black and white painted barrel and stopped dead. He peered nervously out past a vast expanse of heavily smoked cigarette butts and fixed his attention on a tall and prematurely balding man pacing up and down a tiny tarmac path. Plumes of smoke fidgeted around his head as he feverishly dragged on the last millimetres of tobacco in his Embassy.

Abruptly he spat a plethora of choice invectives as his already smarting index finger received yet another burn from the dying embers. Flicking the beige stub across the Camford General Maternity Garden and scoring a bull's-eye on a sadly scorched geranium he whirled on his heel and dashed across to the raincoat flung across the little-used parkbench.

'Fags, fags, quick boy, fags!' he cursed at himself and

with an ecstasy of fumbling he managed to fire his Zippo up. Three desperate drags and he was back on the march again, plumes of nicotine drenched breaths mirroring the deep lungfuls of his secretary panting in the delivery suite.

Calabrese, thrilling with the recollection of past endeavours, clicked his fingers under Lupin's stub nose and brandished a series of carefully mimed gestures at him.

'What's that all about?' he tutted beginning to realise why the race of feyrie was in such a mess if this was what you had to go through to get a date.

Calabrese snarled derisively, pointed at the baseball cap sitting on the bench and made grabbing gestures. In the next second he was off, loping across the cigarette field, keeping the bench between him and the desperately expectant father. Not that he was in much of a state to notice anything.

In seconds his hat and coat were hightailing it off towards the geraniums, its right sleeve pointing skywards as it wrapped itself around the arm of the fleeing feyrie.

'You, stand up and turn around!' barked Calabrese as he looped around the geranium barrel, wrestling with the left sleeve.

Bewildered, Lupin obeyed. With one spring Calabrese was on his shoulders, wobbling precariously. The next second he was picking himself out of a suitable bush.

'Could've warned me,' grumbled Lupin defensively as Calabrese lined up for another go. This time it was far more successful.

With a satisfied flick of his wrist Calabrese donned the Chicago Bears baseball cap and attempted to roll up his sleeves whilst his 'legs' carried him towards the door.

'The top o'th'morning, t'you,' he called cheerfully to the expectant father. 'And may all your troubles be little ones!'

The stream of invective which was hurled over his shoulder could've curdled yoghurt.

Lupin powered them on towards the door, cursing Calabrese volubly. They pushed through the sprung door and slapped along the grey lino'd corridor, Calabrese steering with his knees in Lupin's ears, Lupin peering through the gap between the raincoat buttons. And so it came to pass that it was through this exclamation mark of a field of view that the hormonally fizzing Lupin caught his first sight of real womanhood.

She appeared like a vision from the linen cupboard – a miracle in sensible shoes, a dozen plumped white towels nuzzling as affectionately against her bosom as Lupin would have given his eye teeth to be. Suddenly the mass of Calabrese pressing on his bony shoulders meant nothing to him as he slapped enthusiastically down the corridor, inches behind the pertly bobbing, uniformed backside of Student Nurse Eleanore Jonsson. His eyes twitched up and down in time with the hypnotically entrancing gluteal motion.

'Her! Her! I want her!' panted Lupin in between whimpers of undying infatuation.

Suddenly the vision in Camford Area Health Authority turquoise turned and a dulcet inquiry floated through the raincoat.

'May I help you?' coo-ed Student Nurse Jonsson and Lupin was treated to a horizon spanning eyeful of freshly starched apron hovering above a pair of perfectly formed knees. The two globes of her patellas smiled through a wisp of grey ten denier tights.

'Oh yes, yes, yes!' begged Lupin and had his left ear knee'd for his troubles.

'Yes,' picked up Calabrese. 'We're . . . er, ahem, I'm looking for ward, er . . . ward, er . . . Tom Cruise Ward,' he finished having spotted a suitable signboard above Student Nurse Jonsson's perfectly attached cardboard cap.

'First time?' she asked.

'Eh?' spluttered Calabrese.

'Here? First time? I saw you pacing about in the Maternity Garden before and I thought, "it's his first time". I can always tell,' she wittered away. 'You've got the classic symptoms. Can't get your words out, you're looking pale, flustered . . .'

'Er, yes, I'm fine. Now, Tom Cruise?'

'Second left and follow the little aeroplanes. You can't miss it.'

'Aeroplanes?' spluttered Calabrese.

'Yeah, you know. *Top Gun*.' And there and then Student Nurse Jonsson helpfully mimed a dog-battle in the corridor. 'You can't miss it,' she repeated finally and, retrieving her towels from a convenient trolley she spun on her toes and was away about her business.

'No, no!' barked Calabrese in the tone of desperate frustration heard daily on numerous riding schools throughout the civilised world. He squeezed Lupin's head between his knees by way of command and somehow managed to overpower the feyrie's more basal instincts. 'Second left! Move!'

Muttering a constant stream of obscenities he reluctantly obeyed, slapping his bare feet away down the seemingly endless corridor under a fuming cloud.

Suddenly ahead there was a squeaking of under-oiled bearings and a wheelchair cannoned out of a side corridor, spun and was wheeled towards them by a very determined ancient looking woman in a blue rinse.

Lupin ranted on unstoppably, turning the air inside the raincoat bluer by the minute. Desperately Calabrese attempted to hiss for silence. He was totally ignored.

And so the three beings closed – squeaking, shushing and swearing profusely.

'I *beg* your pardon?' gagged the woman, shocked as she passed into earshot. Her eyebrows made a sudden and ineffectual bid for freedom up her forehead.

Calabrese shrugged, looked woefully apologetic and pointed to his midriff, the apparent origin of the offending monologue. 'Grumbling appendix.'

Behind him there was the sound of a crashing wheelchair, accelerating down a deep stairwell.

Ignoring the cries for help with a wicked sense of satisfaction Calabrese grinned as the string of tiny pink aeroplanes veered off abruptly to the left. Expertly he knee'd Lupin in the side of the head and herded him beneath a large sign which declared that they were 'Now Entering Tom Cruise Ward'.

Lupin was dealt a sharp bruising barrage of blows to his right ear and, on the verge of concussion, he was bundled into a tiny room just inside the environs of the ward. Much to the relief of his shoulders Calabrese unbuttoned the raincoat and leapt off into a convenient pile of strangely holey blankets.

'Help me on with this. Come on!' he snapped waggling a large white cotton object from the third shelf up.

'What's that for?' grumbled Lupin rubbing his ear and beginning to wonder if Calabrese's recollections of the 'Good Old Days' weren't as tall as some of his favourite ballads.

'You'll see. Quick, quick!'

Just under a minute later a tall, thin and worryingly gaunt looking man in a white coat lurched out of the linen cupboard, rings clattering beneath his darkened eyes. He was the vision of any House Officer after a ninety-eight hour stretch on call.

His appearance was greeted with a sprinkle of feminine giggling.

'Nice nap?' asked the Charge Nurse on the desk and the bevy of pale blue uniformed maidens chuckled with unignorable coquettishness.

'A little too much of Doc Deadly's Home Brew at the House Officer's Bash last night, eh?' smiled the Charge Nurse.

Calabrese, understanding perhaps one word in two, shrugged. 'Can't remember?' interpreted the Charge Nurse. 'Ooooh, must have been at least three bottles, then. Short-term memory always goes half way down the third. What d'you reckon, girls?'

'Looks about the right colour,' confirmed a brunette holding a stack of towellelling nappies and sporting a very unflattering blue plastic apron. 'Although I've seen worse.'

'I had three bottles, once,' chuckled a blonde idly chewing a pen as if in distant contemplation.

'You had three?' gasped the Charge Nurse in amazement. 'What happened?'

'Can't remember,' chortled the blonde, slapping the desk with the flat of her hand. The others erupted in a geyser of giggles. It was obvious that the contents of the bottle of Bollinger perched on the desk (courtesy of Her-In-The-Private-Room) had found their way down their throats in the very recent past. Its effects, at just before ten in the morning, were proving quite deadly.

As the giggling became shriller, Lupin and Calabrese edged into the ward, hurried on their way by a dismissive wave from the Charge Nurse naturally assuming it was Her-In-The-Private-Room's time for something-or-other to be checked upon, or something. So many strange folks had popped in and out of there in the last few days she was convinced they'd been making a documentary about it for Channel Four.

Unusually, they had.

His heart pounding faster than a virginal rabbit's with first night nerves, Calabrese reached out a quivering hand and twisted open the door handle. They slapped their way inside, and, pushed the door shut with a satisfying click.

'Ahhhh, at last!' bellowed the perfectly cosmeticised woman in the bed, tugging her mobile phone from her ear and replacing her ear-ring. 'Do you people not keep timetables? I should have had it changed at *least* twenty minutes ago. Now see to it!' She pointed an imperious finger over the top of her laptop and waggled it in the vague direction of the mewling child at the foot of her bed.

Approximately three feet below Calabrese's eyeline, Lupin was rubbing his hands in growing anticipation. Okay, he'd had his doubts, sure, but hey, maybe Calabrese did know what he was on about after all. He had guided him successfully to a place where the women were already in bed. Now, *that* was a definite plus. Now, if he could just get an eyeful of what delights he had lined up . . . Nonchalantly, Lupin shuffled his grey tootsies sideways across the lino.

'Honestly, Fabian,' barked the woman back into the

mobile, 'You said this National Health Birthing Experience would benefit me as much as that month in Tibet. I know . . . I know, you said it would be rustic . . . but this! Why these people put up with such standards I don't know. Precisely . . . that is *precisely* what I think, darling. Sue the buggers! Sue them until they haven't a leg to depilate!'

At a point where any normal human's navel would be sighted, there was a sharp intake of breath. Lupin blinked and instantly questioned Calabrese's taste in the female form. What had possessed him to drag him away from the deliciously aerobatic Student Nurse Eleanore Jonsson in favour of this?

He watched in bewildered confusion as she jabbed angry fingers at her laptop and pulled up the latest Hang Seng figures.

'Okay, grab it!' snarled Calabrese out of the corner of his mouth.

'You must be joking,' snapped back Lupin and shuffled a pace backwards.

'Twenty-two minutes late. And counting! Get a move on!' barked the woman, glaring at them across her Motorola mouthpiece. She wrinkled her eyebrows, mouthed an obscenity and then added in a more conciliatory tone, 'No, not you, darling. You're always right there, when I need you. Now, sell AT&T and buy Mothercare, thirteen thousand shares.'

'Grab it!' snapped Calabrese again. 'Shove it under the coat and we can get out of here. Come on!'

'*Under* the coat?' gagged Lupin trembling at the thought and wondering just how he'd extract her from beneath all the paperwork and humming electronics. 'You mad? She'll never fit . . .'

'Are you going to change that child of mine?' snapped the woman.

'Certainly ma'am,' oozed Calabrese in a way he'd seen a waiter fawn on the CablePix tv. 'I'll bring you another immediately. Grab it,' he added under his breath through what he hoped was a smiling face.

'Grab that? Are you mad? I don't want a squealing . . .' flapped Lupin.

The woman stared at the screaming child thrashing all four limbs in opposite directions. 'No, no. I'll keep that one. It's tolerable enough, I suppose. Apart from the noise. Can't you shut it up? These are important phone meetings.'

'I shall remove it from your earshot immediately, ma'am.' Calabrese reached out and Lupin stepped three paces backwards.

'I think there's some need for explanation,' snarled the lower half of the white-coated figure.

'What is it with this squealing and smelly child? It is smelly, you know?'

'It's traditional,' hissed Calabrese attempting to learn the arts of ventriloquism instantly. He gave up and muttered into his neck. 'Steal a foundling child and bring it up until the appointed time of deflowering when . . .'

'*Hold* on a minute,' interrupted Lupin beginning to smell something of a distinctly rodentish nature. 'Did I hear you just say something about "bringing it up"?'

'Yes, course I did,' snapped back Calabrese his grip tightening on Lupin's shoulders. 'After eighteen years together you can . . .'

'What? Eighteen years! Are you mad? I can't wait that long.'

'It's the way it's done,' hissed Calabrese and attempted to flash a reassuring smile at the mother. She ignored him, busying herself with a complicated breakdown of the last years' trading in base metals on the Nikkei Dow.

'Used to be done,' snarled Lupin. 'I don't want this . . . this thing. I want the goddess that carries the name of Student Nurse Eleanore Jonsson! I will make her mine . . .' He turned and headed for the door, his hormones fizzing wildly through his loins.

'Ahhh, finished at last?' piped up the squealing child's mother. 'There, it wasn't that bad, was it. I'll expect you want a tip now? Pass my wallet and . . . hang on. Why's it still making that awful noise? You haven't changed it, have you? How dare you skimp on essential consumables. We had a contract. Explain yourself!' The aerial of her mobile phone whipped out across the room and ended inches from Calabrese's nose, waggling like the deadliest of fencing foils. 'Explain!'

'Er, well, I . . . that is we . . .' struggled Calabrese.

The woman's eyes narrowed and the tip of her aerial crept towards the peak of the Chicago Bears baseball cap itching to uncover the face of the intruder in a classically flamboyant flick of a swashbuckling wrist.

'You're no doctor,' she snarled prodding Calabrese's chest accusingly with the aerial. 'I knew it all along. No wonder the National Health is in such a state if they have to employ casual labour off the streets. I bet you don't even have any interest in children.'

'Well . . . as a matter of fact . . .' Calabrese held out his hands and leaned forward.

And suddenly, and most unexpectedly for the mobile phone-toting woman, a nerve of maternal instinct was fired. In a millisecond she had assessed the situation, calculated the likelihood that this leering intruder attempting to pass himself off as a doctor was genuinely here for the benefit of her child, decided against it and, with the lightning reactions of a Wall Street Trader, she stabbed the 'Alarm Call' button.

Lupin froze as Tom Cruise Ward was scrambled to immediate action.

'Move!' cried Calabrese desperately looking at his feet. 'Let's get out of here!'

Lupin shuffled nervously, completely unsure which way to go as the claxons echoed outside and a dozen newborn babies joined in. Feet pounded up and down the corridor outside.

'There's no escape,' snarled the woman, already pounding '999' into her mobile. 'You really shouldn't have chosen to mess with me . . . Hello Police . . .'

Calabrese screamed and made a dash for the window. Before her very eyes the impostor doctor split at the midriff and turned into two tiny creatures. She screamed as Lupin

148

blinked and dashed off after Calabrese as he sprang up the radiator and onto the window sill.

The phone was chattering away ignored by the wailing woman. '... no good you just phoning us up and screaming at us,' babbled the receptionist. 'We need a little more to go on than that. Now, name ...?'

Calabrese, like an epileptic escapologist, was thrashing his way out of the white coat and dancing around on the window sill. He peered down the three floors and cringed. They were trapped. Any moment now the Hospital Security team would burst through that door grab them and drag them off to who knows what punishment and embarrassment. ...

Suddenly he had an idea.

'Grab this!' he barked at Lupin and thrust the white coat into his arms. Bewildered and panicking he had no choice but to accept it. Calabrese was swarming up the venetian blinds on the window setting them clattering noisily. Then suddenly he leapt, grabbed at a spring catch and swung on it.

For a sickening moment nothing happened then, jiggling up and down in a far from dignified manner, it unhooked. The entire bottom half of the window swung out into the open air, leaving Calabrese dangling over a deadly drop.

'Throw me the coat,' he cried, barely audibly above the alarms and the screaming of mother and child.

In seconds Calabrese had it in his hands and had somehow hooked it over a thin wire cable attached to the wall above his head.

'Come on!' he urged and mimed Lupin to jump and grab the tail of their erstwhile disguise.

And so, in the very instant that the door of the Private Room was kicked open and Stan Moss, fifty-nine year old Hospital Security man and part-time porter, burst in, two grey-skinned figures slid away down the telephone cabling, one dangling each side of a recently stolen white coat.

'Two of them I tell you, jumped out that window!' insisted the woman minutes later. 'Three feet tall, grey skin, almond-shaped eyes. They tried to steal my baby. Tried to pull her out from under my very nose. But *I* won't let them get her, oh no!' She clutched firmly at her screaming offspring and struggled to fit herself further into the corner.

'I knew childbirth could be a bit of a trauma,' whispered Stan the Security Man to the Charge Nurse. 'But do they always complain about little grey men trying to abduct their babies?'

'Think we might cut down the painkillers,' tutted the Charge Nurse and walked away shaking her head.

A small cardboard box squatted on a table in the back room of *The Monocle and Asparagus* and chirped in the way normally associated with two-day-old hatchlings of the common leghorn.

'I told you, didn't I?' hissed the surly Regan leaning back in his chair and shaking his head dismissively. 'We should've claimed it as our own when we had the chance.'

'That wasn't the plan,' insisted Elijah Sacramento stroking his artistically correct goatee beard.

'Are you certain that's what they said?' asked Farson.

'Absolutely,' hissed Regan tugging one of Tandy's finest radio cassette players out of a capacious pocket and placing it on the table. Triumphantly he flicked the 'play' switch and reached for his Fosters. 'Seven o'clock news on Radio Camford,' he growled. Instantly the artificially enhanced tones of a newsreader rattled forth.

'*. . . break-in at the Splice of Life Patentable Biosciences Ltd Head Offices last night causing several hundred pounds worth of damage and stealing nothing but four insignificant chickens . . .*'

Regan stroked a self-congratulatory finger nail across the stubble of his chin.

'*. . . Whilst the Chief Scientist Professor Crickson was unavailable for comment, Doctor Boscombe of the Camford Constabulary Forensic Department is of the firm belief that the incident was carried out by rustlers. This from our reporter at the scene . . .*'

'*What is the motive for the break-in?*' asked a voice on the tape recorder against a dense confusion of background noise.

'*That I will answer,*' replied the now familiar tones of Doc Boscombe. '*The motive is rustling!*'

There was sudden vacuum of shocked silence from the babbling reporters. It was broken only by the sound of a single pair of hastily retreating footsteps as Boscombe dashed towards a waiting car.

Regan jabbed the 'Stop' button and took another swig of Fosters. 'Rustlers! Told you, didn't I,' he frowned at both of them. 'I said last night this would happen, but oh no, you wouldn't listen. If we'd had the spray cans they'd've known who did it. And all this wouldn't have been in vain.' As if in agreement the four chickens in the box began peeping enthusiastically.

'It's alright,' said Farson. 'It doesn't matter. When Tara writes her article . . .'

'Ahhh, yes. The good Miss Ness,' mused Regan over-theatrically. 'Just how certain are you that she's who she says she is?'

'Well, I . . .' began Farson.

'Are you absolutely sure she's a journalist?'

'Is this leading somewhere?' asked Elijah with a quiver of nervousness.

Regan leant back and stared idly at the ceiling in the manner beloved by screen criminals about to make some stuning observation. 'Didn't any of you get the strange feeling that you'd seen Miss Ness's face before somewhere?'

Farson and Elijah shrugged.

'Or perhaps had it crossed your mind that her surname is a bit familiar? Ness. Goes with monster infested Scottish lochs and . . .?' He let the sentence linger in the air, urging a response from his GAIA colleagues.

It didn't come.

He scowled. 'Doesn't the name Chief Inspector Everett Ness sound familiar?'

'Oh, come on,' choked Farson. 'This is another one of your ridiculous conspiracy theories, isn't it? There's plenty of people with the surname Ness . . .'

'True, true,' agreed Regan. 'But there aren't that many

whose father is the Chief Inspector of Camford Constabulary.' Before Farson could leap to Tara's defence Regan rummaged in his inside pocket and tugged an old cutting from the Camford Chronicle into view. 'Anybody look familiar now, eh?' he grinned idly flicking the picture across the table.

'This could be anyone,' insisted Farson squinting at the aging photograph of a group of dignitaries in front of the police station.

'Look at the caption,' prodded Regan.

'"The new Chief Inspector poses with Camford's Finest Force, his wife Rosemary and daughter Tara,"' read Elijah.

'I don't believe it,' spluttered Farson. 'Where did you get this?'

'I keep good records,' grinned Regan. 'You never know when information just might come in handy.'

'So what conclusions can you draw from this?' asked Elijah.

'Obvious isn't it?' hissed Regan leaning forward enthusiatically. 'She's trying to infiltrate GAIA!'

'Never. I invited her . . .' began Farson.

'*After* you'd invited her to the launch of *Adversity*,' announced Regan cheerfully. '*After* she'd just happened to show up in my shop moments before you popped in with some wild story about being a journalist . . .'

'For a magazine you said you'd heard of!' interrupted Farson.

'Yeah . . . er, well, I *had* to say that didn't I, otherwise . . . er, well, we can keep an eye on her now can't we?' hedged Regan.

'No, this can't be true,' defended Farson. 'She wouldn't . . .'

'We can soon find out what she would and wouldn't,' grinned Regan as a brunette head bobbed by the window.

'How?' gasped Farson.

'We can ask her,' chuckled Regan victoriously. 'Ten seconds and she'll be in that door.'

'How can you be so certain?' asked Farson, his head spinning.

'Phoned her up this afternoon.'

'You've got her number?' Farson bridled with jealousy. 'How?'

Irritatingly Regan tapped the side of his nose, snatched back the newspaper clipping and the object of their discussion strolled into sight. 'Hi, guys,' she waved and crossed over to them. Nonchalantly Regan pulled a Bloody Helga out from under the table and set it down in front of her. Farson scowled suspiciously at the black clad GAIA militant. Something was going on here he didn't understand and he didn't like it.

'Good day at the office, dear?' asked Regan with just a hint of sarcasm.

'Not bad,' offered Tara non-committally and took a swig of her lager and tomato juice.

'Article going fine, is it?' pressed Regan.

'Which one? I mean there's the review and the launch and last night's ...'

'Last night's,' grinned Regan wolfishly. Farson shifted uncomfortably in his chair.

'Well, I haven't done very much on it yet. Er ... I'm trying to find the right angle. As a matter of fact I need a bit more background about ...'

Regan hurled back his head and laughed. 'Background? I bet you do. That's good, very good. A bit more background for daddy?'

Tara looked bewildered and began to feel very uncomfortable.

'I expect you'd like names and addresses of all GAIA members, details of forthcoming raids, that sort of thing?'

'Well as a matter of fact ...'

'There you go, chaps. Just like I said,' declared Regan triumphantly. 'Miss Ness is a mole for her father. She had you all fooled.'

'No, no. It's nothing like that,' gasped Tara.

153

'Oh no? So how come you showed up at exactly the same time the police sign a contract with Splice of Life, eh?' accused Regan.

Tara shook her head. 'What contract?' she mouthed.

'I put it to you that it was your intent to furnish certain local constabularies with vital information in order to prevent GAIA interference with Professor Crickson's Project CFC.'

'What's he on about?' squeaked Tara.

Regan ranted on judiciously. 'In fact it would come as no surprise at all to learn that Chief Inspector Everett Ness owns shares in Project CFC and is therefore using this, his daughter, to ensure its success. What have you to say for yourself?'

'Is this some kind of joke? Like positive vetting?'

'Do you deny that your father is Chief Inspector Everett Ness?'

'Wish I could,' tutted Tara with all the respect teenagers normally hold for their parents.

'There. See? Guilty!' declared Regan and leant back in his chair.

The silence around the table was broken by a bewildered Tara asking, 'Guilty of what? Being my father's daughter?'

Regan nodded in a manner befitting any High Court judge.

'Oh, marvellous,' she spat. 'You might as well hang me for being a girl. Bloody sexist.' Across the table Farson grinned.

Regan sat up suddenly. 'No, no, that's not what I meant. You're the daughter of a Chief Inspector . . .' he flapped.

She shrugged dismissively. 'You called me here to tell me that? I had noticed, you know? The uniform's a bit of a giveaway.'

Regan made a strange snarling noise and took a swig of lager.

'Oh, I get it. You think that because we live under the same roof he knows what I'm up to? You obviously haven't met him and you *obviously* haven't got teenage daughters. Don't worry, he hasn't a clue where I am.' She looked at her watch. 'In fact he probably hasn't a clue where he is right now. He'll be on his fifth gin and tonic already. Dinner with the Mayor, you know?'

'Bloody bourgeois capitalist . . .' grumbled Regan, scowling into his lager.

Tara ignored him and turned to Elijah. 'So, if it wasn't to talk family trees, why am I here?'

'It seems that our motives have been somewhat misinterpreted,' answered Elijah stroking his goatee thoughtfully.

'Just like I said, but you wouldn't listen . . . oh no,' grumbled Regan.

'Listen to this,' said Farson rewinding the tape recorder.

'Spare me,' growled Regan. 'They think rustlers did it.'

'Chicken rustlers?' chuckled Tara. 'You're kidding.'

'I say we get right back in there armed with spray cans and finish the job,' snarled Regan. 'Show 'em who's boss.'

'The place is swarming with police,' coughed Farson. 'I had terrible trouble getting out after work. Seems they don't want to risk any disruption to the DNA Profiling Programme. First county to get all their known criminals typed gets a big bonus, or an MBE, or something. And Chief Inspector Ness doesn't want to miss out.'

'Typical,' groaned Regan. 'We've totally blown it. And all for the want of a can of spray paint. I bet Greenpeace don't have these problems. They're organised.'

'It's not that bad,' suggested Elijah squinting through his rose-coloured spectacles. 'We've already caused a massive disruption to Crickson's latest project.' He tapped the chicken filled cardboard box proudly. 'Without these little chaps he can't progress . . .'

'Until he orders some more,' grumbled Farson glumly. 'Which he can now he's got regular money coming in from Camford Constabulary.'

'I bet they're already on their way,' moaned Regan.

'Along with a whole new set of glassware. Gods, there'll be no stopping him. Nothing'll ever be safe again,' added Farson despondently. 'No creature's genome sacred or

155

unexploitable. And it's all the fault of Camford Constabulary. Damn them!' he grumbled. 'Bloody cash injection, if only we could stop it!' Miserably Farson drained his Fosters and started ripping the beermat apart systematically.

Suddenly Tara sat bolt upright, grabbed her glass and poured a good quarter pint of Bloody Helga down her throat. Wiping her gauze bandage across her mouth and slapping the glass onto the table in the very way she was sure she'd seen John Wayne do, she fixed her GAIA associates with a firm gaze and somehow managed not to go cross-eyed.

'What if we *could* stop it?' she grinned, the whites of her eyes shining with the excitement of inspiration.

'But we can't . . .' began Farson the pilot light of his enthusiasm remaining stubbornly dead.

'What if we could?' repeated Tara thumping the table and setting the baffled foursome of chicks off again. She stared piercingly at Farson.

'Well, Splice of Life wouldn't be able to afford any more genetic research and . . .'

'They vanish as a threat to genetic integrity . . .' interrupted Regan.

'. . . I lose my job and go off to work on that organic kibbutz I've always dreamed about. You know the one just twentyfive miles from the Dead Sea. I showed you the brochure . . .' finished Farson with a wistful gaze and a ripping of beermat. 'Ahhhh, heaven!'

'That's all very well,' mused Elijah Sacramento tugging pensively at his goatee.

'I hear a "but",' interjected Tara.

'But,' frowned Elijah. 'How?'

She took an enigmatic slurp of lager and tomato juice and, with enforced nonchalance asked, 'Name a few traditional methods of stopping folks doing something you don't want them to do.'

'Ask them nicely?' suggested Farson his mind hovering somewhere sunny and communal in the depths of the middle east.

'Semtex,' growled Regan.

156

'Demonstrate!' declared Elijah his eyes beginning to sparkle at the heady thought of endless afternoons placard painting and fly-posting.

'Take too long,' Tara shook her head dismissively.

'Defeatist,' moaned Elijah.

'Semtex is quick,' complained Regan and was ignored.

'Think more *NYPD Blue*,' suggested Tara. 'More personal and attention grabbing.'

Instantly Regan was back with them. 'Murder!' he declared a little too loud. A clot of sales reps at a nearby table scowled at him over their third pint each.

'Er, not quite that attention grabbing and a bit less permanent,' said Tara willing them to get the answer. To her it was so blindingly obvious. In fact she was amazed it had never crossed her mind before. For the first time in her adult life she was beginning to realise that having parents could actually be useful.

'Blackmail?' thought Elijah out loud.

'No, no, no!' erupted Tara. 'The perfect scheme to get exactly what we want is . . .'

'Letter bomb stuffed with Semtex,' enthused Regan.

'No, no, no,' snapped Tara. 'Kidnapping!'

The baffled response from the other three was utterly underwhelming.

'Don't you see it?' she enthused. 'Ransom note drops on the Chief Inspector's desk, you know, made out of cut out bits of magazines and newspapers and stuff. I could do that. I've always been good at collages. And it says, "Cancel the Splice of Life contract or the girl gets it!" He can't refuse. Never could.'

Farson looked at Elijah with the glazed expression of an undergraduate in an organic chemistry lecture. Slowly he shook his head attempting to rid it of utter incomprehension. 'Kidnapping?' he mouthed and a host of attention grabbing headlines on national press began to germinate in his mind.

'Yes,' mused Elijah with similar thoughts blossoming. 'It might just work.'

Two grey-skinned creatures cannoned down a narrow alley-way, ducked behind a suitable row of wheelie bins and hid in the shadows, almond shaped eyes peering out for signs of pursuit.

'Well *that* was a rip-roaring success,' panted Lupin dripping sweat and sarcasm in almost equal proportions. 'The stuff of heroic ballads I really don't think.'

'Alright, alright, so I'm out of practice,' whined Calabrese. 'Let's just wait for all the fuss to die down and we'll try again.'

'What? Not me, no way!' snapped Lupin backing further into the shadow of the wheelie bins.

'Scared, eh?'

'N . . . not in the slightest,' lied Lupin.

'You were rooted to the spot. Admit it.'

'I will admit to a certain raising of the old heart rate . . .'

'Pah! See, there you go, you lily-livered son of a . . .'

'. . . But!' Lupin continued silencing Calabrese with a single raised index finger. 'I put that down to the exertion of the last ten minutes. It's quite some time since I had that much exercise, after all. Jogging's not much fun under-ground, those roots can be a real pain.'

Calabrese made a grumbling noise and folded his arms. 'Terrified,' he muttered under his breath.

'Was not!'

'Then let's get back in there. Best thing you can do after a scare is get straight back in. Just like when you've been tossed off a badger, get straight back on, slap it about the ears a bit and show it who's boss.'

'No way,' tutted Lupin. 'I'm not spending eighteen of the best years of my life bringing up a kid!'

'It'll be worth it, believe me. That first smile, her first words, teething . . .'

'Mucking it out! Teenage problems! Oh, no. No chance. I've seen the hassles on "Rootside". Count me out!'

'Am I detecting a significant change of heart here?' prodded Calabrese. 'And after such enthusiasm last night.

Shame. Eighteen years is such a small price to pay for the privilege of creating one's perfect partner.'

'Perfect partner?' chortled Lupin. 'If they're that perfect how come I don't see one on your arm at this very moment, eh?' Calabrese looked at his toes. It was the one question he had hoped Lupin wouldn't ask. 'It wasn't my fault. I did everything by the book. Gave them all they wanted, whenever they wanted it. New clothes. The latest portraits. The lot. And on their eighteenth birthday, without fail they upped and left.'

'Ungrateful hussies,' tutted Lupin with far less concern than he should have felt. 'What they want to go and do a mean and cruel thing like that for, eh?'

'Could have been that "w" word,' suggested Calabrese. 'Seems that eighteen year olds just don't like the prospect of being a "wife". "Lover", "concubine", "other woman" no problem. Even "bit on the side" suited some of them. That was kind of romantic, you know, sneaking about covertly and arranging sly little meeting places, filling each moment together with the maximum lust, but "wife" – to them, that was sock washing with a kid on the hip. In days they were holed up with some "handsome" young buck with gap teeth, acne and a cupboard full of Puck's Purple Passion weed.'

'All pain, no gain,' chuckled Lupin making lewd gyrating motions with his hips. Calabrese nodded. 'And you wanted to try again?' chuckled Lupin. 'Do you never learn?'

'I thought things would be different this time, okay?' snapped Calabrese, feeling suddenly angry that he'd confessed his failures to Lupin.

'What? How come? You're no different.'

'If you really want to know,' growled Calabrese his eyes smouldering with the shame. 'There just isn't the competition these days.'

'And what does that mean?' barked Lupin, knowing exactly what it meant. Being of an artistic temperament one thing he was good at was spotting an insult when it was hurled his way.

'Well, just look at you. Handsome doesn't really fit, now

159

be honest.' Calabrese stared disparagingly at Lupin's non-muscular i-shaped torso and sneered.

'I'll have you know that in some quarters I am considered to be rugged,' spluttered Lupin defensively and struck what he hoped was a macho pose.

'That the same quarter that are terrified of week-old rabbits and go totally catatonic if anyone so much as comes within ten yards of them with a loaded pussy willow?'

'That's beside the point. I can still pull any girl I wanted,' he bragged. 'In fact that's just what I was going to suggest we do tonight. Someone not unlike Student Nurse ...'

Calabrese was clutching his ribs. 'You can't be serious?'

'Deadly,' snapped back Lupin pulling a face which he hoped portrayed deadly seriousness from every muscle.

'It won't work,' tutted Calabrese.

'Course it will. I'm irresistible.' Lupin admired his features in a wrinkled up scrap of silver foil and tried to perfect the perfect pout.

'I'm telling you, you don't stand a chance. Have you ever stopped to consider why we grab them so young, eh?'

'Er ... 'cause they're easily transportable?' hazarded Lupin.

'No! It's 'cause of size. They've got no idea what's normal when they're two weeks old. If you show up with a chirpy "Hello darlin' Fancy a good time," and draw yourself up to your full two and a half foot ...'

'Two foot eleven and a half.'

'She'll wet herself laughing,' finished Calabrese with a victorious chuckle.

'Size isn't everything,' began Lupin.

''Tis with the type of girl that would be interested in you, believe me.'

'I don't,' frowned Lupin. 'And if that *is* the case, well ...' he fished about desperately for a solution. 'Well ... I can stand on your shoulders. Yeah, you owe me that much at least.'

'Owe you?'

'I carried you around all afternoon on your mad scheme. Now it's my turn.'

'Alright, you're on,' grinned Calabrese. 'I could do with a real laugh. From now on, you're in charge.' And he sat back against the wheelie bin, arms folded, his ribs vibrating with mirth.

'Right ... right ... you asked for it,' spluttered Lupin wagging his finger with far less confidence than he needed. 'You'll see just how it should be done ... you'll see.'

He backed away into a narrow corner and suddenly had the horrible feeling that he had just opened his mouth and planted both feet firmly in it. But now there was no going back. Calabrese would never let him live it down. There was no retreat. The best he could hope for was heroic failure. At least that way he'd be able to hold his head up in public after a few decades or so. Maybe he could hide the actual identities of the folks involved and turn it into a comedy ballad. Maybe Princess Hellebore would like that?

Nothing ventured, nothing sprained, and all that.

The grim cold silence of Camford's Morgue was shattered by the eager clattering of feet and the kicking open of the door. In seconds a figure, bearing a striking resemblance to a very young Boris Karloff, was hurling his lambswool jacket with fifties lapels across the office and, as per usual, scoring a perfect bull's-eye onto the peg.

Chuckling enthusiastically to himself he ran into his forensic den with three plastic bags clutched in his fists. Placing them carefully on the marble workbench he leapt into his white lab-coat and flushed the taps on with a swipe of his wrists. Steaming water cascaded over his hands as he scrubbed up at double speed.

This, more than any other case, was a matter of professional pride. He'd show those genetic meccano-mongers just what a *real* scientist could do. Oh yes, he'd run a blood grouping classification up on that sample on the glass, reference it to his vast database of known criminal groups and have the perpetrator's name, address and inside leg measurement by the end of the week. All the stops would be pulled out on this one. Not just the common ABO and Rhesus systems. No this little spot of rust would have M and N . . . ah, God bless Landsteiner. Then he'd run up a few haptoglobins and followed it with a side salad of G6PD, Tf, GLO I, CA II. Already he was starting to salivate with anticipation as he snapped a pair of surgical gloves on his quivering hands and pounced on the shard of stained glass in the bag.

But just as he sliced a glinting scalpel through the neck and snaked his hand inside, there came an imperious yell of command from the door.

'What is it?' barked Boscombe grating his teeth and spinning around.

'Paperwork?' asked Chief Inspector Ness in the way mothers always ask nine year olds if they've washed their hands.

'Yes, yes, yes,' hissed Boscombe unsheathing the sabre of glassware just a little too hastily.

Ness was instantly suspicious. 'Where is it? I want to see it, now?'

'I'm busy,' fumed Boscombe.

'Not until I see the paperwork, you're not,' snapped Ness. 'Protocol. Remember my memo of last week? Don't you know that fifteen and a half per cent of certain convictions are thrown out of court on simple clerical errors by people filling in the paperwork after the essential tests? It was all in that memo, black and white, clear as day.'

'Really,' tutted Boscombe. Damn this Criminal Justice Charter. It was more trouble than it was worth, getting in the way of his work like this. Paperwork! He wasn't a bloody secretary! He should be uncovering facts not writing the damned things down on endless sheets of ridiculously pedantic forms designed by idiots who hadn't the faintest idea about the fundamental principles of forensic science.

'So where is it?'

'Threw it away, I expect,' muttered Boscombe and edged closer to the arrays of test-tubes and pipettes spread across the worktop. 'Never keep memos after I've read 'em. Clutters the place up terribly, you know. Really impedes efficiency.'

'So does missing paperwork,' growled Ness suspiciously staring intently at Boscombe. He hadn't reached the position of Chief Inspector without not knowing when someone could be lying. All he had to do was stare at the suspect and in a few minutes they'd crack and admit it all.

His gaze burrowed hard into Boscombe's receding hairline. 'I do hope you *have* filled it in. I spent a long time thinking up all the questions for it, you know?'

Boscombe groaned.

'Aha! Just as I suspected!' cried Ness. 'Now what are we supposed to do before we begin any testing, hmmm?'

'Fill in the paperwork,' groaned Boscombe incredibly surprised Ness hadn't grabbed him by the earlobe like some errant schoolbrat and led him into his office.

'I didn't hear that,' complained Ness folding his arms and tapping his toe.

'Fill in the paperwork,' enunciated Boscombe with weary disdain.

'Yes! Fill in the paperwork. And did you?'

Placing the shard of blood-stained glass reluctantly on the worktop and cursing numerous obscenities under his breath Boscombe wrenched off his gloves, hurled them into a waiting bin and stamped into his office. He knew damned well that Ness was in one of his 'just-so' moods. Hell would have to be populated by polar bears, and holding skating competitions, before he could begin grouping that blood without all the necessary paperwork filled out in advance.

The shriek of alarm from the throat of the Chief Inspector told him it was going to be a little longer before he got his pinkies on that particular chunk of forensic evidence.

'Just look at this desk!' shrieked Ness his eyes on stalks as he took in the two foot heap of Boscombe's in-tray. 'This isn't good, you know, not good at all. I want to see at least half of that dealt with before you get to work on those latest samples.'

163

'But, I'm . . .'

'No excuses. Half.'

'It'll take weeks!' cried Boscombe in despair.

Ness smiled smugly and fixed the Forensic Scientist with a self-righteous stare. It was the exact answer he wanted. 'Well, then, the quicker you begin, the quicker you'll be finished, eh!' And he whirled on his heels and stamped out.

Fortunately for Boscombe's promotional prospects Ness never found out just how close he came at that moment to discovering first hand just what it was like to be strangled viciously. Somehow, the fuming Forensic Scientist just managed to control his rising tide of wild fulmination.

Ness was barely out of the door when the mobile phone in his top pocket warbled into life.

'Hello?' he snarled through clenched molars. 'This is the Big Cuddly Uncle Copper Crime Hotline. Nobody's keener to . . . What? Lights in the sky? Yes I've heard about them bloody lights in the sky!' The 'End Call' button was stabbed angrily.

Despite the fact that he was facing a veritable Mount Rushmore of paperwork Boscombe grinned.

Alone and untouched, the sabre of glass with the incriminating blood stain sat quietly and awaited its turn under the microscopic gaze of modern investigatorial science.

Framed in the rear-view mirror of the 1983 VW Golf a pair of pale eyes stared intently backwards down the narrow alley. The eyebrows furrowed irritably as a cat squealed and clattered out of a tumbling dustbin, startled. Elijah Sacramento's knuckles tightened about the rim of his steering wheel and he squinted around desperately, nerves rubbing rosinned bowstrings of fear up his spine. It was two minutes to ten and already he felt certain he had been there far too long. He must have been, Radio Camford had already played the same single off the new Michael Jackson album three times since he'd been parked and waiting.

But suddenly his rear-view vigilance was rewarded.

Exuding an air of calm casualness which he both admired and jealously detested, a tall, slim brunette strolled around the corner. Whistling the theme from *The X Files* in an oddly off key manner, she tripped down the alley, drew level with the Golf and, without the merest hesitation climbed in.

'Well?' barked Elijah, failing totally to hide his state of nervous agitation.

'All set,' coo-ed Tara, feeling as if she had stepped into one of the sixties shows beloved by her mother. 'He couldn't resist, poor dear. We're meeting in *The Monocle* in about five minutes for a swift half then he thinks he's taking me off to a late night showing of *Independence Day* at the local scout group.'

'And you're sure he doesn't suspect a thing?'

'Sure, I'm sure. He almost wet himself when I leant over the Sainway's mint counter and invited him out. Quite touching really. He's fancied me ever since I started buying *New Spaceman*. Can't you kidnap him as well? I've, er . . . borrowed a couple of handcuffs from dad's pocket if you need . . .'

Sacramento shook his head and tried desperately not to think of Tara in handcuffs. 'No it is not a good idea. If we nab him as well then there'll be no witness to go to the police and alert . . .'

Suddenly the rear passenger door was wrenched open and a white coated figure sporting a red pony tail dived in. 'The news! Have you heard it?' he panted pointing at the radio. 'Turn it up!' he insisted as they shook their heads.

Baffled, Sacramento obeyed.

There was a fanfare of orchestral keyboard stabs across a staccato typewritery sound and a female newsreader's voice boomed out of the door speakers.

'This is the Ten o'clock News at Twenty-Two Hundred Hours. You're tuned to Radio Camford 1034 FM. I'm Titian McBride. Hello.'

There was a brief rustling of paper and, sporting a professional air of concerned drama, she launched into the News.

'Later in the programme a growing number of people claiming to have seen lights in the sky. Truth or hoax? We investigate. But first, the latest in the Splice of Life break-in. Police have taken a big step towards revealing the identity of those involved.'

The two in the front seats gasped.

'A spokesman has revealed exclusively to Radio Camford Newshounds that a sample of the criminal's blood has been recovered from the scene and is even now currently in the Forensic Department undergoing tests.'

Tara squeaked and clutched at her bandaged hand.

'Chief Inspector Ness is certain that, once a match is found amongst the extensive criminal records, arrests will follow in days. Hospital staff were congratulated today on their handling of an attempted snatching of a local business-woman's newborn ...'

Elijah reached out a trembling hand and switched the radio off.

'Arrests! Days!' he spluttered. 'Blood samples!' His face was rapidly losing its colour, even his goatee seemed to be limper than usual.

'It's a total disaster!' wailed Farson. 'They'll be onto us, rounding us up and ... what are you giggling at?'

Tara was rocking backwards and forwards, her bandaged palm flat across her mouth. 'Just listen to yourselves,' she spluttered almost incomprehensibly. 'You panic so easily.'

'They're onto us!' repeated Farson. 'Panicking is fine!'

'They haven't a clue,' soothed Tara.

'Course they have. That blood stain, remember?' growled Farson.

'Oh, that doesn't count,' trilled Tara cheerily.

'But ... but what about the Forensic Stuff they can do with it?' spluttered Elijah. 'They can find out your blood group. Then they'll know it's you!'

'How? Look, knowing a blood group doesn't mean you can find a match. For one thing you've got to have a blood group in the records to compare it to. Now, since I'm not a criminal they don't have my group in the records therefore they can't blame me! Easy!'

'How come you know all that?' asked Farson, amazed. 'You're never in when *NYPD Blue* is on and *The Bill* isn't that detailed.'

'Dear old Dad,' she confessed. 'When he got promoted to Chief Inspector he took us all in to Forensics for a look around. Showed us how to do blood groups and stuff. Really dull actually, but he said it was vital. Can't remember why now, though.'

'So, everything's still on for tonight?' said Farson looking through the gap between the seats like an eager three year old.

'Of course,' insisted Tara. 'Ready and raring.'

'Er, well, shouldn't you have already rared?' asked Elijah tapping his watch.

She gasped, snatched at the door handle and jammed her shoulder against the glass.

'Wait, you don't know where it's going to happen,' shouted Farson leaping out of the back seat after her.

'Surprise me. It'll be more effective,' she called over her shoulder in a flurry of brunette hair. 'And wear a good disguise. Don't want to be fingered in the identity parade.' With a final glimpse of Farson in his white coat she vanished around the corner on a beeline for *The Monocle and Asparagus* leaving a cheery wave hovering in the evening air.

'Identity parade?' gagged Farson. 'Arrests?' For the first time he was beginning to wonder if all this was worth it. I mean, so what if Crickson did produce a maize plant that tasted like chicken. It wouldn't hurt Nature too much would it?

Nervously he jumped back into Sacramento's Golf and barked, 'Take me to Proscenium Arthur's Fancy Dress Shop, I need a disguise quick!'

Watched only by a couple of sewer rats out on their normal nightly perambulations, Sacramento's Golf lurched forward down the alley and headed off in search of a new identity for Farson.

In one of the tinier back ginnels which criss-crossed Ancient Camford's compact centre on some medieval architect's whim, two small grey forms squatted in a dense shadow. The taller one continued to hurl abuse and stones in the direction of the mange-ridden cat he had taken an instant dislike to. 'And get a fur-cut, you scruffy bloody . . .'

'Keep your voice down,' hissed Lupin angrily. 'And gimme that baseball cap.' He snatched the Chicago Bears cap off Calabrese's head and swung it onto his own, adjusting its angle to cover his eyes and add to the impending mystery.

'Gods, you're jumpy,' taunted Calabrese. 'What's the matter? Scared?'

'No,' lied Lupin. 'I just don't need you disturbing the local wildlife and kicking up a racket, announcing we're here. If the authorities find us . . .'

He didn't need to finish the threat. Calabrese swallowed nervously and carefully put down the stone he was holding. He knew what would happen. He'd seen it all on the tiny CablePix monitor. At best they'd be kept locked away in tiny cages whilst they were prodded and poked by faceless men in dark glasses and white coats. At worst, it was certain dissection. In that instant he almost wished he hadn't seen that programme on the Roswell Incident. Images of a semi-dissected grey alien swam nauseatingly before his mind's eye.

'Now, bend over and give me a leg up,' snapped Lupin.

'You still think you can pull this off?'

'Of course. And just think of all the advantages. Instant intelligent conversation; a lifetime's experience to draw upon and utilise for ballads and epic poems; no hanging about for eighteen years to find out what they'll end up looking like. I tell you this could be the way of the future. Choice by appearance, not ease of stealing; quality, not availability.' Lupin struggled his way into the white coat from the hospital. 'I'll be hailed as a hero!'

Secretly Calabrese swelled with pride. It was really heartening to hear Lupin fired up so keenly, primed and ready with such enthusiasm to re-establish the name of feyrie where it belonged – the top of the supernatural charts. True, Lupin would almost certainly be hailed as a hero, but it was he that would take all the major credit for starting this New Golden Age.

Now, just one last pre-flight check to make sure Lupin's loyalties were well and truly in the right place.

'It'll never succeed. We'll be caught and dissected, I tell you,' insisted Calabrese with thoughts of his portrait on every wall.

'Where's that sense of adventure you were telling me about?'

'Ahh, times were different then,' shrugged Calabrese in feigned nervousness. 'Things weren't as dangerous. People were scared of us, then. I mean, if I was caught stealing a bawling kid from a woodcutter's cottage I could just pull a face and, whilst the wife was recovering from a dead faint, I'd be off, scot-free. But nowadays . . .' He let the sentence drift away into the evening air.

'Yeah, I know, I know, I saw the programme about the bad press we got from the Brothers Grimm, that Hans Christian Andersen guy and all those blinking Victorian photographs showing us with wings, gah! Well, it's been going on too long,' hissed Lupin fizzing with the desire to rekindle the good old days, his mind filled with a highly romanticised vision of the past. A time when real men were real men and they all knew how to be scared of feyries. 'Look around.' He peered disparagingly around the moss-and-grafitti-covered walls of the ginnel. An eighteen inch rat hauled itself out of a nearby grid, leered at them and relieved itself noisily against the wall. With a surly squeak it shuffled off into the gloom. 'Look at what we're reduced to. Not even the rats take us seriously anymore. Well this is where it stops. It's about time we put ourselves back on the supernatural map. Time we made our presence known. Time we redressed the balance of power!'

Calabrese's eyes lit up in the dark ginnel as he peered at his first recruit to the cause spouting his own words back at him. He squinted into a new and exciting future, his enthusiasm sparking off a cascade of visions of a feyrie domination. Back where they should be. On top.

'I couldn't agree more. No more skulking about in the dark snatching what dregs of femininity we can get our hands on. Oh no, if they were scared of us we could just line 'em up and take our pick. Like the good old days.'

'Of course,' joined in Lupin. 'They'd save the prettiest girls for us. It would be an honour for them to come and service our greatest needs.' A lewd leer leapt across his face as he was utterly captivated with the idea of glorious bikini'd extras from *Warrior Women* waiting upon his every whim in an over-indulgence of decadence. 'We could have a harem. Two. Ten! Give me a leg up,' grinned Lupin.

Rubbing his palms together excitedly Calabrese knelt and, with a deft flick of his cupped hands, hurled Lupin onto his shoulders. In seconds the white coat was buttoned up and, sporting the Chicago Bears baseball cap, Calabrese was knee'd about the head in the general direction of the end of the ginnel and civilisation.

Already in the back of Calabrese's mind, like a spore of cheese mould on a mature cheddar, the fevered visions of his future grew legs and began to run towards the realms of possibility. Ahhh, if only he had an army of such devoted followers . . .

'I must admit to being thoroughly delighted that you are accompanying me on this fine night,' wittered Douglas from the Sainway's magazine section fingering the edge of a David Duchovny poster he was about to present Tara with as a token of his affection. She was bound to like it, he was sure. She was always whistling *The X Files* theme tune, after all.

Nervously he led her out of *The Monocle and Asparagus*. The swift half of Pedigree he'd downed in minutes in the company of Tara had done little to calm his excitement. 'Er, Tara . . . you don't mind if I call you Tara do you?'

'You have been for the last half hour,' she grinned.

'Oh . . . good. Er . . . Tara, I've got you a little present which I'd like to give you before we get to tonight's screening of *Independence Day* at the local scout group hut. I hope you like it. It's . . .'

'Step away from the girl,' growled a voice in the shadows in a tone which clearly showed it was rather unused to growling. Somehow its unexpectedness made Douglas jump with fright. His hand shot skywards involuntarily and dropped his gift of glossy paper. With a squeak he bent to retrieve Fox Mulder from the pavement.

'Leave it!' growled the voice and a thin figure in a white coat made a threatening move forward, collar pulled up high.

Tara stood warily beneath the street light trying to recognise the voice. In the instant she saw the white coat she knew it was Farson. She caught a glimpse of grey skin and stifled a smile of admiration.

'Good disguise' she thought and wondered what he'd done with his hair. Surely he couldn't have fit it all in the top of that Chicago Bears baseball cap, could he?

'Wh . . . what d'you want?' spluttered Tara in her best scared voice.

'You,' growled back the man in the white coat. 'I want you!' A slight tremble of desire quivered as an undertone.

'You can't have her,' piped up Douglas, the half of Pedigree obviously having more effect than first imagined. 'She's . . . she's with me . . . er . . . if that's alright.'

'We're taking her now,' growled Lupin, kneeing Calabrese about the head and making him struggle forward.

'We?' asked Douglas confused. 'There's more than one of you?'

Lupin bit his bottom lip. 'Er . . . er, yes. My partner's closer than you think. And he's watching you.' He allowed himself a brief grin of self-congratulation at wriggling out of that.

'And he's got a gun!' growled Calabrese from beneath the

coat. It was clear that CablePix had affected him quite a bit. He made a noise in his throat which bore an uncanny resemblance to the sound of a Walther PPK having the safety catch unhitched. Lupin squeezed his head between his knees.

'Now look here, darlin'. You're comin' with us, y'hear?' drawled Lupin in a way he hoped was coming across with somewhat more machismo than his normal tone. It wasn't helped by the fact that he suddenly realised that this was the first time he'd actually had a conversation with a real woman. His desperate vocalisations at the sight of Student Nurse Eleanora Jonsson didn't really count.

'I . . . I hear?' pleaded Tara theatrically. 'D . . . don't shoot me.'

'Okay, come over here, closer. Away from the light,' drawled Lupin and beckoned an oddly grey-looking finger.

Acting reluctance, Tara obeyed. A gust of wind rattled down the street and caught the poster. Douglas squeaked as it was shoved twenty feet away from him landing precariously close to the edge of the road.

Tara shuffled into position next to her kidnapper and began covertly rummaging inside her handbag. In moments there was a rattling of metal links and a weight dropped into Lupin and Calabrese's white coat pocket. 'Handcuffs,' whispered Tara out of the side of her mouth. 'I forgot to give them to you earlier. Use them, it'll look more convincing. Oh, by the way, great disguise.'

'Oooh, you think so?' thrilled Lupin intoxicated by the mixed aromas of Tara's perfume and the heady scent of warm anorak.

'J . . . just a little something we picked up earlier.'

'Proscenium Arthur's Costume Hire Shop?' she whispered and then backed away half a step and raised her voice. 'No, no, not the handcuffs!'

Douglas wrestled with his conscience and kept a wary weather eye on his poster. Surely he should be doing something to help her? But what could he hope to achieve against two men one of which he couldn't see and who had a gun on him and the other of which was now shaking as he clipped handcuffs around her wrists. These were professionals, no doubt. What could he do?

'Phone the police,' called Tara and acted as if she was being tugged about violently by the handcuffs. 'Owww. Quick! Before it's too late! Owww, owww you fiendish brute!'

'I can't leave you . . .' began Douglas until another gust of wind picked up the poster and hurled it unceremoniously into the middle of the road. 'Er . . . er . . . I'll call the police!' he announced and sprinted off down the road towards the nearest phone box after bravely saving David Duchovny from a fate worse than death.

But as he turned to snatch one last glimpse of Tara's abductors it was too late. They had vanished down a nearby ginnel Lupin fizzing with barely controllable hormones. Calabrese reeling in amazement.

Half a mile away at the far of an underpass a bored clown with a long red pony-tail sat twiddling his motley gloved thumbs and wished he'd chosen a better costume. A passing student chuckled at him and threw him a coin.

What was taking Tara so long? She did say a quick drink, didn't she? What was that? Two pints? Four?

Miserably Farson settled himself down for a long wait.

A Footprint in the Dust

Feeling like a recent captive in a white slave trading franchise, Tara was tugged by the handcuffs and led off towards a heavily overgrown back alley around the edge of night darkened parkland.

'This way. C'mon,' barked Lupin in as macho a manner as he could muster under the heady effects of his captive's perfume and the animal smell of warm anorak.

'Er, are you sure?' asked Tara looking doubtfully at the growth of privet hedging. 'Isn't it better to go down Vestry Row and . . .'

'This way,' insisted Lupin giving another tug on Tara's handcuffs and wincing. Those wrists, so perfect, so tender.

'But, there's nobody following us. We don't need all this secrecy and besides if we're going to get to Fenland Road aren't we better to cut across . . .'

'That's not where we're going, I'm sorry, but . . .'

And slowly the clear light of understanding dawned in Tara's mind. 'Oh, I see. Change of venue, eh? Good plan. Stops me giving anyone any subconcious clues beforehand. We don't want them finding us *too* soon now do we? Well, not before we get an agreement from Splice of Life.'

Lupin shook his head in confusion.

'Make 'em sweat, that's what I say,' continued Tara enthusiastically, overjoyed that the staged kidnapping had gone so well. Douglas had been totally convinced by it. His phone call to the police would be the perfect confirmation that they needed to make it all work. 'Don't give 'em a clue where I am. Take 'em right to the brink when they're begging to have me back. It's the only way to get what we want. Another victory for GAIA and . . . Hey! Where are you going?'

'Over here,' growled Lupin tugging her behind a large

rhodendron and over a rickety stile. Ahead lay the rapidly darkening expanse of the fens.

"Gods, Farson. Not so fast. It's dark,' complained Tara realising for the first time that the familiar yellow glow of the Camford street lights had disappeared behind them. 'I can't see properly. Do you want me to twist my ankle?'

'No, no, no,' gasped Lupin staring at the shapely nature of her denim-hugged legs. He quickly knee'd Calabrese to a halt. Admiring his choice of companion he caught two almond-shaped eyefuls of moonlit Levi-ed thigh as Tara straddled the stile and descended towards him. It was all he could do to stop himself falling off Calabrese's narrow shoulders. He still couldn't believe that he'd actually managed to pull it off. It had been so easy, so straightforward. It was almost as if she'd wanted to come with him. Almost as if his magnetic personality had totally captivated her in seconds, as if he was irresistible. Yeah, that was it. She'd seen through his disguise and had quite simply been utterly captivated by his devastating good looks. It was bound to be that. He knew some folks just couldn't resist big almond-shaped brown eyes. He'd find out soon enough when he got her exactly where he wanted her. Just him and her alone in a cosy hollow, on a crispy bed of freshly tossed ferns . . .

Snatching another glimpse of her muscular thigh, Lupin caught himself dribbling as she scrambled awkwardly over the crumbling wooden structure and stood in the edge of a fenside field. Already a slight mist was beginning to rise. In the distance ahead the silhouettes of dozing ducks could just be made out standing on one leg, their heads tucked under one wing, looking like some odd type of mushroom.

'Now look here, Farson. Where the Hell are we?' she asked in the tone of voice which normally required the firm placement of fists on hips. Sadly the handcuffs prevented this. 'Is it much further?'

'Not too far,' answered Lupin leading off across the seemingly trackless fens. 'Then you can lie down and I can . . .'

175

'Glad to hear it. I'm knackered. I mean, I've hardly stopped all day. Up to Sainway's to get the newspaper and a pot of Pritt for the ransom note. Back home and start cutting out the letters. Back up to Sainway's to chat up Douglas. Oh, wasn't he a sweetie. "She's with me!" I'll give him a treat when all this is over. Yeah, I'll let him take me out for a Chinese, or something. He'd like that.' The mist rose from the fens and licked affectionately at her ankles. Lupin did his best to stifle a pang of jealousy.

'Anyway,' continued Tara chattering away as if she was on some Sunday afternoon picnic, 'what with all that running about, I'm worn out. Tell you, I really hope all those hundreds of creatures that aren't going to be cloned now, appreciate how much work we've put in. I didn't think arranging your own kidnapping was so time consuming.'

'What?' chorused the feyries simultaneously.

'Arranged your own?' spluttered Lupin. 'H . . . how can you say that?' Underneath the coat Calabrese barely stifled a giggle.

'Well, okay, you helped a bit. I mean, that disguise is pretty good. Nobody would recognise you in that get-up, that's for sure. It's great the way you've hidden that pony-tail of yours. But I did all the hard work. And, don't forget, Farson, it *was* my idea in the first place.'

'Your idea?' gagged Lupin shaking his head. Calabrese grinned inside the safety of the white coat.

'Yes, *my* idea. You were all for giving up and letting Crickson populate the world with God knows how many identical copies of whatever new hybrid he was working on until I came along. Or had you conveniently forgotten that, hmmm?'

Calabrese's curiosity pricked insistently. 'Populate the world' . . . 'identical copies.' What was she on about?

Lupin was struggling with comprehension. Answers weren't very forthcoming. 'Forgotten? I . . . I . . . er . . .'

'Oh c'mon, stop being dense. I even supplied these!' she waggled the handcuffs meaningfully.

'Yes. I meant to ask you about those,' began Lupin. 'Is

176

that a traditional sort of greeting hereabouts, signifying the submission of will towards that of another . . .?'

'Greeting? Submission? What are you on about?' bridled Tara stopping suddenly. 'You know damned well what they're for . . .' And her voice trailed away into the Camford night air, as the word 'submission' jangled in her mind. Her eyes narrowed in irritation, the bridge of her nose wrinkled in disbelief and the muscles at the sides of her jaw clenched in extreme irritation. 'You pervert!'

Lupin stared into her transformed features and felt stirrings in his hormone levels. There was no doubting it, she looked so amazing when she was annoyed. Fiery, spiky, utterly delicious!

'I've seen the way you've been looking at me. Is this the way you always try to get girls. Hmmm? What's wrong with a night at the pictures, or a nice meal for two? You're sick you are . . .' And suddenly Tara thumped what she thought was Farson hard in the face.

Lupin's arms waved desperately for balance, swirling madly as he attempted to stay on Calabrese's shoulders. He failed.

She stood in total catalepsy in the middle of the fens, clutching her cheeks in horror as she watched the figure before her wobble uncontrollably. It flexed in grossly unnatural ways at the midriff, staggering forwards and backwards, until, suddenly centres of gravity got far too much for it. Before her very eyes, like some grotesque circus trick, the figure she was convinced was Farson split across the belt line, his torso somersaulting into the mist complete with white coat and Chicago Bears baseball cap. All that remained was three foot six of grey-skinned creature, staring up at her apologetically through vast almond-shaped eyes, its overlarge head tilted to one side as it pointed its toes together. It was wearing nothing but the carefully positioned green asterisk of an ivy-leaf of modesty.

'Surprise,' offered Calabrese, limply waving an elongated hand in what he hoped was a friendly sort of way.

Tara stood rooted to the spot, unable to believe her eyes,

finding it impossible to close her mouth. The fens spun around her, suddenly unreal, suddenly alien. What had happened to Farson? Had they taken him over?

Miserably rubbing his backside and nose Lupin shuffled out of the mist, the white coat swamping him like a three year old in his father's favourite raincoat.

'What d'you want to go and do that for?' complained Lupin to Calabrese. 'You've blown it now, dropping me like that when we were getting on *so* well.'

Tara just stood staring, her gaze transferring from one of the feyries to the other and then back, looking like a traumatised spectator from the centre court at Wimbledon.

Calabrese prodded Lupin in the chest and crowed, 'I told you it wouldn't work. You've totally screwed it up now! Completely . . .'

'If you hadn't dropped me I'd still be . . .'

Tara made a choking noise. 'Who . . . who are you? What have you done with Farson?' she gagged finally.

Lupin's head spun around and he plastered a hasty smile across his face. 'It's alright. We're your friends. We've come to take you away to a better place.'

'Take me away?' she whispered and stared at the two grey figures. Mentally she ticked off everything she had heard about such encounters. Skin colour, long fingers, almond-shaped eyes, height. 'Why me?' Her mind whirled with a thousand images of first contact scenarios, they leapt from tv screen and glossy magazine with wild enthusiasm.

'Well, I'd, er . . . like to get to know you better. You're a nice looking girl and I'd, er, well fancy spending time with you to, you know, find out what makes you tick and stuff and, er . . . Hope you don't mind,' added Lupin almost apologetically.

Tara trembled as the message was translated in her fizzing mind. It was obvious to her that he was having trouble with language, all those 'er's . . . but, reading between the lines . . . 'nice looking girl' . . . 'spending time with you' . . . her heart skipped as she knew instantly that this creature was in the process of abducting her. And he was asking her

178

permission! Funny the way they never mentioned that bit in *The X Files*.

'Do I mind? N ... no, not at all,' she answered, eyes widening with the mounting excitement of this first contact. She found herself almost curtseying before the pair of aliens. 'I'd be honoured ... er, flattered. Take me, take me, Sir! Er, your honour?'

Already her mind was spinning ahead to the fantastic consequences of being abducted by aliens. She'd heard all about what happened to young fertile women when they were snatched from earth by greys. First she'd be beamed up to the waiting ship in a halo of blinding light then, slowly she'd be stripped naked before a massed audience of thousands of wildly appreciative eyes, each admiring her every curve, lingering on her perfect skin. Then, her young, firm body would be touched all over by hundreds of fingers as she floated weightlessly in a warm bath of gently circulating liquid. For hours she'd lie there in that sensual fluid being caressed, petted, until after all had admired every inch of her anatomy she'd be lifted out and gently cocooned in a warm duvet-like substance before being returned home days from now to begin a career writing science fiction stories based upon her experiences. Oh yes! *So* much better than a quick grope in the back of a Renault. It could last days ... weeks! She couldn't wait to see the inside of that intergalactic spacecraft.

'Which way?' she asked and took an eager step forward. 'Lead me on, lead me on!' Calabrese scratched his head and stared in confused wonder at Lupin. Desperately he ran back over that last conversation, checking and rechecking every word, every nuance, every context. Try as he might he couldn't find what it was that Lupin had said to change her mind. Was this some minstrel magic of which he was unaware? Could it be she actually *liked* him?

'Take me to your leader,' Tara found herself giggling excitedly as she skipped across the Camford fens mere feet behind the two feyries.

'Our leader?' whispered Lupin in shock. 'You want to see Oberon?'

'Obe Wan?' gasped Tara her jaw dropping again as she misheard. So all those Star Wars things were really true. The whole Empire shebang, the Force, all of it! Did George Lucas know? Was he one of them?

'Bad idea,' muttered Calabrese looking up and down Tara's anorak clad figure appreciatively and then recalling the overlarge form of their dear Queen. 'Very, very bad idea. Titania would have a fit. You do know she's the jealous type, don't you?'

'I had heard,' gulped Lupin floating dreamily above the grass as Tara's voice repeated over and over in his mind, 'I'd be honoured, er . . . flattered. Take me, take me.'

Tara scurried after them, her thoughts galloping recklessly across the fens already checking out the interior of the vast, gleaming saucer of extraterrestrial engineering.

She was only disappointed that she hadn't brought her camera with her.

With a quivering of eager fingers Professor Crickson glanced at the clock, clicked his tongue and switched off the current. Expertly he disconnected the electrodes and pulled the eighteen inch long separating gel out of the tank. In moments he had shaken it dry, leapt across the cluttered lab and, hurling three of Striebley's experiments to the floor to make room, he clipped the gel into the lightbox on the wall with an air of actors playing expert consultants in Saturday night hospital dramas.

Striebley made a noise in his throat and detested those damned rustlers, or whatever they were, for turfing Crickson out of his lab. He also aimed an oath at Camford Constabulary for keeping him out. Crickson was a real pain to share a lab with. Even for a day. Already Striebley was convinced that the frontier of scientific knowledge had pushed back hard against him, shoving him at least three months deeper into ignorance. And Crickson was the catalyst.

Somehow vital pipettes gravitated into Crickson's lab-coat

pockets at the most inopportune moments. Four times already that afternoon Striebley had been up to his armpits in a vital titration only to look up and find the pipette he had just put down was now thirty feet across the lab tucked behind Crickson's ear. Irritatingly it didn't stop with pipettes. Pencils, calculators and every single magnetic stirrer in the building was now to be found about Crickson's person.

If Striebley didn't know better he would have concluded that right now, as it rapidly approached the witching hour in that lab, there was something seriously wrong with the very fabric of the Universe. Perhaps, if he had been able to keep his eye on any piece of equipment for long enough, he might have tried to scan for the presence of micro-wormholes centring on Crickson and capable of transporting paper-clips instantaneously across the lab. For a moment he stood rubbing his chin and pondering the revolution that would have in the field of office supplies if he could find it.

He was just proposing the shakiest of primary principles in his head when a cry erupted from the vicinity of the lightbox and his concentration (along with any hopes of setting up Striebley's Instantaneous Office Supplies Ltd) was shattered.

'That's it! That's it!' eureka'd Crickson skipping up and down and pointing at the illuminated gel.

'What precisely is what?' asked Striebley dropping a test-tube back into a rack with a sigh and strolling over towards the epicentre of the excitement. Years of experience had taught him that Crickson in this sort of mood was impossible to ignore. Let him get this breakthrough off his chest and then maybe, just maybe, he'd get some work done. Although, at quarter to midnight, perhaps it was time to call it a night.

'I've found it. I'm certain!' chuckled Crickson squinting over his bifocals. 'There, look. Isn't it beautiful?' He pointed a wildly gyrating index finger at a small area of seemingly randomly arranged horizontal lines stacked in four vertical columns.

Striebley shrugged. He'd seen possibly thousands of such

DNA gels and after a while, as he always said, one square inch of genetic info looked pretty much like any other.

'One square inch of genetic info looks pretty much like any other,' he said much to Crickson's obvious disgust.

'Philistine!' barked the elder Professor. 'Have you never seen another, more perfect arrangement of the four bases of life than this?' He tapped at the gel.

Striebley leaned forward and read off from the tiny lines, 'AGGTCTCAAAGGTTCCAGCTA. What's so special about that?'

Crickson slapped his forehead and raised a pair of imploring hands to heaven in a gesture of which many of the Jewish persuasion would be proud. 'And I expect that you can see nothing special about the simple four notes which so spectacularly open Beethoven's Fifth Symphony, eh?'

'That's different, that's music.'

'Music of the ears,' tutted Crickson. 'This,' he stabbed his finger once again at the gel. 'This is music of the heart. The music of the future of fast food as we know it!'

'Eh?'

'That section of DNA is *the* most important section in the entire chicken genome. And I have isolated it. That is what makes chickens unique!'

'Er . . . don't tell me. It's the gene that codes for that little flap of skin that dangles under a cockerel's beak?' hazarded Striebley.

'No, no, no.'

'The one that makes them wake up at the crack of dawn with the urge to squawk noisily.' And suddenly Striebley's eyes lit up with the obvious profit potential of isolating that gene. 'Hey, if you could take that out of every forthcoming generation there'd be millions of farmers'd love you. Just think . . . totally silent cockerels!'

'No!' screamed Crickson. It was obvious this wasn't going the way he really wanted it to. 'That gene codes for a tiny protein which is unique to chickens. The one which makes chickens taste like, well . . . chicken!'

'I prefer my silent cockerels . . .'

'That code could be worth millions, billions even. That's our future!' And Crickson turned back to stare at the gel like a lovestruck teenage girl with a topless poster of the latest squeaky-clean boy band.

'Er . . . I don't want to sound dense but . . . How is that string of twenty-one letters our future?'

'Fast food!' declared Crickson enigmatically. 'Billions of pounds a week is spent on the humble chicken. Thousands of tons of the beasties are devoured all over the world. Breadcrumbed, nuggetted, spiced, satayed . . . the list is endless.'

'Oh yeah, everyone eats chicken,' grinned Striebley suddenly realising that he hadn't stopped for anything to eat in hours. A trip to the Kenchucky Take-Out for a large portion of Southern Savoury Wings and Fries looked imminent.

'Not everyone!' announced Crickson. 'What about vegetarians?'

'Well, that's obvious, isn't it?'

'And there's others, too. The terrified!' Crickson's eyes were alive with excitement. 'Every time there's another new food scare people stay away in their millions. I'm telling you, one more salmonella worry and it'll be curtains for Kenchucky Fried and the rest of 'em. And that's not all. Another outbreak of BSE and burgers are buggered. There'll be only two survivors. Spud'U'Like and us!'

Striebley raised a finger as if to say that they were scientists not purveyors of fast food, but there was something in the way that Crickson steamrollered on that didn't let him get a word in.

'Believe me,' decreed Crickson with evangelical fervour. 'The fast food industry is wringing its hands in desperation for something new. Something safe. Something that vegans and carnivores can sit down in harmony around the same table and under the same roof and devour in peaceful contentment!'

Crickson paused for breath. Then lashed a quivering finger at the illuminated gel. 'There is that something! Chapter one of Project CFC! Chicken Fed Corn! All we have to do is transfer that gene into the humble maize plant and bingo! A vegetarian substitute for chicken virtually indistinguishable from the real thing. Totally free from any risk of salmonella. And *so* much more efficient. Have you any idea how inefficient the intestines of the average chicken are in taking corn and turning it into a portion of boneless breast?'

Striebley was impressed. For the first time it seemed like Crickson was actually onto something worthwhile. It could be that this would knock the unenviable success of boil-in-the-bag gazpacho into a cocked hat.

'But enough time-wasting. It's time for science!' declared Crickson and whirled on his heels. 'The moment has come to press my amniotic tanks into action!'

And he dashed across the lab. Pausing only to swipe his security card through the slot, he vanished around the corner and off up stairs, his mind already racing across the pastures of possibilities.

The Amniotic Tanks! Without them he'd be back in the genetic stone age of actual gene transfer. Excising a length of DNA, looping it into a plasmid and hoping to get it inserted into the genome of the maize, praying that it was in the right place and the right way round. It was so messy back then. But now it was easy-peasy.

Simply type the required DNA code into the buffer memory of the GENE-Erator (TM), wire it up to the Base-Jumper Delivery System (TM), pipe this output into the fifty gallon drums of the Amniotic Tanks (TM) and in a matter of hours the correct DNA sequence would have been assembled. A complete genome.

But that was just the beginning. Add a few vital enzymes, a few litres of essential amino acids and the biochemical stage was set for the miracle of creation.

Crickson was feet away from his very own miracle. He powered on up the stairs, clattered down the corridor, swiped his security card down the side and crashed into the unopened door.

'What the . . .?' He tried again, cursing as he bruised his nose on the stubborn door to his lab.

'Open up, you bloody . . .!'

The door creaked open.

A pleasantly smiling PC Sim stood in Crickson's way. 'Can I help you?' he asked cradling his truncheon meaningfully.

'No, no. I can manage,' answered Crickson making to head for the GENE-Erator (TM) squatting on the far bench.

'Manage what, may I ask?' grinned Sim deftly stepping in front of the scientist.

'Er . . . no, no. It's science, you wouldn't understand.' He feinted left, ducked right and was tripped by Sim as he leapt through the door.

'You can't come in,' said Sim matter-of-factly and pointed to the cat's cradle of liberally strung blue and white tape festooning the lab.

'"Crime Scene–Do Not Enter"' he read helpfully.

'What? This is my lab, you can't!' shrieked Crickson.

'Can. And have. Police business, you wouldn't understand,' grinned Sim helping Crickson to his feet on the far side of the door.

'But I'm on the verge of a breakthrough.'

'That's very good, sir. We seem to be quite a way off ours, I'm afraid,' confided Sim folding his arms across his back and spreading his legs sentry-like.

'You don't understand. I need my equipment. I'm on the . . .'

'. . . verge. Yes, you said, sir. Well if you talk nicely to Doctor Boscombe in the morning I'm sure we can . . .'

'I need it now!' flapped Crickson.

'Oh, that *is* a shame, sir. But orders are orders, see? Can't let you in.'

'And how long is this reprehensible state of affairs going to be in force?'

'Long as it takes, sir. But it won't be too long. Couple of weeks, maybe a month and you won't know we were ever here. Honest. We've got this new contract cleaning firm we use and they're really good. Do the phones, the lot . . .'

'A month!' shrieked Crickson horrified, images of faceless rival scientists patenting his breakthrough scant days before him. That month could make all the difference. Phrases regarding posts and being pipped at them sprang unbidden to his seething mind.

'I can give you money,' begged Crickson. 'Hundred pounds? Thousand?' He began desperately rummaging in his pockets, hurling pipettes and hailstones of magnetic stirrers in all directions.

'Well, that's very kind of you, sir, but . . .'

'Ten thousand?'

'You can give me as much as you want,' said Sim biting his lip. 'I'm not letting you through. And may I take this opportunity to remind you, sir, that I am the one with the truncheon.'

'Is that a threat?'

'No, sir, an observation. Now, may I suggest you go about your business, there's nothing to see here,' said Sim drawing on Police Crowd Dispersal Phrase Numbers eight and nine.

Crickson snarled and peered over Sim's shoulder with a look that could freeze mercury at a hundred yards. It fell on a current edition of the DN-Aids Inc catalogue, slightly foxed, and suddenly an idea sprang to Crickson's fervid brain.

'Nothing to see,' he muttered almost to himself. 'Yes . . . yes, you're right. Ha, silly me. You're only doing your job after all. Yes.' And, much to PC Sim's satisfaction, he turned on his heel and scurried away off down the corridor. With a cheery wave he vanished down the stairs.

Sim shoved the door shut once again and leant a chair against it. Casually he slouched in the corner, picked up his book and gleefully tumbled back into the world of Inspector Morse only slightly unhappy that he was several thousand pounds down on the last few minutes. 'Scientists,' he tutted and began to read.

Downstairs Professor Crickson had his head in another book. A slightly more pristine copy of the current DN-Aids

Inc Catalogue. Desperately he was filling out a Priority Next-Day Despatch Order Form. Dozens of catalogue numbers flooded onto the sheet. He couldn't wait a month. Not now.

Tugging a calculator out of his top pocket he totalled up the cost and winced. Forty-eight thousand three hundred and ninety-seven pounds and twenty-seven pence. 'This'll test them,' he grunted as he sprinted off towards the fax machine. 'Next Day Delivery Guaranteed or Your Money Back!'

The clock on the fax read 23:57.

It was only as Tara followed Lupin and Calabrese as they leapt out of a hazel bush and into a narrow gravel track that she realised where she was. The strings of oscillating cars probably gave it away: 'Rumpy Row'.

'This way,' hissed Lupin leading them Indian style around the back of a particularly steamy Peugeot and on towards a large privet.

Tara's mind spun in excitement as she followed in the dark. If this was 'Rumpy Row' then, just through that hedge was the thirteenth fairway of the Regal Greens Golf Course. Her heart pounded eagerly. Could it be that a vast alien craft was already squatting on the thirteenth, lights flashing, venting extraterrestrial vapours into the night? Shame they hadn't turned up last night, it would've saved the *Adversity* Team a stack of effort. And suddenly a thought struck her. Maybe that was why they were launching from there. The Sainway's car-park covering their other launch site was just an excuse. Did Farson know more than he was letting on? Tara had seen strange lights in the sky hereabouts on more than one occasion, but she had just put that down to security spots from the golf course or torches from a party of midnight putters. Was it possible that those hovering shafts of photons shimering in the fenland mists had come far further than the security lighting department of B&Q? As she pushed on through the privet hedge she knew that in a few moments she would find out.

'Down here, please,' whispered Lupin and headed off across the third rough.

Tara's eyes strained in the gloom searching for any signs of extraterrestrial visitation, any gleaming saucer of un-laserable alloy squatting in the greenery. Would it be guarded by a single implacable robotic sentinel, or stand on hydraulic legs, glimmering behind fences of fizzing force fields of shimmering crimson?

'C'mon. This way,' barked Lupin and led her off to the left, down towards a string of ancient oaks. In moments they had pushed on into the scrubby ferns and were stood surrounded by the vast trunks of the aged trees, hidden completely from prying eyes.

'Well? Where is it?' asked Tara, wide-eyed. 'I can't see it.'

Calabrese tutted. 'It wouldn't do to advertise our presence, would it?'

'Oh, I get it,' thrilled Tara, her handcuffs jingling with her excitement. 'You've got a cloaking device.'

Lupin looked at the doctor's coat and shrugged.

Tara held out her hands and began tapping the air in front of her. 'Is it here? Can I touch it? Great disguise. I'd swear there was nothing here. I tell you NASA would give their eye teeth to be here right now. And the FBI and . . . ooh, loads of other folks.'

'NASA?' shrugged Lupin to Calabrese.

'FBI?' answered Calabrese with a bewildered expression. She certainly did say some strange things this girl. Although he had heard mention of the FBI somewhere before, some show on his tv. That was it, the one with the chap and the funny messages about 'Codename:Alpha1.A1: Prime.President' or something similar.

'So come on, where is it?' gabbled Tara impatiently. 'Don't keep me in suspense any longer. I want to see it.'

'Very well,' agreed Lupin. 'There it is, right in front of you.'

Tara squeaked and stepped back in shock. There, indeed right in front of her, was a hole in the ground which she could have sworn hadn't been there a moment before. It bore an uncanny resemblance to the cellar access chute at *The Monocle and Asparagus*.

'Th . . . that's it?' she croaked staring into the void. It had to be said, as an entrance to an intergalactic space vessel, it wasn't precisely what she had expected. 'It's not what I expected,' she said.

Lupin ignored her and hopped into the mouth of the shaft. 'Do be careful on the way down,' he announced like some air hostess. 'The steps are a little on the steep side.'

And as Tara descended, Calabrese to her rear, she began to wonder if this wasn't even more impressive than she had at first thought. Could it be that she was being led down to a vast buried spacecraft lying beneath the Regal Greens Golf Course like some enormous interstellar flatfish? What advanced technology could they have possibly harnessed to achieve such a seamless cover-up? What could shift an entire forest of ancient oaks? Matter transference? Geological teleportation?

Her heart leapt at the commercial applications of such a device. If only she could persuade them to give her the technology then she could set up her own landscape gardening business. That *and* Science Fiction stories. She'd be made!

'Here we are,' announced Lupin as Tara descended the bottom step and stood in a small roundish antechamber thirty feet beneath the thirteenth green. 'Reception.'

'Great. Yes, it's lovely. Beautiful natural looking soil-effect wallcovering. Now aren't you going to invite me in, hmm? You know, over the threshold?' enthused Tara.

Calabrese's eyes widened. Whatever it was that Lupin had said to her he had certainly convinced her that here was where she wanted to be.

'Certainly, my dear,' fawned Lupin excitedly, thoughts of ferny beds shimmering closer to the forefront of his mind. 'This way.' He pulled back a curtain of roots and vanished through the wall.

Tara leapt a few inches into the air. 'It's a projection field. Wow! I never would've guessed. Oh, this is *so* exciting!'

A long grey finger poked its way out of the soil wall and beckoned. 'Come, come,' declared the disembodied voice of Lupin.

Tara was already scurrying eagerly forward.

Lupin's voice was swirling around Reception. 'Come forward, my darling. Approach with delight.'

Tara was inches away from the seemingly solid sheet of soil and accelerating.

'Step across this earthen threshold,' encouraged Lupin enthusiastically. 'And enter the kingdom of fey . . .'

'What the . . .?' shrieked Tara as her nose came up hard against the wall and burst messily. 'Hey! Whad's going on? Dhis some kind of joke, eh?' she kicked angrily at the now solid wall, clutching her dripping nose. 'You sick alien gits. Is this how you get your kicks, eh? Is it? Well, ha, ha, very funny!'

Lupin appeared through the wall, shock, alarm and dismay writ large across his grey features. 'I . . . I . . .' he stammered, his gast well and truly flabbered. 'Are you alright? Is it broken? Will you forgive me?'

There was only one creature in the tiny room who appeared to be enjoying himself. Calabrese was rolling on the dusty floor clutching at his ribs hooting desperately.

Lupin was across the room scant seconds before Tara would have set about him. 'What's so funny?' shouted Lupin pinning Calabrese to the far wall. 'Tell me!'

'You sure you want to know?' giggled Calabrese. 'You won't like it.'

'Tell me!' barked Lupin slamming his feyrie friend against the subsoil.

'Yeah! Dell 'im!' sniffed Tara squeezing the bridge of her nose and already feeling a bruise spreading under her eyes.

'I .. er, forgot to tell you one of the other problems with "older" women,' began Calabrese around a fit of giggles.

'Old? Who you calling old?' sniffed Tara.

'What problem?' shouted Lupin. 'What?'

'You could be too late . . . for admission,' and Calabrese erupted in another peal of laughter.

'What's that supposed to mean,' growled Lupin tightening his grip around Calabrese's throat to seemingly no effect.

'She won't be allowed in.'

'What? Why the hell not?' chorused Tara and Lupin like some pier-end music hall act.

'Because . . .' Calabrese could barely speak, but somehow he managed to part the hysterical clouds of mirth and pull himself together for a moment. 'Excuse me madam, but, are you a virgin?'

'How dare you . . .'

'Just answer the question,' smirked Calabrese as he caught the first inklings of understanding in Lupin's eyes. 'Hast thou been deflowered? Art thou no longer as pure as the driven snowflakes?'

Tara looked at the floor between her feet.

'I take it that's "no"?' asked Calabrese.

'He said he'd make the earth move, okay? It was either that or double geography . . .'

'Please. Spare me the details. They're irrelevant,' winced Calabrese.

Lupin dropped him and began to sob pathetically.

'The sordid details matter not,' continued Calabrese. 'Rules are rules. Those of a more, er . . . experienced nature are not allowed in. You might as well show her the door . . .'

'No!' squeaked Tara desperately. She was this close to interstellar beings and a glimpse of the bridge of a vast alien craft, she wasn't going to be shown the door because of some youthful indiscretion during double geography. 'I . . . I can be useful in other ways,' she babbled. 'I can reach tall shelves. I can tell you things. Anything you want to know. Er . . .' Her mind whirled. What would be of interest to visiting alien creatures? What vital facts did she have locked away beneath that mop of brunette hair? Suddenly she had it. 'I can explain all about warp drive and matter transporters and phasers and sub-space communications and . . .' She looked at the blank expressions floating across their faces.

'Ahhh, I guess you already know about that stuff, don't you? I mean, you're here after all.' She fished about in the recesses of her knowledge, grabbing desperately at anything that could interest these visitors. 'Er . . . er, I could tell you all about our science. I'm not very good at chemistry or geography,' she blushed. 'But . . . er, genetics, how about that? Fancy knowing how you can take a teeny bit of DNA and clone a whole army if you want to?

Suddenly Calabrese was on his feet and looking eager. 'A whole army?'

'Oh, sure,' winced Tara feeling herself treading onto extremely dodgy ground. Could she remember enough of what Farson had told her last night after the meeting to make this convincing? He had told her a lot, desperate to ensure she reported all the right facts in her piece about the GAIA raid. Now, where had he started . . .

'Well, there's this stuff called DNA right and it's like little corkscrews of letters, see? But there's only four of them, right. Er . . . letters that is, not DNA, there's millions of them, well, every cell's got loads of this DNA stuff and . . .'

And so it was that the first underground midnight genetics lesson began.

The fax in the Portakabin office of DN-Aids Inc chuckled to a halt and sat quietly in the corner, a sheet of paper protruding insultingly like a tongue between pursed lips.

'Get that,' spat Miles, the managing director, pointing his baseball bat at the machine.

Alistair, the part time delivery man, tugged an excuse for a forelock and ripped the message clear. 'It's an order,' he declared.

'Give, give!' hissed Miles, clicking his fingers impatiently. In seconds he was staring at the shopping list, his eyes widening with thoughts of healthy bouncing baby profits. 'GENE-Erator, Amniotic Tanks, yes, yes.'

It was only as he reached the last line that his expression clouded over.

'Eleven fifty-seven and they want next day delivery? What kind of a nerve have they got?' And then he looked again at where the fax had originated. 'Splice of Life Patentable

Biosciences Ltd. I might have known,' he frowned. 'These things in stock?'

Alistair shook his head and put his hands in his pocket. It wasn't a surprise that forty-odd grand's worth of equipment wasn't in stock. Truth be told there was never anything more than a couple of packets of pipette tips in stock. Anything else was an inefficient waste of financial resources. And Miles should know.

Not for nothing had he done a practical Management course during his time in Wandsworth for shoplifting. Right now he knew all about Nick of Time stock rotation. It was so simple. Keeping the stocks on the shelves down to the absolute minimum decreased any chance of losing money to the very lowest. For DN-Aids Inc this was zero. Miles made absolutely certain that there was nothing on his shelves. He had other sources of supplies.

He was already flicking through his bulging dossier of this month's records of competitors' deliveries to surrounding labs. 'Aha!' he declared and peered joyously at the freshly hacked documentation. 'It seems that Cyto Tech have ever-so recently delivered everything we need to Genesystems Labs.' Rubbing his hands together he smiled at Alistair. 'Fetch the van, my man. I shall bring the glasscutters, pliers and blue-prints!'

Elijah Sacramento launched a flotilla of curses into the night air and flicked off the radio as the dj on Camford FM took a deep breath and announced cheerily. 'And here it is. Released today. The Biggest, the Baddest, the Thriller of a musical generation. The brand new single from Michael . . .' His fingers drummed noisily on his steering wheel and only barely drowned out the sound of his grinding teeth. It was one minute to twelve and there was no sign of Tara and/or Farson. Something had gone horribly wrong he was sure. Farson had forgotten where the rendezvous was, that was bound to be it. Oh, if only he'd insisted they all took mobile phones. It would have been *so* much easier.

Suddenly there was a movement in the Golf's wing mirror.

Sacramento squinted over his shoulder and stared across the car park of Sainway's. A figure that looked like a reject from Billy Smart's Circus was heading his way with a determined lurch.

Nervously he reached around, locked all the doors and checked the key was in the ignition. If it came to a quick getaway, he was ready.

The clown lurched onward, size twenty-five shoes flapping awkwardly before it, kicking up stray Sainway's own brand cola cans noisily.

Sacramento felt alarm rising within. An hour and a half sitting alone in this darkened carpark had done little to soothe his nerves.

Suddenly the clown slapped a bulbous hand on the car roof and peered inside.

'Open up!' he shouted. 'It's me!'

'Who's me?' shouted back Sacramento, one hand on the ignition.

'Farson. Don't you recognise my voice?'

Through toughened glass and a plastic clown's mask it was a little on the difficult side.

'How can I be sure it's you?' barked Elijah.

'Who else would be stupid enough to be walking around like this at near midnight in Sainway's carpark, eh?'

'Good point,' conceded Elijah.

'Well, c'mon then, let me in,' begged Farson tugging plaintively on the door handle.

Sacramento stared at the clown outside the car window and flicked the lock. 'I said choose something inconspicuous!' he shouted as Farson wrestled his feet through the door. 'What's that?'

Bozo, the clown, shrugged. 'All they had left,' he mumbled miserably. 'Some student's do on tonight, or something. Still, it doesn't matter now, does it?'

'Where is she?'

'Didn't show.'

'What?'

194

'Didn't show. I waited until gone closing time, I even went back to The Monocle and trawled the bar, at great personal risk, I might add. No sign of her. Gone!'

'Farson, we've got a problem,' confessed Elijah.

'No. It's that bloody Tara's got the problem. When I get my hands on her, I'll, I'll . . . Do you know how humiliating it is to walk around all night dressed like this?'

Elijah was shaking his head. 'It's our problem. She caught the last post.'

'What?'

'The ransom note's gone. Tara sent it. They'll get it tomorrow. We're ruined!' wailed Elijah. 'GAIA will be a laughing stock. Nobody'll take the cause of Genetic Anti-Interference seriously again when she shows up at breakfast while her dad's opening our ransom note. It's a disaster.'

'Unless . . .' offered Farson, his bow tie spinning involuntarily as he sat on the switch.

'Unless what?'

'What time does the postie call?'

'No,' gagged Elijah. 'You can't be serious?'

'It's the only way. If they don't actually *receive* the note then everything's alright and I get to tell Tara just what I think of her.'

'I'm not doing it,' said Elijah.

'It's your turn, don't you think,' growled Farson, his nose glowing in the light of the Golf's dashboard.

Elijah whimpered pathetically, turned the ignition key and raced out of the carpark.

At almost the very same instant, a sunflower-painted Volkswagen camper trundled into the Sainway's carpark on balding tyres. Two Afghan coated individuals with wispy beards, punctured body parts and dreadlocks clambered out.

'We're lost, man,' said one of them staring at the recently laid tarmac and the gleaming white lines.

'No way, man. This is the place,' answered the other peering up at the stars. 'Constellations are all in perfect alignment.'

'But where's the grass, man?' said the first one staring at the ground.

'Sorry, didn't realise you were without.' He handed over a surprisingly tightly wound cigarette.

'No, no *proper* grass, man.'

'That's good stuff in there. Grew it myself.'

'Grass underfoot, man. We can't go skyclad on manmade tarmac. Interrupts the energy flows, bad karma, can't get to be one with mother earth.'

'You sayin' we can't celebrate entry into the second half of the year?'

'Not here. Oh woe, our traditional site for decades of celebration, another victim of mankind's capitalist intervention.' He scowled at the rectangle of Sainway's supermarket looming atop a confluence of virtually undetectable ley lines.

'Then, let's go to Glastonbury,' offered the one with the cigarette.

'Can't, man. Dole cheque ain't come through. No petrol money.'

'But where can we celebrate . . .?'

'Good question, man.'

As if in answer to that question a sheet of newspaper rolled across the car park on a small midnight breeze. Like a kitten bearing comforting news, it wrapped itself affectionately around a pair of sandalled legs and almost mewled for attention. A slightly grubby hand reached down, took the paper and gasped.

'It is a sign, man. Look!' A finger pointed to the headline of that morning's *Camford Chronicle*.

Bright Midnight Lights Seen Over Regal Greens.

And leaving a curious runic symbol in chalk on the carpark entrance the two figures leapt back into their sunflower-painted VW and headed off to reconnoitre the Regal Greens Golf Course with a view to a night of pagan festivities with a few friends.

The traditional morning aroma of freshly fried bacon, free-range eggs, pork sausages and sizzling mushrooms suffused the whole of the Ness household. Casually, it drifted up the Laura Ashley wallpapered stairs and hammered on the bathroom door. As if in response the door was tugged open and a freshly abluted figure staggered through it, towel dangling around his neck, shirt collar open. He closed his eyes momentarily and breathed deeply through flaring nostrils, looking for all the world like an underenthusiastic holiday camp PE instructor. He exhaled noisily, lurched around on his heel and trudged down the upstairs landing rapping his knuckles noisily on the last door on the left.

'Come on, come. Wakey wakey. The sun is up, it's time you were!' he shouted at the expanse of white glossed woodwork, ignoring the 'Do Not Disturb' and 'Beware-Biohazard. Exercise Extreme Caution!' signs. He slouched off down the stairs and, muttering the traditional morning vow that he would never ever drink that much gin again, took his place at the dining room table, tapping his fingers impatiently.

In seconds the kitchen door was pushed open by a fluffy slippered foot, and his dressing-gowned wife entered bearing the morning's repast and a scowl that could kill.

'Toast?' she barked dropping the plate of full English breakfast on the table and, leaving a brooding fug of hatred, she turned on her heel and headed off to ready a mug of English Breakfast Tea and a jar of Thin Shredded Seville Orange Marmalade. Secretly she plotted a host of punishments for that damned daughter of his. She would pay for lazing about in bed whilst her mother cooked breakfast. Damn that Tara, didn't she know her place?

In the silence of the dining room Everett stared at the cindered chunk of bacon, head in his hands, and began his slow recovery from the excesses of the Mayoral Dinner last night. He was a real believer in starting the day properly. The possibility of facing the world without several portions of dead pig and a pair of unborn baby birds nestling within his stomach was as alien as muesli. 'If mankind had been meant to eat cereals,' he maintained vehemently, 'we would have be born with four stomachs and the innate ability to ruminate!'

'English Breakfast Tea and Thin Shredded Orange Marmalade' he yelled a few moments later as the familar printed humming birds of his wife's dressing gown swept into view and deposited his toast.

Unseen outside, a mysterious figure, sporting an artistically correct goatee beard, skipped over the waist-high front fence and secreted himself behind a suitable bush. He settled down nervously to await the arrival of the postie and desperately wished he could recall if the Nesses had an ankle-philic dog.

Meanwhile, Chief Inspector Ness was sitting in his dining room staring at rapidly cooling breakfast, his arms folded impatiently. 'Where is that girl? Doesn't she realise breakfast's *the* most important meal of the day? Sets you up for all the ensuing trials and tribulations of the workplace.'

'Yes, dear,' nodded Rosemary.

'And besides, it's the height of poor manners to keep us waiting. Has she learnt nothing of what I have drilled into her?' He stood, hurled his one hundred percent linen napkin onto the table and yelled up the stairs. 'Tara, get your arse down here this instant. It's breakfast time!'

Unsurprisingly there was nary an answer.

'Tara? Can you hear me? Tara? This is your father speaking. If you don't get down here in the next thirty seconds I'm coming in. Is that clear?' he yelled in his finest hostage-situation voice. 'Come down now, and I'll forget about it. Tara? You're only making it worse for yourself, you know. No good can come of this.'

Outside, in the laburnum lined street, the chirruping of the resident sparrows was joined by the lilting tunelessness and

198

irregular footsteps of Limp Ron, the local postie. Behind his suitable bush Elijah Sacramento began to tremble. This was it, the time for action was approaching.

'I'm waiting!' shouted Chief Inspector Ness up the uncommunicative stairwell. 'Right. That's it. I'm coming in!' he announced and stormed up the stairs at the very instant in which Limp Ron landed a heavy foot at the front gate, lifted the latch and crunched unevenly down the cotswold gravelled drive whistling a strangely lopsided rendition of Ravel's 'Bolero'.

Once again ignoring the signs advising him to variously, Not Disturb and Exercise Extreme Caution, Chief Inspector Ness burst into his only daughter's room, vocal chords blazing. 'That's it, come on. Up! Now! I'm waiting . . . eh?'

For a moment he stood in the centre of the oddly tidy room and looked around, confused, playing a mental 'spot the difference' game. Something was amiss. Had she actually put things away? He scowled at the top of her cupboards bringing to bear all of his wealth of investigatorial experience. Nope, they were still a mess, strewn with a myriad of cans of hairstyling products, cd cases and a random selection of cult music magazines. Scratching his head he stepped backwards and sat down on the corner of the bed.

And then it hit him. The bed, it was neatly made, pillows bunched, the corner of the duvet turned down. It hadn't been slept in!

Scant moments before the roar of realisation was vocalised in an eloquent string of four-letter effluvium, Limp Ron plucked a pair of letters out of his sack and, pausing only to squint quizzically at the strange array of newspaper letters festooning the front of an otherwise bland manilla envelope, he shoved them part way through the letter box and waved cheerily into the dining room. In his bush Elijah's heart was in his mouth. The clock was ticking now. The race was well and truly on. The future standing of GAIA's reputation hung twitching in the balance. Time seemed to run like molasses as he watched the asymmetric postie crunch down the drive, his gaze flitting between him and the pair of envelopes sticking from the letter box, taunting like a seven year old's tongue.

'Rosemary?' yelled Ness stomping around his daughter's room. 'She's been out all night. Do you know anything about this? Is this a teenage thing?'

Rosemary was trying her best to ignore him as she shuffled her fluffy slippered way towards the door to collect the post. Unbeknownst to her, another was after her letters. At that very instant Elijah Sacramento was crawling SAS style behind a begonia and a couple of geraniums, his eyes fixed on the contents of the Ness letterbox. Suddenly he stopped, alarmed, unsure what to do. Ahead of him, just beyond a clump of rather parched looking pinks, lay twelve feet of deadly gravel. It stretched between him and the twin mock Georgian pillars supporting the porch. Twelve feet of absolute exposure. No cover for love nor money. His heart stopped. Entire squadrons of trained paratroopers had been lost crossing less.

Across the exposed expanse the pair of letters waved insultingly, taunting. He had no choice. He had to make a break for it. Crouching under the pinks, like a sprinter on the blocks, he bit his lip, held his breath and powered out of the foliage.

At the same instant he caught a snatch of motion through the mock stained glass insert of the front door. Squeaking he diverted from his target and hammered to a halt under cover behind one of the pillars. Gasping, eyes bulging, he strained around the plaster cylinder, three feet from target. A scant yard from the ransom note; a million miles from success. It was now or never. He half fell, half exploded from behind the pillar and swooped on the letters, hands grasping. His grip tightened, snatching at his target.

'Post's here, dear,' called a female voice, inches away through the door and tugged the two envelopes through the brush-lipped rectangle as Elijah's fingers closed on thin air.

He bit his lip and sprinted down the Ness's gravel drive hurdling the gate and vanishing down the road. It was something of a shame he didn't hang around, he probably would have found the ensuing discussion rather interesting.

'The post?' barked the Chief Inspector down the stairs. 'My daughter's gone and you're interested in the post?' Much to Rosemary's relief he seemed to have forgotten about his overcooked breakfast, now tepid.

'But, you always like to be informed when the post has arrived, dear,' answered Rosemary, her voice fading as she looked suspiciously at the oddly lettered manilla envelope. Could this be the latest ploy to get folks to open junk mail?

'There's one here addressed to the "Chief Insector",' called Rosemary failing to spot the dislodged 'p' clinging to the letter box's draught excluders. 'It's not from *Entomology Today* again is it, dear?'

'How should I know?'

'Well, it's addressed to you,' she offered helpfully.

'Oh, open it if you're that bothered,' he bellowed peering under Tara's unruffled bed for clues as to her whereabouts. He didn't expect to find out where she was quite so soon.

In a flurry of humming bird print dressing gown his wife erupted into Tara's bedroom waving a strangely lettered ransom note.

'Do keep it down, dear,' barked Ness. 'You know how yelling ruins my concentration.' Rosemary continued to leap up and down in obvious signs of acute agitation.

'Yes, yes, dear. I know for once I shan't be early for work. But this is important,' growled Ness peering under the bed again.

Rosemary stamped her foot for attention. A gesture somewhat sadly lacking in impact. Fluffy slippers striking half inch shag makes not a lot of noise to ensnare the attention. In the end she shoved the note under his nose and waggled it impatiently.

'Oh, do take that ransom note out from under my nose, dear. It really is distracting and . . .' He stopped, grabbed her wrist and peered at the note, swallowing nervously, his eyes widening in alarm as he stared at the unevenly applied letters.

We hAve Your PreCIouS tARa
sHe Is sAfE jUsT noW. fOr tHe mOMenT.
CanCel tHe coNtraCt wiTh sPlIce Of liFE
oR YoU'lL neVer sEe Her aGaIn.
We wIlL bE waTchiNg. GAIA.

'My Tara!' snarled Chief Inspector Ness his face reddening.
'How dare they take her. That's stealing. After all the time
and money I've spent on her, bringing her up, school
uniforms, college fees. Damn them! I will get her back!'

He leapt across the room and snatched at the pink
telephone, scattering cans of firm hold hairspray with
conditioner in all directions. Rosemary watched in amazement as his fingers clattered 999 into the keypad and he
perched himself on Tara's fluffy make-up stool.

'Yes . . . Yes, it's an emergency. Get me Plain!' he barked
into the handset. 'What d'you mean "Which service?" I want
Plain. No, I do not want an ambulance or a fire engine. It's a
kidnapping . . . Of course a kidnapping is an emergency!
How would you like it if your daughter was suddenly . . .
What? Pen and paper? Er . . . yes but . . . 335627. What's
that . . . Hello? Hello?' Snarling he slammed the phone
down. 'They hung up? Can you believe it? Hung up on me?'

'You should try that "Big Cuddly Uncle Copper Hotline"
service that's advertised in the papers,' offered Rosemary
helpfully.

Chief Inspector Ness scowled at his wife, tutted and
stabbed 335627 into the telephone. In the wardrobe of the
room next door a mobile phone warbled. 'No answer,' he
hissed, leapt to his feet and whirlwinded down the stairs
grumbling about dealing with things face to face. Pausing
only to snatch his car keys from the small peg in the
cupboard by the door he exploded into the morning air and
vanished into the garage. In seconds tyres were spitting
gravel as he accelerated towards the police station all
thoughts of breakfast erased from his mind.

'. . . and this is were the actual blood groups are done, Tara.

Hold out your thumb, there's a good little girl.'

Memories of a laboratory redolent of formaldehyde swirled inside Tara's head as she writhed uncomfortably in the unsettled shallows of the oceans of sleep. In the sepia-tinged recollections of her past a dream-lancet slashed into the pad of her thumb, oozing a bead of blood in its wake.

'What'd'you do that for? It hurt!' she heard herself pout, her voice sounding shrill as she wrestled to jam her thumb into her waiting mouth – the place any wounded digit truly belonged.

'It's alright. Police procedure,' placated her father, arm-wrestling her down and sucking the droplet into a capillary for testing. *'We've got to know what blood group you are. You see, now that I've got such an important job there are some people who might not like me any more.'*

'What, like murderers and rapists and money launderers and stuff?' asked the eight year old dream Tara who'd obviously spent far too much time in front of the telly recently.

'Ahem, yes. That sort of people. Well, in the unlikely event that you're ever kidnapped to get at me, we can actually make sure that it's all genuine. We get the kidnappers to send a blood sample. Then we do a quick test, compare it with the records and we can make sure it's really you, see?'

The sepia-tinted Tara was all eyes, quivering with excitement. *'Kidnapped! Ooooh, how exciting! Will they tie me up to a chair? Isn't that what they do when you're kidnapped? . . . kidnapped? . . . kidnapped?'*

There was a brief rustling of anorak, a groan, and, with a shock Tara awoke.

'Good morning. Did you sleep well?' Lupin asked cheerfully, fluttering his eyelids in a way he hoped was becoming.

Tara's head swam as her brain changed gear and scurried to catch up ten years. In a flash she remembered all the events of last night. The kidnapping, the journey back here, her gabbling away incessantly and the alien called Lupin fluttering his eyes at her and edging closer all night. If it had been anyone else, she might have thought he fancied her. But that wasn't the way aliens did things . . . was it?

All of a sudden she became horribly aware that she hadn't spent the night on the comfiest of mattresses. Her buttocks throbbed coldly. She shuffled miserably and cursed as the handcuffs chafed at her wrists. Rummaging about in the inside pocket of her jacket, after a few moments she produced a key. There was a brief rattling of lock mechanisms and the cuffs fell away.

'You . . . you could have taken them off at any time?' gasped Lupin as Tara tucked the handcuffs back in her inside pocket.

'Course I could. You reckon I'd trust Farson to keep his hands to himself with me in handcuffs? No way. They were just for show.'

'So why leave them on all night?' asked Calabrese, rising from the far side of the hollow, his face a picture of feyrie calculation, assessing, hoping for more information of the calibre she had supplied last night.

'There were a couple of other pressing things on my mind, in case you hadn't noticed,' she observed, looking at the pair of short grey creatures. 'It's not every day I meet up with the likes of you.'

'It has been a while since we last popped in for a visit,' mused Calabrese as Lupin checked the tuning on his favourite lute.

Confused, Tara stared at the curious instrument which bore an uncanny resemblance to medieval types she remembered from school textbooks. She shrugged and put it down to convergent musical evolution. After all, if finches on isolated islands can end up doing what lizards do on others, why shouldn't two races separated by millions of light years of empty space discover the musical properties of a vibrating string? It stood to perfect reason. At least, it did in her mind.

Lupin shuffled a little closer and said cheerily. 'Here's a little something that I wrote while you were sleeping which I think you will find eminently delightful. It concerns the unrequited yearnings of a lovelorn prince whose eyes have fallen upon a beauty in the next kingdom and ... well, I'll just sing it shall I, you'll, er, get the message soon enough.'

He pulled a simpering grin, struck a doleful chord and, pausing only to jam a finger in his ear for pitching, launched into the ninety-seventh such lovelorn ballad that he'd written during the night. It seemed that his first night sleeping with a real woman had really inspired him. No mean feat since most of the time she'd been tossing fitfully, grumbling and whimpering.

He launched into the first verse in the irritatingly nasal manner he had.

> As a bee buzzeth in the rose's throat,
> As an ousel whistleth the purest note,
> As the sunlight illumines the smallest mote,
> So do I upon thee dote.
> I dote, I dote, I do, I really, really do dote,
> I'll dote for ever, just you see if I don't
> As a mallard swimmeth on the lillied moat,
> As a weasel isn't really much like a stoat,
> As a ferryman ain't much good without a boat,
> So do I upon thee dote.
> I dote, I dote, I do, I really, really do dote,
> I'll dote for ever, just you see if I don't.
> As I feeleth chill when I'm without my coat
> As the ostrich ...

Suddenly it was too much for Tara this early in the morning. 'Got anything a bit more, er ... tuneful?'

A strangled final chord collapsed off Lupin's lute and nobody ever found out what the ostrich was, much to their obvious relief.

'Is that song not to your liking?' asked Lupin.

'No.'

'I could perform another?'

'No.'

'One which tells the story of two lovers separated by crowbars before they can actually ...'

'No!' pleaded Tara raising her hands in despair.

'Another ditty won't be necessary,' insisted Calabrese. 'Can't you see our dear guest was troubled with a less than restful night?' He turned to Tara. 'Had you not dropped off quite so swiftly in the early hours of the morning, I would have endeavoured to ensure a more comfortable position for you.'

Lupin scowled at the back of Calabrese's head. What was he doing talking to his Tara like that? All smarmy like. 'Er ... me too,' he blurted defensively. He didn't want to give her the impression he didn't care.

Calabrese edged closer. 'I do hope your dreams weren't too bad,' he oozed, desperate for her to resume his rapid education on all things genetic. It had been *so* maddening the way she'd dropped off in mid-sentence like that. 'Of course the thing you've really got to remember about cloning is that ...' and then the gentle sound of snoring. And it had only been 4 a.m.

'Dreams? What dreams?' whispered Tara backing away towards the wall of soil. How did they know about the dreams? Did they possess some kind of alien alpha wave monitor to peek into her slumbering thoughts?

'Something about kidnapping,' offered Calabrese.

Suddenly Tara's mind was filled with sepia-tinted images of the forensics lab again.

'And something about blood?' pressed Calabrese, certain this would have something to do with his crash course in genetics. After all, he now knew that DNA floated about inside bodies and so did blood. They were bound to be connected.

'Blood?' gasped Tara. 'But what's that got to do with ...?' And suddenly her mind was filled with the events of the raid on Splice of Life Patentable Biosciences Ltd. A kaleidóscope of images stampeded through the corral of her mind. Glassware somersaulted across the interior of Crickson's lab shattering into a myriad fragments. A single tell-tale fluff of yellow feather clung accusingly to the top lip of a test-tube. A blood-splattered liquidizer arced into a distant

206

wall in a corona of sparking consumer electronics. A beautiful glinting scythe of glass gleamed on the desktop. Her fingers reached out to snatch her jotter. Another hand snatched for the scythe of glass . . . Then the white hot stab of a punctured palm.

Involuntarily she clutched her bandaged hand as a final image of glinting crimson, perched on the tip of the glass, flashed across her thoughts. A damning millilitre of incontrovertible evidence, ready and waiting to be processed, assessed and blood grouped. Panic hurled her desperate thoughts backwards, conjuring up swirling images of her father proudly showing her around the forensic lab almost a decade ago and in that instant she knew it would only be a matter of time before she was a marked woman. All her biological markers were held on file for use in the event of an offspring-kidnapping scenario.

Tara quivered with terror.

'Anything amiss, miss?' asked Calabrese, desperate to know more about the possible applications of cloning.

'It'll be in Forensics already!' she panicked, staring ahead almost unseeing, focussing on a distant lab bench below Camford Constabulary and a sinister figure which bore an uncanny resemblance to a young Boris Karloff.

'And what might "it" be, pray do tell?' charmed Calabrese, staring at the exact same spot of the soil looking for inspiration.

Lupin's mouth was dangling open, his head snapping to and fro with every change of speaker. If this was Calabrese's way of getting back in Tara's good books he'd hate to see how he made enemies.

'The glass,' shrieked Tara. 'My blood. They'll trace it to me. They'll know I destroyed the lab! They'll know I stole the chickens!'

Calabrese, understanding the tone of panic more than the actual meaning, knew it was high time to act. She was vulnerable, alone, desperate. Perfect!

'My, my, it does seems that you really require our help, my dear gel,' oozed the feyrie.

'Help? What can you do?' flustered Tara biting her nails.

'You'd be surprised,' grinned Calabrese, rubbing an immodest finger tip over his chest. 'Over the last century I have striven to achieve a reputation as the finest burglariser hereabouts. You'll find none finer, I'll wager, dear gel.'

Lupin's derogatory outburst was stifled by a deftly placed heel.

'In, snaffle, out,' finished Calabrese. 'That's the way it should be. None of this creeping about.'

'Burglar, you say?' mused Tara, her attention well and truly ensnared by images of scimitar-shaped slices of glass tipped with her blood. 'Think you could break into Camford Police station, hmmm?'

Calabrese's thoughts whirred back to the last episode of *The Bill* he'd seen on CablePix and conjured up images of a large building peopled by dark-blue uniformed folk. That police station didn't look particularly brimming with immensely high security systems. 'I should consider it a challenge. Name the object of your desire.'

Lupin did his best spaniel expression and fawned up at her pathetically.

'Blood,' whispered Tara with a harshly conspiratorial tone.

'Urgh! Are you a vampire?' spluttered Lupin, who obviously put far too much credence in some of the darker ballads in his repertoire.

'My blood,' snapped Tara at Lupin. 'I need it back. Can you do it?' she asked Calabrese.

'No problem,' he beamed with a dismissive flourish.

'Today? Now?' begged Tara.

'No problem.'

Tara's eyebrows raised. 'No problem? Really?' Her jaw was just readying itself to drop in relief and amazement when suddenly she caught herself and blushed. What was she thinking, of course it would be no problem for these two to break into Camford Constabulary and nick a chunk of glass. After all, they *had* just crossed countless millions of light years in state-of-the-art alien technology, moved an entire

208

forest and buried said alien technology safely beneath. It would be a sad reflection on the state of the galaxy if they couldn't pinch a fragment of conical flask.

'Need anything else?' asked Calabrese much to Lupin's disgust.

'Well, I could do with some breakfast,' she answered as her stomach announced its presence in no uncertain terms.

'No prob . . .' began Calabrese with another expansive gesture before Tara's expression darkened suddenly and the tides of suspicion swept back in.

'Hang on,' she snapped. 'Why are you being so nice, eh? What's in this for you?'

'Yeah, why are *you* being so nice?' hissed Lupin. 'That's my job . . .'

Calabrese smiled his most accommodating smile. 'Oh please. This is just my way of taking advantage of a splendid chance to make amends, dear girl. A golden opportunity to aid a delightful damsel in obvious distress. A once-in-a-lifetime occasion to right a wrong wrought by our own selfish and thoughtless actions.' He fluttered his eyelids again and Lupin growled in protective jealousy.

'And the truth now?' asked Tara.

'I want information,' stated Calabrese matter-of-factly. 'Here's the deal. You tell me absolutely everything else you know about genetics, the application of cloning technology and current advances in embryonic incubative systems and I retrieve any evidence you want from Forensics.'

'No strings?'

'You've got no choice,' stated Calabrese, and knew he had a deal. At a tiny spot, just above his spleen, he felt a twinge of wickedness growing. The morning had definitely started well.

Surfing on a curling breaker of screaming engine revs Chief Inspector Ness's two and a half litre Rover slewed into the back car park of Camford Constabulary. There was a screech of brakes and the dark green monster slid to a halt in his private space. In a second he was out and striding toward the door, zapping his infra-red key fob over his shoulder with a furious jab of his thumb. The Rover dutifully flashed its lights at him, locked its doors and settled down for a day's gentle snoozing in the car park. It would almost certainly be the calmest thing in the whole of the station, all day.

Ness slammed the heel of his hand into the door of the police station and powered on through it unstoppably, his pace barely faltering as the mobile phone in his top pocket warbled into life. It hadn't even begun its second trill before it was jammed against the side of his head. 'You're through to the Big Cuddly Uncle Copper Crime Hotline, hello. I'm really not in the mood to talk to you right now so call back later. Unless you're ringing about lights in the sky the other morning, in which case, go away and get a life. There are no such thing as aliens, clear?' Before the caller could begin to mention the fact that fifty thousand quids' worth of brand new scientific equipment had mysteriously vanished during the night from TechGen Labs, Ness's thumb severed the connection.

Two floors above, PC Plain yawned, glanced at the clock on the wall and began shuffling papers together in readiness for sloping off quick-sharp just as soon as his shift finished. Overall it had been an uneventful night, a few punch-ups at closing time, the odd stolen car, a missing cat, a plethora of complaints about students racing hijacked punts along the River Camf. All routine stuff for any Ancient University City. Easy to deal with, simple to file. A piece of cake to slide off onto someone else's desk. Oh, all except that kidnapping outside *The Monocle and Asparagus*. That was going to require actual work. Plain sighed. How damned inconvenient of them to do it when he was on shift.

Soon he would find out just how inconvenient it really was.

'Plain!' bawled Ness even before the lift doors had opened. Every organ in that PC's body winced and "Uh-oh"-ed in its own unique way. The three-quarter inch pile of his hair stood nervously erect over the whole of his head, giving him the expression of a startled hedgehog. What had he done? Or not done?

'Plain, you idiot! Why was I not informed as soon as it happened?' bellowed Ness striding across the office. Several dozen heads of other officers hid behind numerous desks and computer monitors. 'D'you think it's pleasant to find out about it via the morning post, do you? What are you paid for, eh?' With one final raptorial leap Ness was at the duty officer's desk, hands already eager to close around Plain's throat.

'Perhaps if you could furnish me with somewhat more information, Sir, I ... er, might be able to ...'

'Kidnapping!' snarled Ness pounding his fists on the desk and leering forward like an irate silverback mountain gorilla. 'Why the Hell wasn't I told about it?'

'Told about the kidnapping, Sir?' spluttered Plain wondering for a moment if he hadn't in fact dropped off into a particular lucid nightmare. He winced as he scraped the heel of his standard issue police size ten down the front of his shin. Bad news, this was real. 'It ... It didn't seem appropriate to apprise you of that situation, Sir. Er ... after all, you get little enough time with your family as it is, Sir, without disturbing your evening to report a simple kidnapping.' He tried a simpering smile.

It didn't work.

'Have you even the faintest idea who it was that was kidnapped, hmmm?' A pulse of an artery twitched at Ness's temple. 'Wasn't appropriate, wasn't it?'

'Er, no, Sir, we are still looking into the identity of the young lady who was so unexpectedly snatched from ...' Desperately Plain was rummaging through a sheaf of paperwork on the desk before him. A task not made any the simpler by the blasts of Ness's breath blowing them in all directions. And all the time his mind was whirring with flurried questions. Was this one of Ness's dreaded snap unannounced inspections? Had they reached 'Kidnapping' in the alphabet of crime so soon? It only seemed like yesterday that arson investigations were under Ness's exacting spotlight. Plain grabbed at a sheet of paper and peered at it. 'Er

... as yet, Sir, nobody in the entirety of Camford has reported receiving a ransom note, but her name appears to be T ...'

'*I'm* reporting a ransom note!' yelled Ness.

Plain's eyebrows scrambled up his forehead as if in some desperate attempt to hide in his hair. 'You, Sir, but ...'

Ness slapped the ransom note noisily on the desk, the draught scattering more paperwork in all directions in a blizzard of chaos. Plain's eyes bugged out as he stared at the uneven array of letters. Throughout the office a dozen constables were straining to see the note, stretching like seedlings racing for a crack of light in a cupboard door.

'First post today,' growled Ness jabbing the note with an irate index finger. 'A gas bill and a ransom note! What have you got to say to that?'

'That modernisation scheme at the Sorting Office really did the job, didn't it,' offered Plain.

The Chief Inspector made the type of noise in his throat that you don't want to hear from a wild doberman in a dark alley. 'Why wasn't I informed that my Tara had been stolen from under our very noses?'

Plain felt a trickle of nervous sweat squeeze its way out between his third and fourth lumbar vertebrae and head for the relative safety of his boxer shorts. 'Under your noses, Sir? The report we had was that it all happened outside *The Monocle and Asparagus*' pleaded Plain. 'And the description wasn't exactly a perfect match to your daughter ...'

'Eye witnesses, pah! I know what my daughter looks like! I don't need some spotty teenager telling me,' fumed Ness. 'What kind of a witness did you have anyway? Labrador and whitestick, perhaps? Drugged up to the eyeballs? You know the public always exaggerate when they're talking to us. Makes them feel important, especially drunkards falling out of real ale hostelries at all hours of the night.'

Plain nodded submissively and decided it would be safer for his bodily particles if he didn't mention the fact that young Tiberius Douglas had only necked a half of Pedigree. He also thought it unwise to mention the fact that some eyewitnesses claim to have seen a rather suspicious looking character dressed as Bozo the clown lurking around the vicinity shortly after the actual incident.

'Now let's get this straight,' continued Ness. 'There was only one kidnapping last night, right?' Plain made a show of consulting his papers and nodded warily.

'One kidnapping, one girl missing. QED! Bring that report,' snarled Ness snatching up the ransom note and whirling on his heels. 'And follow me,' he added over his shoulder.

Plain stared at the clock on the wall. 'Sir? May I remind you that my shift finished several minutes ago.'

'No,' barked the Chief Inspector accelerating across the office, seemingly totally unaware that he was still wearing his finest Marks and Spencer's tartan carpet slippers. 'There's no time to lose.' His voice echoed down the stairwell as he clattered off towards the dark cool, clamminess of Boscombe's haunt.

Much to the amazement and irritation of a queue of women in their Vauxhall Corsas, a large, gaudily painted van dripping with tents and firewood stopped suddenly in the entrance to Sainway's car park. The driver leapt out in a plume of incense and a rattling of crystals, stooped low and examined a strange runic symbol chalked on the tarmac. He scratched his head, shrugged and leapt back into the cab. There was a sudden scattering of Corsas as the van crunched its gears into reverse and backed up.

Pausing only to shout a series of indecipherable instructions to the drivers of a 1964 Bedford Coach and an aging Land Rover sporting a quarter-size painting of a killer whale, the van headed off in the direction of the Regal Greens Golf Course.

The women in the Corsas cursed politely and filed into Sainway's for the weekly shop.

Lance Farson slouched against the wall of the lab and cursed as Crickson's voice echoed throughout the whole of the

Splice of Life Patentable Biosciences Ltd building. He had been barking endless orders for the past half hour, haranguing either, or both, of the folks from 'DN-Aids Inc' as they unloaded his order from the back of an unmarked transit and shoved it into a hastily cleared corner of the recently commandeered laboratory. It was disturbing Farson's worries about Sacramento's attempts to divert the course of certain ransom notes. Had he been successful? Or was the credibility of GAIA unravelling at this very instant?

'That's it, that's it. In that lab there to the right. C'mon, I haven't got all day,' shouted Crickson his white coated arm blurring wildly as he pointed down the corridor. 'Come on, come on, get a move on. The tides of science wait for no man, and all that. Mind that step! Have you *any* idea how delicate that GENE-Erator (TM) is? That's precision scientific equipment that is, one knock and the entire sub-helix doubler array will need realignment. And that could take weeks! No, no! Careful with that guanine exciter diode, it's worth over three hundred quid and I only ordered one ...'

Alistair shrugged and Miles uttered a scathing Wandsworthian curse. Farson covered his ears and moaned as the air was bombarded with more words per minute than an overexcited racing commentator could spit out.

But suddenly the piercing gaze of Crickson fell on his inert form huddling in the corner. 'You, Farson! Don't just stand there. Give me a hand with this,' shouted Crickson tearing acres of bubble wrap off the better part of fifty grand's worth of scientific equipment. 'Come on, here, grab this cytosine delivery tubule.' The Professor pointed to an outlet and waggled what looked like an eighteen inch length of B&Q's cheapest garden hosepipe available from all good out-of-town shopping complexes at about a quid and a half. 'Connect it to that output faucet,' he ordered, blissfully unaware that the eighty-seven pounds and ninety-three pence worth of DN-Aids Inc cytosine delivery tubule was in fact an eighteen inch length of B&Q's cheapest garden hosepipe available from all good out-of-town shopping complexes at about one pound fifty.

Farson shrugged, pushed himself off the wall and attempted to put away thoughts of just what he would do to a certain Miss Ness when he laid his hands on her. He attempted to console himself with the thin comfort that the quicker Crickson made his 'culinary breakthrough of the millennium' then the quicker he'd be off staking claims to patents, or whizzing across the world trying to flog Project CFC to the first fast food franchise that so much as licked its corporate lips. And the quicker that he'd be able to get back to cajoling Striebley to continue developing his solar rechargeable King Edward lying forlornly abandoned in its dust-covered tank in the corner. If only he could get the Doc to up the power output tenfold then a geostationary satellite would be back on the cards and . . .

Suddenly his thoughts were shattered as Striebley sprang in through the door. 'Good news,' he announced to Crickson sounding somewhat unconvinced. 'You'll be glad to hear that phone call was from one of Chief Inspector Ness's minions who regrets to inform us that he won't be attending to our own private crime scene today. It seems his daughter's done a runner and he's a bit tied up investigating it.'

Crickson's face wrinkled into a grin.

Behind the bulk of the GENE-Erator, Farson's jaw dropped. 'Done a runner?' What was that girl playing at? How could he have been so stupid to trust her? He should have known that anyone who drank Bloody Helgas and knew the serial number of USS *Voyager* would have been unreliable.

'A day free from the pounding of constabulary boots, ahhhh, bliss!' grinned Crickson. Striebley shook his head, and wasn't sure it would be quite so blissful. A day free from pounding constabulary boots meant another day Crickson's lab was festooned with blue and white tape, and another day that he'd be inhabiting *his* lab. Striebley saw the chances of getting back to his King Edward sailing off towards a very distant horizon. The only way he was going to get rid of Crickson now was to add his not-inconsiderable scientific expertise to Project CFC. Oh, cruel fates!

'Come on,' snapped Crickson slapping eighteen inches of hosepipe against his palm irritably. 'Work, work, work!'

Striebley pushed Farson out of the way, snatched the cytosine delivery tube and, trying his best to ignore the B&Q barcode, jammed it onto the outlet marked with a red 'C'. Next to it were three others, 'G', 'A' and 'T', each corresponding to one of the other three essential ingredients to manufacture DNA, guanine, adenine and thymine.

'Ere, Doc, that's th'lot,' sniffed Miles, the managing director of DN-Aids Inc, dropping an Apple Mac heavily onto the desk. Carefully he tried to hide the barely erased label declaring it to be 'Property of H.M. Prison Wandsworth.'

'Sign 'ere, Doc,' sniffed Alistair and thrust a rusting clipboard under Crickson's scientific nose.

'What did you say?' came the imperious reply.

'Sign 'ere, Doc. C'mon, I've got other orders t'steal . . . er, collect, y'know?'

'"Doc"?' hissed Crickson peering over his half moons and tapping at a radio-sensitive name badge pinned to his breast pocket cuff. 'What does this say?'

'"DN-Aids Inc Curie-Counter Name Badge",' read the delivery man with another noisy inhalation of nasal mucus.

'No, no! The name, the name!' hissed Crickson.

'Oh, Professor Cricks . . .'

'Exactly. "Professor"!' insisted Crickson.

'Yeah, so y'got a promotion. Woopie-doo. Sign'ere,' insisted the delivery man heart-warmingly underwhelmed. A grubby and bitten index finger pounded on the top sheet.

Crickson made a face and scrawled a suitably illegible signature behind the 'X'.

'Bailiffs'll be round for the payment a week on Tuesday, alright? Make it cash, will you, only it's easier t'launder, see?' grinned Alistair and headed out before Crickson had a chance to object.

'Ignorant plebians,' scorned Crickson under his breath and turned his attention back to the Transit-load of equipment scattered in the corner of the lab. If it all worked the way he was certain it would he'd have the Nobel Prize for Culinary Genetics by a week next Tuesday. All he had to do now was assemble the damn thing.

'Right, Striebley, align that Base-Jumper Delivery System (TM) over by the GENE-Erator (TM) and you, Farson, unpack those Amniotic Tanks (TM), clear? Well go on then!'

Crickson peered at the instruction manual open on the bench and rubbed his hands with glee. Oh, yes, Project CFC was coming along very nicely indeed thankyou very much especially today without police interference.

The unmistakable sound of Michelins smearing across tarmac echoed around the environs of *The Monocle and Asparagus* and PC Plain leapt out of the Rover. Already a significant darkening of his chin and eyesockets showed that he'd been awake far too long. With a flourish of eager constabulary efficiency he tugged open the rear passenger door and a string of questions rattled out from Chief Inspector Ness. 'What? What is it? Why've we stopped?'

'We're here,' placated Plain sweeping an inviting hand over a very insignificant looking portion of Ancient Camford's streetage. Ness blinked at the cracked flags. A scrunched up Cheese and Chives Flavour crisp packet trundled across his field of view looking like some odd grazing animal on a vast wasteland savanna.

'And where, precisely is here, hmmm?'

'The site of last night's abduction,' tutted Plain as he ducked around the rear of the squad car and covertly checked his report sheet just to be sure. In a moment he had swept open the other rear door and a figure, bearing an uncanny resemblance to a young Boris Karloff, uncurled itself onto the pavement. He stood clutching his mock-crocodile forensics bag and stared disdainfully at the paving stones pock-marked with chewing gum and the signs that pigeons had been there.

'Not exactly bursting with clues, is it?' complained Doctor Boscombe.

'If it was, I wouldn't need you, would I? You'd still be

working on that Splice of Life case,' snapped Ness. 'I mean, if the kidnapper had just happened to leave a partly used cardboard clip of matches with a conveniently scribbled name and address just *lying* in the road, well, I wouldn't be requiring you to wring the tiniest of clues out of this scene, now would I?'

'You do have a point there,' conceded Boscombe after making a show of giving the matter some thought by tapping his front teeth with the edge of his antique brass-framed magnifying glass.

'Accurate, valid and eminently unquestionable,' he mused.

'So get wringing,' barked Ness. 'C'mon, there's bound to be a fingerprint or ten on that drainpipe, or a footprint over in that dirt there, or a shredded fragment of floral print dress torn from her hem as she struggled bravely with her captor and . . .'

'Do you mind?' admonished Boscombe, his eyebrows arching. 'Melodrama brings me out in a rash.' And with a haughty flurry of professionalism, he donned his protective knee-pads and, like some devoted pilgrim on a mission of inner cleansing, fell as if in prayer and turned his expansive attention to the pavement in hand.

Through the refractive powers of his trusty Victorian lens, the humble expanse of flagging took on a life of its very own, magnified into crystal surreality. The vast baseball bats of ant's antennae swung wildly across his field of vision and their jaws wrestled with the freshly added concretion of a part-sucked Murray Mint. Enormous clumps of ageing moss ballooned from between the cracks and fought for supremacy over stray strips of fur blown from The Feline Groovy Kitten Coiffeurie. And the swirling whorls of a strangely elongated toe-print in the dust nestled around each other like the walls of the Hampton Court Maze, parallel, never touching and . . .

Suddenly Boscombe blinked. Toe-print? His eyes snatched at the image with the manic fervour of a parched Bedouin in a sandstorm. He grasped at every curved ridge, devoured every tented loop and accidental pocket, sucked every ounce of detail from each wriggling bifurcation.

218

And even before he reached for the casting compound in the vain hope of preserving this tangible evidence, he knew that this was a footprint the like of which he had never seen before. 'Found anything?' snapped Ness eagerly, standing far too close for Boscombe's comfort as he poured in the Polyfilla. 'What is it? What've you got?'

Boscombe looked up at the Chief Inspector and wrinkling his forehead meaningfully delivered the very phrase that any forensic scientist would quite simply die for. 'It's a footprint, Chief Inspector. A footprint the like of which I have never seen before.'

Deep in the bowels of Camford Police Station, directly below a large and highly polished stainless steel dissecting table, lay a ten inch cast iron grating. It was innocently minding its own business, quietly happy in the sure and certain knowledge that, over the years it had squatted quietly there in the mouth of the main drainage sluice of the post-mortem room's hermetically sealed flooring, it had never once allowed anything valuable to get past it that shouldn't. It knew that without its lightning reflexes and ready vigilance fifeen scalpels, twelve biros and countless scraps of forensi-cally significant fluff would have vanished forever into the Camford sewerage system. The grating's proudest and most exciting moment had been only a few scant months ago when it had leapt a full millimetre to the right, twisted and saved Doc Boscombe's filing cabinet keys from a very sticky end. It still thrilled with pride when it thought about that one.

Little did it expect that today it would add another sensation to its growing dictionary. The sensation of surprise.

It was minding its own business, contemplating the possibility of a career progression to the heady heights of air conditioning, when *something* stroked its back side. Before it had the chance to take evasive action ten digits entwined themselves about its person and, with nary a by-your-leave, it was unseated and cast cruelly aside upon the cold tile floor. All it could do was watch helplessly as a pair of grey-skinned creatures leapt out of the drain and slapped wetly onto the floor.

'You couldn't have found a better way in, could you?' complained Lupin, dripping sarcasm and stinking water in almost equal proportions.

'Do you want them to know we're here,' hissed Calabrese peeling a sodden tissue off his chest. 'We had no choice but to enter that way.'

'What's wrong with just hurling a brick through the window? That always works. At least it did on CablePix. Quick, not very elegant, but it smells a hell of a lot better. And there's far less chance of catching something nasty. Did you see the size of some of those rats? Did you?'

'A brick through a window,' mused Calabrese stroking his chin as if in deep contemplation. 'A grand plan, Lupin. However, if you would care to take a good look around . . .' He swept a drainage-stained arm around the examination room. 'In case it had escaped your attention, there is a distinct lack of readily smashable windows.'

'Well, what about a chimney to squirm down, or something. There just must have been a less nasally challenging way in. If I don't come down with something nasty I'll be amazed . . .'

'Stop complaining,' growled Calabrese, suddenly losing patience. 'We're here now, we're in. It's time to get down to business. Time to save your dearly beloved.'

A vision in anorak surrounded by romantic pink edging flashed across Lupin's mind. 'Tara. Tara,' he whimpered clutching his hands beneath his chin. It was only by a great effort of will that he tugged himself back to the reality of the situation. 'Now hold on a minute. You never did explain this business properly. How exactly *are* we going to save her?'

'Gah! I see that the playing of ballads and recitation of heroic poetry doesn't stimulate logical thought,' spat Calabrese with a withering tone.

'There's no need to be like that,' muttered Lupin looking at his feet. Upon catching sight of the state of them he suddenly wished he hadn't. There were things stuck to them that he'd rather not know about.

'Are you telling me you can't see this as the chance you've been after? The golden opportunity of your life?' It was a minor wonder that Calabrese didn't snake a conspiratomal arm around Lupin's shoulders. 'Your one big break at overwhelming heroism.'

'Me? A Hero?' gagged Lupin, wondering precisely how a deserted forensics lab could possibly help in the hero stakes. The only thing he could see it raising the chances of so far was contracting any one of a half dozen gut-rotting diseases.

Calabrese was staring at Lupin in that disturbingly overenthusiastic way he had. 'This is your chance to really rise in your dearly belusted's opinion. By the time she sees you again Tara will be deeply in your debt, ready to give you absolutely anything you desire.'

Lupin's ears reddened with anticipation ... 'Absolutely anything?' he simpered, visions of fresh fern beds shimmering before his doting eyes. Had there been a buttercup in reach he would almost certainly have been limply tugging its petals off one by one.

'Absolutely anything. Now pay attention,' hissed Calabrese slapping the fawning feyrie around the cheeks. 'Ten minute's work here and she'll be yours. You'll be her hero. The one who saved her from certain incarceration. In that office, over there,' he pointed a dripping arm, 'is a test-tube and piece of glass she needs to free her from the burden of imprisonment and torture. Go fetch it!'

Calabrese's words stirred something deep in Lupin's heart. He could save her from all that, just by grabbing some bits of glass? Was that really possible? And then he thought of all the heroic poems he had sung. Ninety-odd per cent of them had some muscle-bound hunk galloping off on an endless search for some chunk of crystal, or an axe, or something. Why was this any different? He *was* Tara's hero! She *would* fall for him!

With an eager slapping of bare feet on ceramics he was off in search of the Glass Scythe of Circumstantial Evidence and the Terrible Test-Tube of Truth. This was certain to make a cracking ballad, oh yes! His deeds would be sung about in nasal tones for generations to come.

Calabrese smirked as he watched Lupin go. There were times when he was so easily led. Especially by organs other than his brain.

But he himself didn't remain motionless for long. In the instant that Lupin disappeared into Boscombe's office Calabrese spun on his heels, cracked his knuckles and began searching desperately along the shelves, his mind fizzing with the recently imparted knowledge of all things genetical. He knew he didn't have long to find what he sought. A minute, perhaps two whilst Lupin ransacked Boscombe's desk.

Calabrese's eyes pored eagerly over the miles of shelving, ignoring boxes of gloves, skipping over stacks of beakers, passing vast crates of variously sized plastic bags until, much to his relief, he found them.

It was just as Tara had described them. Thousands of them scattered in a single large corrugated cardboard box. In a blur of grey fingers he had snatched a single tube and stopper out. Then he leapt down the shelving a little further and tugged open another receptacle. In seconds he had ripped the sterile package from the lancet and was standing in the examination room, breathing deeply, the glinting blade raised and pointing directly at his left thumb pad. A tiny grey tongue licked apprehensively at his lips as he readied himself to strike, steeling himself for the short sharp shock. He took a last breath, held it tight and silently the razor-sharp lancet slashed down. Wincing, he twitched at the last second. The blade bounced off his grey thumb with no effect.

Cursing, he tried again. This time with just a little more force. Just enough to pierce the skin but not so much that it hurt too much. It was a hard balance to find.

It was only after three more attempts that he succeeded. A sphere of dark blood oozed from his thumb and was squeezed into the tube. Quickly, punctured opposing digit firmly in mouth, he stoppered the tube and pattered into

Boscombe's office.

'Found it yet?' he hissed at Lupin, thumb behind his back.

'Yes, yes!' cried the diminutive feyrie. 'Look!' joyously he held out the Terrible Test-Tube of Truth and the Glass Scythe of Circumstantial Evidence.

Calabrese snatched the tube, glared at the label and nodded in curt confirmation. 'Where was it?'

'Up there, just next to that pile of bent wire things,' he pointed at a pot of paper clips blissfully unaware that Calabrese was carefully peeling off the label. In a second he had slapped it onto the new tube.

'That's it! Perfect. Let's go,' pushed Calabrese thrusting the Terrible Test-Tube of Truth back into Lupin's trembling hand and shoving him towards the door and the open drain.

Unseen, he hurled something onto the desk and scurried out after him. A test-tube of freshly taken blood landed on Boscombe's desk right next to a small pot of paper clips.

'Can't we go out another way?' whined Lupin staring into the pitch blackness of the drain.

'There's no time,' barked Calabrese.

'But, how can I be a hero and sweep Tara off her beautifully delicious feet if I appear before her smelling like this.'

'She'll love it,' hurried Calabrese lying with desperate improvisation. 'One whiff and she'll really appreciate the lengths to which you'll go to aid her in times of trouble. You will blossom in her estimation!'

'You reckon?'

'No doubt.'

Lupin's face cracked into a beaming smile as he held his nose and dived into the drain, clutching his prizes.

Calabrese shook his head, grinned and followed.

Much to the relief of the grating it was carefully replaced by the strange intruders. And a good job too. Sackable offence that was, not being on duty at all times. Sackable.

Calabrese was only a scant three yards down the drain when the door to the forensics lab was shoved open and a crash helmeted traffic policeman stomped in wearing full leathers and a Dayglo yellow waistcoat.

'Doctor Boscombe?' came the muffled query. 'Hello? Is there anybody here? I've come for the blood tests. Hello?' His boot heels struck sharp echoes off the tiled floor as he marched towards the office. 'Anything needs taking over to Splice of Life besides the DNA files?'

His vast padded gauntlets punched open the door and, moving like some deep sea diver at fifty fathoms, he went in, eyes peering out through tinted visor. In moments his gaze settled on a single stoppered test-tube lying next to a pot of paper clips. There was a muffled noise of relief inside his helmet and five bulbous leathern fingers fumbled their way around the tiny receptacle and popped it into his jacket pocket. He also grabbed a pair of lever arch files containing all the current combined DNA profiles for known criminals and shoved them into his rucksack.

In seconds he had stomped out and was heading for the car park, a muffled whistling emanating from inside his helmet as he thought of his BMW eleven hundred nestling between his leathered thighs.

Twenty feet or so away through several thicknesses of wall, a brunette teenager squatted in a dark alley and kept a careful watch on a square manhole inspection cover. Even though she was expecting it, and had seen the same sight on countless American movies, she still almost jumped out of her skin when the cast iron cover leapt upwards and was hurled suddenly sideways. It landed with a clatter and a dripping Lupin sprang out into the narrow alley standing in his best impersonation of a heroic pose.

'I have it!' he declared to Tara and leapt across to her. With an unnecessary flourish he dropped the Glass Scythe of Circumstantial Evidence and the Terrible Test-Tube of Truth at her feet and looked eagerly up, blinking his almond-shaped eyes with heroic winsomeness. He looked for all the world like some bald grey chihuahua who was overjoyed at having finally learned to fetch.

'That's it, that's it!' she cried with a flood of relief as she instantly recognised the shard of bloodstained glassware.

Unheralded, a dripping Calabrese emerged from the drain.

'You did it!' she thrilled, wrinkling her nose as the aroma of ancient sewerage systems floated unignorably into nasal range.

'Oh, it was nothing. Honestly,' simpered Lupin drawing patterns on the alley floor with the drips from his toes.

Calabrese stifled a chuckle and shoved the manhole cover back into place with a low grating of metal.

'You don't know what this means to me,' smiled Tara. 'If my father had found out, then . . .'

'No details needed,' proclaimed Lupin with a dismissive wave, adding self depreciatingly. 'It was nothing, really. A mere bagatelle. For you I would climb . . .'

'If there's anything I can do . . .' began Tara sensing a song coming on.

Lupin's heart leapt. He looked up at her, fluttered his eyelids and tried desperately to ignore the fact that something brown and mercifully unidentifiable was slithering down between his shoulder blades. 'Well, my dear, as a matter of fact . . .' he began, clenching his fists coyly beneath his chin in as endearing a manner as he could muster under the circumstances. 'I . . . I was wondering if . . . er . . . when I'm cleaned up a bit . . . if you and I could . . . well . . . I was wondering if . . .'

'If you've got a computer we could borrow?' blurted Calabrese suddenly elbowing Lupin out of the way.

'Computer?' repeated Tara, shocked. 'Well, I've got one in my room but . . .'

'Computer?' gagged Lupin spinning angrily on his heel and staring accusingly at Calabrese. 'You can't. Not now. Not while I'm just about to ask her to . . .'

'With modem?' asked the taller, and somehow cleaner, of the two feyries.

'Modem? Er, yes sure . . .' gasped Tara, bewildered.

'And fax?'

'Now hold on just a minute!' objected Lupin, fists planted effeminately on his narrow hips. He was ignored.

'It's got e-mail, but that's near enough, isn't it?' answered Tara, sure that aliens of their calibre were bound to know the difference.

'If you say so. Well, come on then, lead on,' declared Calabrese rubbing his palms enthusiastically and skipping off down the alley.

'Hold on a minute, not so fast. There's something I really have to do.' Tara looked down at Lupin standing forlornly in a growing puddle, his toes angled fourteen degrees too close together. His eyes, almond pools of frustrated misery, stared imploringly back at her like some Madagascan marsupial. He attempted a smile. It squirmed around his upper lip, twitched and mutated into an embarrassing grimace.

But despite this Tara knew in her heart of hearts what she had to do. He *had* gone to all the trouble of fetching that pair of forensically damning glassware, after all. She took a breath, held her nose and bent out of the sky towards him. He watched, amazed as she swept forwards, her hair tumbling wildly around her face, the creaking of her anorak filling his ears, her arm reaching out in embrace . . . He couldn't help it. He closed his eyes, threw his arms wide and puckered up, his dreams surfing in on a neap tide of overwhelming desire.

Tara snatched the shard of beaker and the test-tube, spun on her heels and within three strides was cheerfully smashing them into a cast iron Camford Borough Council litter bin.

'Now, what is it about this computer?' Lupin heard her asking Calabrese a moment later over the clatter of footfalls. With a snarl he opened his eyes and glared at their backs as they ducked away down another little-frequented alley.

'Allow me to explain,' answered Calabrese, his voice already fading.

'That's gratitude,' tutted Lupin miserably, kicking a Sainway's own brand cola can against the wall and wincing. Suddenly he felt very, very alone. 'Here. Hang on, wait for me!' he cried and sprinted off after them trying to hide a limp. With a slapping of feet he vanished around the corner.

In the back carpark of Camford Police Station a motorbike policeman flicked the electronic ignition of his BMW eleven hundred and thrilled as far too much power was blasted noisily from a pair of far too large exhaust pipes. Gently, like a Grand National jockey, he patted the gleaming fuel tank of the beast, clicked it into gear and, with a deft flick of the wrist roared off in the direction of a certain laboratory on Edison Boulevard.

As the bike's echoes rattled into Calabrese's earshot he grinned in the sure and certain knowledge that everything was going just right.

A Postcard from Tau Ceti?

The few cubic litres of air which lurked behind a twenty inch colour monitor were rapidly tending towards the bluer end of the spectrum. Doctor Striebley spat another dozen choice expletives into the atmosphere as the rainbow-loomed scart plug refused, yet again, to nestle snugly in the socket.

'Well? Well? Have you done it yet?' called Professor Crickson hoarsely from the far side of the array of newly delivered DN-Aids Inc equipment.

'Do you think I'd be swearing so profusely if I had?' snapped back Striebley. The last seven hours of Crickson's hectoring instructions had done little to foster patience.

'Judging by the current rate of obscenity delivery, yes,' answered Crickson.

Not for the first time Striebley considered how fatal it would be for Crickson if one of the fifty gallon Amniotic Tanks (TM) were to collide with his head from a height of fifteen feet or so. It was an experiment he was desperate to try out. But sadly, until Crickson was safely back in his own laboratory upstairs there would be no chance of Striebley ever doing any of his experiments. His beloved solar-rechargeable King Edward lay forgotten in the far corner of the lab and it had seemed like days since he had checked on the hypersensitive radio telescope receiver array perched on the roof. Had it received anything useful recently? Could there even now be a single interstellar message waiting on his cosmic answerphone?

It had been one of the first long term experiments he had set up. Wistfully his thoughts frolicked back to the day he had first tried to persuade Crickson of its validity. Every detail of that conversation shimmered before his mind's eye in crystal clear recollection. He had known that it wasn't strictly within the field of research of Splice of Life Patentable Biosciences Ltd but he had to try it.

'You want to do what?' Crickson had spluttered two years previously.

'Mount a hypersensitive radio receiver array on the roof,' Striebley had answered proudly, his confidence fired by a most enlightening chat with Farson. It was so heartening the way his little face had lit up beneath that red fringe of his at the prospect of contacting extraterrestrials. Nice, that.

Crickson had shook his head in disbelief. 'What? So that you can tune in on mobile phone conversations in the University and rip off ideas?'

'Nothing quite so close to home,' Striebley had grinned in as enigmatic a way as he could muster.

'Ooooh, MIT or NASA?' grinned Crickson, suddenly becoming interested. Bugging the Americans was bound to unearth some handy little secrets.

'No. A bit further afield,' trembled Striebley and pointed heavenwards.

'You want to spend hundreds of thousands of pounds on a blinking radio dish so you can sit there listening to the conversations in the ether like some nosey old git next door with a glass to the wall?'

'In a manner of speaking that's more or less . . .'

'What the hell for? What d'you hope to get out of it, eh?'

Striebley, straining behind the colour monitor, smiled with pride as he recalled his answer. Well, actually it had been Farson's answer, but it was so good, bound to get Crickson's attention. 'Secrets,' he had whispered.

'You can get secrets by just hacking into MIT, or . . .'

'Not secrets like *these*. Not the secrets of the vital techniques necessary to achieve suspended animation for deep space travel.'

'Eh?'

'What do MIT know about, for example, the hundreds of subtle steps on the path to tissue regeneration?'

'Nothing the last time I looked.'

'Aha,' grinned Striebley as if he had some inkling into

these matters. 'And who knows what other readily patentable secrets are zipping about in the ether around Tau Ceti or Epsilon Eridani, just waiting to be overheard and claimed as our very own, eh?'

And Crickson's eyes had lit up.

'The patentable franchises on our adaptations of alien biotechnology could be worth millions! Billions,' pushed Striebley.

'Of course!' Crickson had shrieked. 'It's brilliant! Why hasn't anyone thought of it before? We just set up a radio dish pointed at the stars and ... Hang on a minute ...' A dark cloud of despondency had drossed the Professor's face. 'Is this some kind of sick joke?' he had snapped. 'They *have* thought of it before. NASA has just poured millions of dollars into blinking Project Phoenix! How the hell can we compete with that?'

And Striebley had tapped his nose, looked over his shoulder and there and then two years ago had uttered those immortal project launching words: 'Cause NASA've got it *all* wrong, that's why. More money than sense they have. They're looking the wrong way. Tuned to the wrong frequency,' Striebley had insisted. 'Even with the best radio you're never going to hear the top ten if you're tuned to Radio Four, are you?'

'Eh?'

'Look, they're interested in 1.420 GHz. The background hiss given off by hydrogen. They reckon that just because every astronomer on earth gets bugged by hissy hydrogen that alien astronomers would too and so would send a message in with the static, or at half the frequency, or something. They're totally mad. How many radio hams d'you know who tune into the static when they want to talk to their mates, eh?'

'And what frequency do *you* suggest for our first contact?' Crickson had asked warily.

'Ahhh. It won't be first contact though, will it? That's where NASA've got it all wrong, see? They've been here before!' he pointed heavenward.

'Been here before,' Crickson had repeated unconvinced.

'Thousands of years ago. They came just as our first inklings of language was starting, when we were still in caves and furs and stuff. And they left a clue to the correct contact frequency. It was a seed that spread throughout every language.'

'A seed?'

'Yeah, look, you can't deny that every race on Earth has a word for "Sky" right? And it's a reasonable assumption that the vast majority of races have a word for "Pie" – well, except for the Eskimos, of course. But they've always had trouble with languages. I mean, they've got ninety-eight different words for snow. Anyway: "What's this single succulent nub of linguistic wisdom that'll lead us to unlock the contact frequency?" I hear you asking.'

'Get on with it,' Crickson had hissed, his natural overdose of scepticism rearing its ugly head again. 'I haven't got time or this.'

'Pie in the Sky!' Striebley had declared to an underwhelming response from Crickson.

'Have you been at the industrial methanol again?'

'No, listen. Think of all the places where the word "Pie" crops up at vital junctures in mankind's development. What was man's first invention, eh?'

'The wheel?'

'No, no, before that.'

'The axle?'

'No, it's fire! And it's dripping with references to "Pie". Funeral pyre. Pyromania. Pyromancy. And what about geometry, eh? We'd still be in caves without geometry and geometry would be in a pretty sad state without things pertaining to "Pie". Just ask yourself where triangles would be without Pythagoras. Where would circles be without that fundamental mathematical constant Pi? Is this all coincidence? All chance? I think not. This is a message! And it's been waiting thousands of years to show us the truth, but only when we were ready. "Pie in the Sky." It's telling us to tune in to 3.1415 Ghz! That way.' And once again he pointed heavenwards.

Surprisingly Crickson had actually agreed to let him stick a dish on the roof, but only after getting the desperate Striebley to agree that it did not interfere with any business of Splice of Life and that he could get BSkyB on it.

So far, in the two years it had been straining desperately into the vast unknown swathes of cosmic infinity, Streibley's dish had collected nothing but heaps of static, the entire output of BSkyB, several hundred hours of interference from the local taxi company and a liberal smattering of guano from the local pigeon population. As for any inkling of how to make the perfect Tau Ceti souffle . . . nothing.

But somehow, for Striebley, hope sprang eternal. They were out there, maybe today would be the day they called to say 'Hello Again!'

'Hello? Hello? Have you fallen asleep?' shouted the angry voice of Crickson snapping Striebley back to the all-too-present world of a very stubborn scart socket in the back of a mass of scientific gubbins.

'Er, no, no. I . . . ah, there!' With one last knuckle-scraping shove he rammed the twenty-four pin plug home. A lightning strike of static exploded through the laboratory as the colour monitor blossomed into life. Striebley, feeling like some potholer in a high-tech cave system, began to back his way out from behind the bank of equipment, picking his way carefully around festoons of creeping cables and twisted lianas of wire looms.

A good three minutes of writhing later, he emerged from behind the GENE-Erator (TM) to be greeted by an irate looking Crickson stabbing angry fingers at the central control keyboard and swearing.

'Trouble?' asked Striebley reluctantly. He knew the dangers of such direct questioning – another expedition behind the bank of humming hardware. If anything was connected up incorrectly, he would have to go potholing again.

'Damn, bloody thing can't blinking well find the DNA

hybridisation sequence I inputted last night!' snarled Crickson, jabbing at the monitor screen for no apparently explicable reason. 'Look, nothing! How am I supposed to get the damn thing to synthesise DNA strands without the hybrid file, eh? Answer me that. It's impossible. Damn idiots from DN-Aids Inc sent me a duff one! Not a sequence file in any of it!' he glared at the monitor screen and the definite lack of information showing thereon. 'I loaded it in, I did! Why can't the bloody thing read it, eh? What's wrong with the infernal device, eh? Well, they're not getting away with it. Oh no!' And he whirled on his heels and stomped off towards the door.

'Where are you going?' called Striebley, bewildered by Crickson's impatience.

'To order another one! One that works. I'm not having my research held up by their incompetence!' The door slammed behind him with seismic fury.

Striebley groaned and slapped his palm to his forehead. Seven hours to assemble the thing and it's written off in three minutes. Quickly he totted up the looming hassle in his mind. Four hours to strip, repack and shove it outside to be collected. And then the same thing all over again tomorrow. His solar-rechargeable King Edward and his rooftop dish bleated forlornly for attention in the back of consciousness. Another day without them beckoned to him.

There had to be a simple explanation for the lack of sequence information. Wearily Striebley perched himself on a convenient stool, clenched his fist and pressed it firmly to his forehead in the immortal position of one deep in thought.

'Let's see,' he mused. 'Crickson would have taken the genetic information from the sequencing gel and transferred it directly into the Splice of Life local area network using . . .' He glanced around the lab and his eyes fell on a solitary terminal on the far end of a bench. It was almost completely buried beneath a vast stack of paperwork, a huge portfolio of sequencing gels and a printout from the DN-Aliaser. 'Using a terminal,' Striebley completed his thought.

'Now, he would have done all of that last night in

preparation for the arrival of the new equipment so ...'
Striebley's hope exploded into a roman candle of delight and
he was off across the lab like a greyhound from a trap. He
snatched at the terminal, tugged it away from the wall and
yanked an anonymous grey cable from a socket in the wall
and the rear of the Apple Mac. 'It's always difficult
accessing files when you're not networked.'

Victoriously he dashed back across the lab and, peering
behind the mountain of freshly delivered equipment, kicked
the half hidden figure of Farson hard across the backside.
'No ... no apogee plus fifty,' muttered the red-haired
technician, shocked out of his thoughts about exactly how to
pilot a remote-controlled satellite in to a safe landing on the
radio-silent dark side of the moon. This, apart from building
the thing in the first place, was the only snag preventing
SOFA from positioning a hyper-sensitive ear on an interfer-
ence-free spot of the moon.

'Job for you,' announced Striebley and dropped the cable
into Farson's baffled hands. 'Plug it into that socket there,'
he pointed to a wall outlet almost hidden behind the new
equipment, 'and jam the other end into the terminal.'

Farson attempted to hand the cable back. 'Well, go on
then. Plug it up.'

Striebley folded his arms. 'Your turn, I think,' he looked
down at the horror-stricken face of the red pony-tailed
technician.

'Ah, no, no,' spluttered Farson dreading the claustropho-
bia inducing squirm behind the machinery. 'Be far better if
you did it, don't you think? You know exactly where it
should go.'

'I'd love to,' lied Striebley. 'But ...' He pulled the type of
face which somehow told Farson that if he didn't get
squirming behind the equipment quick-sharp then it wouldn't
be too long before small, but significant, parts of his anatomy
began appearing in various experiments. 'Now get to it!'

Farson made the slightest of whimpering sounds and
vanished completely behind the bank of humming technology, cable clamped firmly between his teeth.

Revelling in the sudden tranquility of not having Crickson screaming at him Striebley leaned back against the wall for a few minutes, stared at the ceiling and wondered precisely how long it would be before he got his hands back on his favourite potato. Behind him there was a scuffling of body and not a small amount of judicious cursing.

'Try that,' came the muffled cry from Farson.

Shaking his head Striebley stabbed a series of instructions onto the newly delivered keyboard and grinned as software shook hands with software and performed the type of wary sniffing that labradors meeting for the first time were wont to do. In seconds the two programmes were the best of friends and were cheerfully exchanging megabytes of casual reminiscences over the local area network.

'FIND DNA SEQUENCE FILE,' typed Striebley and in the very instant that a fuming Crickson burst back into the lab, the screen flickered and a list of files cascaded into view.

'Insisted there was nothing wrong with it, but I told 'em straight, I did,' snarled Crickson. 'There'll be a new one here first thing in the morn . . . Hey. It's working! What the hell did you do? No, don't tell me, I don't care.' He shoved Striebley out of the way and, all thoughts of replacement systems evaporating from his head, he pulled up all the necessary genetic info to get back on track with Project CFC.

'Striebley, check the pH and ionic balance in the Amniotic Tanks and calibrate the tryptophan delivery . . .'

'I'd really love to,' Striebley lied. 'But I hear the timer on the DN-Aliaser. *Someone* has to attend to it and download the results if we are to secure payment from those obliging chappies at Camford Constabulary. Bye!' And he was off. One quick swipe of his security card down the side of the door and he was free, bounding into the corridor with all the enthusiasm of a beagle in spring. The door slammed shut behind him, cutting off the plaintive objections of Farson as he clattered wildly up the stairs, swept his card through another security lock and sprang into the safety of the DN-Aliaser room. He slammed the door behind him and collapsed against it panting desperately, exhaustion and relief flooding his body, gathering his wits before delving into the internal memory of the DN-Aliaser.

He was still relatively new to it, having ignored the squat pale grey device as simply a quick way to make some cash. In his mind that type of a commercial service just wasn't science. No way. You didn't get professional portrait painters offering three minute passport quickies from tiny booths in Woolworths, did you? So why should he demean his scientific integrity to earn a few measly quid?

Right now, though, the very prospect of doing something even remotely scientific drew him like a bee to a blooming buddleia. Anything to get him away from Crickson's barrage of instructions. Striebley tugged a stool out from beneath the DN-Aliaser and settled his weary buttocks upon it. Then, booting up another Apple Mac and entering his access code he proceeded to delve into the short term memory of the machine. Over the last four hours the DN-Aliaser had been cheerfully chewing away at the single blood sample brought by the motorcycle cop, slicing the DNA off like wafer-thin slices of cucumber, exposing them to four different cobalt laser polarisations and noting down the results. It was cutting edge technology. The type of whizz-bang genetic analyser that the chappies of the Human Genome Project would have slaughtered for. Eight hundred and ninety-eight times faster, ten times more accurate and, best of all, it came ready loaded with LAB Doss 9.3.

Secretly Striebley had to admit that having LAB Doss 9.3 was a huge advantage. It was this software alone that had really convinced him of the worth of the DN-Aliaser. Scientifically it was utterly useless, of course. But it didn't half make a rainy lunch time fun. He was sure that if Camford Constabulary found out the hours of idle frivolity that could be had from LAB Doss 9.3 they'd be ordering a DN-Aliaser in seconds. It was that good a games package.

With a deft punching of buttons Striebley pulled up the menu of fifty-three state-of-the-art time-wasters, shrugged and settled down for a good few rounds of Hyper-Asteroid Pool. The tiny screen on the DN-Aliaser shimmered and metamorphosed into a three inch asteroid field dotted with half a dozen black holes. Liberally sprinkling his pulsed anti-grav shock cue with three milligrams of beryllium alloy particulates he lined up on a likely-looking ball of granite and squeezed the trigger. A thin fizzing sound simulated the deadly release of an eighty megaton anti-grav pulse, the asteroid launched forward and, charged with just the right amount of top-spin, cannoned off a small moon and vanished in the top corner pocket. There was a ripple of simulated applause and he lined up on a small comet zipping in from the bottom right. It was double bonus points if you could divert a moving comet. Firing thrusters on his cue he swung around just as an alarm went off on the Apple Mac next to him.

'Bugger,' he cursed as the comet slammed into the side of his cue spreading debris in all directions and calling up the 'Game Over' flag. One day he'd actually hit a comet. One day.

Miserably he spun on his stool and stared at the screen of the Mac as it flashed up a message declaring 'SPECIES SEQUENCE NOT RECOGNISED'.

He tutted, quickly typed in 'HUMAN' and pressed return.

Again the message flashed up. 'SPECIES SEQUENCE STILL NOT RECOGNISED'.

Cursing something under his breath about equipment manufacturers trying to be clever, he inputted the words 'HOMO SAPIENS'.

'LOOK, I TOLD YOU . . .' began the computer before he tapped in 'DISPLAY SEQUENCE'. His jaw almost hit the keyboard as the screen filled with row upon row of strangely unfamiliar letters.

In the instant he stared at that screen he somehow knew he was looking at a genetic code the like of which no man had seen before.

He swallowed nervously and all his thoughts shot to the roof. Was this a message from beyond the stars? Had his faith in the 'Pie in the Sky' theory been vindicated? Would this lead to a host of appearances on prime-time chat shows?

*

Chief Inspector Ness was pacing irritably up and down in the cold clammy environs of the forensics lab, his heels spitting echoes in all directions.

'Isn't it ready yet?' he growled for the dozenth time. 'Ten minutes, you said. *Ten* minutes.'

Doctor Boscombe rolled his eyes heavenwards momentarily before sliding them back onto the second hand of his trusty stopwatch and counting off the time.

'Nine fifty-eight, fifty-nine and . . . ten.' With one bound he leapt to his feet, grabbed the irregularly shaped bundle of plasticine currently residing on a hastily constructed nest of Sainway's shopping bags and began tearing it apart.

'Well? Well?' pestered Ness over Boscombe's industrious shoulders. 'Can you get an ID from it? Can we nail whoever did it, eh? Can we?'

'Patience,' tutted Boscombe as he hurled globs of plasticine into a waiting bucket. 'This is an operation of utmost delicacy. One false tug and it will be ruined.'

'Give it here, then.'

'No, no. Only those with the sufficient levels of skill should be allowed to . . .'

'Skill? You've just been playing with plasticine all afternoon. Where's the skill in that?

Boscombe's teeth ground noisily as he tore another three pounds of sticky goo clear of the central cast and tossed it into the bucket. 'Reconstruction modelling is a highly precision oriented art requiring intimate knowledge of comparative anatomy, physiology . . .'

'Comparative anatomy?' squawked Ness shocked. 'And whose anatomy were you comparing, eh?'

'The forensic school provided the models for us to study. I never caught her name. Oh, but it did make Wednesday afternoons a definite highlight of the week. A pleasant change to be dealing with live subjects rather than . . .'

'I don't pay my taxes to send you on courses so you can ogle slender young . . .'

'There. It's done,' announced Boscombe, wishing he hadn't invited Ness in for the grand unveiling.

'Excellent, excellent,' grinned the Chief Inspector and took a few steps back to admire Boscombe's Polyfilla creation standing motionless on the desk. 'Er, what is it?' he asked a few minutes later having stared at the pale grey thing from a variety of different angles.

'I *told* you. It's a reconstruction of the very foot which made the print taken from just outside The Monocle and Asparagus.'

'I guess you failed reconstructive modelling, then,' spluttered Ness dismissing the grotesquely shaped foot standing on the table. Apart from the fact that it bore five toes and was spread out a bit at the bottom, it bore no resemblance to any foot that Ness had ever seen. For one thing it was less than half the size it should've been. For the other it had claws.

'I came top of the class. A distinction!'

'The others must've been distracted by the model, then. All that naked flesh cavorting before their eyes.'

'If you are suggesting that this reconstruction is in any way inaccurate then think again.'

'Oh, come on. Look at it. Are you seriously trying to tell me that something with feet like that kidnapped my daughter?'

'Not kidnapped,' answered Boscombe meaningfully. 'I think the word you're looking for is abduction.'

'Kidnapping, abduction, what difference is there?'

'All the difference in this, or any other world,' answered Doctor Boscombe in the tone of voice that really cried out for a swirling cascade of violins ending in an overly-melodramatic organ chord. A flash of lightning wouldn't have gone amiss either.

'Ab ... abduc ...' gagged Ness as the truth hit. 'You mean like "wooof", gone?' He made a swooping motion with the flat of his hand, like a child imitating Concorde taking off.

Boscombe nodded and helpfully reached a large box file off the shelf. 'I've got a picture of what it probably looks like,' he muttered to himself as he began rummaging through his vast collection of likely movie aliens.

'Nope, not that one,' he tutted hurling a full colour glossy of Jabba the Hutt across the desk. 'Don't think he's got any feet. Er . . . nope, not that. Far too big,' and he rejected a black and white print of a ten foot tall seamless robot standing on the slope of a vast saucer in a park somewhere in America.

'My Tara, abducted! And after I paid all her college fees!' wailed Ness suddenly and, wondering briefly if the life assurance policy he had taken out on her would pay out for alien abductions, he stormed out of the lab.

'Hold on,' called Boscombe waving a photo of a nasty black-carapaced thing with a curling shiny head and extensible teeth that were the stuff of many a nightmare. 'I *have* got a picture somewhere. Don't you want to see it? You know, for the APB or the photofit or whatever it is you do?'

The door slammed shut in the wake of a whirlwind of panicking Chief Inspector.

Already fifteen different pumps were whirring away to themselves as they shoved liquids here, sucked solutions there and generally set about creating a perfect environment within the fifty gallon universe of an Amniotic Tank (TM). It wasn't entirely clear whether this process was currently being helped or hindered by the actions of a certain carrot-topped technician.

'Have you checked the glucose–fructose ratio?' barked Professor Crickson to the sweating blur of Farson.

'N . . . not yet,' panted the red pony-tailed one. 'I've only just finished back-titrating the free sodium quotient and stabilising the potassium baths.'

'How long ago did I ask you to check the glucose–fructose ratio, hmmm? C'mon man. Get your finger out! Time and Tide. Time and Tide!'

'Er . . . D'you want that doing before or after I calibrate the Kreb's Recyclers?'

'After. After! Gods, are you deliberately trying to make things more difficult! Now, what's the current concentration of acetyl choline in the ribosomal header tank? Quick, quick!'

'Thirteen point three five micro-moles.'

'Good, good. Now get those Kreb's Recyclers on line and calibrated before oxygenation sets in. Quick.'

And so the sweating Farson leapt here and there, tweaking this, topping up that, pH-ing the other in a frenzy of last minute preparations and tweaks that would put even the most hastily arranged of society weddings to shame. But somehow, almost miraculously, after dashing hither and yon for upwards of an hour and a half Crickson barked the final order and amazingly it was all set. Solutions that should be bubbling were, liquids that should be brimming with vital cocktails of complex organic molecules did and everything on the biochemical stage was set to the very pinnacle of organic and technological perfection.

All it needed now was the vital code and it would be off. Crickson, perched like a bald headed eagle on a cliff, squatted on his stool and cracked his knuckles theatrically.

'LOAD SEQUENCE CFC-I .BIO', he typed with one finger and pressed 'RETURN'.

Somewhere upstairs a disk drive whirred and spat several dozen kilobytes down the network cabling.

'SEQUENCE RECEIVED' answered the computer as a glob of data was thrust down its throat with all the finesse of a guillemot swallowing a herring.

'INITIATE ANABOLISM CFC-I .BIO', typed Crickson with pedestrian slowness and stabbed 'RETURN'.

'ARE YOU SURE?' checked the Mac.

'Too bloody right,' growled Crickson and fisted the 'RETURN' key for the final time.

There was a single heart-stopping moment of utter silence as the GENE-Erator (TM) analysed the genetic code, performed the digital equivalent of tapping its index finger against its chin and launched into the miraculous process of creation.

Crickson thrilled as valves whirred and spat precise microlitre aliquots of primed bases into the Amniotic Tank and hungry enzymes leapt upon them. In seconds invisible strands of DNA were beginning to form, held like growing strands of kelp on the sub-helix doubler array, each an identical copy of the sequence held in the volatile memory of the GENE-Erator (TM), each growing with unnatural speed under the frantic action of countless millions of anabolic enzymes.

For a few minutes Crickson and Farson stood in awe watching the humming and gurgling machine, captivated by it like six year olds before their first steaming traction engine. But then the Professor shrugged his shoulders and scrambled down off his stool.

'Well, that's all there is to it,' he said. 'Couple of hours and the DNA's done then it clicks over and starts making proteins. By the time you're having your breakfast the seedlings of the world's first chicken fed corn will be uncurling their very first roots. Couple of days and we'll be famous!' And with a strange lightness to his step Crickson whirled on his heel and headed off towards the bike shed.

Farson shook his head and trudged off after him. After all there was nothing he could do. It was totally automated. Temperature control, chemical addition rates, incubation periods, all were carried out by the Mac in the middle. It was just like some strange variation on the domestic washing machine really. It just sat in a corner under the worktop and set about your smalls with unrivalled mechanical determination while you slept peacefully in your bed.

Farson took one last look at it, blinking and gurgling away to itself and had to admit it was damned impressive. A wonder of modern technology. Quietly he closed the door and readied himself to break some very interesting news to Sacramento down *The Monocle*, sure in the very knowledge that nothing could possibly go wrong with it. Nope. Absolutely nothing at all.

In the deep shadow behind a suburban garden shed, a teenage hand was raised suddenly and an anorak-clad girl skidded to a halt with a grunt of irritation. It was the first command that had been given in ten minutes of scurrying covertly around the darker ends of a host of compost heaps and various vegetable patches.

'Damn, damn, damn,' she cursed, rubbing her leg and peering cautiously around a stack of broken pots.

'What is it?' asked Calabrese with a quiver of excitement in his voice. 'Danger? Are they waiting for us? Do they know we're coming?'

'Don't be stupid,' tutted Tara. 'There's never anyone in the garden at this time of day. They'll be having dinner. Always do at half six. On the dot.'

'Then why've we stopped?'

''Cause I've just ripped my Levi's. Look!' she tugged a branch of dog rose out of her ruined legware and waggled it at the pair of feyries behind her. 'Bloody typical. They were my last pair, too.' Lupin's eyes bugged at the sight of pale calf framed between blue lips, he clutched his hands tight to his chest and whimpered desperately.

Calabrese made a tutting noise. 'Such trivia in the face of momentany,' he grumbled to himself then fixed his almond-shaped eyes firmly on Tara's wide browns. 'Apart from the state of your leggings, is there anything preventing us continuing?'

'Well, no, I don't suppose so.'

'Then let's go!' he snapped. Calabrese's insides were knotting faster than a pack of scouts at a summer camp, victims of the floods of excitement coursing through his body. This was more than just the thrill of the chase, more than the elation of simple badness. Calabrese was currently gripped by the highest kicks of pure adventure, its legs can-canning across his field of view shaking the fizzing petticoats of elation with gay abandon. No one else knew what he had in mind. Yet. But soon he would let them in. Soon they'd realise they were on the very brink of a change of history. By then he would be unstoppable.

And right here, in a matter of minutes, it would all begin. The Resurgence of an Ancient Race. The Uprising of the

Downtrodden. The Return of Feyrie to their Rightful Place at the very top of the heap.

'Well? What are we waiting for?' hissed Calabrese behind the garden shed.

'Don't you speak to Tara like that. It's not nice,' snapped Lupin prodding him in the ribs. He received a foot in the head for his troubles.

'C'mon, c'mon,' insisted Calabrese, squirming forwards impatiently.

'Not yet! Quiet!' whispered Tara and pointed up the garden. Calabrese stared in disgust as a woman emerged through the french windows and trudged across the patio, a wicker basket under her arm.

'I thought you said they'd be having dinner?' growled Calabrese as Mrs Ness began bringing in the day's washing. Despite the fact that they had a top of the range Electrolux spin dryer, she always hung the washing out when the weather was fine. Well, how else could she possibly show off her extensive, expensive and highly fashionable mail order wardrobe to the neighbours?

'They always do,' insisted Tara. 'Six thirty, every night. I don't understand it.'

Her confusion was alleviated a second and a half later when the unmistakable sound of a Rover grinding to a frenzied halt on the gravel of the front drive was heard echoing throughout the neighbourhood.

Rosemary dropped her wicker basket and scurried indoors, wagging-finger armed and ready, tongue preparing itself for a pre-emptive barrage of stinging questions. 'What time d'you call this?' or 'Do you *like* burnt cottage pie?'

'Now! C'mon,' whispered Tara, and without waiting for a response she broke cover and sprinted diagonally across the striped lawn, ducked around the side of the house and headed straight for the garage. Lupin watched her go, admiring her athletic form through valentine tinted eyes. In seconds she was half way up the carefully reinforced trellis and heading for her bedroom window, her heart pounding with the effort. Expertly she slid onto the roof, followed by the two feyries.

She stood and was ready to move across it when, suddenly, beneath their feet came the dull thud of a slamming car door and the trudge of weary feet. All of them froze in terror. A pair of motors whirred and the garage door rumbled shut. Standing motionless, helpless and exposed, daring not even risk the tiniest of foot movements, Tara's ears boomed with the sound of her breath as she stared down in terror on Chief Inspector Ness. He crunched across the gravel drive and let himself in through the front door.

Counting to five she let her breath out with a gasp, closed her eyes and hugged the garage roof like a long lost friend. She would have lain there for several minutes, quivering as she calmed down, had it not been for the insistent prodding of a long grey index finger in her ribs.

'Alright, alright!' she barked and under duress, skittered carefully across the tiles and up towards her bedroom window. 'Nearly there,' she grumbled, wishing that perhaps she hadn't been quite so grateful to them for snatching the evidence. Next time – if she was ever that careless again – she would have to agree to *almost* anything.

'Just through this window here and ... Bugger!' she cursed as her fingernails scrabbled at the frame. 'It's shut!'

'Oh wonderful. That's just really great, that is,' said Calabrese in a hoarse whisper. 'All this way and the window's shut. Brilliant!'

'Don't blame me. It was open when I left it.'

'Yeah, don't blame her,' offered Lupin supportively and flashed a simpering grin towards Tara. 'It was open ...'

'I heard,' growled Calabrese, fuming. 'Get a brick. Two bricks. Smash the damned thing. I'll smash it ...'

'Don't be so stupid,' glared Tara.

'Yeah, don't be so stupid,' agreed Lupin heroically.

'They'll hear us.'

'They'll hear us,' parroted Lupin, really feeling important now that he was standing up for his beloved.

'And anyway,' grinned Tara wickedly, 'there's no need for such destruction.'

'And anyway ...' began Lupin.

'Shut it!' chorused Tara and Calabrese.

Lupin stood for a moment, his mouth dangling limply open, then he sniffed and looked pathetically at his feet. They were ganging up on him, it wasn't fair. Miserably he began pulling a nearby piece of moss apart, tossing the fluffy remnants into a convenient gutter.

Meanwhile Tara had rolled up her sleeve, lifted up a loose tile from the roof, extracted a large screwdriver and was busily gouging out the putty around the glass. A few moments later she prised out the pane, angled it carefully and threaded it into the house.

'After nearly spending a night on the tiles when a gust of wind slammed it shut, I made contingency plans,' she grinned and ducked in through the window. 'You coming?' she called out to Lupin after Calabrese had slipped in.

The small grey figure shrugged and trudged into the warmth.

'So where's this computer?' hissed Calabrese looking around Tara's bedroom and fixing his gaze on the interesting looking stack of hi-fi squatting on the chest of drawers. In a flash he was across the room, grey index finger flicking on the power. His eyes filled with brimming excitement as a host of multi-coloured leds sprang into life. 'This one?' he asked his digit hovering above the play button on the cd.

'No!' gasped Tara, too late. With one flick of a stray finger it was spurred into life. In seconds the laser was gaily four-fold oversampling to its glittering heart's content, snatching digits of music off the disc and flinging them at the amplifier. Obeying the laws of audio inevitability floods of power chords surged down speaker cables, blasting into freedom, shattering the still air of Tara's bedroom.

It was a damned good job she had the headphones plugged in. An orchestra of bees trilled ineffectually out of two tiny circular cones, inaudible anywhere beyond the door.

'Idiot! That's my stereo. Leave it alone! If they hear anything . . .' She pointed downstairs towards where she expected her parents to be.

Calabrese pulled a sheepish grin and reached out to switch

it off.

'No, no, don't,' begged Lupin and snatched desperately at the headphones, instinctively jamming them over his head and submerging himself in the stirring metallic tide of power riffing. Perhaps if he could learn some of Tara's favourite songs then a night of delightfully romantic lute serenading might not be too far off the cards. Before the first chorus was through he was cheerily nodding his head, right hand thrashing at the imaginary strings of an electric lute.

Tara tutted then turned and swept a host of empty hairspray bottles away from in front of a spanking new Hewlett Packard Arcturus 911.

One of the advantages that came of her father's sad belief that she was still studying for her A-levels was conning him into shelling out two and a half grand on a whizzbang pc.

Proudly she booted it up, grinning as she ran through its spec. '32Mb RAM, 2.3Gb hard disk and the little darling you're really interested in, an internal 28,800 Modem.'

'Great,' shrugged Calabrese. 'What's it all mean?'

'Haven't a clue,' confessed Tara, 'but it's what you need for the demands of today's office. The guy in Currys told me so, it must be true. What d'you want me to do with it? I've got a stack of really great games. I've just got SimMageddon 2000. It's ace, you've got to set up the biggest series of ecological disasters you can and see how much of the world you can destroy. I'm not very good at it yet. I've only succeeded in wiping out ninety-three per cent of America and burying Europe under a radioactive blanket of hyper-toxic fallout, rendering it inhospitable for ten thousand years or so.'

Calabrese shook his head and scoured the back of his mind for the necessary term. Whilst Tara rabbited on about the way she had accidentally built a twenty-eight kiloton nuclear reactor on the San Andreas fault and been ever so chuffed when a 4.2 Richter earthquake had cracked the core, caused a meltdown and sunk half of middle America, he conjured up the images of a keyboard he had seen on CablePix back in his own private hollow.

He reran all the movements of the fingers, reviewed the letters glinting on the screen and then, as Lupin wailed tunelessly to an unknown song, it came to him.

'Codename:Alpha A1:Prime.President,' he declared, suddenly interrupting Tara's graphic description of the demise of San Francisco.

'Eh?' she gagged.

'Codename:Alpha A1 . . .'

'Yeah, yeah, I heard that. What about it?'

'You type it in there.'

'You want to do some hacking?' she asked her eyebrows curling with excitement.

'Yes! That's what it's called, hacking.'

'Well, why didn't you say?' she grinned cracking her knuckles in anticipation. 'Where d'you want in?'

'Splice of Life' he answered barely stifling a wicked grin.

Tara stared at him sharply quizzical. 'You want in to Splice? What for?'

'Can you do it?'

'Sure. Do it in my sleep. Farson gave me all the security codes. Thought I might need them for a bit of nocturnal journalism. Personally I just think it's an excuse so he can pop round for a quick hack with me, but . . .'

'Get me in and I'll explain as we go,' growled Calabrese.

Tara raised her grubby fingers and was just about to pull the telephone dialling board on-screen when a horribly familiar creak rattled its way through the door.

She froze again, listening, her ears straining in the almost silence. And there it was again, the relaxing groan of the floorboard. There was no doubting it, someone was coming up the stairs.

'Change of venue,' whispered Tara and, grabbing the computer and praying that the telephone cable was long enough, she bounded frantically over the bed and disappeared into the wardrobe. Calabrese clamped a hand over Lupin's mouth and shut off the stereo, snatching the headphones off him and feyrie-handling him into the Laura Ashley draped environs of the wardrobe.

'I was enjoying that,' Lupin protested as the sounds of the bathroom door being locked were heard.

'Well, play with that and shutup,' whispered Tara, thrusting an ageing Walkman at him.

Enthusiastically he slipped the headphones on and pressed play. Tara had commanded him to listen to her music. He thrilled as the hiss of the cassette filled his ears.

For a few moments he frowned as Queen's 'We Will Rock You' whump-whump-smacked its way through a few bars, but then Brian May let rip on his guitar and once again Lupin was happy.

And so it came to pass that as the sounds of flushing cisterns splashed through the walls of wardrobe and Chief Inspector Ness attempted to explain about alien abductions to a wife more concerned with the state of charring on her cottage pie, the security systems of Splice of Life Patentable Biosciences Ltd were greeted by a stream of data cheerily masquerading as an old, old friend. Unsurprisingly, a few brief digital pleasantries were exchanged casually and with the minimum of fuss ACCESS was GRANTED.

The red pony-tailed figure of Lance Farson burst into *The Monocle and Asparagus* and, for probably the first time in his life, swept past the bar without ordering a drink. He bustled into the back room on a beeline for the enigmatic figure in the corner sporting a goatee beard.

'Have you heard?' gasped Farson snatching a chair from under the table and dropping into it a little too fast.

Elijah Sacramento stared into his pint of Ruddles and made a small moaning sound. 'Ruined,' he whimpered. 'Reputation destroyed.'

'Have you heard the news?' tried Farson once more, fidgeting impatiently.

'GAIA will never be taken seriously again,' sniffed Sacramento drawing double helices in a puddle of beer on the table. 'Never.'

'Of course we will, there's nothing to worry about on the reputation front ...'

Sacramento looked up from his pint. 'Nothing to worry about?' he gagged. 'How can you say that?'

'Easy, there's nothing to worry . . .'

'I missed the ransom note,' blurted Sacramento. 'It's been delivered.'

'That doesn't matter, there's . . .'

'Doesn't matter? Of course it matters. How can you hold someone for ransom when they turn up for breakfast like normal?'

'Keep your voice down,' hissed Farson as a bunch of remarkably familiar looking reps glanced up from their fourth lager.

'How can you threaten them when she's sat there large as life munching on her Frosties? Where's the emotional leverage in that, eh? Where?'

'That's what I'm trying to tell you. She's *not* there,' insisted Farson. Sacramento stopped, mouth open, and stared at Farson. 'What?'

'She's gone,' hissed the technician. 'Disappeared.'

'You sure?'

'Ness didn't turn up today because of it and he's got Boscombe working on it.'

Sacramento took a large swig of his beer, wiped his mouth enthusiastically with the back of his hand and suddenly looked as if a massive weight had been lifted from his emotional shoulders. 'So you're saying everything's alright? Back on plan?'

'Well, I wouldn't quite go that far . . .'

Sacramento wasn't listening. 'Ha ha, they'll have cancelled that contract within the week, just you see. They'll come crawling to us on their hands and knees begging for . . .'

'Not necessarily,' growled Farson. 'We could be in one hell of a mess right now.'

Somehow Sacramento noticed. 'What's that supposed to mean, eh? What mess? What are you on about? They've got our ransom note and Tara's disappeared. What more could we ask for?'

'It depends where our dear Tara has disappeared to, doesn't it?'

Sacramento shook his head. 'What are you saying?'

'Nobody knows where she is.'

'Nobody?'

'Well, maybe one person,' growled Farson, his brow darkening with anger. 'Fond of black, militant, owner of a small shop which goes under the name "Fitments of the Imagination".'

'You saying Regan knows where she is?' Sacramento's face brightened. 'Well, then there's nothing to worry about ... Why are you shaking your head?'

'Did you see his face when he found out Tara was going to be our mouthpiece? When he found out that she, a newcomer, was going to tell the world of our cause?'

'Well, he looked a bit miffed,' shrugged Sacramento. 'Nose out of joint, that sort of ...'

'Nose out of joint? He looked like he was going to kill her. And don't think he hasn't already tried. What about the incident with that glass during the raid?'

'Oh come, come. That was an accident. One small slip.'

'It was an accident he didn't scare her off,' hissed Farson. 'If I hadn't stopped him ...'

'Yes, yes, very gallant I'm sure.'

'You don't believe me, do you?' challenged Farson.

'Well, no. He's never done anything to arouse my suspicions.'

'Oh no? Well, what about the three thousand pound shortfall in the shop's profits last year, eh?'

'An accounting error, it's easily ...'

'What about the missing case of four hundred ET loo roll holders with glowing finger tip attachment?'

'A clerical error, it's *easily* ...'

'What about his mysterious secretive trips to Amsterdam?'

'Look, this doesn't concern us stopping the police contract with Splice of Life,' suggested Sacramento trying to steer the conversation onto firmer ground.

'It does if she doesn't turn up safe and sound.' Farson let

the sentence hang in the air.

Sacramento's mind was suddenly filled with a million ways which Chief Inspector Ness could wreak his revenge if anything did happen to go wrong. Nervously he swallowed a good half pint of Ruddles.

'Well . . . well, what d'you want me to do about it?' he spluttered. 'Rough him up a bit and get him to tell us where she is?'

'No, no, no!' panicked Farson thinking of Tara all alone in a basement somewhere at the mercy of that brute Regan. 'Remember those ET toilet roll holders? We never did find them.'

Sacramento swallowed again.

'No leave this to me,' suggested Farson through tightly determined jaws. 'I'll find her,' he announced and, with thoughts of precisely how grateful Tara would be when he kicked down the door of the warehouse, or wherever it was she was being kept, strode across the darkened floor, lifted her desperate body off the cold floor and carried her into the light, he whirled out of *The Monocle and Asparagus*.

A girl was bound to be mightily grateful for that sort of heroic act, wasn't she?

A brief spurt of his plasma thrusters, a modicum of attitude correction and once again his cue was right on target. Palms sweating with excitement Striebley dialled up twenty-three percent back-spin, punched in a thirty-three megaton anti-grav pulse and held his breath. Three hours solid he'd been playing this and right now he was perfectly set for the match of his life. If he could get this asteroid in the middle pocket and leave himself lined up for a thin slice onto the comet he was certain should be appearing from the top corner perihelion in the next few minutes, then there was no doubting it, he would take the Hyper-Asteroid Pool Open Masters.

Closing his eyes in a silent prayer to the God in charge of computer games – if there was one – he thumbed the 'fire' command and heard the simulated fizz as his pulse was released. Squinting nervously out of one eye he barely dared watch as the asteroid lurched in slow motion, spun backwards against the knap of the gravity field and banana'd its way perfectly into the jaws of the waiting middle pocket. He leapt off his stool, punching the air with delight and pirouetting wildly. One more pot and he'd have it. An unbeatable victory. His initials indelibly stamped forever upon the high score board. But he still had to sink it. The pressure was well and truly on, as uncomfortable and unignorable as porcupine-lined boxer shorts.

Shaking the sweat off his palms he righted his stool and snapped his attention back onto the three inch square of almost empty asteroid field.

As his eagerly awaited comet soared in from the top corner and he made final precise adjustments to attitude and yaw, a strange thing started to happen inside the Apple Mac behind him.

A normally inanimate file apparently took it upon itself to open, reach inside itself and extract a quite unique sequence of rather incriminating genetic code.

Then, with all the fuss of a landlord handing over a frothing pint to a thirsty punter, the file dropped the code in front of an expectant looking programme, saluted and shut itself down again.

The programme, momentarily baffled, stopped what it was doing, accepted the new code and quite happily began hurling a totally different set of instructions to all the various bits and bobs of equipment currently under its command.

Downstairs in Striebley's lab an entire three hours' worth of DNA replication was dumped out of the bottom of the Amniotic Tanks (TM) and work began anew, synthesising a genetic code the likes of which only one man had ever seen before.

Striebley, blissfully unaware of the goings-on behind him let rip with a sweeping thirty-two megaton anti-grav pulse, miscalculated the top-spin and simultaneously screwed both his cue into a black hole and his chances of everlasting victory.

'No, no! Referee!' he screamed pounding his fists against the tiny screen as the 'Game Over' flag waggled irritatingly at him.

'It can't be. Give me a bonus cue you damned, blinking, infernal . . .' The screen blanked out.

'Right, right, I'll show you. I don't need a bonus cue. I've got this sussed now, just you watch this!' Feverishly he rolled up his sleeves, stabbed at the tiny keypad and pulled up a brand new game of Hyper-Asteroid Pool.

Three and a half miles away, deep inside a Laura Ashley print filled wardrobe, Tara wriggled her way out of the internal network of Splice of Life security systems and shut down her computer.

'Okay, what was all that about?' she asked half suspecting the answer but not really daring to believe it.

Calabrese tapped the side of his nose in as enigmatic a way as he could. 'How long will we have to wait for a full cycle on the GENE-Erator?'

'Eight hours,' answered Tara pulling the figure from the brochure which Farson had supplied her with and which Calabrese had insisted he had a look at. 'It'll be ready first thing in the morning. Whatever "it" is?'

'So what do we do until then?'

'Fancy a game of SimMageddon 2000? I'll be the eco-terrorists and you can play NATO,' offered Tara enthusiastically booting up again.

Lupin lay in a heap of undies, moaning occasionally to some unheard lyric, his hands strumming and fretting away desperately at his electric lute.

23rd June, Next Year

Into that thin hour of Camford's day reserved for posties, milkies and the drunken dregs of last night's revelries three pairs of feet scampered, two slapping nakedly, one crunching in Doc Martined splendour.

'Look, you don't have to do this,' reiterated Calabrese for the third time as he sprinted alongside Tara. 'We can manage perfectly well on our own now, you know?'

'Oh, you can, can you?' answered the girl, dripping scepticism.

'Yes, yes,' insisted Calabrese, his feet slapping two for every one of Tara's. 'You've been most helpful. Very kind. All debts *more* than adequately repaid.'

Lupin, trotting two paces behind, attempted to smile sweetly back at her. He was ignored.

'It was the very least I could do under the circumstances,' she grinned in a most graceful manner. Inside she was fizzing with excitement. Last night she had broken into her own home, hacked her way into a certain laboratory not a million miles away and tweaked a few programmes, all under the instruction of a pair of interstellar invaders from beyond the trackless wastes of space. It didn't take a genius to think that perhaps something interesting might have been afoot. She wasn't going to miss finding out precisely what that was. Besides, she still hadn't seen inside that spaceship, yet.

'You really don't have to put yourself out any further, honestly,' Calabrese said in as firm a voice as he dared to try without raising Tara's suspicions that he might, just *might* be trying to hide the awesome something that was awaiting him inside the laboratories of Splice of Life Patentable Biosciences Ltd.

'Oh, it's not trouble at all,' she trembled, her stomach hatching a lepidopterist's heaven of nervous butterflies.

'No, no, I insist . . .'

Suddenly Tara stopped dead in her tracks and scowled at Calabrese. 'Listen, pal. If you think I'm bothered whether you can manage on your own, thankyou very much, or not, then you're very, very, very . . . er, wrong.'

Behind her Lupin grinned, thrilling equally with the ferocity of her anger and the suffering of that anger's victim.

'Nobody, repeat *nobody*, gives me *that* bad a night's sleep and gets away without letting me in on why, okay?' fumed Tara. 'I know damned well you're up to something well dodgy and I am going to find out what it is whether you want to tell me or not. Clear?' hissed Tara, her anorak sleeves rustling threateningly.

Lupin's knees were weakening by the second.

'Y ... y ... yes,' spluttered Calabrese barely audibly.

'Good, that's settled then,' announced Tara quivering with relief.

Lupin scowled intense jealousy at the shaking Calabrese. Ungrateful git. How dare he not appreciate such treatment? And why should he have been treated like that? What had he done to receive such personal attention from Lupin's beloved? It just wasn't fair.

'Onward to Splice of Life, then is it?' grinned Tara at Calabrese and trotted off towards Edison Boulevard. 'Well, are you coming?' she called at the pair of feyries rooted to the spot.

Lupin clapped his hands under his chin and stared up at her receding figure, his almond-shaped eyes blinking in devoted admiration. Ahhhh, beautiful, athletic and an undoubted genius ... what a combination! Shame she was just that little bit too tall, though. Still, ninety-eight and a half per cent perfect isn't *that* bad.

It was only as she disappeared around a distant corner at a sprint, Calabrese hard on her heels, that he was shaken suddenly out of his rose-sodden reverie. 'Er ... hey! Hang on. Wait for me,' he cried, as plaintively as a two month old prairie dog pup lost in the endless wastes of the badlands. It took him three whole streets to catch them up, and he only succeeded then when they had to duck behind a convenient van and wait as a gently chinking Dairy Crest milkfloat trundled on by.

And so, after an early morning jog across the dazed suburbs of the Ancient City of Camford, the three unlikely companions dashed into a tiny cut-through and emerged at the back of that corrugated cathedral of scientific research, Splice of Life Patentable Biosciences Ltd.

Barely slowing, they scurried past the bike sheds, skittered around the front corner and stopped dead in their tracks as their eyes fell on a two-ton unmarked Transit, its engine idling boredly in the still morning air.

Tara gasped and dragged the two grey-skinned ones hastily back around the corner out of sight.

'Was that part of your grand plan, eh?' mocked Tara waggling a thumb around the corner.

'What the hell's it doing there? What's it waiting for?' spluttered Calabrese. A tide of panic was rising within him. He knew there were only a few short minutes before the resident scientists rolled up for work and discovered the surprise awaiting them in the turbid nutrient solution of the Amniotic Tanks (TM).

'Deliveries,' she offered matter-of-factly.

'But, we've got to get past it. We've got to get in!' Terror glistened at the very edge of Calabrese's eyes. Was this how it was to end? His cloned brethren trapped helplessly inside Splice of Life at the mercy of scalpel wielding, white-coated scientists; the rise of the New Feyrie Empire stopped by a badly timed two-ton Transit?

'Get past that van? Are you mad? I think the driver might spot you two looking like that. You don't stand a chance . . .' And suddenly a spark of an idea began to hatch in her mind. 'No chance at all . . . looking like that. So why don't you tell me exactly what it is you're after in there, and I'll grab it for you. After all, it's no hassle for me to sneak in unnoticed, especially with, er . . . with . . .' She rummaged about desperately in her inside pocket for a credit card sized security strip – a spare one 'borrowed' from Farson. She was certain it was still there . . . Now where was it?

'Never!' hissed Calabrese. 'You'll never get the credit for it. I masterminded it. Me! And I can get in there myself!' A security card glinted between his elongated fingers.

'How did you . . .?'

'Inside pocket,' he sneered. 'By the way, do you know you snore?'

'I do not!'

'How d'you know? You were asleep at the time.'

Calabrese smiled triumphantly as he scored a minuscule victory.

Suddenly, shattering the drowsy air, a pair of irritable horn blasts sounded from the Transit around the corner, freezing the threesome in a tableau of nervousness. It reminded them, as if they needed it, of their immediate problem.

'So how the hell *are* we going to get past that?' snarled Calabrese.

'I've got an idea,' announced Lupin if anyone was interested.

'Is there a back way in?' pondered Calabrese.

'I know how to do it,' declared Lupin.

'Not one that works with that security card,' Tara answered Calabrese.

Lupin stamped his foot. 'It's obvious,' he hissed.

'What about the windows?' pondered Calabrese tapping his chin.

Lupin tutted miserably and trudged away in the very direction of their problem.

'None of them open,' he heard Tara say behind him. 'Something to do with the air-conditioning,' she added as he peered almost casually around the corner and saw the driver of the Transit stabbing away angrily at the doorbell.

He failed totally to see the flash of grey-skinned creature as it skittered around the back of the van, ran along the far side and, with an effort, scrambled up the sheer cliff of steps and leapt into the cab. In seconds Lupin had grabbed a large fawn overcoat, a pair of sunglasses and, the essential finishing touch, a conveniently discarded black Def Leppard baseball cap.

The other two hadn't moved by the time he returned, his arms overflowing with the jumble sale of clothes.

'So what d'you think, Lupin? Tara distracts him while I sneak around the back and hit him over the head with ... What've you got there?'

'Just shutup and put it on,' tutted Lupin and dropped the collection at his feet.

'Of course! Now why didn't I think of that?' said Calabrese, slapping the baseball cap onto his head.

Lupin made a derogatory noise in his throat and rolled his eyes. Around the corner, Alistair, the deliveryman from DN-Aids Inc was hammering his fists ineffectually against the reinforced tinted doors of Splice of Life.

'C'mon, wakey, wakey! Anybody in there? C'mon! You don't answer soon and I'm goin'. You're not the only delivery I've got this mornin' y'know? Oh no, ten more before I get a coffee break.' Cursing profusely he turned away from the door and folded his arms across his barrel chest, his fists throbbing. 'Bloody scientists, deaf as a blinkin' ... Ahhh, about time too!' He declared, drawing himself up to his full height and marching imperiously towards the brunette teenager and the overcoated one with sunglasses and a baseball cap who had just sauntered casually around the corner.

'You want this stuff, or what?' demanded Alistair tugging up the roll-over door of the van with a rasping noise. 'I've been waiting here hours, you know? Hours!'

Calabrese stopped and stared at the mass of equipment jammed into the dark interior, his mind matching it to the glossy pictures he had seen in the brochure in Tara's wardrobe.

'Well?' hissed the driver. 'D'you want it? You'd better do after keeping me hanging around out here all mornin', I can tell you.'

'I'm sorry, I'm only a technician,' lied Tara, fluttering her eyelids in what she hoped was a placatory way. 'I can't make executive decisions regarding expensive equipment, I'm afraid you'll have to call back tomorrow.'

'Tomorrow? Tomorrow? I can't bloody do ...'

'That won't be necessary,' blurted Calabrese swaying gently atop Lupin's shoulders. 'I'm afraid she's new here,' he confided, his mind positively gyrating with a full oral examination of the gift horse that had galloped into town. 'Now, what, precisely, is it you've got for us?'

'GENE-Erator and all the associated gubbins, just like

what you ordered yesterday. Now, for the last time, are you havin' it, or should I just drive away right now?'

'No, no, I, er . . . we definitely want it.' Calabrese almost begged. 'A GENE-Erator and all the gubbins', there, in front of him, just waiting to be taken away. With this at his fingertips there'd be no end to the numbers of identical followers he could churn out. There would be no stopping him. As many armies of followers as he needed.

'Should hope so, too,' grumbled the driver. 'Now, I'm not deliverin' it any further than this kerb here, you understand? I'm already late for my next customers and my mate's off sick with somethin' he picked up on holiday, so if you expect me to lug this lot inside you're very much mistaken.'

'Don't worry yourself,' grinned Calabrese. 'Here will be absolutely fine. We can sort it out amongst ourselves.'

The driver mumbled begrudging approval and leapt up into the back of the van, flipping down the hydraulic tail with expert ease.

'Are you mad?' hissed Tara under the noise of the whining lift.

'Oh, no,' murmured Calabrese. 'Why have a single trooper when you can have an entire army?'

'What?' Tara's jaw dropped in alarm. 'What d'you mean?'

She never got an answer.

The driver, now feeling a little less het up yelled down, 'Great band, aren't they?'

All three figures on the pavement grunted, 'Eh?'

'Def Leppard,' insisted Alistair over the whining hydraulics, and pushed a chunk of equipment onto the gate, tapping his forehead to indicate the baseball cap. 'Saw 'em at Wembley little while back. You?'

'Er, I . . . yes,' hedged Calabrese as Alistair decended.

'Thought as much. "Wembley" I said to myself soon as I saw that,' he tapped his head again and shoved the chunk of biotechnology onto the herringbone bricks of the pavement. 'And how'd I know it was Wembley?' he chattered, rising slowly from the ground again. 'Black baseball cap, see? They were only selling the black ones at Wembley. Special edition, that is.' He vanished into the gloom and shoved another machine onto the tail. 'I've got one just the same in the cab up front. I can show you if you like?'

'No, no, no! I . . . er I know exactly what it looks like.'

'Ahhh, that you do,' ranted Alistair cheerily without pause for breath, shoving out more and more equipment and informing them, with obvious delight that the black baseball cap was 'exactly the same as what Phil Collen wore on stage. Now that's not Phil Collins out of Genesis, that's Collen the guitarist. Yeah, confusin' isn't it. I was a bit stumped at first. But not as bad as I was when I heard about Paul Young in Mike and the Mechanics and Paul Young him what sung "Wherever I Lay My Hat (That's My Home)".'

Mercifully, before he launched into full discography of all the artists concerned and a brief tuneless rendition of some of each of their more popular hits, he shoved out the final item of equipment.

'That's your lot then,' he announced unnecessarily, zipped the door shut and headed off for the cab. 'And if you've got any complaints about this lot, don't call me!' he shouted and roared off in a cloud of diesel fumes.

Tara was stood with her hands on her hips staring at Calabrese. Lupin peered out through a gap in the buttons and whimpered gently. She looked so stunning when she was angry, the way her eyebrows quivered . . .

'What the hell are you going to do with this lot?' she snapped in amazement.

'Get it out of sight, quick!' barked back Calabrese leaping off Lupin's shoulders and pushing hard at a device which looked remarkably like a washing machine. 'C'mon!'

The other two shrugged. 'What's it worth?' asked Tara.

'How about the man of your dreams?' lashed back Calabrese quickly.

'Eh?'

'Help me and you can have him,' grinned Calabrese a twinkle of excitement phosphorescing at the corner of his eyes.

'Anyone? You mean like . . . .. like Tom Cruise?'

'Anyone,' insisted Calabrese, 'Now, c'mon!'

Tara rubbed her hands together delightedly and thoughts of Tom Cruise all to herself, she began shoving.

Lupin grit his teeth and cursed under his breath. 'Who the hell is this Tom Cruise? And what's he got that I haven't, eh? Bet he can't play the lute or recite one hundred and twenty-three heroic poems word perfect.'

And so, just as a creaking cotterpin and rattling mudguard was heard struggling into the first hundred yards of Edison Boulevard the last of the equipment was tucked away around the little-visited back of Splice of Life.

It had taken him a good six hours of determined concentration, but, after seventy-three attempts starting at level one, Striebley was finally back with one asteroid and a stray comet on his hands.

This time he'd do it. This time he'd get his name on the championship table of Hyper-Asteroid Pool. He was absolutely sure of it, and nothing, not even all that banging on the door and ringing of the bell, would put him off.

The sweat of concentration dribbled down his forehead faster than Andre Agassi's in the full heat of a Wimbledon final. He wiped his palms hastily on the thighs of his thoroughly sweat-stained jeans, took a hasty swig of flat Sainway's cola and stabbed at the buttons with fevered excitement. Instantly his cue's thrusters angled it in for the final approach on the slowly tumbling asteroid. Another tiny blast of pixels spun off into the vacuum of virtual space as he corrected and pushed on forward. Expertly he selected a forty-eight megaton anti-grav pulse, raised his finger and readied himself to launch his penultimate shot. Tongue waggling in a paroxysm of concentration he watched the asteroid tumble into range, his pulse counting off the seconds before launch of the pulse, finger quivering.

Suddenly an alarm erupted into life from the lab below. Striebley jumped, hit the fire button and shot an anti-grav pulse impotently into space. The asteroid rumbled on, its trajectory unaltered. Spitting curses like there was no tomorrow Striebley wrestled with the controls, desperately trying to slew his cue around and catch the runaway lump of granite. He failed.

Helplessly, capable of nothing but profanity, he watched his chance of victory trundle off the edge of the screen and into the arms of oblivion.

'Game Over' confirmed the message.

From the floor below the alarm was still warbling its distress. Kicking the now empty can of Sainway's cola across the lab in disgust he stomped out of the room and clattered down the stairs to find out what damned piece of supposedly advanced biotechnology had run out of what.

Shouldering the door open after the essential zipping of security card in slot he strode in and stood hands on hips glaring at the array of equipment.

'Alright, who is it? C'mon? Who wrecked my game?' Like a cigar chewing sergeant major in a foul mood he strode imperiously in front of the machinery, glaring at every piece. Silently he cursed the manufacturers for not going the whole hog and putting flashing lights on the damn things. It would have made life a shed-load easier.

Eventually, on his third pass when the insistent sound of the alarm had shredded every ounce of remaining patience he had, he found the problem. A single cistern-full of amino acid solution perched atop the Flo-Tein protein generator was empty.

'Damn valves,' cursed Striebley blaming the tool rather than his own judgement as was the true scientific way. He knew Crickson would have supervised Farson as he measured out the correct volume necessary to transfer the current genetic code into all the necessary proteins of life and thus into several hundred tiny chicken fed corn seedlings. The only explanation for running out of tryptophan was a dodgy valve, of course. Stands to reason.

He couldn't possibly have been any further from the truth.

Then suddenly it struck him. Were the seedlings alright? What irreparable damage had the lack of one essential amino acid reaped upon the tender seedlings? And worse . . . could it be fixed without Crickson finding out? The ensuing personal damage didn't bear thinking about.

Panicking he dashed across to the fifty gallon Amniotic Tank and peered nervously into the cloudy primordial soup. Eddies of enzyme-rich nutrient swirled before his eyes as they were slowly stirred and thermostatically incubated. He squinted in, desperate for a glimpse of at least one tiny green seedling. Even a pale yellow one would do.

Suddenly, the alarmingly familiar sound of a security card zipping through the slot rattled into his tender shell-likes. Stifling a scream of alarm he spun around and dived for his stool, frantically trying to adopt some semblance of innocence.

'Well? Well? How are my darling little babies?' shrieked Crickson excitedly as he bounded into the lab and scurried towards the Amniotic Tank, his half moons already in position on the bridge of his nose.

In seconds his aquiline beak was inches away from the toughened glass, his hands spread across the surface as eagerly as a gecko on a Maltese wall. 'Well? Where are they?'

'There, er ... might be a slight ...'

'What?' screamed Crickson spinning to face Striebley. 'A slight what, eh?' The senior professor's eyes lasered angrily over the top of his lenses.

'Er ... p ... problem,' whimpered Striebley.

Crickson whirled back to stare at the Tank concern writ large across his face, as helpless as a father in labour ward. 'What happened? Tell me. I ... I want to know!'

'Just a slight lack of tryptophan, that's all,' muttered Striebley desperately hoping the oil he was attempting to pour upon Crickson's angry seas wouldn't blow up in his face.

'Tryptophan!' came the squealed reply as Crickson stared into the tank. Slowly something loomed towards him.

'It only ran out a couple of minutes ago, it shouldn't be too disastrous ...'

He was cut off in mid-sentence by the scream from

Crickson. Hopping about on the spot he was pointing frantically at the tank his hair turning whiter by the minute. 'My babies! Look at my babies!'

Striebley's jaw dropped in stunned shock as the unmistakable sight of a half-developed fist drifted murkily past, its strangely elongated knuckles scraping the inside of the glass.

'What have you done?' gasped Crickson as a barely completed pair of feet bobbed on by.

'Me? I didn't touch it. You can't blame me for . . . for that.'

'Course I can, you idiot!' yelled Crickson, the neap tide of anger growing. 'You let it run out of tryptophan. You did nothing about it. It's all your fault! You killed my baby seedlings! You! You!' He was prodding Striebley in the chest accusingly.

'But . . . but . . .' It was all he could come up with for the moment. His mind was filled with images of the thing in the tank and a million fizzing questions which didn't seem to make any sense. He knew damn well that lack of an amino acid meant that there'd be a shortage of some protein or enzyme, or other. You'd end up with a weak and feeble version of the something you were trying to grow. Or a dead one. There was absolutely no way on earth that you'd ever end up with something completely different splashing about in the tank. It was just totally, utterly, scientifically impossible, way out, no chance of it ever happening at all . . . unless.

Striebley caught his breath as it hit him. No, surely not. Not this way. It couldn't be. Could it? Ignoring Crickson's squeals for compensation he dashed across to the Apple Mac and stabbed frantically at the keyboard, pulling down menus and selecting files with feverish abandon. In moments the screen was flooded with hundreds of single letters, each either an A, C, G or T. Striebley bit his knuckles and collapsed onto his stool the blood rushing from his face.

'What the hell's that?' blustered Crickson staring at the screenful of unfamiliar genetic code.

'Is that your feeble attempt to change the subject, eh? Well, it won't work you know, I . . . Oi. Are you listening to me? Hey! Pay attention when I'm tearing you off a strip, Striebley. What's so damned fascinating about that bloody ceiling?'

Striebley was shaking his head and staring straight upwards. But his wide-eyed gaze was focused not upon the asbestos lined ceiling. It was fixed way, way beyond the trivial normality of mere man made structures. It looked to the vicinity of Tau Ceti.

'Are you going to tell me what's on this screen?' barracked Crickson, jabbing Striebley in the shoulder.

'Control code for the GENE-Erator,' he answered distantly, his mind already half way beyond our solar system.

'No, it's not,' huffed Crickson. 'That's not the code for Project CFC. What the hell is it?'

'Control code for the GENE-Erator,' repeated Striebley.

'Look, that's not it, alright? Project CFC doesn't start with TGG . . .' Suddenly Crickson stopped. TGG? Now why was that familiar? TGG . . . and then he remembered. Those three letters were the very genetic sequence which coded for tryptophan. Every time it appeared that amino acid was incorporated into the ever growing protein being manufactured under instruction from the DNA. He shuddered as his gaze zipped along the series of letters.

Thousands of TGGs leapt out at him, far, far more than he knew were in the code for Project CFC. So many in fact that if that code had been entered into the GENE-Erator and left running overnight there was no doubt that by about, ooh, eight thirty or so the next morning, give or take ten minutes, the tryptophan cistern would have run completely dry.

Nervously he angled his wrist upwards and peeked at his watch. It was eight thirty-five.

'What is it?' gasped Crickson. 'And what the hell's it doing in my GENE-Erator?'

Striebley pointed beyond the ceiling. 'It's a message,' he whispered in the tone of voice of a prophet who's just been down the pub with his favourite deity – awestruck and intoxicated. 'A message from beyond the stars! They have spoken. To me!'

'A message?' scoffed Crickson. 'You cannot be serious.'

Striebley snatched his gaze away from the light fitting and stared earnestly at Crickson. 'Deadly serious,' he growled and arched his eyebrows to prove the point. 'What did you expect, a postcard from Tau Ceti?'

'Well, as a matter of fact . . .'

'I should have known it would be this way,' ranted Striebley almost guiltily. 'It should have been so obvious. Why risk a ship across the vastness of space when you can simply beam all the necessary information in one single burst of letters. It's so elegant.'

'What are you on about?'

'Don't you see? In that tank is the Ambassador from Tau Ceti, or Epsilon Eridani, or wherever. An envoy from the stars, its mind filled with vital race memories and bursting with technologies beyond our wildest dreams, just waiting to answer all our questions and help mankind a few rungs up the ladder of Interstellar Society . . .' His lungs gave out before his enthusiasm. Gasping he turned red and leant forward panting.

'Shame they didn't tell us to order two extra pintas of tryptophan,' tutted Crickson dryly and began fiddling with the computer.

'Don't be so picky. They can't think of everything.'

'Mmmmm, looks like even aliens from beyond infinity still haven't found a way of hiding their hacking,' grunted Crickson tapping the screen of the Apple Mac. 'From 18.43 till 19.07 we had a visitor, look.'

'That . . . that was them! Oh, God! I was here and I didn't know,' Striebley wailed, staring imploringly at the ceiling again.

'Er . . . I hate to be the one to go shattering any dreams of interstellar communications but,' he grinned a grin that was about to do just that, 'don't you think it's a bit weird, these aliens of yours using a local telephone number to hack in on?'

'What?'

'Here, look.' Crickson angled the monitor towards Striebley and flicked the screen. 'It was good idea of mine to have that 'Hacker Tracker' software installed, eh?'

Striebley stared at the single entry.

18.43 ... 19.07. UNAUTHORIZED ENTRY PERP. 01053 265896.

'Where's that?' he gagged in awe. 'A public call box near a park? Yeah ... it's bound to be. Maybe they came out of hyperspace, landed in the Mayor Keswick Donational Park and rang in from there.'

'Are you telling me that aliens from another galaxy have valid phone cards?' spluttered Crickson dubiously.

'If they've got hyperdrive I'm certain they could figure a way around BT ...'

'You're getting desperate now.'

'But the code? How can you explain that?' begged Striebley feeling the sands of his conviction eroding in the undercurrent of Crickson's scepticism.

'Pass me that phone,' Crickson, commanded and rolled up his sleeve decisively.

Shaking only very slightly Striebley handed it over and hovered nervously as Crickson stabbed away at the buttons. Should he be letting him call up? What if that was a direct link to the vast alien mothership hovering just beyond the nearest jump-gate? Could he trust Crickson with the fate of the entire human race? Was his telephone manner up to it?

Striebley's ears were straining desperately as he heard the ringing tone purr in Crickson's ears. After three there was a series of clicks and a gruff sounding voice came on.

Crickson's eyebrows leapt up his forehead as he heard the answerphone message. 'Hello, hello, hello. This is Chief Inspector Ness. I'm not in right now, probably out solving some vital case or other, you know the way it is. Anyhow, if you've got any info, or clues or stuff that'll help me rid the streets of criminal scum just leave your name and number after the tone and I'll get right back to you just as soon as . . .'

Crickson screamed and slammed the receiver down staring at it as if it had tried to lick him.

'What? What?' shrieked Striebley bouncing up and down impatiently.

'N . . . Ness,' came the gasped reply.

'Eh? They've got Ness on the mother ship?'

'Ness is the hacker!' gagged Crickson shaking his head.

Striebley stood for a moment, dumbfounded, his face the very image of a twelve year old trying to do long division in his head.

'Let's just get this well and truly straight, shall we?' began Striebley a few minutes of confusion later. 'You're trying to tell me that last night Chief Inspector Ness, pillar of the local community, honesty incarnate, hacked into our humble computer network and, with malice aforethought, planted a complex and unique, and up until now secret, sequence of alien DNA in our GENE-Erator?'

Crickson nodded pathetically.

'Ah. Well, there's just one question I'd like answering, if that's at all possible.'

'And that is?'

'What's Chief Inspector Ness doing with a unique, and up until now secret, sequence of alien DNA in his pocket?'

'D'you know, I was just wondering that myself,' confessed Crickson stroking his chin.

Lupin wiped his brow and finally managed to get enough of his breath back to turn on Calabrese and demand, 'Wh . . . what the hell d'you think you're playing at? What are we supposed to do with all this?' He kicked out angrily at the array of equipment collected behind the Splice of Life building.

'Move it quickly,' hissed Calabrese. 'Before we're discovered.'

'Where to?' gasped Lupin.

269

'Away. Far away, out of sight,' mused Calabrese tapping his chin desperately.

'Better not be too far,' complained Lupin. 'It was bad enough just shoving it all around the corner. If you want to go much further, well, I'm not too sure I could . . .'

'And I thought you were made of sterner stuff,' tutted Calabrese shaking his head. 'Now I understand it all. Everything becomes crystal clear.'

'Eh? Understand what?'

'There I was thinking that beneath that unimpressive exterior lurked a muscular integrity to make women go weak at the knees. I can see I was mistaken. Hence your current state of enforced celibacy.' He tossed an idle glance towards Tara who was currently flicking through the GENE-Erator User's Manual.

Lupin's eyes flashed wide with realisation. 'What? You think that I can make an impression by shoving all this stuff . . .'

'Sssssh!' hissed Calabrese suddenly raising his hands for silence as the sound of a two-ton Transit's diesel engine rattled into earshot.

Nervously Calabrese dashed past the bike sheds to the corner of the building and peered around.

Baffled he watched as a strangely familar Transit van executed a natty three point turn in the cul-de-sac and skittered to a halt directly outside the tinted doors of Splice of Life. The driver leapt to the ground, dashed around the front of the cab and accosted a red pony-tailed technician on his way to work.

Fascinated, Calabrese watched as the DN-Aids Inc delivery man repeatedly thrust a clipboard of pink delivery forms under the technician's nose and was met with a barrage of shrugs of denial. The conversation was volleyed ably by the delivery man and returned with a deft waving of palms. Only when the threat of actual bodily harm became obvious did the red haired technician swipe his security card in the door and show the delivery man inside.

Then, staring at the silent delivery van, an idea hit

Calabrese between the lobes. He was on his feet in seconds and beckoning enthusiastically to Lupin and Tara. He spun on his heel and sprinted across the herringbone brickwork of the pavement, skipped eagerly around the far side of the van and was up in the cab faster than a terrier down a sett-full of prime badgers.

Tongue planted firmly in the corner of his mouth he splayed his fingers and carefully traced the paths of power lines running up and down the steering column. Within moments he had sensed a break in the circuitry centred around what looked like a small mechanical knothole.

'What d'you think you're playing at?' stage whispered Tara as she tugged open the cab door and stared in at the feyrie in the foot well, a pair of wires in each hand.

'Can you drive this thing?' he asked waggling the ignition cable out of the steering column.

'Yeah ... I ... I think so, but ...'

'Excellent,' hissed Calabrese stripping the wires with his teeth. He twisted two bare ends together. There was a brief spark and the diesel coughed instantly to life.

'Bring the equipment around and get it loaded,' he barked and sprang out of the cab.

Inside Striebley's lab, the conspiracy theories were getting way out of hand as the two professors stared wide eyed at the strings of letters filling the computer screen.

'You don't think Ness's ...'

'... in with the FBI?' interrupted Crickson.

'... and that's the genetic code from ...' countered Striebley.

'... the Roswell American Air Force Base, Nevada!'

Striebley stood open mouthed for a moment.

'Nah,' he denied a second later. 'Much more likely to be working for Scotland Yard. After all, who's to say that America has a monopoly on aliens, eh? I mean, just 'cause they've got *The X Files* and *Star Trek* ...'

Suddenly Crickson clicked his fingers together, slapped his thighs and leapt to his feet.

'Got an idea?' asked Striebley helpfully.

'Of course, it all makes perfect sense! Why else would Camford Constabulary be using us to test their criminal DNA?'

'Er . . . the Criminal Justice Charter?' suggested Striebley totally lost again.

'How better to keep an eye on us and ensure our silence than by utilising that iron hard grip that comes from the exertion of financial pressure?'

'You mean blackmail?'

'Well, it's like that, but a bit more subtle. He's probably been checking us out for months, bugging our telephone calls and such like . . .'

'No. I know exactly how he's been doing it,' grinned Striebley getting thoroughly into the spinning of conspiracy theories. He hadn't seen every episode of *The X Files* without *something* rubbing off. 'It's someone closer to home. I've suspected it for weeks, the way he's always doing something shifty and hardly ever around when you need him, talking to folk on the phone and . . .'

He never finished that accusatory sentence for at that very instant there was a zipping sound and the door burst open to admit the unmistakably pony-tailed technician leading a confused delivery man from the DN-Aids Inc company.

''Ere look, all I need is a signature on this form an' I'll be off,' announced Alistair the delivery man. 'All that talk about Def Leppard and the bleedin' form went straight out me 'ead. I was 'alf way up Fenland Road when I thinks to myself I haven't got a signature, I thought, so . . .'

'What are you talking about?' growled Crickson.

'Delivery, guv. This mornin'. Dropped it off outside. That chap with the Def Leppard baseball cap and glasses said it'd be fine to leave it out front. Him and that pretty young brunette with the anorak said they'd sort it out later.'

Farson's ears pricked up. It couldn't be, could it? It had to be Tara. But what was she up to?

Crickson and Striebley looked at each other and swallowed. What was going on? Was this Ness's way of tightening the screw of their financial discomfort? Could he keep them quiet with another fifty grand added to their debt?

'Look, I'm not signing for a delivery I didn't get and you can tell your boss that,' insisted Crickson showing the delivery man the door.

'Yeah, yeah, it's a very nice door, guv, but I'm not leaving here without a signature. More than my job's worth, see?'

'And how does your truck being nicked count in a job security sort of way,' asked Striebley looking out of the tinted front door at the shadowy figure in the cab and the plumes of smoke emanating from the exhaust.

'Ahh, no. You can't pull that one on me,' winked Alistair wisely. 'I know what you're up to an' it won't work, see?'

'Oh yes?' answered Striebley as the two-ton Transit lurched forward, stalled and cut out.

'Yeah. I'm supposed to go runnin' out to see what's goin' on an' you lot slam the door behind me an' don't let me in again.'

A plume of diesel erupted once again from the Transit's exhaust as it was re-hotwired by the expert fingers of Calabrese and, with far too many revs for the engine's good, it roared off down Edison Boulevard.

Casually, Striebley zipped his security card down the slot in the front door and with a swish they opened. Helpfully he pointed out the receding van and the delivery man's rapidly vanishing job prospects.

'Why didn't y'tell me!' he shrieked and was out the door in seconds, the door sliding shut behind him cutting off his cries of 'Come back with my van you bast . . .'

On the opposite side of the road two blue overalled figures stood in the doorway of Tyres'R'Us leaning against a stack of Michelins, sipping coffee and shaking their heads.

'Disgusting. Can't leave anything standin' around out here these days,' tutted one of them. 'Shockin',' mused his mate. 'Joyriders these days are gettin' worse. I mean, just listen to the revs on that. Burn out the engine in a few thousand miles if they carry on like that.'

'Disgusting,' tutted the first one again downing his

morning mug of Mellow Birds with a slurp and, being the public spirited chappie that he was, he shuffled off to increase Camford Constabulary's workload by a factor of one reported taking and driving away.

Now familiar with both the camber of Edison Boulevard and the sharp right turn into it, the two drivers of the Camford Constabulary squad cars managed to add a good twelve miles an hour to their entry velocity. The pair of orange and white Rovers screamed in towards Splice of Life Patentable Biosciences Ltd just touching eighty, their wheels barely in contact with the tarmac, their sirens echoing off the row of buildings. Four doors up from the bullet-proof tinted security door of Splice of Life both drivers slammed heavy feet onto brakes, twitched their steering weels and pirouetted gracefully to halt in the now traditional cloud of acrid blue.

Across the road an amazed mechanic in a blue overall peered through the door of Tyres'R'Us clutching a telephone receiver. 'Blimey, that was quick,' he gasped and, much to the confusion of the receptionist at Camford Constabulary the emergency of a stolen Transit suddenly vanished. Idly wondering precisely how many tyres they get through in the average day behind the wheel the blue overalled one trudged off towards an aging Golf and set about re-radialing the thing.

'Open up!' shouted Chief Inspector Ness pounding his fists against the tinted door of Splice of Life. 'This is the law!'

Between hammerings there could just be heard a slight zipping of a card in a slot and abruptly it slid open.

'Aha! The very person I want to see,' declared Professor Crickson stepping out of the door and into the glare of Ness and Boscombe's combined stares. 'You've got some explaining to do I think. Do come in.'

'Hang on. It's you that needs to do the explaining,' insisted Ness. 'We have reason to believe that a vital sample of blood was taken from my daughter ten years ago for the purposes of kidnap verification has ended up here ...'

274

'Tut, tut, Chief Inspector. I really don't think that you should be concerning yourself with such trivial earthly matters as police business. Not today of all days.' Crickson turned away, slid into the leafy green atrium and headed off towards Striebley's lab.

'Did you hear that?' spluttered Ness, his face reddening. 'Police business, trivial? How dare he?' The buttons on his jacket gleaming with judicial rage, Ness stomped across the threshold.

'Interfering with forensic evidence is *far* from trivial,' frowned Doctor Boscombe slapping his trusty Victorian magnifying glass into the palm of his hand in the manner beloved by thugs with baseball bats. He followed in the Chief Inspector's echoing footsteps.

Behind him PCs Plain and Skitting raised curious eyebrows at each other, shrugged and stared after the receding figures. This sounded like it was going to be very interesting. Plain scratched his head and wondered if he had ever heard Chief Inspector Ness explain anything to a member of the public. Curiousity fizzing like a burger on a barbecue they sprinted into earshot.

'Professor Crickson, would you care to explain your wherabouts between the hours of . . .' began Ness imperiously. It was as far as he got before Crickson silenced him with a dismissive flick of his wrist.

'Come, come, Chief Inspector, let's drop this pretence of normality. We all know why you're here. So why don't you just come clean and tell us where it came from, eh?'

Ness stared at the two scientists standing before the now covered amniotic tank. He was stunned. He wasn't used to suspects answering back. Especially not with very accusatory sounding questions.

Unseen behind him PC Plain rubbed his palms together eagerly.

'Tau Ceti? Epsilon Eridani? Venus? C'mon Chief Inspector, where did it come from?' pressed Striebley.

Farson shook his head. What side of bed had he got out of this morning? Things were far from normal.

275

'Would you mind speaking in English?' hissed Ness, massaging his temples with trembling thumbs.

'Come now, you're among friends,' smiled Striebley. 'We know it was you who altered the control file. Just tell us where you got the codes from. Was it shot down over Porton Down? Have the RAF got the remains of the craft?'

'What control file?'

'The one controlling the GENE-Erator. That's why you're here isn't it? To see the results of your handiwork, eh?'

'Am I imagining this?' begged Ness turning to Boscombe. 'Tell me they're asking sensible questions, please.'

Boscombe scratched his head. 'Grammatically they are perfectly constructed,' he replied with a slight quiver in his voice. 'However, they do appear to be somewhat lacking in the sense department.'

'So what are they talking about?' begged Ness.

'You know damn well,' snapped Striebley. 'This!' He tugged the lab-coat off the murky amniotic tank.

There were gasps of confusion all round.

'You hacked into our system and planted the genetic codes to create it. Now, for the third time: Where the hell did it come from?' insisted Striebley.

Curiousity writ large across their foreheads, the visitors from Camford Constabulary advanced on the opaque vessel, peering into the swirling solution.

'Oh my God ...!' gasped Ness as a strangely elongated half-formed knuckle swam into view.

'What ... what is it?'

The wind fell out of Striebley's sails. 'You mean you d ... don't know?'

'Haven't a clue,' shrugged the Chief Inspector. 'Going to tell us what it is, then?'

'We were hoping *you'd* tell *us*,' whimpered Striebley.

Crickson leant forward and, staring across Ness's shoulder at the thing in the tank, said, 'Bit of a conundrum, don't you think?'

'It's ... it's hideous!'

Only one of the forces of Law and Order seemed pleased

by the vision. 'It's just like I said it would be,' cried Boscombe, pointing wildly at the tank as a long thin foot slewed into view. 'Look at that meta-tarsal formation!'

'Aha!' declared Crickson, 'The truth at last!'

Ness stared at the foot drifting by, his attention captured with the revolted fascination of a schoolchild watching a conger eel in an aquarium. Reluctantly he had to admit that it did bear a striking resemblance to Boscombe's Polyfilla sculpture.

'How did you get it looking so realistic?' asked the forensic scientist in raptures of fascination, his eyes wide as they tracked every movement of the foot. 'It's latex isn't it? Have you been taking lessons from the guys who did the special effects for *Aliens*?'

'It wasn't too hard . . .' began Crickson.

Boscombe turned suddenly to the awestricken Chief Inspector. 'You should send me out to a course at Pinewood, then you could really trust my sculptures. Just imagine how realistic I could make my evidence. Might make court fun again, like in the old days when . . .'

'It wasn't too hard making it look real,' began Crickson again, 'Because it is, in fact, totally real.'

'Wait a minute,' cut in Striebley, eyes widening as he snatched at Boscombe's last few sentences. 'Sculpture? What sculpture?'

'Reconstructive modelling of a foot not too dissimilar to that based on the footprint found at the scene of . . .'

'Footprint!' shrieked Striebley clapping his hands together and leaping into the air excitedly.

'Did you hear that? A footprint! My God . . . it's true.'

'What's true,' whimpered Ness, not entirely certain he really wanted to hear the answer. The way this morning was going he was probably destined not to like it much.

'They're here!' declared Striebley.

'Hold on, hold on!' cried Ness clutching at his temples again. 'Who's here? What's going on?' Crickson stared at Ness in disappointed confusion, his brow wrinkling. 'You mean you don't know?'

'Don't know what? Will somebody tell me what's going on?' wailed Ness.

'The aliens have landed,' chorused Striebley, Crickson and Boscombe.

'A . . . aliens,' gagged Ness the whites of his eyes showing around his dilated pupils. 'But my Tara . . .'

'Ah, yes,' began Boscombe. 'Things would be seeming to point towards, er, her being taken a little further away than the distances of which the average kidnapper is capable.'

'Further away? How far?' begged Ness.

'Oooh, no more than a couple of light years or so,' hedged Boscombe. 'Or he might only be in the next galaxy, you never know your luck.'

Somehow this news didn't seem to settle at all comfortably with the Chief Inspector. 'How am I going to explain this to Rosemary? And where am I going to get the resources for an intergalactic house-to-house?'

Streibley was skipping up and down as he listened to this exchange and suddenly made a connection in his head. 'Actually. I don't think she's that far away,' he announced.

'What? Where is she?'

'Well, I don't exactly know that,' admitted Striebley losing a little of his momentum. 'But . . . but I know where she was last night.'

All eyes were glued on him. Not least those bloodshot peepers of the desperate Chief Inspector.

'Where?' he begged.

'In your house!' declared Striebley in the irritating tone of voice beloved by the poorer tv sleuths. He whirled on his heels and began stabbing away at the keyboard of the Apple Mac.

'Chief Inspector Ness, what were you doing between the hours of 18.43 and 19.07 last night?'

'That's my question,' answered Ness.

'Just answer it,' pressed Striebley to the added fascination of the two PC's at the back of the group.

'I . . . I was settling down to watch *Life on Earth*,' admitted Ness. 'BBC 2 are rerunning it

'Just as I thought. And your wife?'

'Washing up, where she should be. What *is* this?'

Striebley triumphantly spun the screen of the Apple Mac around to face his gathered audience. 'Somebody was hacking into our computer system whilst you were otherwise engaged.'

'So?'

'Recognise the phone number, Chief Inspector?'

'Oh, my . . .' Ness slapped a hand across his mouth.

Striebley puffed out his chest triumphantly. 'Does anyone find it more than a little suspicious that the very day after Tara disappears under less than unsuspicious circumstances, a hacker pays us a call from her phone and, without triggering any of the alarms, enters alien genetic codes into our equipment. Genetic codes, I might add, taken from the very forensic samples that were delivered here yesterday morning! The very ones taken from that lab upstairs.'

The shocked silence was as thick as a mature camembert.

'It seems to me,' whispered Striebley in his finest conspiracy theory voice, 'that there is much more to this than meets the eye. Come, it is time we discussed this in more detail. Farson, bring hot sweet tea to the board room immediately. It seems our dear Chief Inspector is in need.'

And with that Striebley led Crickson, Boscombe and Ness away up the stairs. Farson, his head spinning under a maelstrom of whirling questions, headed off for the kitchen. Was that brunette seen by the delivery man this morning the very girl he was supposed to have kidnapped? If so, what was she doing pinching fifty grand's worth of scientific equipment? Who was the strange figure in the Def Leppard baseball cap? And how could that thing in the tank have possibly left its footprint at the scene of Tara's apparent disappearance?

PC. Plain scratched his quarter inch long mat of hair and stared at the thing in the tank. 'What odds would you give on Proxima Centauri?' he mused opening his notebook.

'100–1 against,' answered Skitting. 'Venus?'

'Hmmmm, 9–4 on. Tau Ceti?'

'Where the hell's that?'

'Buggered if I know,' mused Plain licking his pencil. 'Let's give it 200–1 against, eh? What d'you think?'

'Sounds about right to me,' shrugged Skitting. 'I'll give you a fiver on Proxima Centauri, then.'

'Done.'

Hints, Tip and Handcuffs

Grinning like a blunt-scalpel appendix scar, the jagged edge of freshly laid tarmac snaked its way down the pavement of Fenland Road, looped around the avenue of chestnut trees and gruesomely cauterised the dozen or so side streets branching off.

'Beautiful that, in't it?' announced Derrick the Chief Tarmac Operative, sighting down the wriggling black ribbon of trauma. As usual he had to shout above the background racket of the compressor. That and the hundreds of horns blaring their impatience as they sat miserably in three hundred yards of traffic jam piled up behind the red and white tent. 'Yeah, a sheer work of art,' grinned Bob the Operator-in-Charge of Pneumatic Drills squinting proudly at his handiwork. 'D'you know, I think I'm gettin' straighter.' His hand trembled before his eyes, vibrating at precisely the same frequency as his drill.

'Definitely,' confirmed Derrick, shovelling a few hefty trowels' worth of Marvel into the day's fifteenth mug of what passed as tea thereabouts. 'If those trees weren't there that'd make a laser look wiggly.'

'You reckon?'

'Too right,' mused Derrick cheerily smashing the stubborn icebergs of powdered milk floating on the murky surface of the tea.

'You say the nicest things sometimes, you know?' grinned Bob, accepting his tea and scalding his hands as usual. 'I must say your tarmac is really lookin' unusually flat today. And I particularly admire the deft manner in which you succeeded in filling that drainage duct unfortunately uncovered by myself being somewhat overenthusiastic with the tool of my trade.'

'Awww, you're just sayin' that,' answered Derrick coyly.

'No, no. As one artist to another, I *know* when simple roadworks transcend the mundane and take on an artistic worth more at home on the walls of the Louvre.'

'Cooo,' coo-ed Derrick and slurped his tea.

'Take Isambard Kingdom Brunel for example. He would've been quite within his rights to just slap a few bits o' prestressed concrete across the Clifton Gorge and call it a bridge but oh no, not 'im. Not Izzy. You ever seen the Clifton Suspension Bridge? Beautiful that is, poetry in cast iron, a sheer riveted stunner of a . . .'

Fortunately for Derrick, Bob's rapture was rudely curtailed by the sudden unannounced appearance of a two-ton unmarked Transit. It swerved around the back of a large caravan hand-painted in primary colours, burst through a gap in the chestnuts, losing a wing mirror, and swerved barely controllably onto the pavement.

'Now would you look at that,' said Derrick shaking his head and staring at the rapidly approaching van, its door handles striking sparks off the miles of cast iron railings. 'Some people are so impatient. The lengths they'll go to just to get past the car in front.'

'Shocking,' tutted Bob chewing at a particularly thick slice of tea. 'Leads to road rage that does.'

The Transit sprang across a sidestreet, leaping the gap with the agility of a charging rhinoceros. It hit the kerb at full tilt jettisoning a pair of hubcaps and stampeded towards them.

'Dangerous that,' commentated Derrick. 'Didn't even slow down, you know? Could've been anything coming.'

With a squeal of over-revving engine the van shot across another sidestreet.

'I've seen 'em do this so many times,' tutted Bob. 'It never gets 'em far, you know? They always have to stop at the end and squeeze back into the queue. Slow down in a minute, always do, just you watch.'

'Er, you sure?' squeaked Derrick.

With a clatter of metal and an explosion of glass the

charging van lost its other wing mirror and careered on towards them, chewing up the distance at a good sixty.

'Yeah, yeah. Trust me. I know what I'm talking about,' he took a sip of tea. 'Now, take the Forth Road Bridge as another . . .'

The van twitched around a post box with millimetres to spare and roared on down the pavement, its roof smashing chestnut branches in all directions.

It was only as Bob stared straight into the whites of the van's headlights that he realised he might just perhaps have misjudged its intended course of actions. The phrase 'slowing down' appeared not to be in its dictionary of suitable definitions.

Screaming, Derrick tugged the Operator-in-Charge of Pneumatic Drills behind a convenient chestnut, sending his mug flying in a muddy rainbow of tea. As the Transit cannoned through the tea-shower, there was a wet slapping sound, a ravenous revving of diesel, a squeal of tyres and it was gone, lurching onto Fenland Road and heading out of Camford. The souls of many a shattered speed limit writhed dying in its wake.

'Now, would you look at that,' cringed Derrick a few moments later when the relative calm of the compressor and a few dozen impatient horns was all that filled the morning air. 'Just look at my work!' He stared miserably at three-quarters of a mile of tarmac sporting inch-deep tyre tracks and somehow knew that his bonus was out of the window.

'My mug,' wailed Bob peering around the base of the chestnut at a crushed tin mug pressed handle deep into the hot black tar. 'Why does nobody ever appreciate an artist?' he wailed. 'I bet da Vinci never had problems like this.'

Already miles away the screams of anger inside the cab of the Transit was almost as loud as the engine.

'Have you gone mad?' squealed Tara kicking at Calabreae as he clung to the accelerator pedal, pressing it desperately into the floor.

'Just shutup and steer,' came the hissed reply.

'Slow down!' yelled Tara as they turned airborne over the

rise of a humpback bridge. It was the signal Calabrese had been waiting for. Three ... two ... one ...

He leapt off the accelerator pedal and snatched at the steering wheel tugging it wildly and sending the van spinning into a gravel side road on the left. 'Keep going until I say stop,' he hissed peering through the steering wheel at the track ahead.

For the first time Tara saw her chance. Slamming her boot on the brake and pulling the gears into neutral the Transit shuddered to a halt. In a second she had ripped apart the hotwiring and pinned Calabrese to the steering wheel, her forearm across his throat.

'That's far enough,' she hissed. 'I think it's time for some explanations! What d'you want with fifty thousand quid's worth of scientific equipment, eh?'

'D ... drive on,' choked Calabrese. 'Up the track. They'll see us from the road if we stay here.'

'*After* the explanations,' insisted Tara. There was definitely something odd going on here. Was this equipment the very reason these creatures had trekked countless light years across space?

Could it be possible that the human race was actually ahead of these aliens in our knowledge of genetics? If that was the case then she wanted more than to just be an accomplice to robbery. She was in a position to make a deal. And if that was just to see the flight deck of their craft then so be it. It would be kind of nice if she could get the secret of faster-than-light travel out of them though. Now, if she could just work out how important this gubbins in the back of the van was to them ...

'How important is this gubbins in the back of the van, eh?' she demanded.

On the passenger seat, clinging to the seat belt, a wide eyed Lupin stared up at the inquisitorial Tara. His eyes drank in the arch of her eyebrows, the twitching of her delicious cheek muscles. The heady mixture of hormones and the adrenalin from the wing-mirror-wrecking-dash through Camford turned his knees to custard and his heart to racing far faster than it was designed for. Hyperventilating, he slithered down the seat.

'I'll tell you, I'll tell you,' pleaded Calabrese. 'Just move the van. D'you want us to get caught?'

'Not really. Thanks to you I've got more reasons to avoid getting caught. The authorities don't look very favourably on teenagers running off with a Transit stuffed with hundreds of thousands of quids' worth of delicate scientific equipment. And if *they* don't get me, there's always the thugs from DN-Aids Inc. I bet they've already got a contract out on me.'

'All the more reason to m . . . move the van,' panicked Calabrese his eyes wider than ever.

'Tell me what the hell you're playing at?' pressed Tara leaning on her forearm a little heavier.

'Yes, yes, promise!' came the choked reply. 'Move the van.'

'Alright, but just let me handle the accelerator this time, okay?'

'Anything, anything . . .'

With a suspicious growl she dropped the feyrie into the foot well. In seconds he had retwined the bare wires and with a cough the engine erupted into life.

Concentrating on keeping the van on the narrow track she failed to notice Calabrese's deft grey fingers fishing in her anorak pocket.

'Stop here,' barked Calabrese recognising a large oak. Tara depressed the clutch and the van crunched to a halt. Before she had a chance to remove her hands from the steering wheel Calabrese leapt forward, snapping her handcuffs around her wrists, entwining the chain irremovably through the spokes of the wheel. The van leapt forward and cut out as Tara's foot slipped off the clutch and the shouting and chain rattling began. Lupin's cries of innocence were buried.

'Save your breath,' hissed Calabrese standing on the dashboard brandishing a three-quarter inch drop-forged ring spanner he'd found in the foot well. 'I'm in charge now,' he announced through clenched teeth, slapping the spanner meaningfully into the palm of his hands and glaring alternately from Tara to the quivering Lupin.

'In charge of what?' asked Tara. 'What are you trying to do? Make as many enemies as you can in as short a time as possible?'

'Not enemies, no,' grinned Calabrese triumphantly. 'Armies!' he declared, a ring of wildness fizzing at the edge of his eyes like luminous eyeliner. 'I have everything I need in the back of this truck.'

'What?' spluttered Lupin.

'You can't make an army,' suggested Tara. 'You've got the wrong adjective there, you *train* armies. You know, lots of square bashing and manoeuvres and assault courses and stuff.'

'Not me. Not with all that equipment.' His finger waggled towards the rear of the van.

Tara's mind whirred as she tried desperately to recall precisely what was back there. Everything had gone so fast today, it was hard to recall. She squinted into the rear-view mirror, its furry dice still swinging, and caught a glimpse of the tops of the equipment. And suddenly she realised what the mad thing on the dashboard had in mind.

'The GENE-Erator!' she gasped, recalling in worryingly vivid detail her impromptu lesson on all aspects of genetic manipulation and . . . gulp . . . cloning.

'Of course,' grinned Calabrese twirling the chrome vanadium spanner and tucking it under his armpit. He puffed out his thirteen inch chest like a sergeant Major he'd no doubt witnessed on CablePix and strutted up and down the dashboard. 'An army of identical cloned copies, all ready to put our name back into the Dictionary of Terror, all ready to unleash the Forces of Disorder, all created in the exact image of their General.'

'You?' gagged Lupin from the passenger seat beginning to wonder what rhymed with dictatorial lunatic. Perhaps the writing of heroic ballads wasn't as easy as he first thought.

'Who else?' cried Calabrese euphorically. 'Our future is

only safe in my hands. Oberon, Titania, Puck, their time has gone. They've lost it, totally!'

'They're not the only ones,' muttered Tara tugging at her handcuffs to no avail, and all of a sudden Calabrese's actions swam into crystal clarity. The interest in her knowledge of the activities of Splice of Life Patentable Biosciences Ltd. The sudden seizure of chivalry as he offered to retrieve the damning evidence from the Forensics lab. The hacking into Splice of Life. The stealing of all this equipment. It had all been heading one way. The way of the Crazed Alien B-Movie Invasion Flick.

'Is that all you aliens ever think about?' she asked as a wave of disappointment welled up inside. 'Domination, destruction, the subjugation of the human race to your own warped and evil ways?'

'Yes,' grinned Calabrese. 'Sounds like fun.'

'Well it's not very original, you know? Been done millions of times before. From Daleks mining the earth's magnetic core, to whopping great chunks of spaceships zapping the White House with screaming lasers. I *had* hoped they'd all be wrong. That maybe, just maybe, the day would come when we really did make first contact and made friends. Okay, so maybe we haven't mastered faster-than-light travel, or teleportation, or the intricacies of hyperspace yet. But you lot don't know everything. I mean, look at you. You haven't even mastered clothes yet. And as for genetics ... You've already shown your ignorance there. What have you got to gain by trying to wreak havoc all the time?'

Lupin stared up at Tara's furrowed brow and twitching cheekbones feeling utterly helpless, her heartfelt speech stirring him. What had he dragged her into? It was all his fault. If he hadn't kidnapped her then she'd be ... she'd be ... well, she wouldn't be handcuffed to the steering wheel of a two-ton Transit staring at a lunatic feyrie toting a three-quarter inch drop-forged ring spanner, that's for sure.

Calabrese rubbed his chin thoughtfully. 'What have we got to gain by wreaking havoc all the time?' he mused. 'That's a *very* good question. And the answer is, in reverse order. The delight of watching you all suffer. In second place . . . the thrill of inflicting chaos at every turn and, last, but by no means least, being back in charge. Oh yes, it'll be stacks better than the old days. Things are so much more complicated these days. So much more damageable. Just think, a single telephone exchange offers a million times more fun than all the rapidly souring milk churns in the world. And then there's air traffic control! And let's not forget the machines that go ping in those places where people are ill . . .'

'Hospitals,' whimpered Lupin, turning pale.

'And the control systems of fast breeder nuclear reactors! Just unplug them for a few minutes and . . . Wha-Boooooom! And to think, I used to get my kicks out of tugging three-legged stools out from beneath milkmaids. How could I have been so naive?'

Tara cursed herself for introducing the mad thing to SimMaggedon 2000. How could she have been so stupid? She must have planted over half the ideas in its head. This impending wave of chaos would be all her fault. Her mind twitched in panic and filled with images of countless wildly cackling creatures swarming unchecked across the country, wreaking chaos, spreading havoc and loving every maniacal minute of it.

And hard on its tail came a wildly reckless idea of her own. She tugged at her handcuffs and cursed under her breath. It was now or never, all down to her.

Calabrese was still pondering the damage a jumbo could do if it just happened to fall out of the sky onto a packed-out interstate freeway outside New York when Tara took a deep breath and piped up.

'Aren't you getting just a little carried away here?'

Calabrese spun on his heel, swung a scything spanner blow at the furry dice strapped to the rear-view mirror and stared angrily at the source of the interruption.

Tara offered the answer before Calabrese had a chance. 'I mean, it's all well and good dreaming about setting a dozen or so nuclear reactors to meltdown just for the hell of it . . .'

288

Calabrese's eyes flashed with the rapture of devilment.

'But . . . don't you think you're a little, er, short staffed?' she added.

Nervously Lupin scratched his head. Questions twitched apprehensively in the wings.

'Nonsense,' hissed Calabrese. 'It appears you haven't understood me. With the gubbins in the back of this van I can have absolutely just as many members of my army as I want!'

'True enough,' mused Tara. 'It'll take a while though, don't you think?'

For the first time in a very, very long time Calabrese didn't have an answer.

Tara pressed on. 'Let's see, say at the best estimate it takes at least four hours to run through a complete cycle of the GENE-Erator, right? And you need, say, a thousand troops then that'll take . . . oooh, six months or so to get together. And that's assuming you run twenty-four hours a day, seven days a week and aren't found first.'

'Yeah, so?' snapped Calabrese, trying to sound as if he'd already thought of that. 'I've already thought of that,' he added to make sure Tara knew it.

'In that case you won't be bothered about a way to cut that time right down to . . . oooh, a couple of weeks, maybe even faster. I mean, if you're happy about waiting around, twiddling your thumbs for half a year before you can start your frenzy of madness, then I'll just shut up.'

'No, no!' blurted Calabrese, scurrying along the top of the dashboard.

'No, no!' wailed Lupin into his hands. She can't do this. She can't help him. Can she?

'Speed things up?' gasped Calabrese peering into Tara's eyes. 'How? How? Tell me!'

'Shame on you,' taunted Tara. 'I thought you'd read all of the GENE-Erator instruction manual.'

The feyrie stood staring at her, his verdant asterisk of modesty ivy trembling with pent excitement. 'Yes, well, the last few pages were . . .'

'Ahhh, that's why you haven't figured it out.' Tara rolled her eyes to heaven in relief. To Calabrese it looked for all the world as if she was mocking him.

'Figured what?' he snarled slamming the chrome vanadium spanner angrily onto the steering wheel scant inches from Tara's knuckles. In the passenger seat Lupin clenched his fists impotently. If he hurts her beautiful knuckles, I'll, I'll . . .

'"Hints and Tips"? You didn't see that?' she asked, her stomach knotting desperately.

'No. Tell me!' The spanner whistled down onto the steering wheel again. Tara felt the draught on her wrist.

'"Hints and Tips Number Three",' she began to quote. '"By connecting three or more Amniotic Tanks (TM) to the Parallel Cloning Output Buffer of the GENE-Erator a substantial increase in desired biomass can be produced in a shorter time. Additional Amniotic Tanks (TM) are available from your local supplier at a cost of . . ."'

'Oh yes, very funny,' snarled Calabrese obviously finding it the opposite. '"Available from your local supplier", eh? How's that supposed to help me?'

Tara made a show of looking over both shoulders, lowering her voice and, despite the restrictions of the handcuffs, gesturing to the spanner wielding feyrie to come closer.

Captivated, he did.

'What if I was to tell you where there were three more Amniotic Tanks, just lying around doing nothing?' she whispered in her finest conspirational voice.

'Three more? Doing nothing?' gasped Calabrese.

Tara glanced over her shoulders again and nodded. 'Yours for the taking,' she added.

'Where? Where?' begged Calabrese.

On the passenger seat Lupin was rocking back and forth in a ferment of woe. Not only had he been solely responsible for dragging his beloved Tara into this wild conspiracy but, worse, she was actually helping. He couldn't believe it.

Tara cleared her throat and rattled her handcuffs. 'Er, I

would drive you there only gear changing might be a gnat on the difficult side. And as for steering . . .'

Lupin's ears pricked up.

'Just tell me where they are,' hissed Calabrese.

'Sorry,' Tara. 'I've got this terrible memory, don't you know? When I'm behind the wheel I can go straight there, but try and give someone directions and they could end up anywhere, absolutely anywhere.'

The Transit's cab was filled with the sound of Calabrese sucking the inside of his cheek thoughtfully. 'Three more, you say?'

'Just lying around,' tempted Tara dangling the carrot a little closer. 'Just waiting for you.' A few more sucks of Calabrese's cheek set Lupin's nerves a-jangle.

'If you're lying . . .' growled Calabrese unlocking Tara's handcuffs and scrambling down the steering column to re-hotwire the Transit.

In moments she was crunching the gears into reverse and, head out of the window, was backing the wing-mirrorless van down the gravel track of 'Rumpy Row'.

Lupin gazed up at her admiringly. That had to be the first time he had ever seen anybody get the better of Calabrese. If only he knew exactly what she was playing at. Miserably he looked at his toes and wondered, just hypothetically, what life would be like with an army of Taras on his side.

Rocking gently back and forth on a chair in the board room of Splice of Life Patentable Biosciences Ltd Chief Inspector Ness still couldn't believe his ears. Aliens! His eyes stared fixedly through the bottom of the mug which had once contained a dose of hot sweet tea as recommended by Doctor Striebley. Aliens! Even though he'd heard all the evidence, watched Boscombe unveil his sculptured Polyfilla foot and seen the thing in the tank, he still couldn't believe that the simple kidnapping of his daughter had turned into an abduction by intergalactic beings of indeterminate origin.

Around him the conversation whirled and spun with the gay abandon of a hurricane harbouring thoughts of typhoonhood. Farson listened wide-eyed with excitement and alarm. All his SOFA theories had been correct . . . well, except for the bit about them being friendly, it seemed.

At that very moment Striebley was pounding the desk with his clenched fists. 'I'm telling you, we've got to find them. And first!'

'To get Ness's daughter back?' asked Professor Crickson with a surprisingly deft eye towards keeping in with the Chief Inspector. He wasn't going to lose out on the DNA profiling contract if he could possibly help it. Returning Ness's dear daughter would be a whole wingful of feathers in his flat cap.

'Yeah, yeah, her as well,' tutted Striebley dismissively as if flicking an irritating fruit fly from his nose.

'We need them to make damned certain there's a future for Splice of Life.' Crickson swallowed and grabbed at Striebley. Desperately he hissed into his ear, 'Until Project CFC is up and running *he* is our future, remember?' He stabbed a surreptitious finger across the table at the vacantly staring Chief Inspector still peering into the bottom of a mug sporting a transfer of some unidentifiable chunk of essential lab equipent. 'We find his daughter, we're made for life, right? He's bound to be a little on the grateful side.'

'We find the aliens we're made for eternity,' enthused Striebley his eyes glinting with excitement. Crickson stopped shaking Striebley.

'Eh?'

'I'll bet you can't even begin to imagine all the technology just waiting inside that starship. Technology just waiting to be patented by us.'

Professor Crickson's eyes lit up as Striebley continued to weave his spell.

'Just think, once we get their interstellar drive, we get ourselves a contract which might as well say "Start printing money. Now!" Everybody will want it. Every government outbidding every other.'

Crickson glanced across at the Chief Inspector. 'Go on,'

he hissed excitedly, all thoughts of a certain abducted teenager vanishing behind shelves of growing patents.

'Then there's day trips in the spacecraft. Or your very own photo of your very own house taken from geostationary orbit. Or all the documentary deals and chat show appearances for the aliens. Not to mention . . .'

Crickson's pupils were rapidly turning the exact shape of a pound sign as he listened in lucrative heaven. Striebley was absolutely right. Why spend year after year researching the very forefront of science with no guarantee of a licensing deal to rub together when there was even the slimmest of chances that here, on their doorstep, lurked a shipful of aliens with entire bucketloads of unimaginable secrets just waiting for the right offer?

It didn't take Crickson long to make a decision.

'Find them!' he hissed. 'They've come all this way, there must be something they want, something they need, something they undercatered for.'

Striebley stared blankly at Crickson. 'Something they undercatered for?'

'Yes, yes. Long trip like that across the icy wastes of space, they're bound to have run out of something, aren't they?'

Farson hung his head. What was Crickson thinking of?

'Well, I suppose so . . . but, what?' asked Striebley.

'Er, something like . . . like chocolate. Yes, yes, try them with that . . .'

'Chocolate?' gagged Striebley.

'Of course, that's it! Everyone loves chocolate, even my dog goes mad for his daily fix of Choccy Drops. I'll bet that it's hell trying to nurture a decent cocoa bush on Alpha Centauri. Give 'em a few bars of Galaxy or Milky Way or Mars and they'll be ours.'

'What about a Yorkie?'

'Get real,' hissed Crickson. 'Do you expect an intergalactic citizen to get excited about something that sounds like a small terrier?'

'Good point,' conceded Striebley.

'Now go. Find them! Take a fiver out of petty cash and stop off at the corner shop on the way,' ordered Crickson.

'Yes, sir!' Striebley stood turned on his heel and stopped. Embarrassedly he sat slowly down again and leaned over towards Crickson. 'Just one snag,' he whispered.

'What?' barked Crickson impatiently.

'Er . . . how do I actually find them?'

'I believe I may be of assistance,' smiled Doctor Boscombe leaning across the table. He had been waiting for this exact moment to come around.

'You? What d'you know about tracking aliens?' challenged Striebley.

'More than you, it would seem,' grinned the Forensic Scientist.

'Oh, yeah?'

'I do know the exact appearance of their footprints and I am already equipped for the job.' With a deft flourish he waggled his trusty Victorian magnifying glass under Striebley's nose. It steamed up in seconds.

Crickson peered across the table at him, dripping suspicion. 'What's in it for you?' he hissed considering his profit margins on a three-way patent and not liking it that much.

'Besides the thrill of the chase, the excitement of a journey into the unknown and the life enhancing moment of confronting our intergalactic brethren face to face, you mean?'

Crickson and Striebley nodded.

Boscombe glanced theatrically over his shoulders and drew the two scientists closer with a flexing index finger. 'Boscombe's Parameters,' whispered the good Doctor. He was greeted by a pair of blank stares of utter incomprehension.

'This is my big chance to make a mark in the world of forensics,' he continued undaunted, his fists clenching eagerly. 'Years I've been waiting for this, years. And now here it is . . . the opportunity to be up there with the likes of Bertillon and his criminal classification based on body measurements; the chance to be revered along with Sir

William Herschel the very inventor of fingerprints; or be hailed as almost deitical alongside Larson and his portable lie detector.'

Striebley barely resisted the temptation to tap his temple.

'There is no forensic landmark left unbroken ...' expounded Boscombe, '... well, except for a really accurate way to determine time of death that doesn't involve sticking thermometers in embarrassing places ... There's nothing left on this planet without a name on it, d'you see?' Crickson and Striebley shrugged their shoulders blankly.

'Look, if I find the aliens I can start the first real system of exo-biologic forensic science! I get to lay the ground rules, I get my name in the history books! With their fingerprints, their footprints and a whole host of other things I can establish Boscombe's Parameters and once and for all prove categorically the validity of tales of alien abduction. Don't you see? I'll be the expert. This is my big chance. Are you with me?'

Striebley looked at Crickson locked in indecision, while Farson made a mental note to check Boscombe out for SOFA membership. He was certainly keen on the subject of our stellar brethren.

Boscombe leant forward, stop-at-nothing-determination fizzing through every ounce of his body, and whispered, 'I'd say yes if I were you. See, I've got the magnifying glass and, er, don't forget, you're still on trial with your DNA profiling service. I still have to make my report to the Chief Inspector.'

'Dr Boscombe, is that a threat?' gasped Crickson.

'Perhaps,' grinned Boscombe with all the hungry affability of the average hammerhead shark. And while Crickson and Striebley turned Boscombe's suggestions over, frisked them and searched for any possible way they could ensure that they weren't ripped off, a mauve Vauxhall Frontera sporting the meanest looking set of bull bars in the history of vehicular cosmetics growled its way along Edison Boulevard. It was stuffed to the gills with four shaven-headed individuals, each of whom weighed in at just under three hundred pounds in stocking feet and baseball bat.

'There, on the right, that's the place,' declared a panting thug on the back seat. 'Dropped the GENE-Erator off right there, I did, this morning.'

'By those cop cars?' growled Miles, the managing director of DN-Aids Inc from the front passenger seat

'They weren't there then,' replied Alistair the delivery man, reliving the morning's events with apprehension. He still wasn't entirely sure how much Miles blamed him for the loss of the Transit and the several hundred thousands of quid's worth of equipment in the back. Was it simply desperate wish fulfilment on his part or had there actually been a dark chuckle of glee after the heart stopping silence when he had phoned in his report this morning? Alistair knew that Splice of Life Patentable Biosciences Ltd weren't Miles's favourite customers. They paid their bills far too regularly and always just in the very nick of time. But now they'd done it, they'd well and truly exceeded their credit limit this time.

'Dusters on lads, we're goin' in,' grinned Miles, and the Frontera was filled with the sound of knuckles slipping gleefully into a host of various metallic reinforcements.

'But, what about those?' asked Alistair pointing nervously at the two silent squad cars.

'What about 'em?' asked Miles with a grin. 'Just adds to the piquant enjoyment of our little visit, doesn't it? Besides, it's been ages since I beat up a copper. They owe me for thirty years in Wandsworth. Alright, Justin, you know what to do.'

The thug behind the wheel grinned, tugged his three millimetre forelock and aimed the Frontera at the tinted glass entrance of Splice of Life, revving menacingly.

'Seatbelts on, lads,' reminded Miles checking his knuckle dusters and unfurling a thirty denier stocking down his face.

Suddenly Justin dropped the clutch and with a squeal of tyres the Frontera leapt across the road, mounted the kerb and sprang at the tinted glass. Bullet-proof as it was it didn't stand a chance against more than a ton of massed vehicle and occupants.

Upstairs in the board room Striebley and Crickson were realising that Boscombe's proposal left them little choice. If they didn't have him on their side not only would they be depriving themselves of his undoubted forensic expertise but, they'd almost certainly end up racing the entire Camford Constabulary *X Files* Appreciation Society to the aliens.

'Doctor Boscombe, your assistance would be most appreciated upon our search for our interstellar brethren,' grinned Striebley, standing and heading towards the door just as a sound not unlike that which would be made by a Vauxhall Frontera making its entrance through a bulletproof glass door was heard. The tinted door exploded and a large mauve vehicle appeared in the cheeseplant populated atrium of the lab. In seconds, four baseball bat toting shareholders of DN-Aids Inc had erupted from the car and were swarming up the stairs, eyebrows and noses flattened by the lingerie headwear.

'What the . . .' spluttered Striebley and, like a great many film extras in a similar situation, made the dread mistake of tugging open the door to investigate what it was that could possibly have made a sound so uncannily like that of a Vauxhall Frontera making its entrance through a bulletproof glass door. If he had stopped to think about it he probably would have come to the correct conclusion.

As it was he caught only a glimpse of mauve paintwork and a nasty looking set of bull bars before a heavily deniered quartet of baseball bat toting thugs hurtled up the stairs, kicked at the door and swarmed into the board room.

'Good afternoon, gentlemen,' growled Miles a few moments later after wielding his bat a few times in the manner of a deranged majorette, and glaring menacingly around at the foursome. 'It seems we have a little delivery problem.'

'Er, n . . . no, no. Everything's fine,' spluttered Crickson recalling yesterday's wild telephone call and leaping with alarm half way towards the right conclusion. 'The GENE-Erator system which you were so kind as to deliver yesterday didn't seem to have been as faulty as I first thought.' He pulled a cheesy grin of embarrassment. 'If you are unable to deliver the second one which I may just have ordered a *little* too hastily I . . . I will understand.'

'Oh, will you?' growled Miles. 'That is generous, isn't it lads?' Three thugs nodded cheerfully.

'So glad you agree,' smiled Crickson nervously. 'Now, er . . . we are in the middle of a meeting here and . . .'

'Where are they?' hissed Miles through the thigh of his tights.

'Sorry?'

'You know what I mean. Delivery van and the GENE-Erator dropped off this morning. Where are they? What've you done with 'em? You'd better've got a good price.'

'Ahhh, I'm sorry to say that I haven't a clue what it is you are referring to,' confessed Crickson his eyes nervously following the arc of the baseball bat as it tapped away at the interrogator's palm. 'The van and your delivery man were here, true. He was rabbiting on about some delivery earlier and, strangely, the van sort of well, was stolen from outside. I, er, suppose it could be, well, anywhere now.'

'I think you know exactly where it is, and I think we're all going to stay right here around this table until you tell us.' The men from DN-Aids Inc lurched forward and sat down in a neat but threatening row along one edge of the table, sneering as they stared in their finest menacing manner.

'We're all sitting comfortably,' growled Miles the managing director glowering at Crickson. 'So, I think you should begin.'

As usual less than a tenth of Tara's mind was attending to the road ahead. But right now as she piloted two-tons of unmarked Transit through the outskirts of Camford, instead of the more normal distractions like the baby-oiled climax of Big Boys from the Bronx or some bludgeoning riffola of Def Leppard's blasting from the speakers, the thoughts that dominated her were far less fun.

'Up here,' she heard herself say in the privacy of her mind.

298

'Second door on the right, there.' Eerily, across the backdrop of racing streets and two-finger waving students, she watched herself slip a security card through the slot of Crickson's lab and ease open the door. Two ghostly grey-skinned figures, wearing nothing but wild grins and variegated ivy-leaves of modesty, slipped past her and dashed in to grab the three Amniotic Tanks (TM) from the far corner. With a triumphant cry of 'Got you!' the ephemeral Tara slammed the door shut behind them, thrilling as solid steel locks cannoned shut. Her mind's eye peered through the window at the two captives hammering elongated fists against the unyielding metal of the door. One phone call to the scientists at Porton Down and they'd be out of her hair forever. Men in bulbous encounter suits would stride in, capture the grey-skinned creatures and have them drawn and quartered by the end of the week. It was all set to make the infamous Roswell Incident look like a three year old's dissection of his brother's Action Man filmed on a shaky camcorder.

'What are you grinning at?' barked Calabrese from the passenger seat jolting Tara out of her scheming rehearsal, slamming her back to the reality of the situation.

'Er ... er, I'm happy,' she spluttered desperately and tugged at the steering wheel to narrowly avoid a poodle strolling across the road.

'What have you got to be happy about?' hissed Calabrese suspiciously as he clambered out of the footwell.

'The er, honour. Yes, that's it. It's an honour to be helping you out. I'm happy that I came up with the idea of helping you use the extra Amniotic Tanks.' She attempted a reassuring smile.

Fortunately for her Calabrese didn't have the chance to ask any further questions. With cursory attention to Highway Code details like mirrors, signalling and manoeuvring, Tara hauled hard on the wheel and sent the Transit careering off up Edison Boulevard.

It was only as she caught sight of the police cars and the mauve Vauxhall Frontera jammed through the front door of Splice of Life Patentable Biosciences Ltd that she realised perhaps things might not be as straightforward as she had envisioned.

Tara was halfway through a shabbily executed three-point turn and getting ready to high-tail out of there when Calabrese leapt out of the door and began slapping his way across the herringbone pavement towards the Frontera door jamb. Tugging the handbrake on and stalling the van in a ferment of panic she leapt out after the runaway feyrie, sprinting around the front and rugby-tackling the beast inches away from the start of the wreckage of the door.

'Are you mad? You can't go in there now?'

'I need those tanks!' growled the feyrie, his almond-shaped eyes, bulging with eagerness. 'I want them and I want them now!' With a twisting motion which Tara wished she could have worked out, he somehow slipped from her grip and, gesturing frantically at Lupin to follow, vanished around the corner. In seconds he was followed over the glass strewn rubble by the grey blur of the second feyrie.

Tara gasped and huddled against the corrugated wall, her heart pounding with every slap of naked feet on staircase. The temptation of just simply running away chewed ferociously at her ankles, nagging, begging her to succumb. It would have been so easy to disappear, wash her hands of the whole thing, deny ever having seen the damned creatures and quietly hope they were caught, reported to the relevant authorities and dissected.

And then she realised with horror ... they knew exactly where she lived. What if they escaped? How long would it be before the grip of strangely elongated fingers around her throat woke her rudely from the sweetest of dreams? And what other chaos would they have wreaked in the meantime?

She had no choice. Thanks to the warped sense of justice that was Fate, this was her problem. In her lap. And she was running out of time.

Desperately wishing she could have had the chance of watching *Aliens* just one more time to get her in the right Ripleyesque scrapping mode, she took a deep breath, peered around the corner of the door post and checked the coast was indeed clear.

In seconds, more nervous that she had ever been in her life, she was dashing up the stairs, heading for Crickson's lab.

Almost directly beneath her feet, safely hidden behind the remarkably soundproof door of Striebley's lab, PC Plain was dealing yet another hand of Rummy to Skitting and Sim.

'I'm telling you, I just heard something,' repeated Sim pointing out through the door.

'Rubbish,' tutted Plain. 'You're just spooked because of that thing, admit it.' Without losing any flow in his dealing he pointed across at the monstrosity in the murky tank.

'You surprised? It's not everyday you come face to face with a tankful of well, whatever it is. It's kind of disconcerting when you think it's been growing all night while I've been upstairs guarding that other lab.' Sim shuddered as he thought of what might have been. What if it had hatched? Would it have been hungry? Would it have come for him?

With an effort of will he dragged himself back to the present. 'But that's beside the point. I'm telling you I did hear something out there. I'm sure of it.'

'Are you playing?' tutted Skitting. 'Or is this just some pathetic way of trying to get out of it? You're still down fifteen hands, you know?'

'I heard something,' insisted Sim. 'I did.'

Plain tutted, shook his head and made a big show of shoving back his stool and standing up. 'Sim says he heard something. I'll go and have a look.' With an overexaggerated swagger of mock confidence he sauntered off towards the door. 'By the way, no sneaking a squint at my hand,' he warned Sim with a suitably admonitory finger. Idly he turned and peered through the round porthole of a window, his constabulary gaze taking in the randomly strewn details of a million fragments of shattered bulletproof glass. In the midst of it all, looking like some Advertising Agency's failed marketing concept squatted a gleaming mauve Vauxhall

Frontera sporting the nastiest set of bull bars in the history of vehicle cosmetics. A trail of bootprints headed off up the stairs.

'Oh, my . . .' offered PC Plain and slid his temporary security card through the slot.

Three-quarters of the way up the open plan stairs, Tara was on hands and knees crawling towards the open door of Crickson's lab, her breath rasping nervously past her dry lips. Perhaps if she could just slam shut the door, then . . .

Suddenly, she heard the heartstopping sound of voices. Reflexively she stared through the stairs, glimpsing a trio of Camford Constables heading warily towards the Frontera in the atrium, notebooks peeled. Panic welled inside her.

'Told you I heard something,' whispered one of the police officers petulantly.

'Shutup,' snapped the other two drawing their truncheons and sliding warily into any available patch of shadow, creeping towards the offending vehicle with a caution that would have made any viewer of *The Bill* thrill with delight.

For Tara it was too much. Her heart pounding so loud that she was certain the whole of Camford could hear it, she scrambled her way towards the open door of the lab, pattering through it like a toddler on speed and shoving it shut with a collapsing breath of relief.

'So, couldn't stay away, eh?' hissed Calabrese staring at her across the lab, hands on his ten inch hips.

'Hah, no, not at all,' whimpered Tara.

Lupin's face lit up with delight as he peered out from behind a stack of box files balanced on the far end of the central desk.

'Well then, since you're here you can give us a hand with these tanks,' commanded Calabrese and swung up onto the top of the nearest tank with the agility of a gibbon. 'After all, it was your idea.'

'Hah, ha, y . . . yes, of course,' spluttered Tara one eye fixed on the circular window in the door, half expecting it to be suddenly fogged by the impatient breath of an officer of the law.

At the far end of the lab, Calabrese was gleefully tugging colourful pipes and randomly marked connectors out of the back of the Amniotic Tank. In a matter of moments his deft fingers had unscrewed every retaining bolt and had slithered out of sight behind it.

'Get ready to catch this, Lupin,' he barked, a disjointed voice from the depths of the array of equipment. Bracing his back against the wall, the flat of his feet against the tank, he pushed. For a moment nothing happened, then, straining against inertia it twitched, tipped and tumbled off its stand.

Lupin squealed and dashed forwards, hands raised like a desperate prop-forward at his first International, alarm painting his face. He barely had his feet planted before the tank slapped into his palms sending him off uncontrollably across the lab his hands clamped around the tank's midriff. It was all he could do to remain upright. Like some unfortunate waiter on a liner in heavy seas he staggered around knocking a host of box files off the end of the table in an avalanche of genetic data. He rebounded off the far wall, spun once and finally overbalanced into a pile cardboard boxes flung in the corner.

'Ready for the next one?' called Calabrese.

Down the stairs PC Plain's ears pricked up. 'D'you hear something then?' he whispered looking up from a trail of bootprints in the glass, the earnest expression on his face the type that gun-dogs practise years to perfect.

'Oh, not you as well,' tutted Skitting.

'It came from up there. You didn't hear it?'

'Well, I . . .'

'Stay here. I'll be back,' announced Plain heroically and was off up the stairs the quietest he could possibly clatter with his standard police issue size tens. Even before he reached the top of the stairs he knew the noise had to have come from the board room. The lab was under police custody, nobody would be in there.

He pressed his ear carefully against the board room door and listened carefully.

Over the distinctive sound of massed baseball bats

303

slapping against palms he could just make out the voice of Professor Crickson. 'No, no, we're a scientific establishment,' he was pleading. 'We wouldn't involve ourselves in petty thievery to finance our valuable research ... er, no offence.'

Plain heard a deep growling and that was enough. He knew exactly what to do in a situation like this. He hadn't been trained for nothing.

He'd run away and think about it.

Spinning on his heel he crept back down the stairs, gesturing to the other two to get back in the lab, quick-sharp.

In the upstairs lab Lupin had, amazingly, managed to safely drop the second Amniotic Tank onto the floor and was psyching himself up for the third. Hands on his knees he was panting hard, regretting that a life spent strumming lutes and reciting heroic poems didn't prepare one for such physical exercise. He was staring absently at the heap of data and files spilled out of the upended boxes he had knocked over when suddenly, out from beneath a manilla folder, a tiny eye winked at him. Baffled, he stared at the landslide of information, shaking his head convinced he had overexerted himself. The tiny eye of a passport photo caught a spotlight's reflection and winked at him again. Before he realised it his hand had shot out, snatched the picture and was staring at a two by one black and white of an eight year old Tara. He barely recognised her, but it was undoubtedly her. In that instant, as he stared at Tara Ness's 'Kidnap File' he realised he simply had to have it to remind him of her during the long, dark nights alone down in his soily hollow. Nights that were sure to come all too soon.

'Lupin? You there? The third one's coming down,' called Calabrese impatiently.

'Hold on,' he panted, 'Let me get my breath back.' Rolling up the file as small as he could he carefully slid it into a small cranny in the nearest Amniotic Tank and dashed off to fetch the last one.

He was too late.

In the second he skittered around the table leg, the tank overbalanced, quivered and fell off its stand. It was only saved from a disastrous collision with the lab floor by a perfectly positioned Tara. 'Right, that's the last one, isn't it?'

Devotedly, Lupin nodded.

'Thought so,' continued Tara and flashed them what she hoped was a reassuring smile. It was just a little too wide to be entirely trustworthy. 'Well, I'll just scoot off with this one shall I and, er, make absolutely sure that the van's started and ready to go. Give me my security card back would you, Calabrese, there's a dear?' She held out her hand and fluttered her eyelids much to the weakening of Lupin's knees. If she could just get her hands on that card then maybe, just maybe she'd be able to imprison them in this lab. Nervously she hoped they didn't have high energy laser rifles hidden behind their leaves.

Calabrese frowned slightly but nonetheless turned his back, rummaged about beneath his ivy-leaf of modesty and handed over the card.

'Oooh, it's warm,' chuckled Tara trying to hide her stomach-knotting nervousness. 'Now where've you been keeping that?'

Lupin at least had the decency to blush.

Not awaiting an answer Tara snatched up the Amniotic Tank and headed off towards the door, a definite twitch of haste in her step. Trembling, she peered cautiously out through the circular window, slid the card through the slot and tugged open the door. In a flash she was through it tugging it shut, thrilling with the euphoria of success. The door was a scant inch away from incarcerating the pair of feyries and sentencing them to certain slow dissection when, with the deftness of the most persistent sales reps, a foot slammed its way into the rapidly narrowing gap. Tara's hands slipped on the handle and the door was snatched open by a furious Calabrese.

'Forgotten something?' he hissed and glared up at her.

'Me? Er . . .'

305

'You weren't thinking of leaving us in there, were you?' growled the feyrie.

'Ha ha, course not,' lied Tara, pathetically. 'What would I want to do that for?'

'Gimme that card!' snapped Calabrese leaping onto the tank and grabbing it. In a second it had vanished beneath his ivy-leaf.

'Lupin! Grab that tank and follow me. You, pick that up and get out of here,' he hissed at Tara. Miserably Lupin obeyed, his heart suffering under the twin strains of exercise and Tara's attempted betrayal. If she didn't like him she could just say, she didn't have to go to the lengths of imprisoning him.

And so, eyes peeled, under Calabrese's direction the threesome struggled down the stairs with a triplet of stolen Amniotic Tanks. With only the slightest of crunching of feet on glass they slipped out and scurried off towards the waiting Transit.

Had PC's Plain, Skitting and Sim burst out of the lower lab even a second earlier, things would have been far different. For one thing Sim would have been screaming his head off and pointing desperately at the things running off with the tanks, pleading with everyone in earshot to tell him they weren't real and that this was all a very bad dream caused by him working too hard and that he really ought to be sent on a nice relaxing holiday to the Caribbean just him and Sylvia from the typing pool.

Fortunately for Sylvia from the typing pool, Sim caught nary a glimpse of the escaping feyries. Undistracted by things unknown, the three officers swarmed up the stairs and arranged themselves outside the Board Room door, truncheons drawn.

In the oak-lined ostentatiousness of said Board Room the gathered gentlemen from DN-Aids Inc were having little joy ascertaining the whereabouts of their purloined property.

'Where the bloody 'ell's my van?' shouted Miles, the managing director, his nose feeling decidedly itchy beneath the cover of his thirty denier stocking mask. Strictly, of

306

course, it wasn't his van since he had recently nicked it from a building site but, since possession was nine-tenths of the law, he definitely regarded it as his very own.

In response Crickson, Striebley and Boscombe shrugged three sets of scientific shoulders. Angrily Miles sighted down his baseball bat and swung it threateningly along the seated row of 'interviewees'. It settled above the head of one Chief Inspector Ness as he peered into the bottom of his mug.

'You ain't said much,' snarled Miles. 'D'you know, I find that a bit on the suspicious side. Where's my van, eh?'

At that instant the mobile in Ness's top pocket warbled into life. Reflexively he tugged it out, dropping his mug of tea, absently pressed the relevant button and answered. 'You're through to the Big Cuddly Uncle Copp . . .'

In the instant the voice began ranting about certain events at the Regal Greens Golf Course, all images of Ness's dear daughter vanished from before his eyes, her endless torment at the hands of a million mysterious monsters from beyond the stars shattered.

'No, no. I'm not interested in lights in the sky. Go away!' He severed the connection with a deft thumb. For a brief moment Ness stared blankly at the tea splattered surface of the table. Then waves of wild frustration gathered at the edges of his mind, swelling, roiling.

'Where's my van?' snarled Miles yet again, prodding Ness's shoulder with the tip of his bat.

'Eh? What's going on?' croaked Ness looking up at the quartet of enstockinged faces. Dim memories of closed circuit tv pictures twitched in the back of his mind.

'Didn't think you'd been listening,' tutted Miles and prodded him again.

'You'll have to let him off. His daughter's just been kidnapped by aliens,' offered Boscombe helpfully.

'Aliens? Hah! Pull the other one.'

The quartet of DN-Aids Inc representatives chuckled evilly.

Ness's cheek muscles tensed as his molars bit hard together, fragments of black and white memory coalescing into a clump of recollection, surfing forward on a growing swell of frustration.

'No seriously,' answered Boscombe. 'Well, at least we think it's aliens. The evidence gathered so far, from footprints and ...'

'Shutup,' barked Miles slamming his bat hard onto the table and causing a nasty dent. 'I don't care whether his daughter's been sold into bondage and is currently languishing in some middle eastern harem awaiting a damn good seeing to ...'

The Chief Inspector made a feral growling sound as he thought of his daughter's expensive education going to such a waste. He leapt to his feet and, with an inhuman explosion of anger shoved the table hard against the far wall. There was a squeaking of chairlegs on polished pine and in seconds the four visitors from DN-Aids Inc were pinned by the midriffs, gasping helplessly against the oak-panelling.

'Miles Punnet, Managing Director of DN-Aids Inc, I am arresting you on numerous charges of selling stolen scientific equipment, extortion, grievous bodily ...'

'You can't do this,' shouted Miles. 'I'm innocent! An' besides, I don't believe in citizen's arrests.'

'I am Chief Inspector Ness!'

With a flurry of truncheons the door burst open and PC's Plain, Skitting and Sim exploded in. 'And these are my men,' added Ness. 'Nicely timed, chaps. Take them away.'

Handcuffs waggled tauntingly at the stockinged thugs and were slapped around their wrists. Buried beneath the cries of innocence and screams for lawyers as Miles's thugs were dragged away, nobody heard the scream of diesel engine as a certain unmarked two-ton Transit was hotwired yet again and raced off down Edison Boulevard.

On the other side of Camford five pairs of eyes were held in rapt attention by the top of the range Philips twenty-eight inch colour tv in the corner of the perfectly appointed lounge. Each pair stared through one of a variety of visual aids; ranging from pale blue diamante studded hornrims for the more flamboyant of viewers to the latest disposable contact lenses from Boots for those of a more modest nature.

Being the second week of the Wimbledon fortnight, Agatha Maple's regular coffee mornings had been shifted to an hour of the afternoon more appropriate to the enjoyment of the latest exploits upon the hallowed turf of Centre Court. Today was no exception. The men's semi-final.

Rosemary Ness sat upon the edge of Agatha's calf leather suite, knees clenched together, chocolate hob-nob poised an inch from her lips. It was break point in the third set and a white baseball capped Agassi was preparing to serve. He hitched up his shorts, wiped his perspiring brow with the back of his wrist band, jogged up and down a few times on the spot and somehow, amongst all this activity he managed to conjure a lemon yellow ball out of his pocket and bounce it up and down a few times on the baseline.

Far away across the distant net, a terrified unseeded Iranian player was skipping from side to side and daring not to question his luck to have got this far. Okay, so he'd had a few jammy scrapes, Becker retiring with backache, Sampras spraining his ankle and Todd Martin failing completely to turn up after a spontaneous party had mysteriously started in his hotel room the night before. The Iranian knew that various members of his government had reassured him of victory, but this was amazing.

The crowds gathered in Centre Court and Agatha Marple's lounge held their breath as Agassi tossed the ball into the air, leapt after it and with a grunt of effort whacked the thing over the net at something approaching one hundred and thirty miles an hour.

Cringing, the Iranian somehow deflected the ball back in the general direction of the net. Almost before it entered his half of the court Agassi was on it, three strides, a quick slide and he was loosing a killer backhand down the line.

'Forty love,' announced the umpire with tension-building calmness.

'Ooooooh, don't you just love Agassi's backhand,' gushed Rosemary Ness.

'It's the back of his legs I prefer,' chuckled Agatha Marple. 'I mean, just look at those calves!'

'Gimme his backside anytime,' leched the hornrimmed one from number twenty-five crunching on a bourbon biscuit. 'So pert, so firm!'

'All athletes are like that,' challenged Agatha.

'Don't kid yourself, darlin',' countered Barb from number twenty-five. 'You tellin' me that shot-putters have tushes like that?'

Around the lounge there were tuts of disapproval. Barb had only moved into the area three weeks ago, she still had to have her less couth edges knocked off. Put her on bourbon rations for a week or two and she'd soon come round.

On the screen there was a brief skirmish of racketry, the crowd went wild and the umpire nonchalantly announced 'Game Agassi. Agassi leads two sets to love. New balls please.'

'Anyone want another coffee?' asked Rosemary slipping out of the calf-leather suite with difficulty.

'Got anything stronger,' grinned Barb expectantly. 'It's gone half four, definitely time for a sweet sherry or five.'

Agatha frowned and pointed wearily towards the decanter as Rosemary changed her mind and opted for a swift Amontillado. She upended the decanter and tutted disapprovingly as barely enough for a glass was forthcoming. Shaking her head she set off into the kitchen to raid Agatha Maple's supposedly secret store.

Unseen by her, at that exact moment an unmarked two-ton Transit squealed down the road and raced into her drive opposite, shuddering to a halt in a quartet of gouges in the gravel.

Barb was on her feet in seconds and peering across the road. 'Delivery van in Rosemary's drive, eh? Wonder what she's getting.'

'Come away from the window,' hissed Agatha. 'What will they think?'

Barb sniffed dismissively and headed off for her glass of sherry.

'Bet it's a tumble dryer. Lord knows she needs one. D'you now she still hangs her washing out on the line? Shocking! Bet she hasn't even got a microwave.'

It was something of a shame that she hadn't continued peering out of Agatha's uPVC Georgian bay windows, it would have enlivened their conversation a great deal to speculate upon the reasons why their neighbour's house was being entered by an anorak clad teenager and a pair of three-foot, grey-skinned chappies wearing nothing more than ivy leaves. It definitely had far more gossip potential than debates regarding spin-dryers.

In truth they probably wouldn't have got the right answer even if that coffee afternoon had lasted the rest of the year.

As Rosemary slopped a hefty triple sherry into a half pint mug with one hand and shovelled bucketloads of deadly turkish paint stripper into the party size cafetiere with the other, three intruders scampered their way up her stairs opposite.

'You sure there's nobody in?' hissed Calabrese, his feet slapping up the stair carpet.

'Course I'm sure. It's Wimbledon fortnight, mum'll be out over the road ogling Agassi's backside, as usual.'

Lupin, baffled, shook his head and brought up the rear.

'In there,' barked Calabrese and pointed to the bedroom door sporting biohazard signs. Tara allowed herself a wry grin as she kicked it open. How prophetic that had been. If only she'd known just what form that biohazard would take . . .

'The computer. Get hacking,' commanded Calabrese. 'Get me back into Splice of Life.'

'But we've only just left there.'

'You arguing?' hissed Calabrese brandishing his favourite three-quarter inch drop-forged ring spanner and looking at her delicate fingers menacingly.

'Er, no . . . no, no. Wouldn't dream of it,' said Tara, booting up her Hewlett-Packard and firing up the printer.

In minutes she was in, ducking past the security and squirming her way into the central data storage system.

'I'm in,' she declared reluctantly. 'What d'you want?'

'Open the DNA files.'

'What?'

'Do it,' snapped Calabrese.

Behind him Lupin whimpered. How dare he talk to his Tara like that?

A file flipped open on the screen displaying a list of samples in memory.

'That one!' Calabrese pointed a grey digit at the screen. Behind his fingertip lurked the title 'Rustler'. 'Open it!'

A spasm of alarm ran up and down through Tara's spine. A replay of a now-distant radio broadcast echoed around her mind.

'*What . . . what . . . what is the motive for the break-in?*' asked a voice.

'*That I will answer,*' replied the familiar tones of Doc Boscombe. '*The motive is rustling . . . rustling . . . rustling . . .*'

Images of a scythe shaped shard of beaker glinting with her blood flashed accusingly into view. In that instant she knew the DNA in the file titled 'Rustler' was from that glass.

'Open it,' snapped Calabrese patting his palm with the chrome vanadium spanner.

'You promised me that evidence had gone. I destroyed it! What's it doing in their files?'

Calabrese threw back his head and laughed. 'You think I would go back on my word?'

'Well, as a matter of fact . . .'

His brow furrowed angrily. 'Just print it out!' he barked.

'But . . .'

'Print it!'

Trembling Tara grabbed the mouse, highlit the file called 'Rustler' and as casually as she could possibly manage began to tug it towards a small icon of a dustbin lurking in the bottom left hand corner of the screen.

'Print it!' screamed Calabrese slamming his trusty spanner onto the desk, pinning the mouse's lead into sudden immobility and shattering a cassette box.

312

Pondering thoughts of igniting spray cans of hairspray in his face and wondering precisely where her matches where, she reluctantly obeyed.

Behind her the printer suddenly coughed into life and began jetting ink onto virgin screeds of paper for all it was worth. Thousands of letters appeared, clumped in threes, each an 'A', 'C', 'T' or 'G'.

Amazed she read the first few lines and her head began to spin:

FILE: RUSTLER

ANALYSIS TYPE: FULL GENOTYPIC LAB NUMBER: x-093456-L
CRIMINAL IDENT: NEGATIVE   CHROMOSOME No: 14
SPECIESIDENT: NEGATIVE

Across the road, the turkish paint stripper had stewed for quite long enough in the party size cafetiere. Absently munching on a chocolate hob-nob, Rosemary pushed the plunger, slopped the thick black brew into the delicate Royal Doulton cups and, kneeing open the door, carried the tray through.

She was hit in the face by a wall of excitement. All eyes were super-glued to the screen, pupils tracking every tiny motion of the tennis ball.

'C'mon Andre, give it loads!' screamed Barb decorously, already half way down her sherry.

'Smash it!'

'Out,' announced the umpire in his perch.

'What?' shrieked Barb. 'No way, ref. That was in. You blind or something?' she yelled at the tv in a manner more befitting the terraces at Wembley.

'Quiet please,' understated the umpire.

'You talkin' to me? He talkin' to me?' spluttered Barb in a state of shock.

'Yes,' grunted Agatha much to the approval of the other ladies.

Satisfied, the umpire allowed play to resume.

Agassi tossed the ball into the air with his usual panache,

swooped after it and, with an almost feral grunt of effort, blasted another ace into his substantial total.

'Game, set and match, Agassi,' announced the umpire.

'What? Already?' gasped Rosemary standing with the tray of coffee. 'But I've only been out a couple of minutes.'

'That Agassi doesn't hang about when he gets going. Gets in and gets the job done,' said Agatha.

'Ooooh, stop it, you're getting me going,' grinned Barb downing the rest of her sherry and heading off across the cream shag Axminster for another hefty Amontillado from the refilled decanter. 'And haven't you got something to tell us?' she accused, pointing at Rosemary.

'Me?'

'Yes, you secretive thing. Having a delivery this very afternoon and not telling us anything about it.'

'Delivery? But Everett and I hardly ever do that sort of thing . . .'

'No, no. Delivery by van, not stork. What is it, eh? You can tell us. Tumble dryer?'

Rosemary was at the window and staring open mouthed at the unmarked Transit in the drive.

'I haven't ordered anything!' she gasped, slopped the tray of coffee onto the magazine table and fled from the room.

'Secret lover?' pondered Barb peering through the net curtains. 'Little bit of rough?'

Four faces watched from the window as Rosemary shuffled her way across the road attempting to keep her slippers on her feet.

She was barely a third of the way up the drive when the Transit barked into life and raced towards her spitting gravel over the chrysanthemums. It missed her by inches, slewed into the road and screamed away in a cloud of blue diesel.

'Lover's tiff,' tutted Barb through a patch of breath clouded window. 'Classic signs. Never get him back, I'll bet.'

'Looked like a girl to me,' mused Agatha.

Barb's eyes lit up. 'A girl! Oooooh, she kept that quiet, I never would've guessed.'

The van skittered around the corner on two wheels and vanished.

Slouching against a convenient stack of Michelins, supping their third mid-afternoon mug of Mellow Birds, the mechanics of Tyres'R'Us were shaking their heads.

'Disgusting,' tutted the larger and more vocal of the blue-overalled pair. 'Told you it'd happen, didn't I?'

His mate nodded agreement as four stocking masked men were herded out by truncheon-waggling officers of the law. They carefully picked their way past a doorwayful of mauve Vauxhall Frontera.

'Said it was a bad idea letting scientists move in,' ranted the mechanic. 'Irresponsible they are. I mean, just look at the state of the place. Disgusting. Can't even park their cars properly. And just look at the company they keep, I ask you!'

There was a slamming of squad car doors, the cough of ignition and the pair of heavily laden Rovers roared off down the two hundred yards of Edison Boulevard. Somehow, despite the extra bulk of their unexpected passengers, they still managed to top sixty before vanishing around the corner.

Shaking his head disgustedly and desperately trying to think of a way to blame this torrid scene on the Conservatives, the mechanic drained his coffee and trudged into the gloom of his place of employ. A second later his grubby hand dragged his mate after him.

Across the road, three of, allegedly, the finest brains in the area were gathered on the herringbone pavement. Farson lurked just within earshot behind. If he could get any clue as to Tara's whereabouts, he'd be off like a shot.

'Well? What now?' asked Professor Striebley nudging Doc Boscombe in the ribs.

'Aha! The chase is afoot, eh?' enthused the forensic scientist whisking his trusty Victorian magnifying glass from an inside pocket and wishing he was wearing a deerstalker.

'No,' tutted Striebley. 'I just want to know where those aliens are. Our future awaits!'

Boscombe gave him a hard stare and, muttering something

about researchers having no sense of occasion, raised his glass to his eye and set to examining the ground for any clues.

Professor Crickson stood watching, folding his arms, tapping his chin and generally fidgeting about. The bees of his thoughts were buzzing restlessly about the honeypot of Project CFC. He had been away from it for far too long. It was time to assess the damage that had been done, resaddle the investigative horses of science and gallop off towards the distant horizon of discovery. 'Er, I'm just going to see about, er . . .' he hedged and shuffled towards the Frontera in the doorway. Farson hid.

Boscombe and Striebley batted not the slightest eyelid, they were already sifting their way through a thousand and ten clues lurking on the ground like informative diamonds in the very dust of ignorance.

'Right, fine, well, I'll leave you to it then,' announced Crickson and slithered past their recently acquired Vauxhall. Ten eager strides later he was letting himself into Striebley's lab and legging it towards the Amniotic Tank in the corner.

For a few moments he stared at its gently swirling contents, watching distorted limbs loom in and out of the turbid liquid, cursing this alien cuckoo in his nest, hating it for kicking his chicken fed corn into a murky background. Fuming, he leapt at the tank, scrambling up the apparatus, readying himself to overturn it in a tidal wave of destruction.

And he would've done too had he not suddenly realised that there was a far easier way to get Project CFC back up and running again. Simply use another Amniotic Tank (TM). After all, there were three of them hanging about upstairs doing nothing and Chief Inspector Ness was certain to be tied up with stacks of paperwork regarding the arrests he'd made recently. Surely it wouldn't matter too much if he was to just happen to accidentally connect one of those to this GENE-Erator, would it?

Grinning as he flung a lab-coat over the thing in the tank he spun on his heels and clattered off upstairs. It didn't take him very long to discover a slight lack of vital equipment.

'Did you hear that?' asked Striebley on the pavement outside.

'Hear what?' muttered Boscombe, his nose inches away from the tarmac as he examined a set of tyre tracks.

'A scream. I'm sure I heard a scream.'

'Pah, nonsense. Just the wind,' tutted Boscombe. 'Nothing to concern yourself with. Unlike this!' Triumphantly he pointed to the black rubber marks.

Striebley's interest was ensnared faster than a rabbit's in spring. 'Have you found something?'

'Attend!' declared the forensic scientist. 'Here we have the tracks of tyres which are commonly used upon the workhorse of delivery companies throughout the United Kingdom. The two-ton diesel Transit.'

Striebley frowned miserably. 'I thought you had something useful. There's bound to be those tracks here. According to the delivery man he dropped off an entire load . . .'

'Aha! Now you see the importance of these particular evidential residues!'

'Eh?'

Boscombe rolled up his sleeves unnecessarily and handed his trusty Victorian optical over to the Professor. 'Observe this set of tracks here.' The toe of his patent leather brogues hovered in the vicinity of a broken line of black. 'Pay particular attention to the patterning about the proximal and distal extremes.'

'Eh?'

'Just look at the edges,' frowned Boscombe. What did they teach these scientists!

Behind them Farson was eavesdropping for all he was worth, desperate for some clue as to how he could possibly manage to ensure he stayed with them on their search for Tara. Then suddenly he had it. Boscombe, in his undoubted enthusiasm and all the excitement had left his mock crocodile bag inside. Now if he just happened to offer to carry it . . . He whirled on his heel and dashed into the lab.

317

'Now, compare and contrast that patterning with . . . this!' Boscombe's toe flicked irritably at another set of prints.

'Paying particular attention to the proximal and distal extremes?' asked Striebley, waving the magnifying glass before his eyes.

'Of course, of course. Notice anything?'

'Er . . . nope.'

'Call yourself a scientist!' hissed Boscombe rolling his eyes heavenwards. 'The tread spacing and distance between proximal and distal extremes exhibited by this latter track are consistently exaggerated with respect to the former. An exaggeration consistent with an increased axle loading over and above that of the vehicle's own tare rating. It's obvious!'

'You saying it was heavier when it left?'

'Of course. Now, whilst I am not entirely familiar with the practices of delivery vans in and around scientific establishments, is it not entirely unusual for a delivery van to weigh more after its delivery than before?'

'Well, yes.' Striebley scratched his head and looked up from the road. 'Er, just one question,' he began almost dreading the answer. 'What . . .'

'. . . was it that the delivery van took away?' interrupted Boscombe. 'A very good question and one which as yet I have no answer to. However, I feel that I may be permitted to speculate that the van which left these tracks drove away from here laden with . . .'

'My Amniotic Tanks!' screamed Professor Crickson erupting from the building in a ferment of panic. 'They're gone. All three of them, vanished!'

'Correct,' agreed Boscombe. 'I *was* just coming to that.'

'What? You knew all the time?' snarled Crickson.

'Of course,' smiled Boscombe proudly and then caught sight of Crickson's wild expression. 'Er . . . well, I didn't *know*, I mean, I hadn't seen it happen or anything like that, oh no. I deduced it, you see? From available evidence, you know, like a jigsaw?'

'Why the hell didn't you tell me sooner?'

'Oh, come, come. Do you announce scientific findings prior to performing further confirmatory experimentation?'

'Of course not!'

'Exactly!' declared Boscombe snatching his magnifying glass back from Striebley and pressing on quickly in the hopes that no one noticed the hollowness of that fragile victory. 'So we are now certain that we have three Amniotic Tanks and, according to those gentlemen from DN-Aids Inc, one GENE-Erator missing.'

'Yeah, someone's got a system capable of genetic engineering on a grand scale,' agreed Striebley.

'Capable of genetic engineering on a grand scale, but unable to carry it out,' smiled Boscombe in as reassuringly intelligent a manner as he could muster.

'Eh?' announced both scientists.

'Am I not correct in understanding that this GENE-Erator device can only function if precise and detailed genetic codes have been input?'

Crickson and Striebley nodded.

'Codes,' continued Boscombe victoriously, 'which, as yet, said thieves do not possess.'

The contrast of expressions which swept across the scientists' faces took Boscombe somewhat by surprise. Striebley, as would have been expected, displayed great relief, his face relaxing almost to a smile. Crickson, on the other hand, went the opposite way. Snarling, he clenched his fists and kicked a shard of tinted glass across the road barely missing Striebley's left ear.

'The bastards!' he declared. 'That's just bloody sabotage that is! How *dare* they stop me continuing my research when they can't use the Tanks for themselves ... It's ... it's criminal!'

'Ah, but ...' began Striebley. '... at least we are sure in the knowledge that without the vital and specific codes necessary for its programming, their GENE-Erator is completely useless.'

'Er ... excuse me,' came a voice from the door. All eyes turned on Farson, the red pony-tailed technician carrying a mock crocodile Scene of Crimes bag. 'I don't suppose anyone's interested, but I've just noticed that somebody's just hacked into our central data store and stolen a copy of the vital and specific codes necessary for the programming of a GENE-Erator.'

Boscombe and Striebley stared at each other. 'Uh-oh!' they mouthed simultaneously.

Crickson whirled around in a flurry of lab-coat and snatched Farson by the collar. 'What codes? What codes?' he barked, backing him up against the corrugated wall.

'It's alright, we haven't lost anything. They're the same as the one's in the memory buffer of our GENE-Erator.'

Three screams of terror rose above the rooftops of Edison Boulevard.

In a flash of glass Boscombe was off, bent double, following the barely visible tyre marks, his eyes bulging as they peered through his trusty brass-ringed Victorian optical.

'W . . . wait for me!' gasped Striebley and ran off in hot pursuit.

'Er, d'you want your bag?' asked Farson dashing after them before Crickson noticed. He had to find out what Tara was up to. All the equipment and data to carry out genetic engineering on a grand scale stolen from right under their very noses. What could it all mean? Was it just as simple as industrial espionage?

Somehow he was really beginning to doubt it.

Derrick, the Chief Tarmac Operative, trundled his motorised roller over the jagged black appendix scar snaking its way down the pavement of Fenland Road, stood back and, hands on his hips admired his handiwork.

'Beautiful,' he told himself as his gaze lingered on the steaming black surface wriggling around the roots of the avenue of chestnut trees. It was just as good as new. Nobody would ever be able to tell that some mad Transit driver had come screaming along that very pavement, churning up the freshly laid surface and almost running him down.

'Hey, Bob!' he called above the familiar backdrop of horn-toting reps jammed in the half mile traffic conserve. 'Get the kettle on. It's time for a brew.'

He turned, shoved a tiny lever forward and set the roller trundling back towards the red and white haven of their tent. Barely had he covered three feet when, from behind him, he heard the unmistakable sound of a two-ton diesel Transit mounting the kerb, tyres screeching on paving slabs, and the revving of an engine.

Reflexively he squinted over his shoulder, catching his breath as the sinking feeling of deja vu clawed at his ankles. 'Oh, no. Not again!' he whimpered as a horribly familiar vehicle raced down the pavement towards him, two of its wheels churning up his freshly laid tarmac.

Panicking he shoved the roller to full ahead and accelerated to the pace of an arthritic snail. Desperately, eyes bulging with the effort, he tried to shove it along faster. Stubbornly, it refused. Behind him, eating up the feet with a voracious appetite, the Transit leapt across a side road and bounced up the kerb, deceleration an unknown concept.

Several thoughts wrestled for attention in Derrick's mind, the favourite being quite simply 'Leggit!' It was only the thought of how long it was likely to take paying off the debt for the replacement roller which stopped him leaping behind a handy chestnut. Instead, thoughts of intact paypackets uppermost in his seething mind, he shoved hard at the steering handles, slewing the yellow monster through ninety degrees and heading it off towards a suitable gap between two trees.

The Transit roared on, fifty yards away and closing, in a plume of scattered tarmac.

The roller crawled sluggishly onwards, making its break for the trees with all the alacrity of an anaemic sloth. Derrick's eyes were pools of fermenting terror as the Transit thundered on towards him, set on a certain collision course. Five yards . . . three . . .

He stood trembling, shoving hard at the roller, a rabbit speared by the headlights of Death's artic.

One yard . . .

Screaming as the insects splattered on the windscreen of the van swam into focus, he leapt onto the roller, sprang between the trees and landed in a heap on the kerb. The van thundered by on a plume of diesel exhaust, a quarter inch to spare.

Derrick closed his eyes and floated on the shimmering li-lo of relief, twitching with thoughts of what might have been and wincing. 'Why me?' he moaned, wiping his sweating brow with the back of his forearm, sweeping his hand in an arc across his forehead.

He was only shocked to his feet by the advancing mass of the tarmac-stained metal roller, trundling unstoppably towards him. He leapt to his feet, dashed behind it and shut it off. Sadly his reactions weren't quite quick enough to prevent it making a very flat mess of an innocent Robin Reliant standing in its path.

The rogue Transit shifted up a gear and roared off once again into the distance. Minutes later it was spitting random chunks of gravel in every direction as it thundered up 'Rumpy Row' and ploughed through a section of privet hedging of the Regal Greens Golf Course. Barely controlled by a squealing Tara it bounced over a dozen tree roots, shattered the rear axle with a grinding shout of fatigued metal and shuddered to a trembling halt amidst a dense copse of ancient oaks.

'Great, great, bloody marvellous!' spat Tara. 'You've done it now. This van's going no further without a *serious* bill from the AA. I'm sure that'll go down well with the boys from DN-Aids Inc.'

'The van is no problem,' grinned Calabrese scrambling out of the footwell and releasing the accelerator. 'We're here.'

'What? Here? Where's here? It's the middle of nowhere!'

'*Au contraire*,' grinned Calabrese in a very worrying way as he vaulted off the gear lever and landed on the dashboard. 'This is the very centre of a brand new beginning, the focus for a gleaming future, the crux of chaos! Empty the van.'

'You're mad!' gasped Tara. 'You can't just set up

hundreds of thousands of quid's worth of scientific equipment in the middle of a forest like it was picnic or something.'

'Oh no?' Sneering as imperiously as a three foot six grey-skinned feyrie could manage he brandished his ring spanner like a maniacal majorette. 'And who's going to stop me? You?' The spanner slammed down against the steering wheel.

Tara squealed and snatched her fingers clear.

'Empty the van,' hissed Calabrese. 'Unless you want to spend the next few months playing SimMageddon 2000 with your knuckles in a sling.'

Lupin took a sharp intake of breath and winced at the thought of Tara's delicious fists suffering beneath a chrome vanadium onslaught.

'Where d'you want it?' growled Tara who suddenly understood how a certain Thomas Hobson had felt when required to make a decision.

'Over there,' grinned Calabrese, pointing out into the clearing. 'Inside that ring of toadstools, safely out of sight.'

It's Kicking!

It was highly debatable if even the most highly trained of nasally perfect bloodhounds could have kept the trail more accurately than Doc Boscombe and his trusty Victorian magnifying glass. Faultlessly he stuck to the ribbon of tyre tracks, back bent, glass held before him like some maniac frying-pan toting chef. Unstoppably he forged on across mini roundabouts, swept over countless clumps of decorously planted flower beds supplied by Camford Council, looped around traffic lights and eventually settled into an immovable position four feet out from the gutter, mooching down the inner ring road towards Fenland Road.

In the last ten minutes half a mile of angry commuters had gathered behind him in a sluggish string of honking irritation.

Farson struggled along the pavement, his shoulders creaking beneath the strain of Boscombe's mock crocodile Scene of Crimes bag.

'Do you have to stay in the middle of the road?' asked Striebley nervously glancing over his shoulder at the threatening bull bars of some generic four wheel drive thing hovering menacingly close to certain of his more delicate organs. 'Get out the way!' screamed the woman barely visible behind the wheel. 'Some of us are in a hurry. The kids still need collecting from the creche and my frozen yoghurt's melting!' She waggled an irate finger towards the passenger seat groaning beneath at least a dozen Sainway's bags. 'If it's dribbled on my upholstery, you'll be sorry!' Striebley shrugged as politely as he dared and tried once more to chivvy Boscombe along.

'Can't you track the van from the pavement? It's safer you know.'

'What? And risk missing any scrap of vital evidence? I think not,' chastised Boscombe.

'But you haven't found anything new in the last half mile.'

'Precisely,' declared Boscombe as they entered Fenland Road 'All the more reason to continue.'

Striebley shook his head. 'Er . . . run that by me again.'

'Pah! Know you nothing of forensic statistics? Have you never heard of Locard's Corollary?'

'Well, actually . . .'

'Call yourself a scientist? Shame on you,' tutted Boscombe shaking his head and somehow keeping his gaze fixed on the magnified road ahead. He took a breath and, despite being bent double, adopted a full-throated lecturial voice. 'Locard, if you will recall, postulated his "contact trace theory" . . .'

'Aha! That's the one about criminals always carrying away some evidence from the scene of the crime and always leaving something behind,' declared Striebley excitedly.

Boscombe raised an eyebrow. 'So, there is hope for the future of science after all.'

A clot of horn-happy medical reps launched a cacophonous volley of irritation from three hundred yards behind.

'And Locard's Corollary,' continued Boscombe ignoring them, 'states that the rate of evidential exchange is constant throughout a given investigation, see?'

'Actually . . . no,' confessed Striebley, feebly.

'Oh, honestly, do pay attention. We had a vast amount of evidence deposited outside your laboratory, correct?'

The doctor nodded.

'And since that time we have had a definite dearth of extra clues,' expounded Boscombe. 'Now, if Locard's Corollary holds true, then, any time now I should be coming across another and vital clue . . . aha!' Without missing a beat in his strides Boscombe turned sharply left and disappeared through a gap between two ancient chestnut trees. Striebley almost tripped over him.

With a joyous revving of impatient victory the woman in the generic 4WD raced forwards a hundred yards and stopped in a far more solid traffic jam. Deep inside her Sainway's bag the once frozen yoghurt was making a determined bid for freedom. It had already somehow manged to prise the lid off its carton and had spied a tiny hole in the bottom of the beige plastic bag. One more push and it was certain it would be snuggling stickily up against the almost pristine upholstery of the passenger seat.

Striding off along the pavement, Boscombe was thrilling like a big-game hunter with the delicate aroma of glistening rhino fewmets in his nostrils. Ahead of him, as damning an indictment of proof as any typewriter ribbon, snaked a tepid line of tyre tracked Tarmac.

'Good old Locard,' he mused to himself as he stomped past two men arguing over the steaming wreckage of a recently flattened Reliant Robin.

'You were nearly run over?' shouted the flat-capped owner of the Robin, paddling in a rapidly expanding slick of motor fluids. 'I've heard some excuses in my time but that takes the Rich Tea biscuit that does.'

'Twice!' snapped Derrick. 'Twice in one day. The same bloody van. Straight at me!'

'Down the pavement?' sneered the Robin owner. 'You really expect me to believe that?'

'I don't care. You don't have to re-lay that Tarmac, again.'

'No, I've just got to get this fixed.'

'Insurance'll pay for that,' grumbled Derrick.

'Oh yeah, and how am I supposed to explain how I came to be run over by a roller whose top speed is three miles an hour downhill with the wind behind it?'

'Tell 'em it's a GTI.'

'Er . . . excuse me,' began Striebley addressing the pair at the edge of fisticuffs. 'Have any of you gents seen an unmarked two-ton Transit passing this way?'

The angrily quivering lip, clenching fists and roar of tormented anguish which exploded from Derrick, the Chief Tarmac Operative, told him in stunning eloquence that, yes, perhaps he had, no, it wasn't very long ago and, no, he really didn't want to talk about it right now, thankyou very much.

326

Of course, the raw body language as he rolled his sleeves up and advanced through at least ten cormorants' worth of oil slick, wasn't quite as polite as that.

Streibley and Farson decided to be somewhere else, very quickly.

It had taken just over three hours of slave labour under the combined forces of Calabrese's dictatorial thumb and his coercive ring spanner, but it was done. Tara and Lupin had plugged up the stolen GENE-Erator to the four half-inched Amniotic Tanks. A host of electric cables snaked amongst the trees, connecting the various bits of equipment, looping from the central computer to the tops of the fifty gallon tanks like dozens of partying pythons. Uncountable coloured tubes writhed hither and yon between toadstools, looking for all the world like a jungle of lianas which had been on the receiving end of far too much Baby Bio for their own good. Everywhere, tiny leds twinkled blackly, ready and eager to burst into coloured life at the slightest flick of a power switch.

It looked as though Calabrese was ready to explode with barely contained excitement.

'Midsummer night approaches and everything is ready!' he chuckled, his hands running around each other with the eager agility of wrestling otters. 'Such perfect timing, perfect! Can you feel it?'

Lupin licked his finger and held it up, a blank expression on his face.

'Can you not sense the precise balance of the seasons, so finely tuned, so supremely poised? So easily screwed up!' Yellow fizzes of euphoria crackled around the edges of Calabrese's eyes as he plucked a dandelion clock from a nearby hillock. Theatrically he balanced it across his outstretched finger. 'One kick, one single kick . . .' he mused staring at the fluffy-tipped greenery. He took a quick breath and blew. Ephemeral ghosts erupted from the weed, spinning wildly in all directions as the naked stalk overbalanced and tumbled from his finger. '. . . and the future's in tatters, spinning off uncontrollably in a totally new direction. Oh yes, I can do that, you know?' he announced to no one in particular. 'Especially tonight. It's so easy on Midsummer's night when the seasons are so finely balanced.'

'You'll never get away with it!' gasped Tara and cringed. She hated the way her choice of available phrases always leapt for the nearest cliche during times of stress.

'Says who, eh?' he grinned. 'There's nothing to stop me flicking this switch here and creating an entire army in my own image! Nothing!'

'Oh, yes there is,' announced Tara and cringed again, wishing she had a dictionary or pet thesaurus handy. 'You'll never get away with it!'

'And why precisely?'

'Because ... because ...' *Don't say anything rhyming with Wizards and Oz!* she shouted at herself in the privacy of her mind.

Taunting, Calabrese waggled his finger above the main power switch which was Gaffa taped to a suitable oak. 'One flick!'

And then it hit her. 'Power!' she shouted.

'Yes, I'll have all the power I need when my army is up to full strength. And now that you have so generously supplied me with extra tanks, I'll have a battalion by the end of the week! There's nothing to stop me.'

'No, that's what will stop you,' challenged Tara suddenly seeing a fatal flaw in Calabrese's grand plan. After all the scheming, the running about, the stealing and coercion he had, in fact, completely blown it. 'You've got no mains,' she blurted, her finger pointing almost hysterically at the useless mains switch. 'You know 240 volts, 13 amps, that sort of thing.'

Calabrese's eyes bulged in horror as he stared at the mass of utterly useless equipment cluttering the clearing, ready and waiting and totally lacking even the slightest trickle of electrical oomph.

'No, no, no!' he screamed, 'How could I have been so

stupid?' The Amniotic Tanks sat unmoving in the forest clearing, as useful as ice skates in the Kalahari.

'You came close,' grinned Tara, relief flooding through her knees turning them to the texture of rapidly thawing cucumber sorbet. 'Close, but no cigar. World domination next time, eh?'

'How could I have missed it? That's ruined a bloody good speech that has,' wailed Calabrese.

But, then, somehow, he pulled himself together. 'Still, never mind, there'll be plenty of time to make up for that.' His mind swam with images of countless identical faces peering up at him as he fired an infinite army of clones into a fever of chaotic frenzy. What did it matter if these two witnessed one dodgy speech? Come the revolution and they'd be first against the tree anyhow.

'Oh, well, never mind . . .'

Tara and Lupin watched in complete confusion as he fell to his knees, patted the ground a few times and suddenly began clawing away at the leaf litter like a deranged squirrel who's remembered about a handy packet of peanuts he'd once buried. Clods of soil flew everywhere as he burrowed down a good eighteen inches, snatched at a thick plastic looking root and tugged. Hard.

A quarter of a mile away a floodlight on the top of the Regal Greens Midnight Putting Complex twitched sideways and was snatched off the roof.

'Silly me,' tutted Calabrese stripping the insulation off the power cable with careful incisors.

'Fancy forgetting about a mains supply, eh? That's what comes of getting carried away, always lose track of the details.' With three bare tips of cable showing and the odd spark arcing between them he shrugged his shoulders, dashed around the computer console and shoved them into the back.

Instantly a whole array of leds sprang into eagerly anticipated life. A hard disk whirred into action and four peristaltic pumps began churning over in readiness. A thrum of power throbbed in the oaken clearing, humming contentedly at fifty hertz.

'There now. That's better, isn't it?' smiled Calabrese dashing around the central console and thrilling as tiny constellations of red and green flickered cheerily on and off.

Tara's heart sank as she stared at the gathered equipment blinking and gurgling. There was no stopping the mad pair of alien invaders now. The world would never be the same again. And thanks to her, it would all happen that much faster. How could she have been so stupid? Helping them all this way? Believing that there might just have been a chance of something useful coming out of this? How could Spielberg have got it *so* wrong with ET?

At that instant a quartet of magnetic stirrers twitched into life and began swirling the cloudy fluids in the Amniotic Tanks (TM).

Suddenly it was too much for her. Teeth grinding in desperation, tears queuing up behind her eyes ready to jump ship, she whirled on her heels and, in a blur of anorak, sprinted off into a dense patch of ancient forestry.

'Tara!' shouted Lupin staring forlornly after her disappearing form.

'Let her go,' cackled Calabrese. 'It's too late for her to do anything now.'

'But, I . . .' Lupin's shoulders sagged as the truth prodded him with the feral glee of a jester with a pig's bladder on a stick.

She'd gone. Run off and left him alone. Woefully his almond-shaped eyes peered into the woody cover desperately hoping for a last lingering glimpse of her fleeting form, yearning for a final eyeful of her sprinting figure.

That she had left him didn't come as too much of a surprise. After all, he hadn't treated her that well and they had got off to a pretty poor start. Abductions may have been all the rage at some point in history, but for the modern girl about Camford they were something of a no-no.

Miserably Lupin ticked off all his missed opportunities. If only he'd had the time for some real romance, you know, given her some bunches of flowers, or fidgeted nervously beneath midnight balconies staring besottedly up towards her nightied form. If he'd only had the chance to play her all of the doting ballads he'd written especially for her, it would all have been so different, wouldn't it? It seemed that Fate had doomed them from the start.

Sniffing, he looked at his toes.

'Run out on you, did she?' mocked Calabrese quivering his bottom lip grotesquely.

'You'd know all about that wouldn't you?' growled Lupin.

'She kicked up enough leaf litter. Couldn't get away from you quick enough. But, chin up old thing,' he slid a consoling arm about Lupin's shoulders. 'Plenty more pike in the pond, and all that.'

Lupin made a strange noise in his throat.

'Good, good, that's the spirit. Now, while you're fishing about for another victim for your sickly devotion, make yourself useful and get entering those DNA codes quick-sharp. No time to waste, c'mon, c'mon, chop, chop!' He slapped a bundle of printouts into Lupin's chest, kicked him sharply across the backside and hustled him off towards the humming expectancy of the central console.

'I want all that in there. Go!' ordered Calabrese pointing from the stack of paper to the terminal.

'And check every letter!' he snapped and was off to check on a dozen or so different connections.

Lupin stared blankly at the waiting screen flashing an 'ENTER CODE' command. Sighing wistfully he opened the pile of papers, shrugged and, in the greatest tradition of all storytellers, began at the beginning.

He hadn't got much past the first 'TGG' before his attention wandered back to thoughts of Tara. Already he felt as if her face was fading from his memory, eroding before his eyes like a melting wax effigy at Gas Mark 4. Desperately he tried to pull her into focus, tracing the curve of her ears, caressing her Doc Martined ankles. He was running a finger of memory across her smiling lips when, in an explosion of recollection the image warped, twisted and, with a tinkling of snapping heartstrings, exploded.

It seemed his imagination just wasn't good enough to maintain a mental portrait of her smiling. She hadn't done a great deal of it recently. Now scowling, tutting, looking at him blackly, they were a piece of cake. He could conjure them up in the twitch of a neurone. He had loads of material to work on there ... But smiling? ... If only he had something he could refer to, something solid, tangible. He *had* seen her smiling somewhere, recently. If only he could remember where.

He slammed his eyes shut and thought hard. Her face floated before him, looking different, younger, black and white ... And then he had it. The photograph of her he had grabbed from the lab. Now where was it?

In a flash of grey he was off, searching the nooks of every Amniotic Tank for a tightly folded up file shoved hastily out of sight.

He found it jammed into the base of the second tank, a tiny spot of manilla. With a struggle and the snapping of a fingernail, he tugged it out, tucked it under his arm and dashed back to the terminal like a schoolboy with a dubiously adult magazine hidden inside his geography exercise book.

Thrilling cheerfully he spread the file out, eased it open and stared at the smiling monochrome of a younger and far less anoraked Tara. His heart skipped a beat as he tore the photo from the file and held it inches from his nose, humming his unused ballad at her.

'Done yet?' called Calabrese from the far side of the clearing.

Lupin jumped. 'Er ... n ... not quite. I was just checking on something.'

'Well, get on with it!'

Flustered he flicked the paperwork back to where he had stopped and found the code. Readying his fingers over the keyboard he looked up and stared at the coding on the screen before him, cursor flashing impatiently.

A wrinkle of confusion wriggled across his forehead. None of the letters matched what he should have entered.

Every single letter of DNA was wrong. Tutting to himself, and cursing the things they call spellcheckers, he erased the few letters and, relieved that Calabrese hadn't seen his sloppiness, began typing once again, stopping every three lines or so to take a glance at the tiny photo.

A quarter of a mile away an extremely dischuffed Reg Treadly, Head Groundsman of the Regal Greens Golf Course, was on his knees crooning pathetically at a small patch of grass just next to the Midnight Putter Complex.

'There, there,' he soothed picking up the lamp which had undoubtedly fallen from the roof. He winced as he saw the sharp gouge which had been torn out of his beloved grass. 'You can have some extra fertiliser,' he cosseted. 'That, and a bit of bonemeal and you'll be right as rain, you'll see. And then I'll be getting onto the police. I've had just about enough of these damned vandals wrecking the place.'

Muttering irritably to himself he headed off back to his small hut at the edge of a distant patch of green where he was sure there was a freshly opened pot of Baby Bio.

Announced by nothing other than a barely visible left indicator and a wisp of steam, a rickety Daimler van turned into the lane know locally as 'Rumpy Row'. The gaudily painted vehicle hauled a large caravan up the track and, following tiny notched directions carved into the bark of suitable trees, trundled onwards. For just over a quarter of a mile it hugged the perimeter of the Regal Greens Golf Course, curved away from the fens and disappeared into a slight hollow, out of sight of prying eyes.

And as the Daimler trundled to a halt, half a dozen fur seal cubs grinning Dulux smiles from its sides, a whoop of delight went up from the gathered party. In seconds folks had poured out of the Land Rover, the two caravans, the ageing VW camper with a killer whale on the side and the particularly non-functional looking coach, and were heading for the latest arrival.

'What kept you, man?' asked a wispy bearded figure in an Afghan coat and matching dreadlocks.

'Serious business up north,' answered the one from the Daimler jumping onto the grass with a jangle of crystal necklaces. The unmistakable aroma of ylang ylang floated out of the cab at almost the same speed as two girls sporting tie-dyed headscarves and at least a kilo of beads each. 'Festival of Tir-na-N'ogg up Kilcarney Stone Circle way.'

'Well special,' nodded the gathered crowd, beads and talismans rattling appreciatively. And now that Moonshine was here amongst them, they knew that tonight's Midsummer celebrations would also be well special. All parties attended by Moonshine were always well special.

It probably had something to do with the constantly bubbling still in the back of the Daimler.

Doctor Boscombe, ace Forensic Scientist, peered through his trusty magnifying glass and continued to sing with far more enthusiasm than pitching ability.

'So take a good look at my face. You'll see my smile's way out of place. It's oh so easy to trace, the tracks of these tyres.'

'Is that really necessary,' grumbled Striebley who had rapidly become heartily sick of Boscombe's irreligious massacring of a number of hits, twisting as many lyrics as he could to bring in something to do with the pneumatic part of vehicles. Already Striebley had cringed to 'Tyre Yellow Ribbon Round the Old Oak Tree', winced at 'Video Killed the Radial Star' and almost strangled Boscombe when he struck up with 'Like a Firestone Cowboy' in full irritating Texas drawl.

'Necessary?' asked Boscombe. 'It's vital. On tracking sessions like this, which may last for days, it is a matter of utmost importance to maintain the highest level of mental awareness. Apaches always did it. Besides, having a singalong always makes things go faster, don't you think?'

Striebley made a face and followed the good doctor over the humpbacked bridge in the midst of the fenland. This wasn't a damned school outing. This was perhaps one of the most important journeys of his life. This trail was leading him towards his first contact with creatures of an unknown origin, beings from beyond the stars. There were a vast number of vital things to consider without wasting brain power whiling away the hours screwing up perfectly reasonable songs.

His mind was beset with problems. For one thing, what would he say when he met face to face with travellers from a distant galaxy? Should he smile, take a step forward and inquire, 'Hi there. D'you come here often?' Would he be better off with the familiar standard, 'Take me to your leader'? Or should he have brought his portable Bontempi and treated them to those infamous five notes from *Close Encounters*?

First impressions were oh so important after all. Get it even slightly wrong and the whole planet could be lasered in seconds, death rays strafing the countryside, demolishing everything faster than the strimmer from Hell. These things mattered.

'Striebley, it's no good. I need your help,' announced Boscombe still striding out along the road, bent double. 'I've got a real problem.'

'Yes? What is it?' asked the doctor eagerly. He'd do anything that would hurry them on towards their first meeting, anything!

'Try as I might,' grunted Boscombe, 'And I have tried very mightily for the last mile and a half, I cannot think of a single misuse of the word "Michelin". Can you think of one with "Michelin" in, eh?'

'No, no!' cried Striebley.

'Come, come, don't give up so easily. Rack those brain cells, you'll be amazed if you . . . oh, ho!' Boscombe's face creased into a grin of professional intrigue, he turned sharply to the left and began rummaging around at the opening of a narrow gravel track.

'What is it? What, what?' gasped Striebley. 'Found something?'

Boscombe didn't answer. Instead he pulled a Motorola

mobile phone out of his inside pocket and began pressing away at the thick layer of plastic covering the digits.

A dozen yards behind, Farson struggled up with the mock crocodile bag.

'What've you found?' pestered Striebley staring at Boscombe as he held the telephone to his ear and awaited the connection.

'Er, oh, the tracks,' mumbled Boscombe massaging the small of his back with his free hand, 'the ones we've been following for the last few hours, well they turn off up . . . aha.' The phone made a series of strange beeping sounds. 'Hello? Get Chief Inspector Ness on will you? . . . What d'you mean this is Chief Inspector Ness? How did you get him to answer so quickly . . .'

Almost four miles away across the guano encrusted splendour of ancient rooftops, the unmistakable figure of a certain Chief Inspector barked into his mobile. 'Because this is my own mobile number. It's not hard to answer quickly when the bloody thing is warbling away in your inside pocket, now is it?' he snapped and continued pacing irritably around the darkened interior of an unsavoury office near the lower holding cells of Camford Constabulary. He glowered at the vast of heap of paperwork stacked up on the desk and was almost relieved at Boscombe's untimely distraction. Truth be told he'd clean forgotten quite how much effort there was in filling out the necessary documentation pertaining to four simultaneous arrests, especially ones like this that sort of just seemed like a really good idea at the time.

It had been years since he'd actually made a real arrest. Chief Inspectors simply didn't do that sort of thing, well not normally. Shout at a few uniformed minions, let them smell the glove and send them off into a drug trader's terrace like dark blue scud missiles, yes, that was what he was used to. None of this interminable nonsense associated with 'opportunist collars'. He sneered as he stared at a clump of questions currently being scribbled at by PC Plain. 'What was it that alerted you to the suspicious nature of the arrested individual?' He shook his Inspectorial head as he read

Plain's answer. In his finest hand, he had written 'Stocking masks, baseball bats and a very large mauve Vauxhall Frontera'.

Almost ignored, Doc Boscombe was rabbiting away in Ness's ear, dutifully reporting his position like the very finest of trackers.

'... evidential sightings point to the stolen transit's rapid alteration of course into the tiny gravel byway known hereabouts by the colourful colloquialism of "Rumpy Row". I am proceeding to follow around the edge of the Regal Greens Golf ...'

'Yes, yes, yes. How very exciting,' tutted Ness. 'Do inform me when you find anything more significant than tyre tracks. Out!' He slammed an irritable thumb onto the 'End Call' button and folded the mobile back into his pocket. He was definitely beginning to regret ever having agreed to carry this phone around. The Big Friendly Uncle Copper Crime Hotline was rapidly become a pain. The bloody thing hadn't stopped ringing in the last few days. Mainly crank calls about lights in the sky a couple of days back over the Regal Greens Golf Course.

His mind spinning with thoughts of his daughter, aliens and a quartet of recently apprehended miscreants lurking in a nearby cell, Ness turned back to the interminable occupational therapy of his police paperwork. Shaking his head, he peered over PC Sim's shoulders and squinted at his progress. His eyes drifted towards question 15 c (ii) *Had you any prior notions pertaining to the imminent incarceration potential of the above named*? He blinked, rubbed his eyes and stared again at his answer hoping it had simply been a hallucination. It hadn't. Wincing he turned away from the cheerfully scribbled reply 'Well, it was Miles Punnet, wasn't it? Most wanted of Camford's Scientific black marketeers, we had to nick him, didn't we?'

Still, there was one consolation, he thought as settled down into his stool. At least his answers would look good when handed to his superior. He licked his pencil, rolled up his sleeve and readied himself to begin.

He didn't get far.

Lead had barely touched paper when an eruption of unignorable warbling trilled from his inside pocket. Snarling, he snatched the Motorola gasping into the air, stabbed an angry thumb at it and barked, 'Who is it? What d'you want?'

'Well that's a fine greeting from our Big Friendly Policeman, I don't think.'

Ness wrestled back a scathing diatribe of dubious expletives just in case it was a random check up from the bigwigs at New Scotland Yard. Instead he launched into his rehearsed answering greeting. 'Hi there, you're through to the Big Friendly Uncle Copper Crime Hotline. Nobody's keener to solve that misdemeanour. How can I be of service?' His teeth ground irritably.

'Cut the crap, Ness,' rattled the voice of Reg Treadly in his ear. 'It's happened again, I tell you! You're not serving anyone. Not out here at the Regal Greens Golf Course anyhow. We pay good money for rent and rates and council tax and . . .'

'What seems to be the problem, Mr Treadly?' snarled Ness through heavily clenched jaws.

'Vandals again! I tell you, it's getting worse! If it's not pot-smoking philosophy students stubbing out their joints on my grass and staring bog-eyed at the stars, it's bloody *X Files* junkies leapin' over my privet in the hopes of catching a glimpse of the weirdy lights in the skies . . .'

'You really shouldn't have reported it to the *Camford Chronicle*, should you? You've only yourself to blame for that.'

Treadly, with a growl, did his best to ignore him. 'I'm telling you, they've even been on the roof. One of my floodlights, ruined. Ruined! Not to mention the poor blades of grass it hit when it landed. I want to set up a Golf Course Watch . . .'

'I'll send somebody round,' groaned Ness.

'You'd better. I pay my taxes and . . .'

The line went dead, as in a fit of desperation, Ness

wrenched the phone out of its leather posing pouch, spun it around and unceremoniously disposed of its battery.

'The nerve of that man!' growled the Chief Inspector. 'What the hell does he think we're here for? Jumped up little officious groundsman!'

'Let me guess,' suggested PC Plain, sucking thoughtfully on the rubber of his pencil. 'The charming Reg Treadly?'

'Got it in one!'

Plain grinned and made a little tick on a scrap of paper. Sim looked crestfallen, there was another round in the bar he was down.

'Complaining about yet another petty bit of youthful exuberance?' pressed Plain.

'Phones me up on the Big Friendly Uncle Copper Crime Hotline to tell me a floodlight's fallen off and bruised his grass! I ask you?'

Sim winced as Plain added another tick to the paper. How the hell did he do it? Was he telepathic?

Plain was shaking his head in condolence. 'Never been the same since that report of lights in the sky hit the media a few days back. If you ask me it's just a cheap publicity stunt by the Regal Greens Golf Course trying to cash in on the current fetish for anything alien. Me, I'm not so sure. I reckon it's . . .'

'What did you just say?' blurted Ness. 'Alien?'

Mutely Plain nodded and stared dubiously at Ness's glazing eyes. Suddenly things didn't look very stable any more.

'Tara!' cried the Chief Inspector as the events and phone calls and ransom notes of the last few days fell into place with all the tumbling chaos of a performing jigsaw. Why hadn't he seen it before? Boscombe hot on the trail of the runaway van heading due east out of town; the lights in the sky above the thirteenth green of a sporting complex sited where the dawn rose; the weird reports of strange vandalism from the groundsman of the Regal Greens Golf Course.

It could all mean only two things.

The aliens were holding Tara somewhere in the Regal Greens Golf Course. And . . . They liked golf!

'Leave that paperwork!' yelled Ness leaping to his feet, sending the stool flying across the room.

'Plain, fire up the Rover! Come on!' He whirled out of the office followed by the three PCs.

Behind them a quartet of stockinged faces peered out through bars and yelled. 'Oi, come back. What about us? What about my phone call? We ain't criminals, you know? We were catering to market needs!'

The door slammed shut on a storm of sprinting constabulary feet.

Even though she knew precisely what each individual portion of the GENE-Erator complex was designed, built and assembled to do, Tara was still having real difficulty believing what her eyes were trying to tell her. Whether it was the fact that she was witnessing such jaw-dropping events within spitting distance of the thirteenth green, or more the fact that the manufacturer's claims were actually true that amazed her more, she wasn't entirely sure. She shivered involuntarily as she lay on her belly in a clump of oak twigs and stared on from beneath a suitable bush, captivated and horrified.

In the last three-quarters of an hour, as the light had begun to fade, a thin otherworldly mist had begun to rise from the very leaf litter of the ancient oaken clearing, shimmering with the tacky mysticism of a bucket of dry ice at an am-dram Frankenstein night. Despite its chilling appearance she could still see the fifty gallon Amniotic Tanks incubating their deadly offspring. And, almost worse than those slowly revolving and growing shapes, was the pair of grey-skinned monsters revelling in their creation.

Cursing in silent helplessness she watched Calabrese spin cartwheels of delight around the clearing, maypoling strands of mist around the static quartet of tanks. He was chanting wildly, touching the tips of each of the crimson mushrooms gathered in the clearing, skipping between them.

Suddenly, out of the corner of her eye, something caught her attention. She was certain that there had been a spasm of motion in the far tank, a twitch of life, a wriggle of ... of what? Squinting through the heavy gloom of the gathering night she focused hard on that spot, straining her eyes in a way that would make her optician wince. A forelock of mist licked its way across her forehead, clouding her vision, trying to keep the dread truth from prying eyes.

It failed.

There before her eyes, across the clearing, a leg quivered unmistakably and kicked against the glass.

Tara snatched her breath. *Oh God!*, she thought, *it's kicking!* Revulsion reared inside her, spurring her into a ferment of agitation. Her nails dug into the ground, clawing in wild frustration. What should she do to put an end to this? What *could* she do?

Suddenly the answer came. Her fingertips uncovered a long abandoned five iron buried in the leaf litter. In seconds it was snatched from its leafy scabbard, clutched tight in Tara's fist and was being wielded in whooshing arcs about her head. Without thinking she leapt from the cover of her bush, scything the rusting club in circles.

Calabrese stopped dead in mid-chant, quivered and screamed in a way far from befitting the putative Lord of New Chaos.

Tara stormed into the clearing, plumes of mist swirling around her boots as she headed for the nearest tank. An anorak-clad Joan of Arc.

Lupin looked up from the central console, his almond-shaped eyes widening in delight. She had come back for him. Running away into the trees like that had simply been her way of playing hard to get. But now, she was back, glorious and ready to deal with Calabrese. His heart skipped and his hands clenched excitedly beneath his chin.

'No more!' shouted Tara spinning the five iron above her head. 'This has gone too far! Too far!'

Somehow Lupin decided that perhaps his first impression

wasn't as accurate as he had hoped. Maybe an idyllic future with her wasn't on the cards after all.

Mist and leaf litter swirled around her feet as she charged forward, rusting five iron rampant. Calabrese sprinted across the clearing, alarm showing around the rims of his eyes.

With a wild cry Tara swung the club towards the cylinder of glass, screwing her eyes shut and bracing for impact. There was a whoosh of splitting air, a desperate squeal from Calabrese and, with a motion that would have made the finest polo players weep with delight, Tara struck something solid.

The only thing missing was the roar of a watching crowd. That, and the satisfying sibilance of smashing glass.

Blinking, Tara opened her eyes and stared down at Calabrese, teeth grit, clutching at the golf club. Steel quivered inches from glass.

'It's too late,' hissed Calabrese showing his teeth.

'Let go, let go!' snarled Tara, desperately trying to wrestle the five iron free, images of shattering glassware flashing across her mind.

Behind the feyrie's head, the thing in the tank twitched and waggled a bare toe at Tara. For a moment, she stood, repelled and enthralled, her attention gripped by the naked, hairless thing gestating before her very eyes as it swirled past like a mallard on a spit.

It was the split second of confusion Calabrese needed.

Too late, Tara squealed as the pair of handcuffs closed around her wrists and a heavy oak branch slammed across the back of her neck.

There was a flash of black, the sound of chuckling and she hit the leaf-litter.

Just outside the north-west corner of the Regal Greens Golf Course a clump of variously tie-dyed, beaded, dread-locked and en-Afghanned folk watched intently as the bearded figure of Moonshine raised a wishbone of yew, held it loosely before him and began to rotate on the spot. A low chanting of something which sounded suspiciously like Bob Dylan dribbled from between his working lips.

There was a kind of hush all over the crowd as they

watched Moonshine perform his Ritual of Finding. Many of the gathered had seen this numerous times before as he focused in on the local earth magic, assessed the alignment of positive crystalline deposits beneath his feet and sussed out the best spot to party, party, party.

It only took him three complete revolutions that night, of which any whirling dervish would be proud, before he spun to a deft halt, held out his hand and pointed to a large privet covered concrete wall.

'Over there,' he announced pointing at the Regal Greens perimeter fence. 'It will be wonderful!'

With almost military precision a dozen Afghanned revellers formed a pyramid next to the wall and, in moments, hoiked Moonshine over the top.

'Bring the still,' he called as he set off through the trackless extremities of the Regal Greens Golf Course in search of the perfect place to party.

At that precise moment he was blissfully unaware that his left sandal had brushed against a carefully concealed wire. Even now, not half a mile distant, alarm bells were jangling in Reg Treadly's hut.

With the stage presence of a troup of terrified fireflies, consciousness crept back into the blackness of Tara's mind. First there was a single flash of sentience, then back to inchoate nothing. Then another spark. Soon there were clumps of brightness heading their way towards understanding. And suddenly, twitching and snatching breath like a drowning teenager, Tara leapt upright.

She didn't get far. The handcuffs around the steering wheel of the Transit saw to that.

'Damn you!' she cursed across the night-dark clearing.

'Ahhh, back with us, I see,' grinned Calabrese. 'And just about right on time, too.' He swept an elongated hand around the tanks and grinned wildly.

In the half hour or so that Tara had been out of it, gestation had proceeded apace. A foursome of figures squatted cross-

343

legged in the tanks, rotating gently, their features obscured by the cloudy fluid surrounding them.

'It seems the first of my troops are almost ready for active service!' chuckled Calabrese. 'Isn't that right, Lupin?'

'Almost,' agreed Lupin nervously. He nodded and continued to stare at the screen of the central console, assuming the type of expression which he hoped conveyed an image of understanding.

'You'll never succeed,' bleated Tara from the van, wriggling her hands through the steering wheel and down towards the bare wires of the ignition. If she could just start it up then surely two tons of well aimed Transit would soon put a stop to this madness. It would be messy, yes, filled with personal risk, obviously, but for the future of mankind she had to try. After all, what chance did earth stand against such selfish creatures? It would be hell being conquered by a race of aliens who wouldn't even let her see the flight deck of the mother ship.

Her thoughts fizzed with a million B-movie images of an invaded earth. The skeletons of charred buildings stretched bleakly in suburban desolation. Shining death machines stalked the rubbled streets, laser cannons armed and ready, hunting. All of mankind huddled grubbily by the barren chocolate machine in Goodge Street tube station . . .

And it could all be prevented. If she could only reach those bare wires and fire that diesel.

'You've picked the wrong planet to mess with,' shouted Tara, her fingers straining to grab at the ignition wires. 'Take yourself back into orbit and you might just survive. Stay here and you'll be dead as a . . .'

'Back into orbit?' spluttered Calabrese. 'What's that supposed to mean?'

'Go back where you came from. Mars or Jupiter or Tau Ceti, I don't care where it is. Just get back in your ship and blast off back up there . . .'

'Up there?' gagged Calabrese, beginning to wonder if he might have hit her just a little too hard across the back of the head. 'What do we want to go there for?'

'Clear off! You are not wanted! Go back to wherever it is you came from!' Tara's index finger brushed a thin red wire.

'This is where we came from,' challenged Calabrese baffled. Okay, things had changed a bit, what with the Golf Course and roads and such, but he was pretty certain it was the right place.

But then suddenly, a realisation dawned on him. 'Oh no, don't tell me you thought we were from . . .' He pointed a grey index finger skyward and a wry grin flashed across his face. 'Elsewhere?'

Tara scowled as her finger brushed the wire again.

Shrieking with delight Calabrese whirled on his heel and prodded Lupin in the ribs. 'You see what you could've landed yourself with? You see the dangers of not training them properly? They get ideas. That's why we feyries always steal infants. So much less hassle.'

In the driver's seat of the Transit, Tara's ear pricked.

'It didn't feel hassle free to me,' grumbled Lupin with thoughts of maternity wards and security guards.

'Ahhh, but that is all part of the delight of feyriedom. The excitement, the thrills, the action,' crowed Calabrese. 'Soon, there will be more to anticipate. Soon, my first generals will hatch. And then I shall start my reign of chaos. How long, Lupin?'

'Er, er . . .' Lupin ran a sweating finger down the screen. 'Five minutes,' he hedged.

'Excellent! Excellent!' enthused Calabrese. 'And once those four have hatched, I can start the next batch whilst my first team head off in search of new supplies. Why, in a matter of hours I could have ten Amniotic Tanks in action. Twenty. A hundred!'

'You'll never get away with this!' growled Tara. 'There's things you haven't got a clue about. The SAS. Kalashnikov Rifles . . .'

'Chieftain tanks, nuclear war heads,' interrupted Calabrese rubbing his hands. 'I know, I know. Amazing the amount of information you can pick up from stray newspapers and CablePix. Just think of the fun that could be had by casually chewing through the control systems of a dear little stealth bomber just before it goes on a taunting mission over Chechenya. I'm certain there'll be some small amount of armed exchange when it goes down in enemy territory, aren't you?'

'You're mad!' spat Tara.

'Conceivably. Years spent twiddling one's thumbs down a hole does that to one!' He struck a tragic theatrical pose, back of hand to forehead, then spun around and snatched Lupin by the throat. 'How long?' he hissed, inches from his face.

'T ... two and a half minutes,' gasped Lupin and was dropped back onto the stool.

Tara's head was reeling, rattling with the after echoes of the words 'twiddling one's thumbs down a hole does that to one'. It couldn't be true, could it? Those creatures weren't aliens at all, but ... but distant cousins of Tinkerbell?

She stared out of the windscreen at the thrumming array of equipment. But how come mythical creatures knew so much about modern laboratory techniques and gene manipulation? Guiltily she instantly knew the answer to that one. Not far behind that knowledge came a veritable avalanche of answers to nagging doubts that had been festering unconsciously at the back of her mind. She suddenly knew why she had never seen the flight deck of the mother ship and why they had never drilled her teeth or probed her body or investigated her in any of the interesting ways that she was certain aliens did. And she knew without a shadow of a doubt the very reason they didn't have high-powered laser blasters strapped to their hips.

The truth hit her like a baseball bat to the shin. She been abducted by feyries. Oh, the embarrassment! Here she was handcuffed to the wheel of a Transit at midnight in the middle of nowhere and it was all because of a pair of three foot creatures from a Brothers Grimm Omnibus. In a flash of misery her career as a science fiction writer vanished, a dozen appointments on mid-morning chat shows evaporated and a lifetime's honorary membership of SOFA collapsed.

346

Gritting her teeth with the type of determination that would have made Sigourney Weaver proud, she strained for the bare wires of the van's ignition. She simply had to get the thing started now. This was personal.

Unseen, three others were making their way around thickets of oak, one peering intently through an ageing brass-ringed Victorian magnifying glass as he followed some clue or other invisible to the naked untrained eye, one struggling with the weight of a mock-crocodile scene-of-crimes bag, and one pacing impatiently in circles.

'Definitely went this way,' whispered Doctor Boscombe striding past a crumpled looking fern and squinting at the tyre-tracks in the leaf-litter.

'Tell me something I don't know,' hissed Striebley his insides knotting with impatience and absolute terror. For every ounce of his being that desperately wanted to meet the invading aliens face to face, sit down and offer them tea and buns, there were thirty-odd grams that wanted to scream and run away.

Suddenly, Striebley halted in mid stride, gasped and pointed at a strange aura of lights swirling in the trees ahead. Ignored by the doubled-over Boscombe he leapt forward and feverishly tapped him on the shoulder. Behind him Farson almost dropped Boscombe's bag.

'Not now,' hissed the forensic scientist. 'Can't you see I'm busy, on the trail of . . .'

'Th . . . they're here!' whispered Striebley with a quiver in his voice.

'Yes, I know. *That's* why I'm tracking them. Now leave me alone to get on with . . .'

'Th . . . they're here!' insisted Striebley tapping once again at Boscombe's shoulder and pointing through the nocturnal forest

For the first time in far longer than his lumbar region would have liked, Boscombe stood up, took the magnifying glass from his eye and stared blurrily at Striebley. 'My good man, whilst I'm sure that scientific protocol allows such ill-mannered behaviour, I am a forensic scientist and do not

347

appreciate being poked and prodded on any given whim to be told what I already know . . .'

'B . . . but they *are* here!'

'Yes, yes, yes. And we are very close to them, too. I have a nose for these things, don't you know?' Tutting he started to turn around. 'Now if you will just let me get on with things my way I'm certain we will . . . ooooooh, now will you look at that.'

Ahead of them, in the precise direction of Striebley's and now Farson's quivering index fingers, an eerie glow of a far from natural origin was illuminating a pale corona of mist.

Indian fashion, Boscombe led off cautiously through the undergrowth, tugging a trusty Edwardian telescope from his bag held by the sweating Farson.

'Fascinating,' he mused a few moments later, peering through the clouds of Spielbergian mist at the complex array of thrumming equipment.

'What is, tell me?' gagged Striebley his throat dry, his heart pounding.

'No obvious power source. Utterly fascinating.' Boscombe peered on through the telescope.

'Amazing the way nature can be broken down into such simple codes. Very elegant. Very.'

'But what about the aliens? What are they doing?'

'Er . . . haven't the foggiest. Can't see them properly, telescopes aren't that good at night unless you're looking at stars and such like. But, but . . . ohhh, I say, there's some girl over in a Transit, handcuffed to . . .'

Striebley could stand it no longer. He snatched the telescope, slammed it against his eye and stared hard into the trembling image. Slowly his eyes adjusted and scenic details swam into view with the reluctance of a camera-shy grouper.

Behind him Farson was squinting into the gloom, his eyes straining to see the Transit and its captive contents. He felt certain it had to be Tara. It was too much of a coincidence that there could be someone else kidnapped hereabouts, wasn't it?

Suddenly, at the very threshold of his vision, there was a

tiny spark on bare wires, a scream, and a diesel engine sprang into life.

Almost instantly Farson was sprinting through the undergrowth, Boscombe's bag clutched unconsciously in his hand.

'Aha! Action,' whispered Boscombe excitedly and snatched back his telescope. 'Won't be long now.'

'What won't be long?' gasped Striebley.

'Mother ship,' answered the forensic scientist with complete assurity.

'M . . . mother ship?' stuttered Striebley looking skywards. 'You sure?'

'Absolutely,' grinned Boscombe, telescope pressed tightly to his eye. 'Young girl in peril, aliens nearby . . . logical outcome?'

'Er . . .'

'Come, come,' whispered Boscombe. 'Begins with "A", ends in media stardom, if you've got the right agent.'

'Ahhh, abduction, of course.' And then realisation came a-knocking on Striebley's shoulder.

'What? Her?'

'All they're waiting for is the imminent arrival of the mother ship,' insisted Boscombe in his practised tone of voice which somehow beggared facetious comments.

'You sure?' was the best Striebley could come up with.

'Course I'm sure,' hissed Boscombe. 'Now keep your eyes peeled. Any sign of the mother ship?'

'Er . . . well, apart from that bank of red and blue lights heading this way at high speed through the trees, er . . . no.'

Striebley stared at the blinding lights spinning in all directions, tumbling over one another as they slid rapidly through the mist, four feet off the ground. It, whatever *it* was, was heading their way. Very, very, rapidly.

'Run away!' yelled Streibley, tugging Boscombe to his feet. Maybe first contact could wait until next time.

'STAY EXACTLY WHERE YOU ARE!' barked a harsh electronic voice and a pair of four hundred kilowatt spots blasted Boscombe and Striebley into quivering silhouettes, freezing them to the spot. With expert skill the bank of lights slewed to a halt and continued to hover four feet or so above the ground. Stray leaves roiled in the beams of halogen white.

Calabrese and Lupin screamed and dived under cover of a handy Amniotic Tank.

'You'll never take her!' shouted Boscombe bravely. 'Well, not without me giving you a thorough examination first!'

Despite Boscombe's apparent motionlessness, deep inside he was trembling desperately. He was sure First Contact wasn't going to be like this. They shouldn't be so, well ... argumentative. It was obvious they'd never seen *Close Encounters?* It might not be quite as easy as he had hoped to persuade them to donate a few organs for tissue typing and blood grouping. Perhaps he could just work his way up from fingerprints and such like.

'DON'T TOUCH ANYTHING!' shouted the voice.

'Oh come on, that's not fair!' wailed Boscombe squinting into the light. 'All I want to do is look at a few things, take a few measurements and that sort of thing. And ... and he'll offer you a decent franchise deal on a couple of bits and bobs like, you know, hyperdrive ... er, that voice box is pretty good too. Very imposing.'

'IT'S MEANT TO BE.'

'Yeah, we could start with that. I'm sure there's a few British Rail announcers who'd give their eye teeth for something that clear and loud and ...'

'BOSCOMBE, HAVE YOU BEEN DRINKING?' snapped the voice.

'You ... you know my name!' he whimpered and his knees gave way. 'Fifty trillion light years across the heavens and you know *my* name?'

'COURSE I KNOW YOUR NAME, IDIOT! YOU'VE BEEN WORKING FOR ME FOR YEARS!'

Boscombe's mind whirled in a maelstrom of incomprehension. Could it really be true that he *had* been working for an alien force for years? Camford Constabulary could seem a strange place at times but ... alien? Well, they did know his name and it didn't really make that much sense for them to zip halfway across the galaxy to lie to him, did it?

But, how had he been working for them? What form had this alien aid taken and who had been his contact?

'ARE YOU GOING TO TELL ME WHAT THE HELL'S GOING ON HERE?' bellowed the voice.

And suddenly, through the clipped harshness of the electronics, in a heart-stopping moment, Boscombe recognised the unmistakable tones of Chief Inspector Ness.

Fear splashed across his face as he stared at the flashing lights hovering imposingly in the night. Ness, was an alien? How many more of Camford's Constabulary were not of this world? How far had their influence spread?

He didn't expect an answer to that one quite so soon.

At that precise instant three figures slhouetted by lights and idling exhaust gases stepped into view and began marching forward into the clearing, the half inch fuzz of hair shimmering like a corona above the crown of PC Plain's head.

Across the clearing, a few hundred yards away, the cab of a Transit was filled with obscenities. Tara was having dreadful problems getting the damn thing out of neutral. She had discovered that shifting a gear lever was not a simple task when one was handcuffed to the steering wheel.

Grunting she slammed her right foot onto the clutch pedal, squirmed around and kicked the gear stick with her left Doc Martin. There was a sickening grinding of metal somewhere beneath her and once again it jumped out of first.

Farson crashed through inconveniently placed branches, storming towards the van, determined to prevent it getting away.

There was another grinding of metal, a squeal of irritation and, with a noise that would make the average garage mechanic wince, the van was jammed into gear. It lurched three feet forward and stalled.

Cursing and stretching through the wheel, Tara snatched at the ignition wires, desperate to refire the engine. Her fingertips worked at the bare wires, feverishly unpicking and

351

sparking them together, left foot hard on the clutch. Suddenly, with a roar of diesel and a scattering of mud the two-ton Transit powered forward on a collision course for the collection of thrumming equipment in the clearing ahead. Tara's knuckles turned white as she gripped the wheel and wrestled the van against the branches and troughs beneath the worn Michelins, sending toadstools and leaf-litter flying in all directions.

Farson grit his teeth and accelerated, swerving around an oak and heading straight for the cab window. Leaping like the finest of movie heroes he sprang forward and somehow managed to get a grip on the handle, his feet dragging the ground. Biceps straining he hauled himself up, reached through the window and grabbed at the wheel. He knew that if he could only achieve full lock they'd never get away with her. Sweating, he tugged hard.

The van slewed sideways, pirouetted wildly and slammed into an innocently watching oak. Vibrations rattled through every fibre of the tree, shaking loose a couple of hundred leaves, several dozen of the less sturdy branches, and a recently launched cylinder of amateur rocketry. *Adversity VI* clattered onto the roof of the Transit, bounced once and ended up nose down in the ground, quivering.

Normally these events would certainly have had everyone's attentions gripped in stunned awe. Sadly, this time it was not to be. In the clearing, strange things were beginning to happen.

All four of the Amniotic Tanks suddenly began bleeping noisily and flashing lights. The final few millilitres of fluids were added to the Tanks with a foetal gurgling and, with the precision of a fairground rocket ride, the lids eased open.

'What ... what is this?' spluttered Boscombe. 'What's going on?' he asked of the flashing lights hovering four feet from the ground.

'HAVEN'T THE FOGGIEST,' confessed Ness.

Spellbound, everybody stared, unsure precisely what to do.

Beneath the tanks Calabrese was trembling with wild

excitement and intense frustration. He hadn't intended this moment, the birth of his troopers fashioned in his own image, to have an audience. Nobody was supposed to see this miracle of technology until it was far, far too late. When he had an unstoppable army of like-minded devotees standing amassed behind him, *then* they should have seen this.

Snarling and cursing in ways no feyrie should know, Calabrese leapt into a suitable pool of shadow and dashed off behind the trunk of an oak to watch events unfold.

The lids locked open with a series of clicks and an extremely uneasy silence settled on the clearing like a freshly fluffed duvet. All eyes stared at the open tanks.

Suddenly there was a splash of movement and, from the glass cylinder furthest from the flashing squad car, like some twisted final scene from *Carrie* a hand curled out of the liquid and clasped onto the rim. It was followed moments later by another.

Calabrese boiled with excitement, his heart racing with thoughts of the impending devilment he could cause with this, his first wave of troopers. Ohhh, what would Oberon and Titania say if they knew what he was up to right now?

The knuckles of the emerging hands tightened around the metallic rim of the Amniotic Tanks and began to pull. It was only then that Calabrese noticed that perhaps something hadn't gone as utterly perfectly as he had hoped. For example, why did the skin not look a good healthy grey like it should? And was it just a trick of the light, or did those hands really look twice the size they should be? It was his mind playing tricks, it had to be, stress and all that.

Alarm spread among the ranks of the gathered forces of Camford Constabulary as suddenly and without any sign of exhalation, a head broke surface and began to rise from the tank.

Calabrese's eyes shot wide open as he watched cloudy liquid dribble down the flowing locks of brunette hair, plastering it tightly to the ascending scalp. Rivulets ran down the glinting expanse of emerging forehead and, suddenly, with nary a twitch of dramatic music, she opened her eyes.

In that instant he knew that something had gone horribly wrong. Nowhere was there any sign of even a passing resemblance to his heroic features. And besides, she was a girl. A very familiar looking girl.

A brief glance at Lupin showed that he too had indeed spotted the similarity. He was lying beneath one of the tanks staring up at her, his hands clenched beneath his chin, eyes pools of desire.

She stood demurely in the Amniotic Tank, its metal rim hovering at a perfectly tasteful bikini-line, and watched her sisters' appearance.

'Quiet,' hissed Moonshine suddenly and raised his hands to the band of fellow party-goers.

'What is it, man?' came a whispered query.

'We are not alone. Look!' He pointed through the trees towards the flashing blue and red lights and the eerie glow of biotechnology.

'Hey, it's a rave, man! Well special!'

'I think not,' whispered Moonshine meaningfully, his branch of yew twitching in his inside pocket. 'For one thing, where's the music? I can hear nothing but a curious humming.'

'Ohhh, wow . . . a silent rave. Sit in a circle and hum. Well communal, man! Let's get in there. I can feel the lotus position coming on.'

Curiosity burning, Moonshine crept forward towards the clearing.

All around the clearing jaws were sagging and knees weakening as four apparently teenage brunettes clambered gracefully out of their tanks as shimmeringly naked as a kitten's backside. Much to Lupin's immense, overwhelming, delight and no little surprise, they were utterly perfect. Each curve a treat for the eye, every contour just aching to be caressed. His almond-shaped eyes licked every detail of their bodies, revelling in their pert flawlessness.

Well, except for the slight omission of a bellybutton each,

but, hey, he could live without that. Upon such imperfections were goddesses created. If in doubt just grab an eyeful of the Mona Lisa.

Skipping up and down on the spot he was in raptures of lust as all around him four dripping beauties climbed into the midnight clearing. Sparing no thoughts as to how any of this had happened and conveniently forgetting the fact that he had inadvertently entered the wrong genetic codes he lapped up every delicious moment, revelling in the fact that he could have an audience of four to try out his latest ballads upon. If he played his cards right, of course. With a spasm of chivalry he dashed over to the nearest girl held out his grey-skinned hand and offered to help her down the final step.

'My dearest, allow me to welcome you to ...' Still dripping, her hair plastered half way down her curvy back, she stared at Lupin as he drew himself up to his full two foot eleven and a half and puffed out his chest.

'Sod off, shrimp. Gimme the guys in the uniform!' With a deft flick of a beautifully engineered ankle she sent Lupin spinning into the disgrace of a rhododendron.

Simultaneously the cloned sisters strutted across the oak clearing, their wet skin throwing a million captivating highlights in all directions. 'I'm dreaming,' whimpered PC Plain, 'tell me I'm dreaming!'

'...' offered Sim helpfully and straightened an imaginary tie.

On the far side of the clearing a bush rustled and Moonshine peered through. 'Well, now, would you look at that.'

'I'm lookin', man. I'm lookin'!' A dozen of his dread-locked companions nodded with an enthusiastic clattering of beads, their eyes filled with a vista of matching buttocks. And without a further word passing between them, the group of travelling revellers began to peel off their clothes.

'Such a long time since I went skyclad on Midsummer Night,' grinned Moonshine hanging his astrologically deco-rated boxer shorts on a nearby bush and stepping into the clearing. 'Excuse me, miss ...' he began with a raised finger.

It didn't take long for the police searchlights to swing around onto him.

'YOU! WHO THE HELL ARE YOU?' barked Ness through the amplifier. 'IDENTIFY YOURSELF!'

The travellers froze in a tableau of shuffling embarrassment.

'Who the hell are you?' came a voice through an angry loudhailer. 'What are you doing on my Golf Course?' fumed Reg Treadly, Head Groundsman of the Regal Greens Golf Course, swinging Betty, his trusty baseball bat.

'INSPECTOR NESS!' announced the idling Rover. 'I'M ... ER, INSPECTING'

Treadly stared at the collection of thrumming scientific equipment. 'Inspecting? Is that what you call it? What happened to the good old days of the bobby on the beat, eh? What's all this lot for, eh? Forensics, is it?'

'WELL ...'

'No, no ... I don't want to know. I really don't,' he fumed as he caught sight of the gouged tracks made by the Rover tyres. 'Get out of here before you do any more damage to my beloved grounds.'

'BUT, WHAT ABOUT THAT LOT?' the spotlight wiggled accusingly at the skyclad travellers.

They grinned sheepishly at Reg Treadly and one or two offered him a chummy drag on a gently smouldering joint. He saw none of this, of course. Four smiling teenage girls caught his attention by the lapels and wrestled it to the ground.

'They look fine to me,' he answered distantly.

'THEY'RE NAKED. THERE'S LAWS AGAINST THAT SORT OF THING, YOU KNOW.'

'Not on private land,' barked Treadly through his loudhailer. 'Now get out! And take all that stuff with you!' He pointed to the humming biotechnology and quickly calculated the damage that removing it would cause, the arrival of heavy lifting gear, a succession of vans ripping up his beloved turf. 'On second thoughts, leave it there. Now go!'

'BUT ...'

'Go!' yelled Treadly and stood tapping Betty meaning-fully. 'And you!' he scowled at Boscombe and Striebley.

Muttering something about gratitude and community policing Ness switched off the amplifier and gestured angrily at his PCs. In moments the Rover was reversing slowly back the way it had come.

'Good call, man,' grinned Moonshine holding out a glowing joint and a glass of steaming liquor. 'What's your pleasure?'

Shrugging in a definite if-you-can't-beat-them kind of way he reached for the glass and one of the four matching Taras. He'd missed out on the sixties setting this place up, it was about time he found out what it had all been about. After all, it can't have been that bad, every single generation of student had since tried to recapture it.

'C'mon, I know the perfect spot for a party,' he grinned and headed off for the slightly scorched expanse of the thirteenth green, leading the slightly enlarged band of travelling revellers away.

In the Transit, Tara wailed and struggled against her handcuffs.

'Hold still,' grumbled Farson picking at the locks with some small spiky implement he had found in Boscombe's bag.

'You shouldn't've stopped me,' she growled.

'How was I to know you were driving?'

'They couldn't reach the pedals, who else would be driving?'

'I didn't know aliens couldn't drive Transits.'

'They weren't aliens!' hissed Tara, tears of shame twinkling at the edge of her eyes.

'Oh no! Sound like it to me. Little grey-skinned beasties, two of them, three foot high. That's what you said, wasn't it?'

'They were *feyries!*' sobbed Tara. 'I was abducted by feyries!'

'No, no. You get abducted by aliens, they were aliens, alright?' insisted Farson. 'You're confused.'

'I didn't get any probing,' she moaned forlornly not really listening as Farson finally got to grips with the handcuffs. 'I wasn't probed, or examined, or anything!' she wailed slamming her fists on the steering wheel.

'Is that what you wanted? A bit of attention?'

'Well, it would make a change,' she sulked. 'Nothing interesting ever happens to me.'

'I know where there's a good party going on,' smiled Farson. 'Fancy coming?'

Tara nodded.

'There's only one snag, though. You're just a teeny bit overdressed for it.'

'Guess so,' she smiled playing with the top button of her blouse.

In the deep dark of a Camford night two three foot grey-skinned creatures forged on through the ferns and scrub at the bottom end of the thirteenth's rough.

'Well, it wouldn't have worked would it?' suggested Lupin two feet behind the fuming Calabrese.

'Shutup.'

'I mean, you? Lord of Chaos, c'mon.'

'Shutup.'

'Now if we'd been gremlins, or something, then fair enough. Gremlins are more sort of, well, wicked, aren't they?'

'Shutup.'

'Still, it'll make a good heroic ballad when I've finished with it. You'll see.'

'Shutup!'

'Might even be good enough to get the interest of the dear Princess Hellebore,' he mused and knew the very chord with which to start this. Yes, maybe, just maybe, with a brand new tale of personal derring-do and a catchy sing-along chorus he might be in there. Failing that, he could always try his hand at Student Nurse Eleanora Jonsson.

Enthusiastically he began scribbling on the back of a piece of paper.

'What's that?' hissed Calabrese suddenly. 'Where did you get that from?'

'Er, it was just lying around on the top of the console when I was putting all that code . . .'

Calabrese snatched the paper off a bewildered Lupin.

Instantly, as soon as his eyes beheld the first 'TGG', he recognised his very own genetic code. He whirled on his feet and was off through the undergrowth the first flicker of hope rising in his heart. It was a long shot, but, if there were just enough reagents left in the Amniotic Tanks then maybe, just maybe . . .